P9-CEL-647

TWISTED

Books by Jonathan Kellerman

FICTION

Twisted (2004)

Therapy (2004)

The Conspiracy Club (2003)

A Cold Heart (2003)

The Murder Book (2002)

Flesh and Blood (2001)

Dr. Death (2000)

Monster (1999)

Billy Straight (1998)

Survival of the Fittest (1997)

The Clinic (1997)

The Web (1996)

Self-Defense (1995)

Bad Love (1994)

Devil's Waltz (1993)

Private Eyes (1992)

Time Bomb (1990)

Silent Partner (1989)

The Butcher's Theater (1988)

Over the Edge (1987)

Blood Test (1986)

When the Bough Breaks (1985)

NONFICTION

Savage Spawn: Reflections on Violent Children (1999)

Helping the Fearful Child (1981)

Psychological Aspects of Childhood Cancer (1980)

FOR CHILDREN, WRITTEN AND ILLUSTRATED

Jonathan Kellerman's ABC of Weird Creatures (1995)

Daddy, Daddy, Can You Touch the Sky (1994)

WITH FAYE KELLERMAN

Double Homicide (2004)

JONATHAN KELLERMAN

TWISTED

A NOVEL

BALLANTINE BOOKS

NEW YORK

This is a work of fiction. Names, characters, places, and incidents are the products of the author's imagination or are used fictitiously. Any resemblance to actual events, locales, or persons, living or dead, is entirely coincidental.

A Ballantine Book
Published by The Random House Publishing Group

Copyright © 2004 by Jonathan Kellerman

All rights reserved under International and Pan-American Copyright Conventions. Published in the United States by Ballantine Books, an imprint of The Random House Publishing Group, a division of Random House, Inc., New York, and simultaneously in Canada by Random House of Canada Limited, Toronto.

Ballantine and colophon are registered trademarks of Random House, Inc.

www.ballantinebooks.com

Cataloging-in-Publication Data is available from the Library of Congress.

ISBN 0-345-46525-3
Text design by Meryl Sussman Levavi

Manufactured in the United States of America

First Edition: December 2004

2 4 6 8 9 7 5 3 1

To Faye

Acknowledgments

Special thanks to: John Ahouse, Rick Albee, P.I., Det. Miguel Porras, Terri Porras, and Susan Wilcox.

TWISTED

1

May brought azure skies and California optimism to Hollywood. Petra Connor worked nights and slept through the blue. She had her own reason to be cheerful: solving two whodunit murders.

The first was a dead body at a wedding. The Ito-Park wedding, main ballroom of the Roosevelt Hotel, Japanese-American bride, Korean-American groom, a couple of law students who'd met at the U. Her father, a Glendale-born surgeon; his, an immigrant appliance dealer, barely able to speak English. Petra wondered about culture clash.

The body was one of the bride's cousins, a thirty-two-year-old CPA named Baldwin Yoshimura, found midway through the reception, in an unlocked stall of the hotel men's room, his neck twisted so hard, he looked like something out of *The Exorcist*. It took strong hands to do that, the coroner pronounced, but that was where the medical wisdom terminated.

Petra, working with no partner once again, talked to every friend and relative and finally unearthed the fact that Baldwin Yoshimura had been a serious lothario who'd made no distinction between married and unmarried conquests. As she continued to probe, she encountered nervous glances on the bride's side. Finally, a third cousin named Wendy

Sakura blurted out the truth: Baldwin had been fooling with his brother Darwin's wife. The slut.

Darwin, a relative black sheep for this highly educated clan, was a martial arts instructor who worked at a studio in Woodland Hills. Petra forced herself to wake up during daylight, dropped in at the dojo, watched him put an advanced judo class through its paces. Stocky little guy, shaved head, pleasant demeanor. When the class was over, he approached Petra, arms extended for cuffing, saying, "I did it. Arrest me."

Back at the station, he refused a lawyer, couldn't wait to spill: Suspicious for some time, he'd followed his wife and his brother as they left the wedding and entered an unused banquet room. After passing behind a partition, said wife gave said sib enthusiastic head. Darwin allowed her to finish, waited until Baldwin went to the john, confronted his brother, did the deed.

"What about your wife?" said Petra.

"What about her?"

"You didn't hurt her."

"She's a woman," said Darwin Yoshimura. "She's weak. Baldwin should've known better."

The second whodunit started off as bloodstains in Los Feliz and ended up with d.b. out in Angeles Crest National Forest. This victim was a grocer named Bedros Kashigian. The blood was found in the parking lot behind his market on Edgemont. Kashigian and his five-year-old Cadillac were missing.

Two days later, forest rangers found the Caddy pulled to the side of the road in the forest, Kashigian's body slumped behind the wheel. Dried blood had streamed out of his left ear, run onto his face and shirt, but no obvious wounds. Maggot analysis said he'd been dead the entire two days, or close to it. Meaning, instead of driving home from work, he'd made his way thirty miles east. Or had been taken there.

As far as Petra could tell, the grocer was a solid citizen, married, three kids, nice house, no outstanding debts. But a solid week of investigating Kashigian's activities gave rise to the fact that he'd been involved in a brawl two days before his disappearance.

Barroom melee at a place on Alvarado. Latino clientele, but Kashigian had a thing for one of the Salvadoran waitresses and went there frequently to nurse beer-and-shots before retiring to her room above the saloon. The fracas got going when two drunks started pounding each other. Kashigian got caught in the middle and ended up being punched in the head. Only once, according to the bartender. An errant bare fist and Kashigian had left the bar on his feet.

Kashigian's widow, dealing with her loss as well as the new insight that Bedros had been cheating on her, said hubby had complained of a headache, attributing it to banging his head against a bread rack. Couple of aspirins, he'd seemed fine.

Petra phoned the coroner, an unconscionably cheerful guy named Rosenberg, and asked if a single, bare-knuckle blow to the head could be fatal two days after the fact. Rosenberg said he doubted it.

A scan of Bedros Kashigian's insurance records showed hefty whole life and first-to-die policies as well as medical claims paid five years ago, when the grocer had been involved in a nine-car pileup on the 5 North that had shattered his skull and caused intracranial bleeding. Brought into the E.R. unconscious, Kashigian had been wheeled into surgery where a half-dollar-sized piece of skull had been sawed off so his brain could be cleaned up. That section, labeled a "roundel" by Rosenberg, had been reattached using sutures and screws.

After hearing about the accident, Rosenberg had changed his mind.

"The roundel was anchored by scar tissue," he told Petra. "And the darn thing grew back thinner than the rest of the skull. Unfortunately for your guy, that's exactly where he took the punch. The rest of his head could have withstood the impact but the thin spot couldn't. It shattered, drove bone slivers into his brain, caused a slow bleed, and finally *boom*."

"Boom," said Petra. "There you go again, blinding me with jargon."

The coroner laughed. Petra laughed. Neither of them wanting to think about Bedros Kashigian's monumental bad luck.

"A single punch," she said.

"Boom," said Rosenberg.

"Tell me this, Doctor R., could he have driven to the forest out of confusion?"

"Let me think about that. With shards of bone slicing into his gray matter, a slow bleed, yeah, he could've been hazy, disoriented."

Which didn't explain why Angeles Crest, specifically.

She asked Captain Schoelkopf if she should pursue homicide charges against the guy who'd landed the punch.

"Who is he?"

"Don't know yet."

"A bar fight." Schoelkopf flashed her the *are-you-retarded?* look. "Write it up as an accidental death."

Lacking the will—or the desire—to argue, she complied, then went to inform the widow. Who told her Angeles Crest was where she and Bedros used to go to make out when they were teenagers.

"At least he left me some good insurance," said the woman. "The main thing is my kids stay in private school."

Within days after closing both files, the loneliness set in. Petra had made the mistake of getting intimate with a partner, and now she was working and living solo.

The object of her affections was a strange, taciturn detective named Eric Stahl with a military background as an Army special services officer and a history that had unfurled slowly. The first time Petra had seen his black suit, pale skin, and flat, dark eyes she'd thought *undertaker.* She'd disliked him instinctively and the feeling appeared mutual. Somehow things had changed.

They'd started working together on the Cold Heart homicides, co-ordinating with Milo Sturgis in West L.A. to put away a scumbag psychopath who got off on dispatching creative types. Closing that one hadn't come easy; Eric had nearly died of stab wounds. Sitting, waiting, in the E.R. waiting room, Petra had met his parents, learned why he didn't talk or emote or act remotely human.

He'd once had a family—wife and two kids—but had lost everything. *Heather, Danny, and Dawn.* Taken from him cruelly. He'd resigned his military commission, spent a year doped up on antidepressants, then applied to the LAPD, where connections got him a Detective I appointment, Hollywood Division, where Schoelkopf had foisted him on Petra.

Whatever Schoelkopf knew he'd kept to himself. Uninformed, Petra tried to get along, but faced with a partner with all the warmth of ceramic tile, she soon gave up. The two of them ended up splitting chores, minimizing the time they spent together. Long, cold, silent stakeouts.

Then came a night full of terror. Even now, Petra wondered if Eric had been trying to commit Suicide by Perp. She'd never brought it up. Had no reason to.

She had not been the only woman in his life. During the Cold Heart investigation, he'd met an exotic dancer, a bubble-headed blonde with a perfect body named Kyra Montego aka Kathy Magary. Kyra was there in the waiting room, too, stuffed into too-small duds, sniffling into her hankie, examining her nails, unable to read the dumbest magazine out of anxiety or what Petra suspected was attention span disorder. Petra outlasted the bimbo, and when Eric woke up, it was *her* hand holding his, *her* eyes locking with his bruised, brown irises.

During the months of recuperation, Kyra kept dropping in at Eric's rented bungalow in Studio City, bearing takeout soup and plastic utensils. Offering plastic boobs and batting eyelashes and Lord knew what else.

Petra dealt with that by *cooking* for Eric. Growing up with five brothers and a widowed father in Arizona, she'd learned to be pretty handy around the kitchen. During the brief time her marriage lasted, she'd played at *gourmet.* Now a nighthawk divorcée, she rarely bothered to switch on the oven. But healing Eric with home-cooked goodies had seemed terribly urgent.

In the end, the bimbo was out of the picture and Petra was squarely in it. She and Eric went from awkwardness to reluctant self-disclosure to friendship to closeness. When they finally made love, he went at it with the fervor of a deprived animal. When they finally settled into regular sex, she found him the best lover she'd ever encountered, tender when she needed him to be, accommodatingly athletic when that was the daily special.

They split up as partners and continued as lovers. Living apart; Eric in the bungalow, Petra in her flat on Detroit off Sixth, near Museum Row. Then September 11 hit and Eric's special forces background made the department look at him in a new way. Transferred out of Homicide to the newly formed Homeland Security Squad, he was sent overseas for antiterrorist training. This month it was Israel, learning about suicide bombers and profiling and things he couldn't tell her about.

He called when he could, e-mailed her sporadically but couldn't receive electronic messages. She'd last heard from him a week ago. Jerusalem was a beautiful city, the Israelis were tough and tactless and reasonably competent, he planned to be back in two weeks.

A postcard picturing the Citadel of David had arrived two days ago. Eric's neat, forward-slanting script.

P.

Thinking of you, all's o.k.

E.

Working solo suited her just fine, but she knew it was only a matter of time before some new transfer was foisted on her.

After closing Yoshimura and Kashigian, she took a couple of days off, figuring on a little downtime.

Instead, she got a bloodbath and Isaac Gomez.

CHAPTER

2

It happened the day she started painting again. Forcing herself to get up by ten and using the daylight to copy a Georgia O'Keeffe she'd always loved. Not flowers or skulls; a gray, vertical New York city scene from O'Keeffe's early days.

Pure genius, no way could she hope to capture it, but the struggle would be good. It had been months since she'd lifted a brush and starting out was rough. But by two P.M., she was in the groove, doing pretty well, she thought. At six, she sat down to appraise her work and fell asleep on the living room couch.

A call from the station woke her up at one-fifteen A.M.

"Multiple one eighty-sevens at the Paradiso Club, Sunset near Western, all hands on deck," said the dispatcher. "It's probably on TV already."

Petra flicked on the tube as she headed for the shower. The first network she tried was running the story.

A bunch of kids shot outside the Paradiso. Some sort of hip-hop concert, an altercation in the parking lot, gun-barrel poking out of a car window.

Four bodies.

By the time Petra got there the area had been cordoned and the victims were covered with coroner's tarp. A quartet of bundles, lying at random angles under a blue-black Hollywood sky. The corner of one of the tarps had blown loose, revealing a sneakered foot. Pink sneaker, smallish.

High-intensity lights turned the parking lot glossy. What looked to be over a hundred kids, some of whom were way too young to be out this late, had been divided into several groups, shunted off to the side and guarded by uniformed officers. Five groups, all potential witnesses. The Paradiso, a movie theater–turned–evangelical church–turned–concert venue, could seat over a thousand. These kids were the chosen few.

Petra looked for other detectives, spotted Abrams, Montoya, Dilbeck, and Haas. Now that she was here, five D's for five groups.

MacDonald Dilbeck was a DIII with over thirty years' experience and he'd be the boss on this one.

She headed over to him. When she was ten yards away, he waved.

Mac was a sixty-one-year-old ex-Marine with silver, Brylcreemed hair and a gray sharkskin suit just as glossy. Skinny, rounded lapels marked the garment as a vintage collectible, but she knew he'd bought it new. A five-eight fireplug, Mac wore Aqua Velva, a faux-ruby high school ring, and an LAPD tie-bar. He lived in Simi Valley and his civilian ride was an old Caddy. On weekends he rode horses and Harleys. Married for forty years, *Semper Fi* tattoo on his biceps. Petra judged him smarter than most doctors and lawyers she'd met.

He said, "Sorry for screwing up your vacation." His eyes were tired but his posture was perfect.

"Looks like we need all the help we can get."

Mac's mouth turned down. "It was a massacre. Four children."

He drew her away from the bodies, toward the double-width driveway that led out to Western Avenue; they faced thin, early-morning traffic. "The concert ended at eleven-thirty, but kids hung around in the parking lot smoking, drinking, the typical shenanigans. Cars were leaving but one reversed direction and backed up toward the crowd. Slowly, so no one noticed. Then an arm stuck out and started shooting. Security guard was too far to see it but he heard a dozen shots. Four hits, all fatal, looks like a nine millimeter."

Petra glanced at the nearest group of kids. "They don't look hard-core. What kind of concert was it?"

"Your basic lightweight hip-hop, dance remixes, some Latin stuff, nothing gangsta."

Despite the horror, Petra felt a smile coming on. "Nothing *gangsta*?"

Dilbeck shrugged. "Grandkids. From what we're hearing, it was a well-behaved crowd, couple of ejections for alcohol but nothing serious."

"Who got ejected?"

"Three boys from the Valley. White, harmless, their parents picked them up. This wasn't about that, Petra, but what it *was* about, who knows? Including our potential witnesses."

"Nothing?" said Petra.

Dilbeck covered his eyes with one hand, used the other to blanket his mouth. "These are the kids unlucky enough to be sticking around when the black-and-whites arrived. All we've got out of them is a relatively consistent description of the shooter's car. Small, black or dark blue or dark gray, most likely a Honda or a Toyota, with chrome rims. Not a single digit of license plate. When the shooting started, everyone dropped or ducked or ran."

"But all these kids hung around."

"Uniforms arrived within two minutes, Code Three," said Dilbeck. "Didn't let anyone leave."

"Who called it in?"

"At least eight people. The official informant's a bouncer." He frowned. "The vics are two boys and two girls."

"How old?"

"We I.D.'d three: fifteen, fifteen, and seventeen. The fourth, one of the girls, had no paper on her."

"Nothing at all?"

Dilbeck shook his head. "Some poor parents are going to worry a lot and then hear the bad news. It stinks, doesn't it? Maybe I *should* fold my tent."

He'd been talking retirement for as long as Petra had known him.

She said, "I'll fold before you will."

"Probably," he admitted.

"I'd like a look at the bodies before they get taken away."

"Look to your heart's content and then have a go at that nearest group, the one over there."

Petra learned what she could about the victims.

Paul Allan Montalvo, two weeks from his sixteenth birthday. Chubby, round-faced, plaid shirt, black sweatpants. Smooth olive skin where it wasn't distorted by a gunshot under his right eye. Two other holes in his legs.

Wanda Leticia Duarte, seventeen. Gorgeous, pale, with long black hair, rings on eight of her fingers, five ear-pierces. Three chest shots. Left side, bingo.

Kennerly Scott Dalkin, fifteen, looked closer to twelve. Fair-skinned, freckled, shaved head the color of putty. Black leather jacket and skull pendant hanging from a leather thong around the neck that had been pierced by a bullet. His getup and scuffed Doc Martens said he'd been aiming for tough, hadn't even come close. In his wallet was a card proclaiming him to be a member of the honor society at Birmingham High.

The unidentified girl was probably Hispanic. Short, busty, with shoulder-length curly hair dyed rust at the tips. Tight white top, tight black jeans—Kmart house brand. Pink sneakers—the shoes Petra had spied—not much larger than a size five.

Another head shot, the puckered black hole just in front of her right ear. Four others in her torso. The pockets of her jeans had been turned inside out. Petra inspected her cheap leatherette purse. Chewing gum, tissues, twenty bucks cash, two packets of condoms.

Safe sex. Petra kneeled by the girl's side. Then she got up to do her job.

Eighteen know-nothings.

She addressed them as a group, tried coming on gently, being a pal, stressing the importance of cooperation to prevent something like this from happening again. Her reward was eighteen blank stares. Pressing the group elicited a few slow head shakes. Maybe some of it was shock, but Petra sensed she was boring them.

"Nothing you can tell me?" she asked a slim, redheaded boy.

He scrunched his lips and shook his head.

She had them form a line, took down names and addresses and

phone numbers, acted casual as she checked out their nonverbal behavior.

Two nervous ones stood out, a serious handwringer and a nonstop
foot-tapper. Both girls. She held them back, let the others go.

Bonnie Ramirez and Sandra Leon, both sixteen. They dressed
similarly—tight tops, low riders, and high-heeled boots—but didn't
know each other. Bonnie's top was black, some sort of cheap crepelike
fabric, and she'd caked her face with makeup to cover up gritty acne.
Her hair was brown, frizzy, tied up in a complicated 'do that had probably taken hours to construct but managed to look careless. Still wringing
her hands, as Petra reiterated the importance of being open and honest.

"I *am* honest," she said. Fluent English, that musical East L.A. tinc-
ture that stretches final words.

"What about the car, Bonnie?"

"I told you, I didn't see it."

"Not at all?"

"Nothing. I gotta go, I really gotta go."

Wring, wring, wring.

"What's the rush, Bonnie?"

"George's only babysitting till one and it's way after that."

"You've got a kid?"

"Two years old," said Bonnie Ramirez, with a mixture of pride and
amazement.

"Boy or girl?"

"Boy."

"What's his name?"

"Rocky."

"Got a picture?"

Bonnie reached for her sequined handbag, then stopped herself.
"What do you care? George said if I don't get home on time he'll like
just leave and Rocky sometimes gets up like in the night, I don't wanna
him to be all like scared."

"Who's George?"

"The father," said the girl. "Rocky's a George, too. Jorge, Junior. I
call him Rocky to make him different from George 'cause I don't like
how George acts."

"How does George act?"

"He doesn't give me nothing."

◆

Sandra Leon's blouse was skin-hugging champagne satin, off one shoulder. Smooth, bare shoulder stippled by goose bumps. She'd stopped tapping her foot, switched to hugging herself tightly, bunching soft, unfettered breasts to the center of her narrow chest. Dark skin clashed with a huge mass of platinum blond hair. Deep red lipstick, an appliqué mole above her lip. She wore cheap, fake-o gold jewelry, lots of it. Her shoes were rhinestone mules. Parody of sexy; sixteen going on thirty.

Before Petra could ask, she said, "I don't know nothing."

Allowing her eyes to drift to the victims. To pink sneakers.

Petra said, "Wonder where she got those shoes."

Sandra Leon looked everywhere but at Petra. "Why would I know?" Biting her lip.

"You okay?" said Petra.

The girl forced herself to meet Petra's gaze. Her eyes were dull. "Why wouldn't I be?"

Petra didn't answer.

"Can I go now?"

"You're sure there's nothing you want to tell me?"

The dull eyes narrowed. Sudden hostility; it seemed misplaced. "I don't even have to talk to you."

"Says who?"

"The law."

"You have experience with the law?" said Petra.

"Nope."

"But you know the law."

"My brother's in jail."

"Where?"

"Lompoc."

"For what?"

"Stealing a car."

"Your brother's your legal expert?" said Petra. "Look where he is."

Sandra shrugged. The platinum hair shifted.

A wig.

That made Petra take a closer look at her. Notice something else about the girl's eyes. Dull because they were yellow around the edges.

"You okay?"

"I will be when you let me go." Sandra Leon righted her hairpiece. Slipped a finger under the front and smiled. "Leukemia," said the girl. "They gave me chemo at Western Peds. I used to have real nice hair. They say it'll grow back but maybe they're lying."

Tears filled her eyes. "Can I go now?"

"Sure."

The girl walked away.

CHAPTER

3

Over the next week, five detectives worked the Paradiso shootings, interviewing family members of the dead teens, recontacting potential witnesses. None of the victims had gang affiliations, all were praised as good kids. No relatives had criminal histories; no one had anything of value to say.

The girl in the pink sneakers remained unidentified, a personal failure for Petra. She'd volunteered to do the trace, worked at it, came up empty. One interesting fact from the coroner: The girl had undergone an abortion within the last few months.

Petra asked Mac Dilbeck if she could go to the media and he said sure. Three stations ran sketchy renderings of the girl's face on the evening news. A few calls came in, nothing serious.

She worked the shoes, figuring maybe an item like that was unusual. Anything but: Kmart special, made in Macao, shipped to the States in huge lots for over a year, she even found them for resale on eBay.

She tried to recontact Sandra Leon because Sandra had given off an uneasy vibe, though maybe it was just tension about being sick. Resolving to go gently with the poor kid, Lord knew what she'd been through with her leukemia. The phone rang but no one answered.

Ten days after the mass murder, the team still hadn't developed any leads, and at the next sit-down Mac Dilbeck informed them they'd been cut from five D's to three: he'd remain as the principal and Luc Montoya and Petra would do backup.

After the meeting, Petra asked him, "What does that mean?"

Mac collected his papers and didn't look up. "What does what mean?"

"Backup."

"I'm open to ideas."

"The unidentified girl," said Petra. "I'm wondering if she's the key. No one's reported her missing."

"Funny, isn't it," said Mac.

"Maybe someone wanted her really gone."

Mac smoothed his glossy hair. "You want to try to chase her down some more?"

"I can try."

"Yeah, it's a good idea." He frowned.

"What?"

He touched the front of his flat, seamed brow. "I got a big fat what-if floating around in here. As in what if there was no motive. Just a bunch of bad guys out to kill some people."

"Wouldn't that be lovely," said Petra.

"It could be, though."

"It sure could."

Two days of working the anonymous girl proved maddening. Petra was at her desk eating a hot dog when the sound of a throat clearing made her look up.

Isaac Gomez. Again.

He stood off to the side, wearing his usual blue button-down shirt, pressed khakis, and penny loafers. Black hair parted and plastered down like a choir boy's. Smooth, brown face all freshly scrubbed. He held a stack of old murder books to his chest and said, "I hope I'm not bothering you, Detective Connor."

Of course, he was. Of course, she smiled up at him.

Every time she saw Isaac, Petra thought of a Diego Rivera kid grown up. The hair straight as brush-bristle; the nutmeg skin; the huge, liquid, almond eyes; the clear hints of Indian blood in the elevated cheekbones and finely boned nose.

Isaac was five-ten, maybe one-fifty, with square shoulders, bony wrists, and a deliberate but awkward way of moving.

Chronologically, he was twenty-two.

Twenty-two and a year from his Ph.D. Lord only knew how old he was intellectually. But when conversation veered away from facts and figures, he could end up mired in aw-shucks adolescence.

Petra was sure he was a virgin.

"What's up, Isaac?"

She expected a smile—the embarrassed smile she seemed to elicit from him. Nothing about happiness, everything about the jitters. More than once, when they were together, she'd spotted a tenting of khaki in his crotch area. The flush around the ears, the quick cover-up using a textbook or his laptop. When that happened, she pretended not to notice.

No smile this evening. He looked tense.

Eight-fourteen P.M. The detectives' room was nearly empty, reasonable people had gone home. She'd been playing with the computer, logging on to missing kids' databases, still trying to trace the girl in the pink shoes.

"You're sure I'm not intruding?"

"I'm sure. What are you doing here at this hour?"

Isaac shrugged. "I got involved . . . started with one thing and ended with another." He hefted the pile of blue notebooks. His eyes looked hot.

"Why don't you put those down," said Petra. "Pull up a chair."

"I'm sorry if this is disruptive, Detective Connor. I know you're working Paradiso, and under normal circumstances I wouldn't intrude." Flicker of smile. "I guess that's not true. I've intruded quite a bit, haven't I?"

"Not at all," Petra lied. The truth was, babysitting Brain Boy could be a butt-aching disruption when things got busy. She motioned to a side chair and he sat.

"What's up?"

Isaac played with a collar button. "I was working on my multiple regression analysis—plugging in new variables . . ." He shook his head. Hard. As if emptying it of extraneous information. "You don't need to hear all that. The essential point is I was searching for additional ways to organize my data and, serendipitously, I came across something I thought you should see."

He stopped. Took a breath.

She said, "What, Isaac?"

"It's going to sound . . . on the surface, it may look like nothing, some kind of coincidence . . . but I've done statistical tests—several tests, each one covering the mathematical weaknesses of the others—and it's obvious to me that it's not just factitious, not just a quirk. As far as I can tell, this is real, Detective Connor."

Unblemished, brown cheeks were suddenly slick with sweat.

Petra sat there.

"It's totally weird," he went on, suddenly sounding like a kid, "but I'm sure it's real."

He began flipping open murder books. Started off talking softly, at a near whisper. Ended up shooting out words, like an automatic weapon.

Assault-brain.

Petra listened. Brilliant or not, the kid was an amateur, this had to be nonsense.

As if reading her mind, he said, "I promise you, it's genuine."

She said, "Why don't you tell me about those statistical tests of yours?"

4

Irma Gomez had been working for the Lattimores for nine years before she said anything about the problem with Isaac.

Doctors Seth and Marilyn Lattimore lived in a nineteen-room Tudor on Hudson Avenue in Hancock Park. Both Lattimores were surgeons in their sixties, he a thoracic man, she an ophthalmologist. Both were no-nonsense perfectionists, but pleasant and generous when not weighed down by professional concerns. They cared deeply for one another, had raised three children, all presently in various stages of medical training. Thursdays they played golf together because Thursday was co-ed day at the country club. In January they traveled for one week to Cabo San Lucas and every May they flew to Paris on Air France, first class, where they stayed at the same suite at the Hôtel Le Bristol and made the rounds of Michelin three-star restaurants. Back in California, every third weekend was spent at their condo in Palm Desert, where they slept in and read trashy novels and wore copious amounts of sunblock.

Six days a week, for ten years, Irma Gomez had taken the bus from her three-room apartment in the Union District and showed up at eight A.M. at the Lattimore mansion, where she let herself in through the kitchen door and disarmed the security system. She began by cleaning the entire house—the prettying-up chores, the surface work. Detailed tasks—polishing, scrubbing, serious behind-the-davenport dusting—were divided up, per Dr. Marilyn's suggestion, because the house could be overwhelming.

Monday through Wednesday, the downstairs; Thursday through Saturday, the upstairs.

"That way," Dr. Marilyn assured her, "you can end the week on an easier note. What with the children's rooms being closed off."

The "children" were twenty-four, twenty-six, and thirty, and they'd been out of the house for years.

Irma nodded assent. As it turned out, Dr. Marilyn was right, but even if she hadn't been, Irma wouldn't have argued.

She was a quiet woman, made quieter by her failure to learn English better during the eleven years she'd lived in the United States. She and her husband, Isaiah, had three kids of their own and by the time Irma began working for the Lattimores, Little Isaiah was four, Isaac two, and baby Joel, a rambunctious infant, active as a monkey.

At age twenty-three, Irma Flores made her way from the village of San Francisco Guajoyo in El Salvador, up through Mexico, and across the border into the United States, just east of San Diego. Prodded along in the darkness by a vicious *coyote* named Paz who attempted to black-mail her for more money than they'd agreed upon, then reacted to her refusal with an attempted rape.

Irma managed to free herself and, somehow, found her way to downtown L.A. To the door of the Pentecostal church where sanctuary had been promised. The pastor was a kind man. A janitor when he wasn't preaching, he found her night-work, cleaning downtown office buildings.

Church was her solace and it was in church that she met Isaiah Gomez. His quiet demeanor and shabby clothes brought out something soft in her. His job was dying sheets of fabric in an East L.A. plant, leaning over steaming vats, inhaling toxic fumes, trudging home pale and weary in the early-morning hours.

They married and when Irma became pregnant with Little Isaiah she knew night-work would no longer do. Acquiring false papers, she registered with an agency on Larchmont Avenue. Her first boss, a film director living in the Hollywood Hills, terrified her with his rages and his drinking and his cocaine, and she quit after a week. God was good to her the second time, delivering her to the Lattimores.

Midway through the ninth year of Irma's employment, Dr. Marilyn Lattimore came down with an uncharacteristic cold and was home for two days. Perhaps that's why she noticed the expression of Irma's face. For the most part, Irma labored in solitude, humming and singing and setting off echoes in big, vaulted rooms.

It was in the breakfast room that the conversation took place. Dr. Marilyn sat reading the paper and sipping tea and dabbing at her red, drippy nose. Irma was in the adjoining kitchen, had removed the covers of the stove-burners and was scrubbing them single-mindedly.

"Do you believe this, Irma? A week of surgeries and I come down with this arrogant little virus." Dr. Marilyn's voice, normally husky, now bordered on masculine.

"Back in medical school, Irma, when I rotated through pediatrics, I caught every virus known to mankind. And later, of course, when I had the children. But it's been years since I've been sick and I find this positively insulting. I'm sure some patient gave it to me. I'd just like to know who so I could thank them personally."

Dr. Marilyn was a pretty woman, small, with honey-colored hair, who looked much younger than her age. She walked two miles every morning at six A.M., followed that with half an hour on an elliptical machine, lifted free weights, ate sparely except when she was in Paris.

Irma said, "You strong, you get better soon."

"I certainly hope so . . . thank you for that bit of optimism, Irma . . . would you be a dear and get me some of the fig preserve for my toast?"

Irma fetched the jar and brought it over.

"Thank you, dear."

"Something else, Doctor Em?"

"No, thank you, dear. . . . Are *you* all right, Irma?"

Irma forced a smile. "Yes."

"You're sure?"

"Sure, yes, Doctor Em."

"Hmm . . . don't spare me because of my cold. If there's something on your mind, get it out."

Irma started to head back to the kitchen.

"Dear," Dr. Marilyn called after her, "I know you well, and it's obvious something's on your mind. You wore that exact same look until we had your papers taken care of. Then you did it again, worrying about whether or not the amnesty would take effect. Something's *definitely* on your mind."

"I fine, Doctor Em."

"Turn around and look me in the eye and tell me that."

Irma complied. Dr. Marilyn stared at her. She had sharp brown eyes and a determined mouth. "Very well."

Two minutes later, after finishing her toast: "Please, Irma. Stop sulking and get it off your chest. After all, how often do you have anyone to talk to, what with Dr. Ess and me always gone. This is such an isolating job, isn't it— Is *that* what's bothering you?"

"No, no, I love the job, Doctor—"

"Then what is it?"

"*Nada.* Nothing."

"Now you're being stubborn, young lady."

"I— Is nothing."

"*Irma.*"

"I worry about Isaac."

Alarm brightened the sharp brown eyes, turned them vulpine, vaguely frightening. "Isaac? Is he all right?"

"Yes, he very good. Very smart."

Irma broke down in tears.

"He's smart and you're crying?" said Dr. Marilyn. "Am I missing something?"

They had tea and fig jam on thin toast and Irma told Dr. Marilyn all of it. How Isaac kept coming home from school crying with frustration and boredom. How he'd finished all of his sixth-grade work in two months, taken it upon himself to "borrow" seventh- and eighth- and even some ninth-grade books and had sped through them as well. Finally, he was caught reading a prealgebra workbook slipped out of a supply room and was sent to the principal's office for "unauthorized study and irregular behavior."

Irma visited the school, tried to handle it on her own. The principal had nothing but disdain for Irma's simple clothes and thick accent; her firm suggestion was that Isaac stop being "precocious" and concentrate on conforming to "class standards."

When Irma tried to point out that the boy was well ahead of class standards, the principal cut her off and informed her that Isaac was just going to have to be content repeating everything.

"That's outrageous," said Dr. Marilyn. "Absolutely outrageous. There, there, dry your eyes . . . three years ahead? On his *own*?"

"Two, some three."

"My eldest, John, was somewhat like that. Not quite as smart as your Isaac seems to be, but school was always tedious for him because he moved too fast. Oh, dear, we had some dustups with him. . . . Now John's the chief resident in psychiatry at Stanford." Dr. Marilyn brightened. "Perhaps your *Isaac* could be a physician. Wouldn't *that* be fabulous, Irma?"

Irma nodded, half listening as Dr. Marilyn prattled.

"A child that bright, Irma, there's no limit. . . . Give me that principal's number and I'll have a little chat with her." She sneezed, coughed, wiped her nose. Laughed. "With this baritone, I'll sound positively authoritative."

Irma didn't speak.

"What's the number, dear?"

Silence.

"Irma?"

"I don' wan no trouble, Dr. Em."

"You've already got trouble, Irma. Now we have to find a solution."

Irma looked down at the floor.

"What?" said Dr. Marilyn, sharply. "Ah. You're worried about repercussions, about someone taking this out on you and your family. Well, dear, don't be concerned about that. You're legal. When we arranged your papers we were extremely careful about buttoning up every detail."

"I don' understand," said Irma.

Dr. Marilyn sighed. "When we hired that attorney—the . . . *abogado*—"

"No that," said Irma. "I don' understand where Isaac come from. I not smart, Isaiah not smart, the other two not smart."

Dr. Marilyn pondered that. Nibbled toast and put it aside. "You're smart enough, dear."

"Nah like Isaac. He always fast, Isaac. Walk fast, talk fast. *Ocho*— eight month he talk, say *papa, mama, pan, vaca.* The other two, was fourteen, fifteen—"

"Eight months?" said Dr. Marilyn. "Oh, dear. That's astonishing, even John didn't utter a word until a year." She sat back and thought, leaned over, and took Irma's hands in hers. "Do you realize what a *gift* you've been given? What someone like Isaac could *do?*"

Irma shrugged.

Dr. Marilyn stood, coughed, trudged to the kitchen wall-phone. "I'm going to call that fool of a principal. One way or another, we'll get to the *bottom* of this mess."

Dr. Marilyn confronted public school bureaucracy and fared no better than Irma.

"Astonishing," she exclaimed. "These people are mindless cretins."

She conferred with Dr. Seth and the two of them took it upon themselves to confer with Melvyn Pogue, Ed.D., headmaster of the Burton Academy, where John, Bradley, and Elizabeth Lattimore had earned nearly straight A's.

The timing was perfect. Burton had come under fire from some of its progressive alumni for being lily-white and elitist, and though plans had been drawn up to increase diversity, no steps had been taken.

"This boy," said Dr. Pogue, "sounds perfect."

"He's extremely clever," said Dr. Seth. "Nice, religious little fellow to boot. But perfection's a bit overreaching. We don't want to pressure the lad."

"Yes, yes, of course, Dr. Lattimore." In Pogue's top desk drawer was a freshly signed Lattimore check. Full tuition for an entire year, with money left over for gymnasium refurbishment. "Clever is good. Religious is good. . . . Um, are we talking Catholic?"

Isaac arrived at the Burton campus, on Third near McCadden, just a brief walk from the Lattimore mansion, freshly barbered and wearing his best church clothes. A school psychologist ran him through a battery of tests and pronounced him "off the scale."

An appointment was made for Irma and Isaiah Gomez and the boy to meet Dr. Melvyn Pogue; Pogue's assistant; Ralph Gottfried, the chairman of the faculty committee; and Mona Hornsby, the chief administrator. Smiling people, white-pink, invariably large. They spoke rapidly and, when his parents seemed confused, Isaac translated.

A week later, he'd transferred to Burton, as a seventh grader. In addition, he received individual "enrichment"—mostly reading by himself in Melvyn Pogue's book-lined office.

His brothers, happy and recalcitrant in public school, thought the whole deal was weird—the Burton uniform with its silly blue, pleated pants, white shirt, powder-blue jacket, and striped tie; taking the bus to work with Mama, hanging with Anglos all day. Playing sports they'd never heard of—field hockey, water polo, squash—and one they knew about but believed unattainable—tennis.

When they asked Isaac about it, he said, "It's okay," but he was careful not to display too much emotion. No reason to make them feel deprived.

In reality, it was better than okay, it was fabulous. For the first time in his life, he felt as if his mind was being allowed to go where it wanted. Despite the fact that most of the other Burton students regarded him as a little dark-skinned curiosity and he was often left alone.

He *loved* being alone. The leather-and-paper smell of Melvyn Pogue's office was imbedded in his consciousness, as fragrant as mother's milk. He read—chewed up books—took notes that no one read, stayed in school well past dismissal time. Waiting, with a bag full of books, for Irma to come by to pick him up, and the two of them embarked on the long bus journey back to the Union District.

Sometimes Mama asked him what he was learning. Usually, she dozed on the bus as Isaac read. He was learning about wondrous, strange things, other worlds—other universes. At age eleven, he saw the world as infinite.

By the time he was twelve, he'd made a few casual friends—kids who invited him to their glorious homes, though he was unable to reciprocate. His apartment was clean but small, and the Union District was grimy, urban, a high-crime neighborhood. Even without asking, he knew that no way would Burton parents allow their progeny that far east of Van Ness.

He accustomed himself to a double life: Burton's beaux-arts buildings and emerald playing fields by day, by night the burp of gunfire and screams and static-scratchy salsa outside the window of the closet-sized bedroom he shared with his brothers.

At night, he thought a lot about the differences among people. Rich and poor, light and dark. Crime, why people did bad things. Was there a fairness to life? Did God take a personal interest in everyone's life?

Sometimes, he wondered about his mother. Was hers a double life, too? Maybe one day they'd talk about it.

By age fourteen, he smiled and spoke like a Burton student and had zipped through Burton's high school math curriculum, all of sophomore biology, and two years of advanced placement history. Four years of high school were compressed to two. At fifteen, he graduated with full honors and was accepted as a "special circumstances" student at the University of Southern California.

It was in college that he decided to become a doctor, and he earned a 4.0 as a bio major with a minor in math. USC wanted to hold on to him, and by the time he graduated summa cum laude, Phi Beta Kappa, at barely nineteen, he'd been accepted to the Keck School of Medicine.

His parents celebrated, but Isaac wasn't sure.

Four more years of lectures with no respite in between. Everything had moved so fast. Deep down, he knew he wasn't mature enough for the responsibility of tending to other human beings.

He requested and received a deferral, needing a break—something leisurely, less structured.

For Isaac that meant a Ph.D. in epidemiology and biostatistics. By age twenty-one, he'd fulfilled all his course requirements, earned a master's degree, and began work on his doctoral dissertation.

"Discriminating and Predictive Patterns of Solved and Unsolved Homicides in Los Angeles Between 1991 and 2001."

As he sat and composed his hypothesis, hunched in a remote corner of the Doheny Library subbasement, memories of gunshots and screams and salsa filled his head.

◆

Though care had been taken by the university to shield its boy-wonder from publicity, news of Isaac's triumphs reached the desk of City Councilman Gilbert Reyes, who promptly issued a press release in which he took credit for everything the young man had accomplished.

Upon the strong advice of his faculty adviser, Isaac attended a luncheon where he sat next to Reyes; shook the hands of big, loud people; contradicted nothing the councilman said.

Photo opportunities were Reyes's meat; pictures appeared in the Spanish language mailings his campaign distributed prior to the next election. Isaac, looking like a shell-shocked Boy Scout, was labeled *"El Prodigio."*

The experience left him vaguely unsettled, but when the time came to request access to LAPD files for his research, Isaac knew who to call. Within two days, he had an authorized long-term visitors' badge, a jerry-built "internship," guaranteed access to inactive homicide files— and anything else he came across in the basement archives. His desk would be at Hollywood Division, because Gilbert Reyes was a serious buddy of Deputy Chief Randy Diaz, the new Hollywood Division overboss.

Isaac showed up at Hollywood bright and early on an April Monday and met with an unpleasant police captain named Schoelkopf, who looked like Stalin.

Schoelkopf regarded Isaac as if he were a suspect, didn't even pretend to pay attention as Isaac rattled off his hypotheses, nor did he listen as Isaac offered profound thanks for the desk. Instead, his eyes focused on a distant place and he chewed his big black mustache as if it was lunch. When Isaac stopped talking, a cold smile stretched the facial pelt.

"Yeah, fine," said the captain. "Ask for Connor. She'll take real good care of you."

5

It was nothing Petra would have ever noticed. Even if it had stared her in the face.

Isaac's neatly typed sheet lay flat on her desk. He sat in the metal chair by the side of her desk. Drummed his fingers. Stopped. Pretended to be nonchalant.

She read the heading again. Boldface.

June 28 Homicides: An Embedded Pattern?

Like the title of a term paper. And why not? Isaac was just twenty-two. What did he know about anything other than school?

Below the title, a list of six homicides, all on June 28, on or near midnight.

Six in six years; her initial reaction was *big deal*. For the past decade, L.A.'s annual homicide rate had fluctuated between 180 and 600, with the last few years settling in at around 250. That averaged out to a killing every day and a half. Meaning, some days there was nastiness, others nothing at all. When you considered summer heat, June 28 would most likely be one of the high-ticket dates.

She said all that to Isaac. He shot out his answer so quickly she knew he'd been expecting the objection.

"It's not just the quantity, Detective Connor. It's the quality."

Those big, liquid eyes. *Detective Connor.* How many times had she told him to call her Petra? The kid was sweet, but there was a certain stubbornness to him.

"The quality of the killings?"

"Not in the sense of a value judgment. By quality I mean the inherent properties of the crimes, the . . ." He trailed off, plinked a corner of the list.

"Go on," said Petra. "Just keep it simple—no more chi square, pi square, analysis of whatever. I was an art major."

He colored. "Sorry, I tend to get—"

"Hey," she said, "just kidding. I asked you to tell me about your statistical tests and you did." At breakneck speed, with the fervor of a true believer.

"The tests," he said, "aren't any big deal, they just examine phenomena mathematically. As in the likelihood of something happening by chance. One way to do that particular analysis is to draw comparisons between groups by examining the distribution of . . . the pattern of the scores. I did exactly that. Compared June 28 with every other day of the year. You're right about homicides clustering, but no other date presents this pattern. Even summer effects tend to manifest on weekends or holidays. These six cases fall on various days of the week. In fact, only one—the first murder—took place on a weekend."

Petra reached for her mug. Her tea had gone cold but she drank it anyway.

"Would you like some water?" said Isaac.

"I'm fine. What else?"

"Okay . . . another way to look at it, is to simply examine inherent base probabilities—" He'd punctuated his words with index-finger jabs. Now he stopped, blushed even more intensely. "There I go again." Another long, deep inhalation. "Let's take it issue by issue. Start with weapon of choice, because that's a discreet— It's a fairly simple variable. Firearms are the clear favorite of L.A. murderers. I've looked at twenty years' worth of one eighty-sevens and seventy-three percent have been carried out with handguns, rifles, or shotguns. Knives and other sharp objects are next, at around fifteen percent. That means those two modalities account for nearly ninety percent of all local murders. The FBI's national figures are similar. Sixty-seven percent firearms, fourteen percent knives. Personal weapons—fists, feet—account for six percent and the rest is a mixed bag. So the fact that neither a gun nor a knife was used on any of the June 28 cases is notable. As is the nature of the fatal injury. In every data bank I've checked, blunt force homicides never rise above the level of five percent. They're a rare occurrence, Detective Connor. I'm sure you know that better than I."

"Isaac, I just closed two cases. A bare-fist blow to the head and a broken neck via martial arts."

He frowned. "Then you just closed two rare ones. Have you seen many others?"

Petra thought back. She shook her head. "Not for a while."

Isaac said, "If we get even more specific, cranial bludgeoning by unknown weapon accounts for no more than three percent of L.A. homicides. But it makes up one *hundred* percent of these cases. When you add the other similarities—identical calendar date, same approximate time, probable stranger homicides, and look at the probability of a chance cluster, you're moving way past coincidence."

He stopped.

Petra said, "That it?"

"Actually, there is a bit more. LAPD homicide detectives solve between two-thirds and three-quarters of their cases, yet all *these* cases remain unsolved."

"That's because they're stranger homicides," said Petra. "You've been here long enough to see the kind of stuff we clear quickly. Some moron holding the smoking gun when the uniforms get there."

"I think you're selling yourself short, Detective Connor." Saying it sincerely, not a trace of patronizing. "The truth is you people are very effective—imagine a major league slugger hitting seven hundred. Even stranger homicides get solved. But not one of these. All that supports my thesis: these are highly irregular events. The final incongruity is that during the same six-year period, gang homicides rose from twenty percent of all homicides to nearly forty. Meaning the chance of a nongang murder lowered proportionately. Yet not one of the June 28 cases appear gang-related. Add all that up and we're talking a combination of highly unusual circumstances. The likelihood of it boiling down to chance is one over so many zeros I don't have a name for it."

Bet you do, thought Petra. *Bet you're going easy on me.*

She slid the list out from under his hand, took a closer look.

June 28 Homicides: An Embedded Pattern?

1. 1997: 12:12 a.m. Marta Doebbler, 29, Sherman Oaks, married white female. Out with friends at Pantages Theater in H'wood, went to ladies' room, never returned. Found in own car, backseat, depressed skull fracture.

2. 1998: 12:06 a.m. Geraldo Luis Solis, 63, widowed Hispanic male. Found in his house, breakfast room, Wilsh. Div, food taken but no money, depressed skull fracture.

3. 1999: 12:45 a.m. Coral Laurine Langdon, 52, single white female, walked her dog in H'wood Hills, found by patrol car, under brush, six blocks from home. Depressed skull fracture. Dog ("Brandy," 10 y.o. cockapoo) stomped to death.

4. 2000: 12:56 a.m. Darren Ares Hochenbrenner, 19, single black male, Navy ensign, stationed in Port Hueneme, on shore leave H'wood, found in alley, Fourth Street, Cent. Div, pockets emptied. Depressed skull fracture.

5. 2001: 12:01 a.m. Jewell Janis Blank, 14, single white female, runaway, found in Griffith Park, near Fern Dell, by rangers. Depressed skull fracture.

6. 2002: 12:28 a.m. Curtis Marc Hoffey, 20, single white male, known gay hustler, found in alley, Highland near Sunset. Depressed skull fracture.

Petra looked up. "There doesn't seem to be any pattern victim-wise."

"I know," said Isaac, "but still."

"I have a friend, a psychologist, who says people are walking prisms. We see with our brains, not our eyes. And what we see depends on context."

Now *she* was pontificating. Isaac sat back. He looked crushed.

"My point is," she said, "that it all depends on how you look at it. You've raised some interesting points—more than interesting . . . pro-vocative." She pointed to the list, ran her finger down the names. "These people are all over the place in terms of sex, age . . . social class. We've got urban and semirural dumpsites. If this is some kind of serial thing, there'd most likely be a sexual angle, and I can't see what a sixty-three-year-old man and a fourteen-year-old girl would have in common as sexual targets."

"All that's true," said Isaac. "But don't you think the other factors are too blatant to be ignored?"

Petra's head began hurting. "You've obviously put a lot of time into this and I'm not dismissing it, but—"

"Why," he interrupted, "does there have to be a sexual angle?"

"That's the way it tends to shake out."

"The FBI profile. Yes, yes, I know about all of that. Their basic thesis is that what they call organized killers—really just a dumbed-down version of what psychologists call psychopaths—are motivated by a combination of sexuality and violence. I'm sure that typically there's some truth to that. But as you said, Detective, reality depends on which prism you're using. The FBI interviewed imprisoned killers and compiled data banks. But data are only as good as the sample, and who says killers who get caught are similar to those who don't? Maybe the FBI's bad guys got caught because they were psychologically rigid. Maybe it was their predictability that tripped them up."

His voice had climbed. Heat in the brown eyes made them something quite other than liquid. "All I'm saying is that sometimes exceptions are more important than rules."

"What motive are you proposing for these killings?" said Petra.

Long pause. "I don't know."

Neither of them spoke. Isaac slumped. "Okay, thanks for your time." He scooped up the list and stashed it in the shiny brown briefcase he carried around. Petra had seen detectives smile disparagingly at the case. She'd heard the comments behind Isaac's back. *Brainiac. Boy wonder. Petra's little day-care project.* When she felt assertive, she silenced the noise with an icy stare.

Now she found herself feeling protective of the kid but annoyed. The last thing she needed was some theory that got her dredging up six years of cold cases. Not with four victims down at the Paradiso, one of them a girl she couldn't even identify.

On the other hand, Isaac was smarter than she was, much smarter. Dismissing him out of hand could turn out to be one of those *big* mistakes. And what if he went over her head to Schoelkopf—to Councilman Reyes. If that happened and he turned out to be right . . .

Headlines danced in her head. *Young Wizard Uncovers Unsolved Killings.* The text: *LAPD detective failed to investigate . . .*

Isaac got to his feet. "Sorry for wasting your time. Is there something I can do for you? On your main case?"

"My main case?"

"The Paradiso. I've heard it's been tough going."

"Have you?" she said. Hearing the chill in her voice, she coerced her lips to form a smile of her own. Stratospheric I.Q. or not, he was a kid. An overly enthusiastic, pain-in-the-butt politically *connected* kid. "It's been a tough one," she agreed. "All those kids mowed down, no one willing to talk. What could you do for me?"

"I don't know," he said. "Maybe look at the data." Now he was blushing again. "That was totally presumptuous of me. You're the professional, what do I know? Sorry, I won't bother you again—"

"Do you know anything about pink Kmart sneakers?"

"Pardon?"

She told him about the unidentified girl.

His posture relaxed. Thinking—analyzing—did that to him. "You're thinking she might've been the intended victim and the others were innocent bystanders?"

"At this point, Isaac, I'm not thinking anything. I just think it's odd that no one's come forth to I.D. her."

"Hmm . . . yes, that would imply some kind of . . . turmoil in her background. . . . It sounds as if you took the shoe-thing as far as you could. . . . I'll give it some thought. I'm sure I won't come up with anything, but I'll give it a try."

"I'd appreciate it," she said. Not meaning a word but keeping the damn smile on high-beam.

Nearly nine P.M. The kid was working late, too. And not getting paid for it.

She said, "How about some dinner—a burger, whatever."

"Thanks, but I need to get home. My mother made dinner and it's a big deal to her if we don't all show up."

"Okay," she said. "Maybe another time." The genius still lived with his folks . . . the Union District, she recalled. Probably some shabby little apartment. Huge contrast to the green lawns and towering trees at USC. Getting all that attention as boy-genius. Working here, his own desk in the detectives' room. No reason not to stay late.

"Make me a copy of that list," she said.

"You're not dismissing it?"

"Let me think about it some more."

Biiiiig smile. "Will do. Have a nice evening, Detective Connor."

"You, too." *Professor Gomez.*

He left and Petra's mind shifted back to the Paradiso slaughter. Gun as "weapon of choice." At least in that way it was typical. Which, for some reason, made her feel worse.

6

A copy of the list was on Petra's desk the following afternoon. Yellow Post-it in the upper right-hand corner: *"Detective C: Thanks. I. G."*

She put it aside and spent the next two days talking to Missing Persons cops throughout California, faxing morgue shots of the girl in the pink shoes, getting a few callbacks but no leads. She thought about expanding to neighboring states. The chubby girl appeared Hispanic, so the Southwest seemed a good bet.

Phoning her way through Arizona and Nevada took another full day, then she moved on to New Mexico, where a Santa Fe P.D. detective named Darrel Two Moons said, "She might be a girl who went missing from the San Ildefonso pueblo last year."

"Our vic had a recent abortion."

"Even better," said Two Moons. "There was a rumor of an unwanted pregnancy. A married man, not a good guy. We've been wondering if he got rid of her, but so far no body. It's the tribal police's case but they called us in. Send the photo."

"The father," said Petra. "Is he the kind of guy who'd drive to L.A. to shoot her?"

"In terms of amorality, sure. Would he work that hard? Can't say."

Twenty minutes later, Two Moons's partner, a guy named Steve Katz, called back and said, "I know Darrel talked to you about Cheryl Ruiz. Sorry, the picture's not her. Also, the tribal police didn't think to tell us they found Cheryl. She took Greyhound to Minnesota, had a baby, has been living with her aunt all this time."

"Interagency cooperation. So what else is new?" said Petra.

"Yeah," said Katz. "L.A., huh? I used to be NYPD, worked midtown Manhattan. I remember what it's like to be busy."

"Miss it?"

"Depends."

"On what?"

"On how long the night stretches. On what else I've got going on in my life."

Another shift full of nothing made her grouchy. Some nice, athletic sex with a touch of romance wouldn't have hurt, but it had been a week since Eric's last call, she wasn't even sure where he was.

Time to pack it in; go home; take a long, hot, gel-lubed bath; maybe actually cook herself something decent and healthy. That meant stopping off to buy veggies and whatever and she decided she just wasn't up to cold, fluorescent supermarket aisles and other lonely people. She'd snarf whatever was in the fridge, hopefully have the energy to take a stab at her O'Keeffe project.

Big, tall New York buildings that turned the city into a shady warren.

Buildings, no people. Painted long before tall New York buildings meant *target*.

What a world.

Just as she locked up her desk, her cell phone squawked from inside her purse. She fumbled past her gun, tissues, makeup, caught it on the third ring.

"Hi," said a voice she'd once thought flat, mechanical, freakishly unemotional.

Nothing about the tone and timbre had changed, but he meant something different to her now. *We hear with our brains, not our ears.*

She said, "Hi. Where'd they send you now?"

"I sent myself. I'm down in the parking lot."

Her heart leapt. One sentence could do that to her?

"The parking lot? Here?"

"Right here."

She said, "I'm coming down."

Eric stood next to Petra's Accord, half-concealed in the shadows. Arms at his side, looking in her direction, not moving. He had on a black nylon windbreaker, half-zipped over a white T-shirt, pipestem black jeans. Those black, crepe-soled shoes he liked for stakeouts.

He looked even thinner than usual. Pale and hollow-cheeked, eyes so dark and deep set they receded into the evening. Dark hair cropped even shorter—back to the military cut.

A middle-sized, skinny guy with the pallor of a seminary student. No attempt to posture, but still the James Dean thing amped big-time, filling Petra's head.

How could she ever have thought him anything but sexy?

She hurried to him and they embraced. He pulled away first, touched her face. Buried his face in her hair, held her tight—the pressure of a needy child.

She said, "You okay?"

"Now, I am."

"Why didn't you come upstairs?"

"Technically, I'm not here."

She took his face in her hands, kissed his eyelids, held him at arm's length.

"Where are you supposed to be?"

"Jerusalem."

"What, you went AWOL?"

"Technically."

"Meaning?"

"The Israelis took a break because they've got business to take care of in Jenin. A chance came up to hitch a ride on a plane."

"A plane."

His smile was fleeting, barely perceptible. "You know. With wings."

"How long can you stay?"

"I need to leave tomorrow P.M."

"One night," said Petra.

"Is that okay?"

"Of course." She kissed his nose. "You have a car?"

He shook his head. "Took a taxi."

They got into the Accord. Petra started up the engine and noticed the dark smudges under his eyes. "How long have you been in transit?"

"Twenty-three hours."

"Some hitch."

"Part of it was a hitch. I flew commercial from Heathrow. Old ladies in wheelchairs were getting frisked while guys who look like Usama's favorite swimming sperm walked right through. You hungry?"

Petra wanted to play house but no food in the apartment meant dinner out.

They went to an Italian place on Third near La Brea, an old-fashioned chianti-bottles-dangling-from-the ceiling taverna, ordered veal marsala and spaghetti with clams and slices of spumoni for dessert. No wine; Eric never drank.

She asked him about Jerusalem.

He said, "I was there years ago, back during Riyadh. I thought it was beautiful then. It's more complicated now. Assholes wearing bomb-packs kind of ruin the ambience."

He coiled pasta on his fork, paused midair. "I met a guy who knows you. Superintendent Sharavi."

"Daniel," said Petra. "We worked a case together. He and Milo and me."

"That's what he said." Eric put the fork down, took her hand in his, played with her fingers.

"You really have to go back tomorrow?"

"That's the plan."

"Through London?"

He hesitated. The instinctive secrecy. "I'm booked on Jet Blue out of Long Beach to New York."

"One night," she said.

"I wanted to see you."

◆

Back in Petra's apartment, they sat on the couch, listened to a Diana Krall CD, and made out.

Eric started off gently, the way he had since their first few encounters. Usually it turned Petra on—the slow simmer, all the erotic ballet. Tonight she was impatient, but she slowed herself down. Then she didn't. Stripping him down to pale, bony nakedness, then ripping off her own clothes so hastily she nearly tripped on a pants leg.

Cool move, Detective Klutz.

Eric hadn't noticed. His eyes were closed and his flat chest heaved. In the flesh, he looked younger. Vulnerable.

She touched him and he opened his eyes, took hold of her shoulders, trailed his hands down her hips and cupped her ass. Lifted her adroitly and settled her on him. Taking his own initiative: moving her up and down, slowly, then faster. Kissing her nipples, biting down gently. Throwing his head back and letting out a long, deep-in-the throat sigh. Clenching his face as he held back.

She said, "Do it, baby." But he kept fighting it. So she sped up, ground against him. And when she came, panting and gasping, her hair over her face, he was bucking up at her and shouting "God!"

Later, in bed, snuggled under the covers, she pinched his butt and said, "Didn't know you were religious."

"Not the religion I was raised with."

His dad was a minister. Reverend Bob Stahl, a kind and gentle man, determined to believe the best about people. Eric's mom, Mary, was no less positive. Petra had come to know both of them in the E.R. waiting room. Petra benefiting from the disapproving glances the Stahls shot at the bimbo's skimpy clothing.

Bonding some more when the bleeding crisis resolved and Eric was moved to a private room, still unconscious. The three of them sitting by Eric's bed as he slept and healed. When Petra offered to leave to give them privacy, they insisted she stay.

Once, just before Eric woke up, Mary Stahl hugged Petra and told her, "You're just the kind of girl I wish he'd bring home."

If you only knew.

Eric began rubbing the twin soft spots just inside her shoulder blades. The places she'd told him always got sore.

"Oh, man," she said. "I'm not sure I'm gonna let you out of here to-morrow."

"You tie me up," he said. "It would be an excuse."

"Don't tempt me."

She tried to get him talking about work.

He said, "You don't want to know."

"That bad?"

He rolled over, stared at the ceiling.

"What?" she said.

"I look at the Israelis' situation and it worries me. They're up against September eleven every day, but they can't do what they need to do. World opinion, diplomacy, all that good stuff."

His mouth snapped shut and he flung his arm over his eyes. Petra was sure he was going to clam up. Instead, he said, "Politics can be poison. Too much politics and you can't protect yourself."

Eric, the most taciturn of men, sometimes mumbled in his sleep. But what woke Petra in the middle of the night was her own, internal voice—some kind of warning. She turned, stared at his face, saw calm. The faint, contented smile of a well-nurtured kid.

The second time she awoke it was just after noon and Eric was up and showering. By twelve-thirty Petra was cooking eggs. They ate and read the paper—Lord, wasn't this domestic.

At one-thirty, Eric kissed her and headed for the door.

"I'll drive you," she said.

"I called a cab."

He'd arrived with no luggage, was leaving the same way. Wearing pressed blue jeans and a dark blue button-down shirt, the same black windbreaker, the same crepe-soled shoes. Fresh duds selected from the clothing he'd left in her guest closet.

Zipping halfway across the world with nothing but a wallet. Like it was a jaunt to the market.

Here and back. To see her.

She said, "Cancel the taxi. I'm taking you."

◆

She hung with him in the cozy, turquoise, modern coffee shop above the Jet Blue terminal until a young man stuck his head in and announced the flight's imminent departure.

Eric got up, shrugged, looked embarrassed. Petra gave him the most intense hug she could muster. One more kiss and he was gone. She left the terminal with aching eyes.

Traffic on the 405 was ominous and she didn't arrive at the Hollywood station until six twenty-five P.M. Two D's were at their desks—Kaplan and Salas—and greeted her with nods.

No messages from Mac Dilbeck or anyone else on the Paradiso case. She headed for a free computer and tried some national databases for missing kids that she'd already contacted, not really expecting anything. Not getting anything.

What to do, now?

A voice from across the room said, "Detective Connor."

Isaac Gomez, wearing an olive suit, yellow shirt, green-and-red rep tie, hair parted and shiny and brushed flat to his scalp, toted his briefcase toward her desk.

"Very spiffy," she said. "Heavy-duty meeting?"

The predictable blush darkened his neck. "Not really. Have you had a chance to consider my hypothesis?"

Changing the subject too quickly. That pushed Petra's mischief button. "C'mon, tell me about it. You get honored again by Councilman Reyes?"

"Not hardly." Mumbling. Tugging at his tie knot.

"Something better than being honored?"

He kicked one shoe with the other.

"C'mon, Isaac," said Petra. "We common folk don't get the chance to hobnob with the powers-that-be. I'm living vicariously through you." She cupped her hand around her mouth. "Is it true what they say about Reyes? Is there a slight flatulence problem?"

Isaac smiled weakly.

Petra said, "What can I do? Mr. Gomez is the soul of discretion."

He laughed loud enough to make Kaplan and Salas turn. Then he grew serious. "A date," he blurted. "I had to go on a lunch date."

"*Had to?* You make it sound like homework."

Isaac sighed. "In a sense it was. I was assigned by my mother. She thinks I need to get out more."

"You disagree."

"I'm social enough, Detective Connor. I just don't need— The problem is my mother was of the firm belief that once I entered college, some golden gate of sociability would open. Sometimes I think she's more concerned about that than academics."

"Mothers care," said Petra. What did she know? Her own had died pushing her out.

"They do—she does, but . . ." Isaac rubbed his cheek. When his hand dropped, Petra saw a red, raised spot. Fulminating zit. Brains or not, he was clinging to adolescence.

He said, "My mother's notion of maximal personal success is that I meet a girl who elevates me socially. She was never comfortable visiting my school—it was an upscale private school. She felt herself inferior, which was nonsense, she's an incredible woman. But I couldn't convince her, so she refused to have anything to do with the parents of my classmates. But I believe part of her would have liked me to hook up with one of those girls. It's the same with her employers. They're doctors, they've been mentoring me. They think she's fabulous but she won't step out of the servant role . . . there's a whole Pygmalion thing going on. It's complicated and I'm sure you're not interested."

He bit his lip. One eyelid ticced. Poor kid was under real pressure. Petra felt bad about ribbing him.

"Hey," she said, "you're smart in all kinds of ways. You'll do what's best for yourself."

"I try to tell my mother. My plate's full enough, I'm not ready for a relationship."

Petra pointed to the chair alongside her desk. He sat down heavily.

"Lousy date, huh?"

He grinned. "I'm that obvious."

"Well," she said, "I figure Mom sets you up with a high I.Q. beauty queen, maybe you'd forget about your plate."

"The girl was nice enough, but not—We had absolutely nothing in common. Her family's new in our church. She's religious and modest, and for my mother, that's enough."

"No beauty queen," said Petra.

"She looks like a mastiff."

"Ouch."

"That was cruel," said Isaac. "But so what? She was also aggressive. Sweet in church but take her to dinner and watch out." He shook his head.

"Aggressive about what?"

"Everything. She had opinions on matters about which she knew nothing. Religion really got her going. Nuclear-strength dogma. We'd barely sat down and she was telling me I needed to go to church more often. Instructing me what to believe. And not with any particular theological elegance."

"Oh, boy," said Petra. "You're not even married and she's running your life."

He laughed again. "You sound like a guy. I mean, that's something one guy would say to another." Blushing deeply. "Not that you're not feminine, you're very feminine, it's just that— Are you married?"

"Used to be. It didn't end because I tried to run his life. I was the most perfect spouse in the universe but he was a lout."

He said, "You're joking but I bet that's true." He looked at her, helplessly.

"In terms of sounding like a guy," she said, "I grew up with five brothers. You pick stuff up."

"That must help in terms of working here—the predominantly male environment."

Somehow the subject had changed. She said, "It does help."

He said, "Anyway . . . about those June 28 cases. I neglected to mention that four of six took place here, in Hollywood Division. I'm not sure yet if it adds another layer of statistical significance to the—"

"We're a high-crime district, Isaac."

"Several divisions have higher homicide rates. Ramparts, Central, Newton—"

"Maybe you've got a point, Isaac. I promise to take a look, but right now I'm kind of tied up."

"The Paradiso shootings."

"Exactly."

"Has that girl been identified?"

"Not yet."

"Okay. Sorry for—"

"She had an abortion within the last month or two. That say anything to you?"

"The obvious thing," he said, "is a possible source of conflict. With the father."

"Over the abortion?"

"I was thinking of the pregnancy itself. In certain situations, an unwanted pregnancy would be a pretty robust motive for homicide, wouldn't you say? Theodore Dreiser wrote a wonderful book about it—"

"She terminated the pregnancy, Isaac."

"But maybe she kept that fact to herself."

Petra considered that. Why not? "It's an angle. Thanks. Now all I have to do is figure out who she is."

She flashed him a smile and turned back to the mess on her desk.

"Detective Connor . . ."

"Yes?"

"Would it be feasible for me to ride with you? To observe what you do firsthand? I promise not to be intrusive."

"It's pretty boring, Isaac. Lots of routine, lots of dead ends."

"That's okay," he said. "The longer I'm here, the more I realize how ignorant I am. Writing a dissertation about crime and I don't know the first thing about it."

"I'm not sure riding along will help you much."

"I think it will, Detective."

A trickle of sweat made its way down his left hairline and reached his ear. He swiped at it. How long had he been building up the courage to ask her? Behind the precocious pronouncements was so much anxiety.

"Okay," she said. "Tomorrow morning, when I recontact some of the witnesses on the Paradiso case, you can come along. But only on one condition."

"What's that?"

"Start calling me Petra. If you don't, I'll start calling you 'Dr. Gomez.' "

He smiled. "I'm a ways off from earning that."

"I've earned my title but I'm forgoing the honor," she said. "You're making me feel old."

CHAPTER

8

The bus that Isaac took to the Union District was a big, loose-in-the-rivets, half-empty, diesel-fed dinosaur that rumbled and bumped through dark city streets, brakes squeaking, belching pollution. Brightly lit; a crime-reduction measure.

By car, the ride from Hollywood would be twenty minutes. Using the MTA, an easy hour.

He sat at the back, read the latest edition of Davison's *Abnormal Psychology.* His fellow riders were mostly cleaning women and restaurant workers, a few drunks. Nearly all Latino, mostly illegal, he figured. Just as his parents had been until the Doctors had intervened.

And now he was wearing his father's hand-me-down suit and playing at scholar.

There but for the grace . . .

When he got home, his father would probably be at work. Lately, Papa had been taking a second shift dipping sheets into noxious vats, wanting to earn a little extra money. Isaiah, home from his roofing job, would be sleeping, and Joel, of late a gadabout, might or might not be around.

His mother would be in the kitchen, changed from her uniform to a faded housedress and slippers. A pot of *albondigas* soup simmering on the stove. A rack of tamales, both savory and sweet, fresh out of the oven.

Isaac had barely eaten all day, taking care to be hungry for her food. He'd learned the hard way his freshman year, eating a late lunch on campus and arriving home with insufficient appetite. Not a word of protest from Mama as she wrapped his uneaten dinner in foil. But those sad looks . . .

Tonight, he'd gorge as she sat and watched him. Eventually, he'd try to get her to talk about her day. She'd claim it was boring and want to know about the exciting world he lived in. He'd resist, then finally parcel out a few details. Not the crime stuff. The numbers and polysyllables.

A few well-chosen polysyllables always impressed Mama. When he tried to simplify his language, she stopped him, told him she understood.

She didn't have a clue what he was talking about. In any language *multiple regression analysis* and *percentage of variance accounted for* were incomprehensible except to the initiated. But he knew better than to patronize her.

Sensitive guy that he was.

One of the initiated.

Whatever that meant.

He'd dozed off and dreamed when the bus came to a quick stop. Jolted awake, he looked up in time to see the driver throw out a homeless man who'd failed to produce the fare.

Angry words and clenched fists shot through the bus's wheezing door as the wretchedly filthy evictee stood in the gutter and howled vengeance. Isaac watched the man, bent over in shame, turned tiny by the bus's departure.

The driver cursed and put on speed.

The cusp of violence. So much of the crime Isaac had studied began that way.

Not the June 28 murders, though. They were something different, he was sure of it. You could lie with numbers, but the numbers he'd divined weren't lying.

Now to convince Detective Connor.

Petra.

Thinking of her by name was unsettling; it reminded him that she was a woman.

He sat lower in his seat, wanting to sink out of view. Not that any of his co-riders were the least bit interested in him. Some were regulars and surely recognized him, but no one spoke.

The geek in the borrowed suit.

Occasionally someone—a woman not unlike his mother—smiled as he boarded. But for the most part everyone wanted to rest.

The Somnolent Express.

Before being wakened, his dreams had been pleasant. Something featuring Detective Connor.

Petra.

Had he been in it? He wasn't sure.

She had. Lithe and graceful, that efficient helmet of black hair.

The crisp features. Ivory skin, blue vein tracings at the periphery . . .

She wasn't anywhere close to the contemporary female ideal: blond, busty, bubbly. She was the antithesis of all that, and Isaac respected her doubly for being herself, not giving in to crass social pressures.

A serious person. There seemed to be very little that amused her.

She always dressed in black. Her eyes were dark brown, but in a certain light, they appeared black as well. Searching eyes—*working* eyes—not vehicles for flirtation.

The overall impression was a young Morticia Addams, and Isaac had heard other detectives refer to her as Morticia. But also as "Barbie." That he didn't get.

There was plenty about Hollywood Division, about police work in general, that continued to elude him. His professors thought academia was complex, but now, after time spent with cops, it was all he could do not to burst out in laughter at departmental meetings.

Petra was no Barbie.

Just the opposite. Focused, intense.

He'd lain awake in bed more than once, imagining what her breasts looked like, only to shake himself out of that, appalled at his vulgarity.

Small, firm breasts—stop.

Still . . . she was a beautiful woman.

9

Petra stayed at her desk until well after midnight, forgetting about Isaac and his theories and anything else that didn't relate to the Paradiso shootings.

She talked to some Hollywood gang cops and their cohorts in Ramparts. They'd heard nothing about the killings being turf-related but promised to keep checking. Then she attempted to recontact all eighteen kids she'd interviewed in the parking lot.

Twelve were home. In five cases, scared and/or indignant parents tried to block access. Petra charmed her way past all of them but the teens reiterated complete ignorance.

Among the six she didn't reach were her two nervous ones, Bonnie Ramirez and Sandra Leon. No answer at either number, no machines.

She got on the computer, figuring to surf her way through some more missing kid sites. Her mail tag was up so she checked that first.

Departmental garbage and an e-mail from Mac Dilbeck.

p: luc and i were out in the field today nothing at our
end, what about yours? there's talk if we don't make
progress of giving it over to HOMSPEC wouldn't that be

```
fun. maybe we should pick your genius kids brain we
could use a good brain to pick around here. m.
```

She e-mailed back:

```
nothing plus nothing equals you-know-what. going home.
tomorrow i check out a couple of nervous w's. planning
to take the genius along. though if you want him you
can have him. p.
```

But once she logged off and got her purse from her locker, the thought of an empty apartment repelled her. Filling herself a cup of detective-room coffee, she bought some insomnia.

Someone had left half a box of sweet rolls out by the machine. The pastries looked none too fresh—the custard ones were hardening around the edges. But the apple seemed passable so she brought it back to her desk along with the mocha-flavored Liquid Plumber.

Kaplan and Salas had left and no one had replaced them. She sat there alone, going through old messages and nonessential mail, filling out a long-overdue pension form and one for departmental health in-surance.

What remained was Isaac's summary.

June 28.

She separated the Hollywood cases from the others, copied down the vics' names, got back on the computer, and logged on to the sta-tion's stat file.

Just as Isaac claimed, all four remained open. Of the four primary D's assigned to the case, she recognized two.

Neil Wahlgren had caught the most recent murder—Curtis Hoffey, the twenty-year-old male hustler. Jewell Blank, the runaway teen blud-geoned in Griffith Park had been assigned to Max Stokes.

Neil had transferred to one of the Valley divisions, wanting to cut down on drivetime. A while back—not too long after Hoffey. And Max Stokes had retired nearly a year ago.

Meaning both cases could have gotten short shrift.

Both Neil and Max were competent, by-the-books guys. Would they have taken the time to work whodunits hard knowing they were leaving soon?

Petra wanted to think so.

The cases were certain to have been transferred but the computer didn't list the newly assigned detectives.

Onward to the next one. Coral Langdon, the woman who'd died with her dog up in the Hollywood Hills.

That one had been handled by Shirley Lenois. Seeing her name made Petra's eyes ache.

When Petra had started at Hollywood, Shirley had been the only other female Homicide D. A short, stocky, fifty-two-year-old woman with a corona of yellow-gray hair, Shirley looked more like a substitute teacher than a detective. Married to a motorcycle vet in Traffic Division, she had five kids and treated Petra like the sixth, going out of her way to make things smooth for the Homicide virgin.

Making sure there were tampons in the ladies' room because no one else would give a damn.

Last December, Shirley had died in a skiing accident up at Big Bear. Stupid tree, stupid goddamn tree.

Petra cried silently for a while, then wiped her eyes and moved on to the fourth Hollywood murder. First of the six, chronologically. The killing that began Isaac's alleged series.

Marta Doebbler, the woman who'd gone to the theater with her friends. Six years ago, well before Petra's time. Two detectives she'd never heard of, a DIII named Conrad Ballou and DII named Enrique Martinez.

Cops were leaving the department faster than they were coming in. Maybe another couple of retirees.

Maybe Ballou and Martinez had done their best, anyway.

Sometimes that didn't matter.

CHAPTER

10

When Petra showed up at ten the following morning, Isaac was at his corner desk, poring over documents, pretending not to notice her arrival.

She felt hungover and queasy, in no mood for babysitting.

By ten-twenty, she'd swallowed two cups of coffee and was ready to pretend to be human. She got up, waved Isaac toward the door, and he followed her, carrying his briefcase over. No more suit, but not the button-down and khakis. Dark blue slacks, navy shirt, a navy tie. Dressing for ride-along. That monotone thing young guys did nowadays. Cute, though on Isaac it looked a bit like a costume.

They exited the building together but didn't talk. Petra left her Accord in its spot and took the unmarked she'd signed out from the motor pool. No-smoking regulations had been in effect for years, but the car reeked of stale cigars, and when she started the engine, it protested before kicking in.

"Bad equipment," she told Isaac. "Talk to Councilman Reyes about that."

"We don't talk on a regular basis."

She steered out onto the street. He wasn't smiling. Had she offended him? Too bad.

"What we're going to do today," she said, "is recontact two witnesses. Both are sixteen-year-old girls, both seemed nervous when I interviewed them the first time. One might have a reason to be nervous that has nothing to do with the case. She's got leukemia."

Isaac said, "That would do it."

"You okay?"

"Sure."

"I'm asking because you seem a bit quiet."

"I don't have anything to say." A beat. "As opposed to most of the time."

"Nah," she said, "you're not gabby, you're smart."

More silence.

She steered the unmarked clunker through smoggy Hollywood streets. Isaac looked out the window.

Eric did that when she drove. Eric noticed things.

She said, "Smart people have a right to talk, Isaac. It's the dummies who get on my nerves."

Finally, a smile. But it faded quickly. "I'm here to observe and to learn. I appreciate your taking the time."

"No prob." She headed down Hollywood Boulevard to Western, then over to Los Feliz, figuring to catch the Golden State Freeway then switch to the 10 East all the way to Boyle Heights. "The first girl is named Bonnie Anne Ramirez. She lives on East 127th. You know the area?"

"Not well. It's mostly Mexican, there."

And he was Salvadoran.

Telling her subtly, *We're not all alike?*

Petra said, "Bonnie's sixteen but she's got a two-year-old baby. The father's some guy named George who doesn't sound like a prince. They don't live together. Bonnie dropped out of school."

No comment for half a block, then Isaac said, "She was nervous?"

"A defiant nervousness. Which could just mean she doesn't like the police. She has no record, but in a neighborhood like that you could get away with plenty of stuff without having your name on a file."

"That's the truth," said Isaac. "The FBI estimates that for every crime an apprehended criminal commits, another six go undetected. My preliminary research shows it's probably higher."

"Really."

"Most crime doesn't even come close to being reported. The higher the crime rate in a given area, the more that's true."

"Makes sense," said Petra. "The system doesn't come through, people stop believing."

"Poor people are dispirited in general. Take my neighborhood. In fifteen years, we've had our apartment broken into three times, my bike's been stolen, my father's been mugged and had his car ripped off, my little brother's been held up for lunch money, and I can't tell you how many times my mother's been threatened by drunks or junkies when she comes home from work. We've been spared anything serious, but you hear gunshots at least twice a week and sirens a lot more often than that."

Petra said nothing.

"It used to be worse," he went on. "When I was a little kid, before the CRASH units got active. There were blocks you just didn't walk. Wear the wrong shoes and you were dead. CRASH worked pretty well. Then, after the Ramparts scandal, antigang policing was cut back and the bad stuff started to rise again."

His mouth set and his hands had balled.

Petra drove for a while. "I can see why you'd study crime."

"Maybe that was a mistake."

"What do you mean?"

"The more I get into it, the more it seems to be a waste of time. Most of my professors are still hung up on what they call 'root causes.' To them that means poverty. And race, even though they consider themselves liberal. The truth is, most poor people just want to live their lives, like anyone else. The problem isn't poor people, it's *bad* people who prey on the poor because the poor lack resources."

Petra mumbled assent. Isaac didn't seem to have heard. "Maybe I should've gone straight to med school. Get out, finish my specialty training, make some money, and move my parents to a decent neighborhood. Or at least get my mom a car so she doesn't have to fend off the drunks and the junkies." A beat. "Not that my mother would ever learn to drive."

"Scared?"

"She's kind of set in her ways."

"Mothers can be like that," said Petra. *How would you know?* "Okay, here we go. The freeway looks pretty good."

◆

Bonnie Ramirez lived with her mother, three older brothers, and little Rocky in a tiny, yellow clapboard bungalow that sat behind rusting chain link. Block after block of similar homes comprised the tract. Built for returning GI's, the houses ranged from decrepit to sparkling.

Effort had been made to keep up the Ramirez home: the two-pace lawn was sunken and brown but trimmed, and impatiens in uneven beds struggled with the early, spring heat. A baby stroller sat on the wooden porch, along with a plaster pedestal spray-painted gold that served no apparent purpose.

Bonnie wasn't home and her mother was caring for Rocky. The toddler slept in a crib set up in the nine-by-nine living room. The floors were wood and the ceilings were low. The house smelled of good food and Pine Sol and just the merest whiff of dirty diaper.

Anna Ramirez was a short, broad woman with hair dyed red, puffy cheeks, and flabby arms. The cheeks were so bountiful they pushed her eyes up and turned them to slits. It gave her a suspicious look, even though she took pains to be cordial. Her voice and speech inflections were that same Boyle Heights singsong.

She invited them to sit and brought out cans of soda and a bowl of pretzels and told them Bonnie's dad was a Vietnam vet who'd survived the war only to die in a heavy equipment accident while excavating the foundation for a downtown office building. Removing his photo from the wall, she brandished it like a religious article. Nice-looking guy in full-dress uniform. But bad skin—unfortunate legacy for Bonnie.

Petra said, "Any idea when Bonnie's returning?"

Anna Ramirez shook her head and frowned. "You just missed her. She comes and goes. She was out last night, slept till ten, left."

"Out late?"

"Always."

Rocky stirred in his crib.

Petra said, "I don't want to wake him."

"It's okay," said Anna. "He sleeps good." She glanced at the pretzel bowl in Petra's lap and Petra ate one.

"Can I get you something else to eat, Officer?"

"No, thanks, ma'am. Do you know why we're here?"

"That shooting in Hollywood. Bonnie told me about it."

"What'd she say?"

"That it happened out in the parking lot. She heard the shots but didn't see anything. She said she talked to a lady cop. That was you?"

Petra nodded.

Anna Ramirez looked over at Isaac. Studied him. "You look like my nephew Bobby."

Isaac smiled weakly.

Petra said, "One of the kids who was shot was a girl we still haven't been able to identify."

"No parents asking about her?"

"No one's come forth, ma'am."

"That's sad."

Little Rocky peeped. Shifted. Bellowed. Anna Ramirez went over and removed him from the crib. Poor kid was flushed and dyspeptic-looking. Swaddled in too many blankets for the heat.

Anna sat back down and lay her grandson across her commodious lap. Rocky burped, frowned, went back to sleep. Circular dumpling of a face, curly black hair. Very cute. Petra noticed that his nails were trimmed and the blankets were spotless.

She said, "He's beautiful."

Anna Ramirez sighed. "Very active. So . . . this girl . . ."

"I was wondering if Bonnie knew her," said Petra. Realizing she'd used the singular since entering the house. Should she include Isaac? He was sitting there, upright and stiff, looking like someone waiting for a job interview.

"You didn't ask Bonnie if she knew her?"

"I did and she said no. I'm just following up."

Anna Ramirez frowned. "You don't believe her."

"It's not that—"

"It's okay. Sometimes I don't believe her."

Petra hoped her smile was empathetic.

Anna said, "Her brothers all finished school, two of them are in J.C., but Bonnie never liked school. Down deep, she's a good girl . . ." She glanced down at Rocky. "This was kind of a— So now I'm being Mama again, so okay, it's okay. It's hard to tell Bonnie anything, but I'm insisting she's definitely gonna have to get at least her GED. What kind of job can you get without that?"

Petra nodded.

Anna sighed again.

"Anyway, ma'am, when she gets home, if you'd be so kind as to give me a call."

"Sure," said Anna. "This girl, you think she could've been with Bonnie?"

"I really can't say, ma'am."

"What did she look like?"

"Short, a little heavy. She wore pink sneakers."

"That could be Jacqui," said Anna Ramirez. "Jacqui Olivares. She's short and she used to be much fatter till she lost weight. But she's still not skinny. And she's got problems."

"What kind of problems?"

"Two kids. A boy and a girl. And she's only seventeen."

"Have you ever seen her in pink sneakers?"

Anna touched a finger to her mouth. Rocky stirred again and she bounced him gently on her knees, smoothed sweaty hair off his little brow.

"No," she said, "I never noticed that. But Jacqui doesn't come around here no more. I told Bonnie I didn't want her here."

"Bad influence," said Petra.

"You bet."

"I have a picture of the unidentified victim, ma'am, but I need to warn you it's not pretty."

"A dead picture?"

"Yes, ma'am."

"I seen dead people, saw my Rudy dead, go ahead."

Petra produced the least deathly of the morgue shots and handed it to her. Anna said, "That's not Jacqui, I never seen this girl."

The address Sandra Leon had given wasn't far from the Ramirez home, but when they got there, Petra knew she'd been had.

The numbers matched a boarded-up bodega on a run-down stretch of abandoned homes backed by weed-choked alleys. Graffiti everywhere. Angry young men with shaved heads and eye-filling tattoos cruised the rutted streets, bopping, staring, sneering.

Petra got out of there fast, drove to Soto Avenue, not far from the county morgue, and into the lot of a busy-looking gas station where she bought coffee for herself and a Coke for Isaac. He tried to pay her back but she wouldn't hear it. As they drank, she got the number for Western Pediatrics Hospital, asked for Oncology, and waited a long time to be connected.

The secretary on the other end said "That's confidential" when she asked for Sandra Leon's address.

Petra lied easily. "I have reason to believe that Ms. Leon is in danger."

"Because of her illness?"

"Because of a crime. A multiple murder that she witnessed."

Long pause. "You need to speak to her physician."

"Please connect me."

"The last name is . . . Leon . . . okay, here it is, Sandra no-middle-name. That would be Dr. Katzman. I'll put you through."

What Petra got on the other end of the line was a soft, male voice on tape. "This is Dr. Bob Katzman. I'll be traveling for the next two weeks, but I will be picking up messages. If this is a medical emergency, the Oncology on-call extension is . . ."

Petra hung up and reconnected to the secretary. "Dr. Katzman's gone for two weeks. All I need is Sandra Leon's address."

"You're with the police?"

I am the police, honey. "Detective Connor." Petra spelled it. "Hollywood Division, here's my badge number and you can call to verify—"

"No, that's okay, I'll give you Medical Records."

Five minutes later, Petra had the address Sandra Leon had listed on her intake form.

The girl had signed herself into care.

"Is she an emancipated minor?"

"I wouldn't know," said the records clerk.

"Is there any adult's name on the form?"

"Um . . . doesn't seem to be, Detective."

"Who pays her bills?"

"CCS—Children's Cancer Service, it's a county fund."

"No family members," said Petra.

"She's not the only one," said the clerk. "We get runaways all the time. This is Hollywood."

The other address Sandra had used was on Gower north of Holly-wood. Minutes from the station. If you were in an energetic mood, you could walk.

Petra got back on the freeway. "See what I mean," she told Isaac. "Tedious."

"I think it's interesting," he said.

"What is?"

"The process. How you go about putting it all together."

Petra didn't believe she'd put anything together. She glanced over at Isaac. Not a trace of irony on his face.

He said, "I also find it interesting the way people relate to you. Bonnie's mother, for example. She clearly saw you as an authority figure and that caused her to be respectful. She's a conventional woman, proud of her husband's military service, takes her responsibilities seriously."

"As opposed to her daughter."

"Yes."

"Generation gap," said Petra.

"Generational breakdown," he said. "People in Bonnie's generation see themselves as free from convention and regulation."

"You think that's bad?"

Isaac smiled. "I've been instructed by my dissertation committee not to make value judgments until the data are all in."

"We ain't in school. Go a little crazy."

He fingered his tie. "I think an extremely open society is a double-edged sword. Some people take advantage of freedom in a healthy way, others can't cope. On balance, I'd opt for too much freedom. Sometimes, when I can get my father to talk, he tells us about El Salvador. I know the difference between democracy and the alternatives. There's no country as great as America in the twenty-first century."

"Except for people who can't cope with too much freedom."

"And they," said Isaac, "have you to contend with."

Gower Street. Unit eleven of a twenty-unit apartment complex the color of honeydew melon set midway between Hollywood Boulevard and Franklin Avenue.

"Okay," said Petra, getting out of the car. "Let's see what our little fibber has to say for herself."

When she scanned the mailboxes near the front door, unit eleven was registered to *Hawkins, A.*

No *Leon* on any of the slots.

The front door was unlocked. They climbed the stairs and walked to the rear of the hallway where number eleven was tucked. Petra rang the bell and a very tall, black man in a green sweater and brown slacks answered the door. White snowflakes were printed at the neck and cuffs of the sweater, a ski-thing in June. An intricate zigzag cornrow sheathed his high-domed head—one of those architectural master-pieces NBA pros liked to sport. Rapidograph pen in one hand, ink stains on his fingertips. What Petra could see of the apartment was spare and well-kept. Drafting table pushed up against a window. A cloud of incense drifted out to the hall.

"Yes?" said the man, twirling the pen.

"Afternoon, sir," said Petra, flashing the badge. "I'm looking for Sandra Leon."

"Who?"

Petra repeated the name. "She listed this apartment as her address."

"Maybe she lived here once upon a time, but not for at least a year, because that's how long I've been here."

"A year," said Petra.

"Twelve months and two weeks to be exact." Twirl, twirl. Big grin. "I promise you, my name's not Sandra."

Petra smiled back. "What would it be, sir?"

"Alexander Hawkins."

"Artist?"

"When I'm allowed to be. Mostly I work at a travel agency—Serenity Tours, over at Crossroads of the World." Another grin. "If that matters."

"It doesn't," said Petra, "unless you know Sandra Leon."

"Is she an attractive young lady who appreciates art?" said Hawkins.

"She's a sixteen-year-old girl who may have witnessed a murder."

Hawkins turned serious. "No, I don't know any Sandra Leon."

"Is there an in-house landlord or manager?"

"I wish. These luxury accommodations are shepherded by Franchise Realty headquartered in the golden city of Downey. I was just on the phone with their answering machine. Little insect problem. I can give you the number, know it by heart."

Back in the car, Petra called the company. The previous occupant of unit eleven had been a family named Kim and they'd been there for five years. No Leons had rented any apartments in the building during the seven years Franchise had managed the place.

She hung up, told Isaac. "Sandra lied twice. And that makes me *real* interested in her."

Back on the phone, she left a detailed message for Dr. Bob Katzman.

Isaac said, "Now what?"

Petra said, "Now we return to the station and I try to locate little Ms. Leon. When I hit a wall, which will probably be sooner rather than later, I'll take a closer look at those files of yours."

"I've been looking into June 28 to see if there's some sort of historical significance. The best criminal link I've come up with is that John Dillinger was born on that day. I suppose that could be inspirational to a sociopath. But Dillinger was a bank robber, a grandstander, very dramatic, the epitome of a conspicuous felon. From what I can tell, this killer's just the opposite. He's been picking a variety of victims in order to embed his pattern."

This killer. Pattern. The kid was convinced of one dark hand behind all six cases. Ah, impetuous youth.

As Petra began the short drive back to Wilcox, Isaac said, "Something else took place on June 28. The assassination of Archduke Franz Ferdinand. June 28, 1914. Essentially, that began World War One."

"There you go," said Petra. "Someone's declared war on the good folk of L.A."

11

I t was the wound pattern that snagged her.

Six P.M. As predicted, she'd hit the wall on Leon sooner rather than later. She phoned a nearby Mr. Pizza and called out for a small deep-dish with everything on it.

Across the room, Isaac remained at his corner desk, scribbling, punching his laptop, jotting down notes. Making a big show out of being inconspicuous. When the pie came, she went over and offered him a slice. He said no thanks, tailed her back to her desk, hung around as she opened the greasy box.

Petra selected a slice and began picking cheese off the pointed end.

Isaac said "Have a good evening" and left the station.

She poured herself more coffee, played with strings of mozzarella, picked up one of the files. Drank and ate and began to read. Getting grease on the folders. Being a little cavalier about it.

Until she came to the autopsy reports.

Six autopsy reports written by six separate coroners. The language was nearly identical.

Compression injuries of the occipital skull.

Hit from behind.

In every autopsy report, the weapon was described as heavy and tubular, approximately 77 centimeters in diameter in three murders, 75 in one, 78 in two. Which was close enough, given varying bone densities in people of different ages and sexes.

Two pathologists had been willing to speculate that the bludgeon was metal or hard plastic, because no imbedded wood fragments had been found.

What *had* been found was lots of blood and bone frags and gobbets of brain matter.

To Petra the weapon sounded like a length of pipe. Seventy-seven centimeters matched three inches on her old-fashioned ruler. Nice, hefty chunk of pipe.

Deep compression injuries, all that gore.

Someone—if there was a someone—liked braining people.

She started with the detective she knew still on the job.

Neil Wahlgren, the D on the Curtis Hoffey case. All she'd heard was he'd transferred somewhere in the Valley.

It took a while, but she located his extension at Van Nuys Auto Theft. Petra's job trajectory had been just the opposite, from chop shops to chopped humans, and she wondered why Neil had switched.

He was away from his desk, but the V.N. desk officer gave her his cell and she reached him.

"Hey," he said. "Barbie from Ken and Barbie, right?"

Remembering Petra and Stu Bishop. Those had been good days.

"That's me," she said.

"Hey," Wahlgren repeated. He had a hearty voice that sounded genuinely warm. Petra recalled him vaguely as a big, ruddy Nord with a bulbous nose. The kind you imagined ice-fishing and quaffing whatever ice fishers quaffed.

"Chasing chrome?" she said. "No more d.b.s?"

"Ten years of d.b.s was enough. Give me a nice boosted Lexus with GPS any day. What's up?"

"I've been looking at some cold cases and came across one of yours. Curtis Hoffey."

Right away Wahlgren said, "Male pross, hit over the head."

"That's the one."

"Messy."

"Messy in terms of crime scene or detection?"

"Both. Couldn't make an inch of progress," said Neil. "Which is no surprise, I guess, a vic like that. Twenty years old and from what I could gather he'd been on the streets since twelve. Poor kid probably serviced the wrong john, but there was no talk on the street and no prior similars."

"I might have one—emphasize *might,*" she said. "Someone was combing through old files and came up with half a dozen head-bashes that match in terms of wound pattern and weapon guestimology."

She paused. Should she go all the way, give him the June 28 tie-in? No, too weird. Not at this point—the guy worked Auto T, anyway, why would he care?

Neil said, "That so? Well, I didn't hear anything about that at the time." Defensiveness had crept into his voice.

Petra said, "No way you could, it's probably nothing."

"Who found it?" said Wahlgren.

"An intern. Who else would have the time?"

"What, one of those Eagle Scout types, all gung-ho?"

"Yup. So who caught it after you left?"

"Don't know. Schoelkopf said he'd handle the transfer. He still there? Still being a total asshole?"

"Still here," she said. "If he did transfer the case, there's no record."

"No surprise," said Neil. "Even at the time he didn't want me spending too much time on it, said we needed to pay attention to gang murders, this was a 'West Hollywood case.' You know what I mean."

"Gay."

"Gay hooker, low probability of closing it, and the city council was making noise about gang stuff. You get a whodunit with no serious forensics, no relatives or politicians breathing down your neck . . ." Neil trailed off.

"Sure," said Petra.

"The truth was, Schoelkopf was right. About it being a likely dead end."

And you didn't care to test the assumption.

"So Curtis had no family?" she said. Using the vic's name. Wanting Neil to think about Hoffey as a human being, at least for a moment.

"No one claimed the body. He got bashed up pretty good. If I never see another one like it, I'll be none the worse off."

12

Jewell Blank, the fourteen-year-old girl murdered in Griffith Park, had relatives, but according to Detective Max Stokes's notes, they hadn't been helpful.

The mother was Grace Blank, twenty-nine, single, a barmaid, living with her boyfriend, Thomas Crisp, thirty-two, an unemployed trucker and "biker type." Neither had seen Jewell for over a year, since she'd run away from their double-wide on the outskirts of Bakersfield. Neither, it appeared, had searched for her with any enthusiasm.

Twenty-nine years old meant Grace had given birth to Jewell when she was fifteen and Petra had a good idea of what came with that.

Another kid in Griffith Park. That made Petra's stomach knot up, as she thought of Billy Straight. Same background, same escape. Billy had lived in the park, like a feral child, scrounging Dumpsters for food and narrowly avoiding death. But for a happier ending, he could've been sitting on a cloud next to Jewell Blank.

Petra had rescued Billy. For the first year, after his grandmother took him in, they'd stayed in touch—regular phone calls, occasional outings. Now, Billy was fifteen, nearly six feet tall, and a prep-school junior. On his way to Stanford, Mrs. Adamson confided. She'd already talked to the dean.

It had been months since Petra had heard from him. Which was probably good, at least from his perspective. His life was in order, what use would he have for the police?

She found no record that Jewell Blank's case had been transferred to another detective.

Max Stokes appeared to have worked the case hard, getting help, as it turned out, from Shirley Lenois. The two veteran detectives had scoured the streets, interviewed scores of other runaways, checked the shelters and the churches and the agencies.

Jewell had squatted, on and off, in some of Hollywood's last remaining abandoned buildings and was known to her street-kid peers as "stuck-up," an assertive panhandler, an adroit shoplifter. No one could say if she'd prostituted herself for money, but she had slept with boys for drugs.

Multi-drug user: weed, pills, meth, acid, Ecstasy. Not heroin, though, everyone agreed. Needles scared Jewell. Petra returned to the autopsy report, avoiding the photos of the little girl's head. No needle tracks. The tox screen revealed significant levels of cannabis, alcohol, and pseudoephedrine, probably from an OTC decongestant.

According to the other kids, Jewell frequented the park when she got in a bad mood and didn't want to hang with anyone else.

No, she'd never spoken of meeting anyone there.

No, there were no boyfriends or regular johns in her life. At least, not that she'd ever mentioned.

She'd been found fully clothed with no evidence of rape. The coroner's conclusion was that she'd been sexually active for some time.

A premortem snapshot had been stapled to the file. What looked to be a school photo of a kid around nine. Jewell Blank had been darkhaired, wan, freckled, reluctant to smile.

Grace Blank and Thomas Crisp wanted to know if the city would pay for funeral expenses. Max Stokes's notes were terse on that subject:

"I informed them that death arrangements etc. were the family's responsibility. Respondents were displeased by that info., said they'd get back to me."

Jewell Blank's body had sat in the morgue for a month before an Inglewood mortuary had picked it up for cremation.

Was there any point talking to Max? Disrupting the poor guy's retirement by reminding him of one that had gotten away?

She looked around the room. Three detectives hunched over piles
of paperwork. That young, good-looking one, Eddie Baker; Ryan
Miller, another stud; and Barney Fleischer, gaunt, bald, ancient, near-
ing retirement himself.

Petra walked over to Barney's desk. He was filling out a requisition
form for office supplies. Demi-glasses perched on his beaklike nose.
His handwriting was tiny, pretty, almost calligraphic.

She asked him if he knew where Max Stokes was.

"Corvallis, Washington," he said, continuing to write. "He's got a
daughter up there, Karen. She's a doctor, never got married so you can
probably find her under Stokes."

No curiosity about why Petra wanted to know. Petra thanked him
and returned to Jewell Blank's file. Skimming a bit more, she put it
aside, called Corvallis, and got office and home numbers for Karen
Stokes, M.D.

Max answered the phone.

"Petra Connor," he said. "We were just sitting down for dinner."

"Sorry, I'll call back later."

"No, it's fine, just cold cuts. To what do I owe the pleasure?"

Picturing Max's ruddy, mustachioed face, she told him about reviewing the Blank file, gave him the same nosy-intern story.

"You're thinking of reworking it?" he said.

"Don't know yet, Max. Depends on what I learn."

"I hope you decide yes. Maybe you can do better than me."

"I doubt that."

"You never know, Petra. New blood and all that."

"You and Shirley, that's a lot of detective ability."

"Poor Shirley. So . . . what can I tell you?"

"I really don't know, Max. Seems to me you guys did all you
could."

"I thought we did . . . I still think about that one from time to time.
Poor little girl. Everyone said she was aggressive, had a temper, but
looking at her . . . such a tiny little thing. It was brutal."

The autopsy report stared up at Petra. Jewell's stats. Five-one,
ninety-four pounds.

Occipital injuries . . .

What was the point of all this?

Max Stokes was saying, ". . . with the parents—actually just one parent, the mother. Plus that boyfriend of hers."

"Solid citizens," said Petra.

"My gut pegged him, Thomas Crisp, as the bad guy. Your typical trash boyfriend scenario, maybe gets a little too close to the daughter, you know? The coroner said Jewell had been having sex for a few years. I'd bet Crisp abused her, that would be a good reason for running away. I never asked him directly, just hinted around and he got squirrelly. Plus, he had a felony record. Bad checks, attempted welfare fraud. I know it's not sex crimes or murder, but lowlife is lowlife. His attitude in general was bad—he didn't even fake caring about Jewell. I checked him out carefully, even drove up to Bakersfield. Guy had an alibi. During the time of the murder, he'd been on a three-day bender with a bunch of other lowlifes. First they bar-crawled, then they bought more booze and went back to the mother and Crisp's trailer. Neighbors in the trailer park complained and the police paid a call. Crisp was definitely in Bakersfield the whole time, everyone saw him."

"What about the mother?"

"She was there, too. Borderline retarded, if you ask me. She did seem to care a little, but every time she started to cry Crisp nudged her in the ribs and she shut up. His big concern was who was going to pay for the burial."

"I read your notes," said Petra.

Max sighed. "What can I tell you. Sometimes you don't win."

"Ain't that the truth. Enjoying retirement?"

"I dunno. I've been thinking of getting a security job. Just to get me out of the house."

"Sure," said Petra. "Makes sense."

"Anyway, good luck on little Jewell."

"One more thing, Max. I don't see any transfer."

"I wanted to transfer it to Shirley and she wanted to take it. Because she'd already started. Actually, it was she who came to me, wanting to partner. Because she'd caught another case, couple of years before, that probably wasn't the same guy but there were some similarities."

"Really?" said Petra.

"Yeah," said Max. "Another head-bashing, but not a kid, some woman, up in the Hollywood Hills. That one, a dog got killed, too, what was the name . . . I'm having a senior moment."

The name was Coral Langdon. Petra said, "Shirley thought the cases might be tied in?"

"At first she did, but in the end, she didn't. Too many differences, what with Jewell being a poor runaway and the other one—what was her name—being a financially comfortable divorcée with a nice house. That one—Lambert, Lan-something . . . anyway, that one Shirley had worked the ex-husband as the main suspect because the divorce hadn't been friendly. Plus, neighbors said he'd always hated the dog. He claimed an alibi, too, but it wasn't much of one. Sitting at home watching the tube, no one else in the apartment. But Shirley never found anything to contradict him and one neighbor did say his car had been in his driveway around the time of the murder."

"How come Shirley didn't get Jewell Blank's case?"

"I assumed she did," said Max.

"If she did, there's no record of it."

"Hmm. Don't know what to tell you, Petra."

"In the end Shirley didn't think Blank and the woman with the dog were similars."

"The only thing similar was head-bashing—Langdon, that was it. Something Langdon. So Shirley didn't work Jewell, huh?"

"Doesn't appear so."

"That's kind of funny," said Max. "You remember Shirley. Tenacious. Real tragedy what happened to her, I didn't even know she skied."

She thanked Max, apologized for interrupting his dinner, hung up, and turned to Coral Langdon's file.

The murdered woman's ex was an insurance salesman named Harvey Lee Langdon. Insurance tipped you off to the best of motives, but Harvey had sold property casualty, not term life. Shirley had taken a close look at Coral's papers anyway, and contacted a bunch of insurance companies. No juicy policy, anywhere. No financial ties at all between Coral and Harvey since their divorce three years ago, except for five hundred a month alimony. Coral Langdon had worked as an executive secretary to an aerospace honcho, made a fine living on her own.

The dog, Brandy, had been a bone of contention in the Langdon marriage. Harvey had expressed dismay at his ex-wife's demise but had smirked when hearing about the cockapoo. Shirley had transcribed his comments verbatim, quotation marks and all:

"Stupid little bitch. Know what her motto was? The world is my toilet."

A shrink could have fun with that. Harvey had definitely been worth looking at, but Shirley had made no progress along those lines.

The modus and the crime scenes—two females bludgeoned in wooded areas of Hollywood—had caused the tenacious Detective Lenois to make a connection between Langdon and Jewell Blank. Had she been unimpressed by the June 28 angle?

Most likely she hadn't noticed.

Would Shirley—astute, dogged, dedicated—have missed something like that?

Sure. The date of a homicide was something Petra never paid much attention to. As a detective, Shirley would have zeroed in on crime scene details.

The head-bashing. Like Isaac said, it was rare.

In the end, Shirley had decided the cases weren't linked, but she hadn't known about two previous head-bashings on the exact same date.

And now Shirley was dead and, once again, there was no evidence the case had been transferred.

Petra studied the photocopied driver's license attached to the file. Coral Langdon had been an attractive woman with a tan, oval face under a short cap of blond hair. Five-seven, one-thirty. Slender. Probably strong, too. According to Shirley's notes, Coral had worked out at a gym, studied kickboxing.

Meaning whoever had brained her was in good shape. And stealthy enough to get her from behind.

Petra visualized it. Langdon taking the cockapoo out for a night-time stroll, he steps out of the shadows . . .

Jewell Blank would've been a whole lot easier. A tiny little girl in the park.

No doubt, Shirley had wondered about that, decided it wasn't a match.

But *six* cases on the same date, that was different.

Like Isaac said, statistically significant.

Like Isaac said.

Petra figured that phrase would be adhering to her brain for a while.

She went back and studied the first two murders in detail. Marta Doebbler, the twenty-nine-year-old housewife who'd gone to see a play at the Pantages, left for the ladies' room and didn't return, and Geraldo Solis, the Wilshire Division case. Elderly man found sitting at his breakfast room table, brains leaking onto a plate of sausage and eggs. Now there was a charming detail.

Nothing else about the Solis file sparked her interest, but a notation on Marta Doebbler gave her pause: Doebbler had been called out of the theater by a cell phone squawk, and the detectives had traced the call to a pay phone around the corner from the theater.

Had someone lured her out? The fact that she'd complied, coupled with her body being dumped in her own car—unlike the others—said it was someone she knew. The detectives had interviewed the husband, an engineer named Kurt Doebbler, and remarked that he seemed "overly calm." Doebbler had an alibi: home with his and Marta's nine-year-old daughter, Katya.

She reread the Solis file. No sign of breaking and entering. Someone the old man had known as well?

No apparent connection between the victims but *could it have been* the same person?

She jotted down the names of the D's on both cases. Conrad Ballou and Enrique Martinez on Doebbler, another unfamiliar name on Solis, DII Jacob Hustaad, Wilshire Division.

Barney Fleischer was still at his desk, pen in his hand, but reading. Blue folder of his own. She'd always thought of Barney as end-of-career deadweight. Was he still working cases?

She approached him again, said, "Sorry, but I was wondering if you knew any of these guys."

He closed the murder book—a file labeled "Chang"—and examined the list. "Got a cold-case assignment?"

"Self-imposed assignment," said Petra. "The kid, Gomez, thought I should look at a few old files."

"The genius," said Barney. "Nice kid. I like him."

"He talks to you?"

"From time to time. He likes to hear about the old days." Barney smiled. "And who better than a geezer like me?" He put the Chang file on his desk. "That's one I did five years ago. No one gives me anything, anymore. I should leave but I'm not sure it would be good for me."

He peered at the list again. "Connie Ballou's a real old-timer. He was here well before I arrived, probably has ten years on me. He left around five years ago." Barney frowned.

"What?" said Petra.

"Connie left under somewhat . . . clouded circumstances."

"What kind of circumstances?"

"He had a bit of a drinking problem. We all knew about it, we all covered. One night he tanked up, got behind the wheel of an unmarked, and crashed it into a building on Cahuenga. That was kind of hard to cover for."

"How was he as a detective? When he was sober."

Barney shrugged. "That wasn't too often."

"No Sherlock," said Petra.

"More like Deputy Dawg, when I knew him. But I heard he used to be okay in the early days."

"What about his partner, Martinez?"

"Enrique had no big problems, but was no great talent, either. He got tarred by Connie's brush. The brass decided he should've reported Connie's drinking and demoted him down to uniform. The obvious question was what about all those other partners Connie had ridden with. But Enrique was the goat. I think he went over to Central Division as a deskman, but who knows how long he lasted there."

"He's living in Florida now."

"Makes sense," said Barney. "He's Cuban."

A lush and a no-talent. There was a good chance Marta Doebbler's murder hadn't been worked to the max. Nor, as far as Petra could tell, had it been transferred. She asked Barney about that.

Right away, he said, "Schoelkopf."

"He doesn't transfer cases?"

"He doesn't like to, if they've gone cold. What with all the manpower problems and the gang issues. You wouldn't know about that because you tend to solve your cases." Barney removed his reading glasses and massaged the ridge they'd etched into his nose. His eyes were wide, clear, blue, nested in a thatch of wrinkles.

"I know you don't like him, Petra, but I can't say as I'd do it any different. It's always a matter of priority. Cases go cold for a reason."

"Who says I don't like him?"

Barney grinned and Petra returned the favor.

He looked at the list again, said, "Jack Hustaad's dead. Suicide. Not job-related. We played golf together once in a while. Jack was a four-pack-a-day smoker, got lung cancer, started chemotherapy, decided he didn't like it, and ate some painkillers. It's not a completely irrational decision, right?"

"Right," said Petra.

"Anyway."

"Thanks, Barney."

"I assume," said the old detective, "that you want your research kept private."

"That would be good," said Petra.

"No problem," said Barney. "I don't like him either."

13

The next day Mac called a noon meeting on the Paradiso shooting. He and Petra and Luc Montoya ate sandwiches in a small conference room and compared notes. Montoya was forty, bald, muscular, with a movie-star face and the longest eyelashes Petra had ever seen on an adult. He wore a cream-colored sports coat, beige linen slacks, white shirt, pale blue tie. Very natty, but his expression was defeated and he didn't say much.

Mac had on the usual gray sharkskin and unreadable face.

He and Luc had dived into the witness pile, come up empty, and no local gang rumors were flying.

Petra told them about Sandra Leon's lies.

Luc gnawed his lip. Mac said, "So we have no idea where this kid lives."

Petra shook her head.

Mac said, "That doctor of hers, think he might know?"

"I've got a call in."

"Maybe you can find him before his vacation's over. Meanwhile, I'm heading over to Compton. They had a shooting last year, bangers, rap concert, cruise-by in the parking lot. Three down on that one. No solve, but they have ideas and I figured we'd compare notes. Misery and company and all that."

Petra called Dr. Robert Katzman's office again, talked to the machine, switched to the Oncology office, and got assertive with a secretary who transferred her to the department administrator, a woman named Kim Pagionides.

"Sandra Leon," said Pagionides. As if she knew the girl. As if she disapproved of the girl.

Petra said, "You've seen her recently?"

"Oh, no." Small, nervous laugh. "No, I don't think so. I'll have Dr. Katzman get in touch when he gets back."

"I need to speak to him now."

"I'm sure he's busy."

"So am I. Where, exactly, is he?"

"Traveling. To a bunch of cities. He's delivering papers at four scientific meetings. Important papers. We're talking about saving lives."

"And I'm talking about destroyed lives. So maybe the good doctor will be able to relate."

Silence.

Kim Pagionides said, "Let me check his calendar."

A few moments later: "He's in Baltimore, at Johns Hopkins. Here's his cell phone."

"Thank you."

"You're welcome."

Punching the cell number elicited an identical "Dr. Bob" Katzman message, mellow and reassuring. The physicians who'd treated her dad before he died from Alzheimer's could've learned something from Katzman about bedside manner.

Petra tried to keep her own voice serene, but she felt she'd barked at Dr. Bob. So be it.

◆

It was one forty-three P.M. and Isaac hadn't come in yet and that was just fine with Petra. Less distraction. She called the LAPD pension office and asked for current stats on retired detectives Conrad Ballou and Enrique Martinez.

Martinez was living in Pensacola, Florida, but Ballou was relatively local. Out in Palmdale, a one-hour freeway drive if you danced around the speed limits.

With nothing more to do on the Paradiso case and feeling lonely and itchy, a one-hour drive didn't sound half-bad.

She decided to take her own car. Wanted to listen to her own music.

As she headed for her Accord, someone called her name. For the merest, foolish moment, she hoped it would be Eric. The last time, they'd met in the lot. In a movie, he'd be back.

She turned, saw Isaac jogging toward her, wearing a white shirt, khakis, and sneakers, briefcase slapping against his thigh.

"Hey," she said. "What's up?"

"I got held up at school, hoped I'd get here in time to catch you."

"Some new bit of data?"

"No, I just thought if it was okay, I could ride with you."

Petra didn't answer and Isaac flinched. "That is, if it doesn't pose a problem—"

"It's fine," she said. "Actually, I'm heading out to talk to someone on one of your June 28 cases."

His eyes widened. "So you do see the validity of the—"

"I think you've put together something interesting. And seeing as I've got nothing else to do, why not check it out?"

Heading toward the 5 on-ramp, she said, "There's one thing we need to keep clear. This isn't an official investigation. It's important to be discreet."

"About . . ."

"Talking to anyone else. Period."

Her voice had stiffened. Isaac shifted his body toward the passenger door. "Sure. Of course."

"Especially Captain Schoelkopf," said Petra. "He doesn't like me, never has. Going off on a tangent when I've got a big-time active case could complicate my situation further. Also, it looks as if he had specific feelings about the June murders. In every case, the investigating detective left for one reason or another. Some retired, some moved to other divisions, some died. By itself, that's not unusual. Since the riots and the Ramparts scandal, there's been tons of turnover in the department. What is a bit unusual is that none of the files were transferred to new detectives. That's because Schoelkopf doesn't like transferring cold cases. So on the infinitesimal chance that we actually learn something about any of these murders, it's not going to reflect well on him."

A long silence filled the car before Isaac said, "I've complicated things."

"That's okay," said Petra. "Truth is, these victims deserve more than they got."

A few moments later: "Why doesn't he like you?"

"Because he's got poor taste."

Isaac smiled. "I don't think he likes me either."

"How much contact have you had with him?"

"The initial interview and we pass in the hall from time to time. He pretends not to notice me."

"Don't take it personally," said Petra. "He's a misanthrope. But he does have poor taste."

"Yes, he does," said Isaac.

She hooked onto the 210, then shifted to the 114, driving northeast through the beginnings of Antelope Valley. Passing through Burbank and Glendale and Pasadena along the way. The rocky outcroppings and green belt that were Angeles Crest National Forest, the site of Bedros Kashigian's final moments, and every psychopath's favorite dump spot.

Pretty, today, under a true-blue sky barely blemished by wispy clouds.

Nice scene to paint. She should get her portable easel out here, find a cozy plein air spot, and go to town.

It had been a long time since she'd painted anything with color.

◆

As the drive stretched on, she told Isaac about being impressed by the wound patterns and everything else she'd learned about the six murders.

He said, "Similar dimensions. *That* I didn't notice."

And none of the detectives had noticed June 28. "You'd have to be looking for it."

"I'll be more careful in the future," said Isaac.

The future?

He said, "That call from the phone booth is interesting. The possibility that it might be someone Mrs. Doebbler knew. What if Mr. Solis knew him as well? Someone familiar to all the victims."

"I thought of that," she said. "But it's a leap."

"Still, it's possible."

"If our killer was acquainted with all six victims, he had a pretty wide social network. We're talking runaways, male hustlers, executive secretaries, retirees, and that Navy ensign, Hochenbrenner. I haven't even looked at his file yet."

Isaac was staring out at the desert. If he'd heard her little speech, it wasn't apparent. Finally, he said, "Mr. Solis had breakfast food on his plate but the murder occurred around midnight."

"People eat at odd hours, Isaac."

"Did Mr. Solis?"

"Don't know," she said. "What, you think the bad guy dished up sausage and eggs after bashing in Solis's head and served it to a corpse?"

Isaac squirmed. She'd grossed him out and it gave her perverse satisfaction.

He said, "I really don't have much of a database from which to make a judgment—"

"A culinary killer," she cut him off. "As if it's not complicated enough."

He kept quiet. The car got hot. Ten degrees warmer out here in the desert. A warm June to begin with.

June. Today was the fourth. If there was anything to this craziness, someone else would die in twenty-four days.

She said, "So have you come up with any other notable June 28 occurrences in the historical archives?"

"Nothing profound." He spoke quietly, kept his eyes aimed at the window. Intimidated?

Bad Petra, mean Petra. He's just a kid.

"Tell me anything you've found," she said. "It could be important."

Isaac half turned toward her. "Basically, I've been logging into various almanacs, printed some lists. Long lists. But nothing jumps out. Here, I'll show you what I mean."

Snapping open his briefcase, he groped around, removed a batch of papers.

"I looked at birthdays and the farthest back I got was June 28, 1367, which is when Sigismund, the emperor of Hungary and Bohemia, was born."

"Was he a bad guy?"

"Your basic autocratic king." Isaac's finger trailed down a long row of small-print items. "Then there's Pope Paul IV, the artist Peter Paul Rubens, another artist, Jean Jacques Rousseau, a few actors—Mel Brooks, Kathy Bates . . . like I said, it stretches on. That's how I came up with John Dillinger."

"Any bad guys other than Dillinger?"

"Not on the birthday list. When I looked at June 28 as a date of death, I found a few more. But none of them appear connected to this type of thing."

"This type of thing?" said Petra.

"A serial killer."

The term set her teeth on edge. Too TV. Too damn hard to solve. She kept her voice light and pleasant. "Which bad guys died that day?"

"Pieter van Dort, a Dutch smuggler. They hanged him on June 28, 1748. Thomas Hickey, a Colonial soldier convicted of treason, was hung in 1776. There's not much more until 1971, when Joseph Columbo, a New York mafioso, was gunned down. Ten years later, Ayatollah Mohammad Beheshti, a founder of the Iranian Islamic Party, was killed in a bomb explosion. Though I suppose his being a bad guy would depend upon your political persuasion."

"Anything of a more wacko criminal nature? A Ted Bundy, a Hillside Strangler?"

"No, nothing like that, sorry," he said. "In terms of historical events, there's been plenty of misery on June 28, but no more than any other day. At least I can't find any statistically significant difference.

History's based on tragedy and upheaval, as well as on the accomplishments of notable people."

He rolled the papers into a tight tube, drummed his thigh. "I can't believe I missed similarities in the weapon dimensions."

"Stop beating yourself up," said Petra.

She switched on the radio, tuned to a station that played harder rock than she was accustomed to. Filled her head with thunder-drums and guitar feedback and screaming testosterone-laden vocals, until the mountains got higher and static buried the noise.

June 4.

She drove faster.

They were well past Angeles Crest now, zipping past canyon after canyon at eighty-five miles an hour, passing low, gray-brown bowls of high-desert to the east. A small-craft airport hugged the freeway, followed by scatters of white-box storage buildings and factories. Then tracts of red-tile-roofed houses in the distance, laid out neatly in the dirt. Between the structures, Petra spied tiny green lawns, the occasional turquoise pool. Lots of space between developments. Antelope Valley was booming but there was still plenty of room to move.

A sign heralding the approach of Palmdale came into view and Petra pronounced the city's name.

Isaac said, "It used to be called Palmenthal. Founded by Germans and Swiss. It got anglicized around the turn of the century."

Petra said, "Really."

"As if you needed to know that."

"Hey," she said. "Education's good for the soul. Where do you pick up stuff like that?"

"I had an advanced geography placement in high school, mostly independent study. I researched several cities in L.A. County and the surrounding areas. It was a surprise, you'd think everything had Hispanic roots, but many places didn't. Eagle Rock—that used to be called the Switzerland of the West. Back when the air was good."

"Ancient history," said Petra.

He said, "Extraneous information tends to float in my head and sometimes it seeps out through my mouth."

"And sometimes," she said, "you come up with interesting stuff."

◆

She exited at the first Palmdale exit, checked her Thomas Guide, and drove toward the address on Conrad Ballou's retirement forms, around three miles east.

Knowing about Ballou's alkie-burnout history, she figured him to be living in a depressing pensioner's SRO or worse, and the first few neighborhoods she passed were pretty sad. But then the environment took a swing upward—the same kind of tile-roofed tracts she'd spotted from the freeway, some big houses, gated enclaves.

Ballou's place was a medium-sized Spanish house in a pretty development named Golden Ridge Heights, where the trees—palms and paper-barked things—had grown sizable and some of the lawns sported mature shrubbery. Lots of motor homes and motorcycle trailers, pickups, and SUVs. The streets were wide, clean, and quiet, and the houses had rear yards that looked out to desert panorama. Sharp-edged mountains served as a backdrop. Too quiet for Petra's taste, but she imagined warm, silent, star-studded nights and thought that might not be too bad.

She pulled to the curb and crows scattered. A ten-year-old Ford half-ton sat in Ballou's driveway. The neighbors on both sides sported basketball hoops over the garage, yards that were more cement than grass. Ballou's place was done up beautifully with creeping dwarf junipers, impeccable mounds of mondo grass, lush Sago palms, and little cross-cut tubes of bamboo lining the pebbled walkway. A length of bamboo dipping toward a stone pot served as a fountain and the water trickle was a continuous soprano.

A Japanophile?

It didn't look like an alkie's place. Maybe the pension office's data bank was out of date, as was so much LAPD data. She should've phoned first before wasting the time and the gas. Now she'd look like a doofus in front of Mr. Genius.

Japanese letters were etched into the teak panels of the front door, above a weathered brass knocker shaped like a fish. A carp—koi—the type Alex Delaware kept in that cute little pond of his.

Petra used the knocker. The man who opened the door was short, bandy-legged, lean but for a protruding belly that hung over his belt buckle.

Koi belt buckle.

Sixty-five to seventy, with a shaved, sunburnt head and drooping white mustaches. He wore a denim work shirt, jeans, red suspenders, and lace-up boots. A white handkerchief flapped from his rear pocket.

He looked Petra and Isaac over, rubbed his hands together as if he'd just finished washing them.

Clear eyes, pale blue, no booze-blear. Sharp eyes, actually.

He said, "I only sell on the weekend."

"Detective Ballou?"

The man's hands stopped moving. Now the eyes were twin specks of granite. "Been a long time since anyone called me that."

Petra showed him her I.D.

He shook his head. "I'm out of all that. Breed and sell fish and don't think about the past." He started to step back into the house.

Petra said, "Marta Doebbler. Ever think about her?"

Conrad Ballou moved his jaw around. "Can't say that I do. Can't say that I give a damn about any of that."

"It hasn't been that long, sir. Six years. I'm looking into some cold cases, including Doebbler. If I could pick your brain . . ."

"Nothing to pick," said Ballou, rubbing his bald head. "According to the shrinks the department sent me to." He looked ready to spit. "I could've saved them the trouble. I wasn't nuts, I was a drunk. Thank God I didn't kill anybody." He shook his head. "They should've tossed my can out long before they did. Damn department."

"So you miss police work," said Petra.

Ballou glared at her. Smiled. Laughed. "You like fish?"

"To eat?"

"To look at. C'mon in. And bring the intern with you."

The house was rescued from tract-cliché by a trove of Asian furnishings. Vegetable-dye rugs, rosewood tables, porcelain vases and planters, paper screens on the walls, all portraying brocaded koi.

Way too much stuff for the space and to Petra's eye, nothing pricey. The kind of gaudy, overlacquered stuff you could pick up in any Chinatown or Little Tokyo tourist trap.

Ballou led them past all that, through rear double doors and out to the backyard. What had been a backyard. Every inch of the quarter-acre space had been converted to fish ponds. Sheets of mesh on stakes roofed the entire area, casting shade, cooling the desert air. Beyond the water was a high bamboo fence and a neighbor's RV.

Lots of burbling, but the ponds weren't attractive like Alex's. These were simply rectangular cement tanks, a dozen of them, arranged in a grid with a walkway between them. Not clear like Alex's, either. Green water, soupy. The only movement on the surface was created by aeration tubes.

But when Conrad Ballou approached the first pond, the surface broke and scores—no, hundreds—of little golden and pinkish fishy faces popped through, flapping, gulping, gasping.

Ballou pointed to the nearest wall where bright blue plastic bins were piled in a heap next to a mess of nets. Nearby stood a gumball machine. Instead of candy, the glass bell was filled with little rust-colored balls, half the size of a pea.

Ballou motioned them over to the machine. "Toss in a quarter."

Petra did. He took her hand and cupped it below the spout. Turned the handle and little balls tumbled out and her nose filled with the aroma of ripe seafood.

"Feed 'em," said Ballou. "It's fun."

"Which pond?"

"That one. They're babies, need the nutrition." Motioning toward the first pond, where the little fish were still clamoring. Petra walked over and tossed in the pellets and a finned riot ensued.

Isaac was already three ponds ahead. Bending low and examining the fish that had risen to greet him. Larger ones, red and black and gold and blue.

He said, "Mr. Ballou, do you use domestic stock or are these from Niigata?"

Ballou lowered his gaze and stared at the kid. "You know koi."

"I've admired them," said Isaac. "My mother's employers have a pond."

"Admire them, huh?" said Ballou. "Then get into it yourself."

Isaac laughed.

"Something funny, son?"

"It's a bit beyond my budget. And space. I live in an apartment."

"Hmm," said Ballou, "then get yourself a good job, work your tail off, and buy a house. Pay down the mortgage a bit and reward yourself with a Japanese garden and a pond full *of nishikigoi.* Nothing like 'em to lower your blood pressure."

Isaac nodded.

"You do all that, son, come back and buy some fish from me and I'll give you a free *karasu*—that's the black one. Symbol of good luck."

Petra said, "I could use some luck. On Marta Doebbler."

Ballou said, "Here we were talking about pleasant things . . . you drink tea?"

Back in his kitchen, he poured steaming green liquid into three stoneware cups.

"Don't think I'm some fanatic. Asian culture soothes me. When I got out of rehab a koi dealer, a nice old man in Gardena, hired me to mop up his place. I mopped for two years, kept my mouth shut, started asking questions by the third year, learned a bit. He died and put me in his will. Left me some of his breeding stock. That motivated me to buy this place, set up a little weekend business. It's real peaceful. I don't think about my other job with fondness."

Petra sipped the hot, aromatic tea.

"Marta Doebbler's a good example," said Ballou. "Ugly scene. When I think of the things I got used to working Homicide." He placed a thumb under his suspenders, gazed absently through the window. Then back at Isaac.

"You seem like a nice kid. Why would you wanna do this to yourself?"

Petra said, "Isaac's going to be a doctor. Meanwhile he's getting a Ph.D. in biostatistics."

"Meanwhile?" said Ballou, appraising Isaac all over again. "We're talking Einstein?"

Isaac muttered, "Hardly." Flushed clear through his nutmeg complexion. Pink as medium-rare beef.

Petra said, "Can we talk about Doebbler?"

CHAPTER
14

What I remember," said Conrad Ballou, "was that the husband was interesting."

He returned to his tea, gave no indication of having more to say.

Petra said, "Interesting as in prime suspect?"

The old guy nodded. "There was no evidence tying him to it. Everyone said him and the vic were getting along fine. But I liked him for it."

He put his cup down. "His reaction to his wife's death was off. Stone-face, not a tear. When I did the notification call, I brought a pocket full of tissues, like I always did. Didn't end up using one. Doebbler just stood there, with this flat look in his eyes. Sometimes that happens before they fall apart, I kept waiting. He just stood there staring. For a second I thought he'd gone into one of those whatchamacallit seizures. Then he says, 'I guess you'd better come in.' "

"Guy's an engineer," said Petra.

"So what?"

"It doesn't explain it but sometimes that type . . ." Remembering her days as a faculty brat. Dr. Kenneth Connor, professor of anthropology at the University of Arizona, Tucson, squiring his little daughter to academic soirees. Meeting the tenured crowd. Finding most of them regular folk with slightly higher I.Q.s, a few crashing bores. A few really reprehensible jerks.

"The type?" said Ballou.

"Engineers, physicists, mathematicians, all those megabrains. Sometimes they don't react emotionally the way the rest of us do."

Ballou glanced at Isaac, as if wanting confirmation straight from the source. Isaac pushed a smile onto his lips.

Ballou said, "Well, Doebbler was a kind of rocket scientist, I guess. Worked over at Pacific Dynamics, electronics stuff, some sort of computer job."

"Anything else besides his demeanor make you suspect him?"

"She was called out of the theater. It had to be someone familiar with her schedule, who else would know where she was? And who else could've gotten her to leave the theater without telling her friends where she was going."

"The husband claiming an emergency," said Petra. "Maybe about the daughter."

"That would've brought her out," Ballou agreed. "The kid was Doebbler's alibi. He'd been home with her all night, Marta was having a girl's night out. I talked to the three friends she went with. No one had anything juicy to offer about Marta's private life, but when I pressed them I could tell they didn't like Kurt. One even said she thought he'd done it."

That hadn't been in the murder book.

Petra said, "That's pretty strong."

"She didn't like him. No one seemed to."

"How'd he and Marta meet?"

"Germany. She was a brain, too, studying astronomy. He was a foreign exchange student. After they got married, she dropped out and became a full-time mom."

"That could be frustrating."

"Sure, that's what I thought," said Ballou. "Maybe she tried to reduce her frustration the old-fashioned way. But if she was having an affair, I never found evidence of it."

Petra said, "Did you talk to the daughter?"

"Poor little thing, didn't want to pressure her." Ballou tugged at his mustache. "She sure reacted, crying all over the place. You'd think Doebbler would've tried to comfort her. All he did was offer her juice."

"Juice?"

"A glass of orange juice: 'Here, drink, you'll feel better.' Like vitamin C would help with losing her mother." Ballou emitted a dry, hoarse laugh. "I would've loved to make him for it . . . how come you're reopening it?"

"It may be related to some others."

"Others you suspect Doebbler did?"

"Others with some similar forensics."

Long silence. You could hear the burbling of the fish ponds, here in the kitchen. Then a loud splash.

"Spawning season," said Ballou. "They jump. Sometimes they jump clear out of the pond and if I don't get there in time, I've got a dead fish."

He got up, peered out the window. Sat back down. "So far, so good. You want to tell me about these others?"

"Five other brainings," said Petra. "Yearly intervals. All on June 28."

Ballou gawked. "You're putting me on."

"Wish I was."

"Before Marta?"

"All after Marta. From what we can tell, she was the first. If it's a series."

"If?" said Ballou. "All on the same day? That sounds pretty convincing."

"But the victims are all over the place in terms of sex, age, and race." She gave him a few details.

"See what you mean. Still . . . so, how'd you discover this? Department finally doing something about working cold ones?"

"Mr. Gomez, here, found them."

Ballou studied Isaac, yet again. "Did you?"

"By accident," said Isaac.

"Bullshit. I don't believe in accidents. My smashing into a building was no accident. It was stupidity. And your finding all this out wasn't an accident, it was smarts." He leaned over suddenly, clapped the kid on the shoulder. "You're definitely going to deserve a pond one day—a big one. You're going to afford it and you're going to build it and I'm going to stock you with beauties."

"I hope."

"Forget hope. Smarts and hard work does it every time. That's how

I pulled myself out of the shit pile." To Petra: "There's one more thing you'll want to know about Marta. We recovered some blood in the car that wasn't hers."

Petra didn't recall that from the chart. As if reading her mind, Ballou said, "It came out later, after the autopsy report, just a speck. The tech who scraped the upholstery mislaid it and it got filed in the wrong place. By the time it got to me, I might not have been in a state to keep good records."

He pulled out his handkerchief, blew his nose, said, "All I remember is it wasn't hers. She was A positive and this was O negative. Kurt's O positive, so it didn't mean much. But maybe if she had a boyfriend." He shrugged.

Petra said nothing.

"Yeah, yeah," said Ballou. "It wasn't my finest hour, but big deal. Real life ain't *The Forensic Files.*"

"Where's the blood sample?"

"If it's anywhere, it's at the coroners'."

"Okay," she said. "Thanks."

"Any fluids on any of your other cases?" said Ballou.

"Doesn't say so in the M-books, but stuff doesn't get in there." Irritated and not afraid to show it.

Ballou got to his feet, heavily and slowly. "That's all I can tell you, so have a nice day. Pleasant lady, Marta, from all I heard. The family's back in Germany, they came over—mother, father, sister. Took the body back, had that shell-shocked look. I think I put their addresses and numbers in the murder book."

"You did," said Petra.

"Good," said Ballou. "Sometimes I'm not sure what I did and didn't do back then."

As they drove away from Golden Ridge Heights, Isaac said, "Someone Marta knew. And home with his daughter isn't much of an alibi."

"Not much," Petra agreed. "With the girl sleeping, he could've phoned Marta with some ruse, lured her, done the deed, and come back. None of her blood in the car says she was killed elsewhere and pains were taken to keep the vehicle clean."

"Doebbler's car."

"Or just a neat-freak murderer. But before we jump on that, we'd need to assume the techs didn't miss anything."

"That happen a lot?" said Isaac.

"More than you want to know. One thing intrigues me, though: Marta was the only victim whose dead body was then moved by the killer. So maybe that does synch with someone who knew her."

She retraced the drive through the outskirts of Palmdale and got back onto the 114.

Isaac said, "A man killing his wife and then going on to kill strangers is pretty unusual, right?"

"Can't say that I've ever heard of it. More commonly, you get some slimeball serial balancing a wife or a girlfriend—raising kids, having barbecues—with a secret life."

"The human mask," said Isaac.

"We all wear 'em."

Petra exited the 210 at Brand Boulevard in Glendale, drove north to a quiet, pretty part of the street, and pulled over. She'd brought copies of Ballou's notes and rifled through them until she found Kurt Doebbler's work and home numbers. It was just after five, meaning he could be either place.

The home was on Rosita Avenue, in Tarzana, clear across the Valley to the west. At this hour, at least an hour's drive. She ran a DMV check. Doebbler was listed as still there. Two cars registered in his name. A two-year-old Infiniti coupe and a three-year-old Toyota wagon. If he'd coveted Marta's Opel sedan, it hadn't been to keep the darn thing.

The daughter, Katya, would be fifteen, too young to drive, but Kurt had indulged himself with two sets of wheels.

Secret life?

She asked Isaac, "What's your schedule like?"

"When?"

"Now."

"I was going to work on organizing my source material. It can wait."

"I can drop you off just as easily as go on."

"Go on, where?"

"To Kurt Doebbler's house."

"Now?" said Isaac.

"Ain't no time like now," she said.

"It's okay if I come along?"

"Sure."

"Let's do it," he said. Excitement in his voice. Then: "Could I borrow your phone, please? I'll let my mother know I won't be home for dinner."

CHAPTER

15

Busiest freeway in the state, busiest time of day.

From Burbank to Encino, they rolled and stopped and waited, averaging ten miles per. Petra finally managed to exit at Balboa. She took Ventura Boulevard the rest of the way, encountered gridlock, foul tempers, distracted cell phone gabbers, some truly frightening risk-taking.

By the time they reached Tarzana, she was too grumpy to talk and Isaac busied himself by pulling a book out of his briefcase, reading and underlining in yellow marker. She glanced over, saw pages full of equations, vowed not to look again. Math had been her worst subject in school. Except for geometry, where her artistic pretensions had kicked in and she'd excelled at drawing complex polygons.

Someone behind her leaned on his horn. *What am I supposed to do, moron? Drive through the ass-end of the Escalade in front of me?*

She realized her hands ached from gripping the wheel and forced herself to relax.

Isaac smiled. What could be funny about equations?

She said, "This is the exciting part of police work."

His smile widened. "I like it."

"Do you?"

"At least you've got time to think."

"That's one way to rationalize," she said.

He looked up from his book. "Actually, I like everything about your job."

Kurt Doebbler's house on Rosita Avenue was a pale gray, two-story tra-ditional set in a low spot on the street, higher properties behind. The front yard was mostly brick and asphalt. The door and the shutters were a deeper gray. Doebbler's Infiniti, a champagne-colored coupe, was in view, sparkling clean. Parked in front of it was the gray Toyota wagon, with one flat tire and a veneer of dust.

The man who answered the door was nice-looking. Tall, late thirties to early forties, with a broad-shouldered, angular build and a thick mess of wavy dark hair, graying at the temples. Prominent chin and nose, generous mouth. The kind of sun-seams that enhanced some men. Petra couldn't think of any women who benefited from aging skin.

He wore a baggy plaid shirt, sleeves rolled to the elbows, faded jeans, white running shoes. A dinner plate dangled from one hand. In his other was a dish towel. Droplets on the plate. Single dad doing his chores?

From inside the house Petra smelled broiled meat. Dinner was over. The drive had taken them that long. She could use a steak.

"Mr. Doebbler?"

"Yes." Friendly brown eyes, slouching posture. Pinch-marks on his nose said he wore glasses. A couple of shaving nicks stippled his neck.

Nothing weird, so far. Let's see how he reacts when she shows him the badge.

He smiled. "I thought you were Jehovah's Witnesses." Looking over at Isaac.

Well-scrubbed kid, Petra could see that.

Doebbler said, "Is there some kind of trouble in the neighbor-hood?"

"I'm a homicide detective from Hollywood Division, sir. I'm look-ing into your wife's murder."

"My wife?" The smile finally melted down. "I'm sorry, it's my brother Kurt you want. I'm Thad Doebbler."

"You live here, too?"

"No, I live in San Francisco, had to be down here on business. Kurt insisted I not stay at a hotel. You're reopening Marta's case?"

"Marta's case never closed, sir."

"Oh . . . well, let me get Kurt for you. He's up with Katya, helping her with her homework. Come on in."

Petra and Isaac followed him through a small, empty entry foyer into a modest living room. Up ahead was a narrow walkway that led to the kitchen. Thad Doebbler said, "One second," loped to the kitchen, and returned minus the plate and the towel.

To the left was a right-angled oak staircase. Human speech filtered down from the second floor. A high girlish voice going on for a while, a single baritone grunt.

Thad Doebbler walked to the bottom of the stairs and stopped. "I don't want to meddle, Detective, but my brother . . . he's been doing pretty well the past few years. Has something new come up? Can I tell him that?"

"Nothing dramatic," said Petra. "We're just doing our best to clear cases."

He rolled his shoulders. "Got it. Make yourselves comfortable, I'll go tell Kurt you're here."

Petra and Isaac sat at opposite ends of a seven-foot sofa. Very soft sofa, tufted exuberantly. White cotton printed with huge red roses and serpentine green vines. Rolled arms and piped seams and a gold-and-red fringe running along the bottom. Catty-corner the couch were two of the starkest black leather chairs Petra had ever seen—tight black skin on chromium frames.

No coffee table in the middle, just a faded brown needlepoint ottoman that served host to a TV tray and a remote control.

The entire room was like that, feminine touches coexisting uneasily with the obvious signs of male inhabitance. One wall was dominated by a big-screen TV, maybe seventy inches wide, and nearly empty bookcases. Nearby was an antique sewing table covered by lace. Prints of Flemish still-lifes hung on the white walls along with two huge, brass-framed photos of space shuttles blasting off and one of a fighter jet slicing through the wild blue yonder. The carpeting was gray—the same gray as the house—and looked as if it hadn't been cleaned in a while. The broiled-meat smell pervaded.

The man who came down the stairs was even taller than Thad Doebbler—six-four was Petra's estimate. Thinner, too. The same thick wavy hair as his younger brother but completely gray. Darker complexion. Thick eyeglasses in silver frames. Huge hands dangled. Similar features to Thad, but on Kurt Doebbler they didn't add up to handsome.

He wore a white polo shirt, brown slacks, black shoes.

Pausing at the same spot where his brother had stopped, he stood there looking at them. Past them.

Petra said, "Mr. Doebbler?"

"You know that, already." The line should've been accompanied by a smile. Kurt Doebbler just kept staring.

"Sorry to interrupt your evening, sir."

Doebbler said nothing.

"Do you have time to talk, sir?"

"About Marta."

"Yes, sir."

Doebbler pressed his hands together, shifted his eyes to the ceiling, as if searching for divine inspiration. Petra knew that kind of movement as indication of deception.

Doebbler said, "What about, specifically?"

"I know it's been difficult, sir, and I'm sorry—"

"Sure, let's talk," said Kurt Doebbler. "Why not?"

He took one of the black armchairs, sat all tight and hunched up, long legs drawn up close. Bony knees. Shiny brown doubleknit slacks; when was the last time she'd seen that?

She said, "This is going to sound like a stupid question, but is there anything you've thought of, concerning Marta, that you didn't tell the original detective six years ago?"

"Conrad Ballou," said Doebbler. He recited a phone number that Petra recognized as a station extension. "I called Ballou often. Sometimes he even called me back."

Even seated he was tall enough to gaze well over Petra's line of vision. It made her feel small.

"Was there anything—"

"He was a drunk," said Doebbler. "I could smell it on him. The night he came to tell me, he reeked. I should've complained. Is he still working as a detective?"

"No, sir. He's retired."

Doebbler didn't budge or blink.

Petra said, "Did you feel better about Detective Martinez?"

"Who?"

"The other detective assigned to the case."

"The only one I ever talked to was Ballou. And not very often." Doebbler's lips shifted suddenly to a very unpleasant smile. You couldn't even call it a smile. "Obviously, you people are well-organized."

Petra said, "I know this is tough, Mr. Doebbler—"

"Not tough. Futile."

Petra said, "The day your wife disappeared, you were here."

Doebbler didn't answer.

"Sir?"

"That was a statement, not a question."

"Is it a true statement?"

"Yes."

"What were you doing?"

"Homework," said Doebbler.

"With your daughter?"

"She was sleeping. My homework."

"You were in school?"

"I take work home. My job isn't limited to nine-to-five."

"You work with computers."

"I develop aerospace software."

"What kind of software?"

"Aircraft guidance systems, integrated spacecraft landing systems." Doebbler's tone said she couldn't hope to understand.

Isaac said, "Circular wave guides? Storage rings?"

Doebbler turned toward the kid. "Aerospace physicists and engineers design storage rings. I write the instructions that enable them to be used in a human-to-machine context."

"Human factors," said Isaac.

Doebbler's hand waved. "That's psychology." To Petra: "Have you or haven't you learned something new about Marta?"

One knee bounced. His mouth was set tight.

Petra said, "It would help me if I had a feel for what Marta was like."

"Like?"

"As a person."

"Are you asking what kind of music she liked? Her taste in clothes?"

"That kind of thing," said Petra.

"She liked soft rock and bright colors. She liked the stars."

"Astronomy."

"That, and she regarded the stars as aesthetic objects," said Doebbler. "She wanted the world to be pretty. She was smart, but that was stupid."

"Naive?"

"Stupid." Doebbler stared at her.

She pulled out her pad and made a show of writing stuff down. *Soft rock. Bright colors.*

Kurt Doebbler said, "Why are you here?"

"We're looking into some of our open cases, trying to see if we can resolve them."

"Ballou's cases. You're looking at them because he was a drunk and he made serious errors and now you're afraid of scandal."

"No, sir. Just open cases, in general. Only Marta's was Ballou's."

"Open," said Doebbler. "That's a euphemism for failure. To you, Marta's a statistic."

"No, sir. She's . . . was a person. That's why I'd like to know more about her."

Doebbler seemed to consider that. He shook his head. "It's been a long time. I can't see her face anymore."

"The night she went out," said Petra, "what was her mood?"

"Her mood? She was in a fine mood."

"And she gave no indication of planning anything but seeing a play."

"That's what she told me," said Doebbler. His knee pumped faster. The hands grasping them were white-knuckled.

That question had gotten to him.

"What she told you," Petra echoed.

No answer.

"June 28," she said.

"What about it?"

"Does the date have any significance—"

"It's the date my wife was murdered. What is this, some kind of game?"

"Sir—"

Doebbler sprang up, made it to the stairs in three long strides. Ascending the flight, two steps at a time, he stopped midway. "I have to help my daughter. See yourselves out."

He disappeared. Isaac began to get up but when he saw Petra remain in place, he plopped back down. Finally, she got up and he watched as she paced around Doebbler's living room, widened her circle, peered down the passageway to the kitchen. Took in as many details as she could before footsteps sounded on the stairs and she motioned Isaac to the front door.

Her hand was on the knob when Thad Doebbler said, "Sorry. Kurt's been under stress."

"New stress?" said Petra, turning to face him.

"Work. It's a high-pressure job. Really, there's nothing more he can tell you about Marta."

"Did he just tell you that?"

Thad shook his head. "He didn't say a thing, just went into his room and closed the door. I'm sorry if he's a bit . . . Kurt's done his grieving."

"How's your niece?"

Thad blinked. "Kurt works hard for her."

Petra said, "The whole single-father thing." On some topics she was an expert. Professor Kenneth Connor had been a jewel of a single dad. She could only imagine what growing up with Kurt Doebbler would be like.

Thad said, "Exactly."

Petra turned the knob and stepped outside.

Thad called after them: "I'm sure he'll want to know if you learn anything."

Even outside, walking to the car, the broiled-meat smell hung in her nostrils and she craved dinner. Isaac had called Mama, letting her know he'd be missing his home-cooked meal, but Petra had an inkling Mama would leave something out for her golden boy.

"Do I drop you back off or should we hit a coffee shop for some grub?"

He said, "I'm not really hungry but I'll tag along."

Not hungry? Petra realized she'd never seen him eat. Then she remembered: This one rode the bus, wore the same three shirts over and over.

Eating out was probably a once-in-a-while McDonald's jaunt.

She said, "Let's go."

She upgraded to a steak-and-seafood place near the Encino-Tarzana border, because it looked unpretentious and not too expensive. When she examined the menu she found it higher-priced than she would've cared for. But so what, she was in the mood for substance.

The dining room beyond the busy bar was cozy and dark, set up with red booths, dark wood walls, and thirty-year-old head-shots of near-celebrities. The waitress who came to serve them was a strawberry blonde, young and cute and buxom, and Petra saw her give Isaac the once over. Then she studied Petra and curiosity sharpened her eyes.

Wondering: *What's the relationship here?*

When Isaac slid as far from Petra in the booth as was possible, and Petra ordered for him, the way you do with a child, the waitress smiled. After that, she flirted shamelessly with the kid.

He seemed oblivious to all the smiles and hair flipping and back-arching and arm-brushing with an ample bosom. Smiling politely and thanking Strawberry Shortcake profusely for every smidge of service. When the food came, he kept his head low, studied his steak, finally cut into it.

Nice, thick filet mignon. He'd claimed to crave a burger but Petra had insisted and Strawberry had backed her up on that.

"Good for strong bones." Smile, flip, arch, bosom-brush.

Almost as an afterthought, Petra ordered two glasses of Burgundy. Corrupting the youth of today. When the wine arrived, she decided to forgo the whole sniffing, swirling thing, not wanting to overwhelm the kid.

She was ravenous and attacked her surf-and-turf as if it was Schoelkopf's face.

After a bit of silent snarling, she asked Isaac how his food was.

"Delicious. Thank you so much." He'd finished his meat, was looking at a baked potato the size of a dog's head.

"Big," said Petra.

"Huge."

"Probably radioactive. Some nefarious DNA-scramble scheme in Idaho."

He laughed. Cut into the potato.

"So what do you think of Mr. Doebbler?"

"Hostile and asocial. I can see why Detective Ballou called him strange."

"Anything else about him set you off?"

He thought. "He certainly wasn't cooperative."

"No, he wasn't," she said. "But that could've been our popping in unannounced. After all those years of no progress, I wouldn't expect him to be a big police groupie."

A drunk and a no-show. LAPD at its finest. She wondered what Isaac thought about that.

Would any of this show up in his dissertation?

How was *she* coming across?

She said, "Unfortunately, there are guys like Ballou and Martinez. Fortunately, they're in the minority." Little Miss Defensive. "What intrigues me about all that is Mr. Kurt Doebbler never complaining to their superiors. All that resentment but he kept it to himself."

Isaac put down his knife and fork. "He wouldn't, if he wanted the case to stay unsolved."

Petra nodded.

"Amazing," he said. "I'd never have thought of that."

They ate some more. He said, "That comment he made, about not remembering what his wife looked like? Sometimes borderline personalities have a problem maintaining mental images of those close to them. Flat affect, also. Except when they feel they've been betrayed. When that happens, they can get pretty emotional."

"Betrayed as in the wife having an affair," she said. "That was just Ballou's offhand comment and I'm not sure he's worth paying attention to."

He nodded.

"What are borderline personalities?" she asked him.

"It's a psychiatric disorder involving problems of identity and intimacy—difficulty connecting with other people. Borderlines have higher-than-average rates of clinical depression and they're more likely to get involved in substance abuse. Females tend to punish themselves but male borderlines can get aggressive."

"Do they kill their spouses?"

"I've never heard that specifically. It's just something that came to mind."

Petra heard herself saying, "Doebbler's an odd one, all right, but when you lose someone close to you, time does have a way of easing things. You forget. It's protective. I've heard other relatives of victims say the same thing."

Talking calmly while keeping a lid on what was blowing through her consciousness; all those hours poring over snapshots. Mom and Dad dating as college students. Mom tending to her brothers as infants, toddlers, little boys. Mom in a one-piece bathing suit looking gorgeous at Lake Mead. Despite the photos, it was all she could do to conjure up the merest hint of the woman who had died birthing her.

Her face must've betrayed something because Isaac looked confused.

She said, "Anyway, before we get too psychological about Kurt, let's remember that his blood type didn't match the sample they scraped off the seat, there's absolutely no evidence linking him to the crime, and he does have an alibi, of sorts."

She returned to her steak, decided she was no longer hungry.

Isaac said, "So what's next?"

"Haven't figured that out. Assuming I want to work the case. Any of them." She shot him a fierce smile. "Look what you got me into."

Another classic Isaac blush. The kid's emotional barometer was fine-tuned, everything rose to the surface.

Polar opposite of Kurt Doebbler. The guy *was* weirdly flat.

Isaac was saying, ". . . sorry if I've complicated—"

"You have," said Petra. "But that's okay. You did the right thing."

He kept quiet. She cuffed his arm lightly. "Hey, I was just having a little fun at your expense."

He managed a mini-smile.

"The truth is," she went on, "diving into a half dozen cold cases that are probably unsolvable wasn't what I had in mind when I programmed my day planner. But you're right, there are too many similarities to dismiss."

When had she decided that?

The wound pattern.

Or maybe sooner. Maybe she'd known right away and had just been denying it.

She said, "Letting it drop would put me in the same box as guys like Ballou and Martinez. So I'm fine with it. Okay?"

He murmured something.

"Pardon?"

"I hope it works out for you."

"It will," she said. "One way or the other."

Listen to her, Little Miss Karma.

"You up for dessert?" Before he could answer, she was waving at Little Miss Strawberry.

CHAPTER

16

Isaac knew he'd made a mistake.

He'd had Petra drop him off at Pico and Union. Near the bus stop where he usually got off, four blocks from his building. Not wanting her to see the liquor stores and abandoned buildings that lined the route. The crumbling wooden houses converted to by-the-day rooming houses. Four-story stucco slabs, like the one his family lived in, marred by the acne of graffiti.

His mother kept an immaculate flat and his building was no worse than any others in the neighborhood. But bad enough. Sometimes homeless guys wandered in and used the entry hall for a toilet. When Isaac walked the squeaky stairs up to his family's third-floor space, he avoided touching the brown-painted handrail. Painted so often, it felt gelatinous. Sometimes it *was* gelatinous. Wads of gum stuck to the wood. And worse.

For a brief time, as an undergrad, his head filled with biology and organic chemistry, he'd taken to wearing plastic gloves when entering the building. Careful to shed and hide them before entering Mama's domain.

The noise, the smells. Generally, he could shut it all out.

This morning, leaving for campus, he'd noticed that the front façade was looking especially shabby.

Most nights, he could forget all that, let his mind drift to the stately trees and brick loveliness of USC, the old-paper fragrance of Doheny Library.

His other life.

The life he'd have one day. Maybe.

Who was he kidding? Petra was smart, she had to know the Gomez family didn't live in a mansion.

Still, there was something about her actually seeing his home base that repelled him.

So he walked.

A quick right turn at the late-night liquor store favored by old winos, then down dark side streets, past alleys, the usual sprinkle of lolling street people and addicts.

Passive in their misery. A few of them, he talked to. Sometimes he gave them lunch leftovers. Mom always packed too much anyway.

Mostly he ignored them and they returned the favor.

He'd been doing it for years, never had a problem.

Tonight he had a problem.

He was unaware of them till they started laughing.

A hoarse, high-pitched hooting, behind him. Close behind. When had they started following him? Had he been that spaced-out?

Lost in thought: Marta Doebbler. Kurt Doebbler.

June 28 getting closer.

Petra. Those dark eyes. The way she'd taken on that enormous steak. *Attacking* it . . . slender hands, but strong. Aggressive in such a feminine way.

More laughter behind him. Closer. Glancing over his shoulder, he saw them clearly as they passed under a streetlamp.

Three of them. A loose-limbed, giggly entourage, maybe twenty feet from his back.

Chattering. Pointing and bumping into one another. Laughing some more. Mexican-accented Spanish interspersed with rude English "Fuck," the operative word—the all-purpose noun/verb/adjective.

He picked up his pace, hazarded another quick look back.

From the round outlines of their heads, shaved domes. Not tall. Baggy clothes.

One of them drove a fist toward the sky and howled. Soprano howl, like a girl.

Maybe it had nothing to do with him. Maybe they just happened to be walking the same street.

They shuffled and bumped into one another some more. Young voices. Slurred. Punk kids. High on something.

Two more blocks till home. He turned.

They stayed with him.

He walked faster.

One of them shouted, *"Yo. Maricon."*

Branding him queer.

All these years, despite the rotten neighborhood, he'd never had to deal with this before. Generally, he was home by eight. But tonight it was well after ten. He and Petra had returned to the station late and he'd hung around some more. Pretending not to pay attention as she worked at her desk.

Pretending to work, himself. Just wanting to be there. For the ambience.

Petra.

The day had shot by so quickly. Tagging along, observing her, listening. Picking up the nuances of detective work, the things no book could communicate. Offering opinions when she asked—and she'd asked a lot more frequently than he'd expected.

Was she just being nice to him or did she really think he had something to offer?

It had to be the latter; Petra didn't suffer fools.

"Yo, you, maricon—hey faggot, whuh time izzit?"

Isaac kept walking.

One more block.

Dinner, dessert, espresso—he'd never had coffee like that. Even the Faculty Club, when Dr. Gompertz sometimes treated him to lunch, didn't have coffee like that.

"Hey, you, puto, why you move you ass so fast?"

He began to jog and heard them shouting and whooping and running after him. He picked up speed, was drenched by a sudden, clammy, full-body sweat.

Thank God Petra wasn't here to see this.

Something hit him from behind, low in his back. Hard boot to the kidneys. Pain shot through him, he buckled yet managed to stay on his feet, but his rhythm had been disrupted, and by the time his legs were ready to move someone was yanking at his briefcase.

His notes. His laptop. He held on but another hand clawed at his neck and as he stepped away from the blow, the case flew out of his hand.

The clasp opened, papers scattered. The computer, heavy, remained inside.

His handwritten calculations lay static, in the curb. Pages of multiple regression analyses of subethnic populations in high-crime regions. He hadn't had time to enter any of it into his hard drive, stupid stupid! If he lost it, it meant hours down the—

A fist—hard, sharp knuckles—grazed the side of his head. He teetered and tripped backward.

Regained his balance and backed away and faced them.

Even younger than he'd thought. Fourteen, fifteen. Small, ghetto-stunted kids, two skinny, one a bit chunky. Same age as cousin Samuelito. But Sammy was a good, churchgoing boy and these three were shaved-head, baggy-pants scum.

The fact that they were kids was meager comfort. Adolescents could be the most dangerous sociopaths. Poor impulse control, insufficiently developed conscience. He'd read that if you didn't change their behavior by twelve . . .

They were surrounding him, a trio of malignant dwarfs shuffling and cursing and giggling. He moved, trying to keep his back clear. The spot on his cheek where he'd been punched smarted and grew hot.

The heaviest of the three planted his feet and held up his fists. Small hands and knuckles. Like something out of *Oliver Twist.*

A night breeze coursed through the street and sheets of calculations billowed.

The heaviest one said, "Gimme your fuckin' mawney, *puto.*" Nasal, barely pubescent voice.

Individually, he could pound each of them to oblivion. But together . . . as he weighed his alternatives, one of the others, the smallest, flicked his wrist and flashed something metallic.

Oh God, a gun?

No, a knife. Flat in an open palm. The kid rotated his hand in small arcs. "I cut you, *puto.*"

Isaac backed away some more. Another gust of breeze; one of his sheets blew a few feet up the block.

The heaviest one said, "Gimme the fuckin' mawney you wanna fuckin' get *cut*?" His voice squeaked and cracked.

Gutted by an idiot with no pubic hair . . . the little one with the blade danced closer. Stepped into the light and Isaac saw the weapon clearly. Pocketknife, cheap thing, dark plastic handle, maybe a two-inch fold-out blade. The kid's wrist was thin, fragile. He smelled bad, all three of them did. Unwashed clothes and weed and jumbled hormones.

Jumpy little sociopaths. Not a good situation. The thought of that stupid little blade entering his flesh enraged him.

He drew out his LAPD authorized visitors badge and said, "Police, assholes. You walked right into a stakeout."

Hoping they watched TV. Hoping they were that stupid.

A nanosecond of silence.

A hoarse *"Huh?"*

"Police, motherfuckers," he repeated, louder, reaching down in his chest to produce his lowest baritone growl. Reaching into another pocket, he drew out his pen case because it was dark and around the right size. He pressed it to his mouth, said, "This is Officer Gomez calling for backup. I've got three juvenile two-eleven suspects. Probable narcotics violation as well. I'll hold them here."

"Fuck," said the heavy one, sounding breathless.

Isaac realized he hadn't even called in an address. Could they be *that* stupid?

Skinny looked at his knife. Grim little urchin face. Deliberating.

The second one, the one who hadn't spoken or done anything, edged away.

Isaac said, "Where you going, shit-face?"

The kid took off and ran.

And then there were two. Better odds. Even with the blade he might be able to escape with just a flesh wound.

Chunky was bouncing on his feet. Skinny had edged back but made no move to leave. The dangerous one, not enough fear in his chemistry. And *he* had to be the one with the knife.

That was *why* he had the knife.

Isaac brought out his pen case again. Held it this time, in an outstretched arm. Walked toward Skinny pointing the stupid thing and ordered, "Drop that fucking nail-file, junior, and get the fuck down on the ground before I shoot your ass. *Do it!*"

Chunky turned heel and ran.

Skinny kept contemplating the odds. Threw the knife at Isaac.

The blade whizzed by his face, just short of his left eye.

He said, "You're toast, motherfucker," and the kid bolted.

He stood there in the silence. Putrid silence; they'd left behind their stink.

Waiting until he was sure they were gone before he began breathing normally. He went to retrieve his briefcase. Collected the errant paper, stuffed the rest of it back in. Then he sprinted the block to his building, ran around to the side, chest tight, stomach churning, chilled by the post-adrenaline shakes.

He leaned against the stucco, feet ankle-high in the weeds that grew there. Dry-heaving, he thought that would be it.

It wasn't. He vomited until the bile burned his throat.

When all his dinner was gone, he spit and headed toward his building.

Tomorrow, before he took the bus to the Hollywood station, he'd visit Jaramillo.

Once upon a time, before the Burton Academy, before all the strange, wondrous, terrifying turns his life had taken, he and Jaramillo had been friends.

Maybe that would count for something.

17

Kurt Doebbler's weirdness stuck in Petra's head and after a few more days of nothing on Paradiso, she found herself thinking about him.

It was just after noon; no sign of Isaac.

No word from Eric. And the mellow-voiced Dr. Robert Katzman hadn't called her back.

Why *hadn't* Doebbler complained about Ballou's drunken incompetence?

The more she thought about how shoddily the case had been worked, the less confident she felt about the integrity of the original file.

Like the blood scraped from Marta Doebbler's car—O negative. And Doebbler was O positive. According to Ballou.

How much was that worth?

She paged through the file, finally found a note of the sample in a small-print coroner's addendum.

She decided to track it down.

The coroner's clerk was sure he had it. Till he didn't. He transferred her to a coroner's investigator, a young-sounding guy named Ballard.

"Hmm," he said. "I guess it could be in the bio division of your evidence room. Over at Parker."

My evidence room.

Petra said, "You guess."

"Well," said Ballard, "it's not marked as leaving here, but it's *not* here, so it must've gone somewhere, right?"

"Unless it's lost."

"For your sake, I hope it isn't. Parker had some evidence problems a while back, remember? Lost samples, spoilage."

She hadn't heard about that. Yet another snafu that had somehow evaded the evening news.

"Anywhere else it could be?" she said.

"Can't think of any. Unless it was sent up to Cellmark for DNA analysis. But even then, we'd keep some here and mail them a sample. Unless there wasn't enough to be divided up—yeah, that could be it . . . okay, here it is. Two centimeters by one and a half. That's about three-quarters of an inch by half an inch. Says here it was attached to a square of vinyl auto upholstery. Meaning it was thin, all we probably got were a few flakes. I guess it's possible Cellmark got the whole thing. Why do you want it?"

"For fun," she said, and hung up and phoned Sacramento.

The Department of Justice lab had no record of receiving any bio sample from Marta Doebbler's murder. Parker Center's Evidence Room hadn't logged it in.

Big-time screw-up, but get anyone to admit it.

Time to take a closer look at the other June murders.

In Geraldo Solis's murder book she found an interesting notation by Detective Jack Hustaad: According to Solis's daughter, the old man had been expecting a cable repairman the day he'd been bludgeoned.

No sign Hustaad had followed up.

She phoned Wilshire Division and learned that, unlike the Hollywood cases, Solis had been transferred after Hustaad's suicide. But not until two years after the murder had gone down. Hustaad must've held on to the file all that time, including a three-month lapse between his medical leave for cancer treatment and his suicide. A week after Hustaad's funeral, Solis had been passed to a DI named Scott Weber.

Weber was still at Wilshire and Petra reached him at his desk.

He said, "I never got anywhere on it. How come you're asking?"

She told him about a possible cold-case similarity, talked about the wound pattern on Marta Doebbler, made no mention of the other murders or June 28. Weber wanted to hear more but when she gave him a few details, he lost interest.

"Don't see any match," he said. "People get hit on the head."

Not that often fatally. According to my expert.

"True," she said.

"What do you figure for the weapon on yours?"

"Some kind of pipe."

"Same here," said Weber. "Any physical evidence on yours?"

Just a missing blood sample. "Not so far."

Why was she being evasive with another detective? Because she still wasn't comfortable with all this.

"Anyway," said Weber.

"One question. There was a note about a cable repairman—"

"You have a copy of the file?"

"One of our interns, doing research, pulled it and made a copy."

"From here?" said Weber.

"I think from the duplicate at Parker."

"Oh . . . yeah, it could be duped, being cold and all that."

"The cable call," she prompted.

"There was a cable call on yours?" said Weber.

"No, I was just wondering if that led anywhere, but obviously—"

"You're wondering if I followed up on it." Weber laughed, but the sound wasn't friendly. "I did. Even though it was two freakin' years later. Solis's cable company had no record of any visit. I talked to the daughter, turns out she maybe remembered something about the old man maybe saying something. Turns out no one saw any cable truck near the house. Okay?"

"Okay," said Petra. "Sorry if I—"

"I couldn't get anywhere on it," said Weber. "It's in the icebox."

No cable appointment. Did that mean a phony call had led Geraldo Solis to expect a visitor? If so, that could be a match to the phone booth call that had lured Marta Doebbler from the theater.

Cable appointment at midnight?

Petra recalled an incident in her own life that had spooked her. Two years ago, in the midst of a one-week vacation, a doorbell ring at eleven P.M. had jolted her out of bed. Some joker claiming to be a UPS deliveryman. She'd told him to go away, he'd persisted, said he needed a signature on a package. She'd grabbed her gun, tossed on a robe, and cracked the door. Found a haggard, brown-clad zombie. Actual UPS guy, with an actual package. Cookies from one of her sisters-in-law.

"Running late," he'd explained. Twitching and tapping his foot. Not even noticing the nine-millimeter held down against her right flank.

She knew delivery services put their drivers under pressure but this guy looked ready to blow.

So it *was* possible. A bad guy calls Geraldo Solis with the cable story, shows up late, Solis opens his door. No cable truck in the neighborhood didn't mean a thing. At that hour, in Solis's quiet, residential neighborhood, who'd be looking?

Geraldo Solis's daughter's address and phone number were duly listed in the murder book. Maria Solis Murphy, age thirty-nine, Covina. A DMV check put her current residence in the city. Right here in Hollywood, Russell Street off Los Feliz.

Her work number matched an extension for Food Services at Kaiser Permanente Hospital. Also Hollywood, an easy stroll from Russell.

She was on shift, came to the phone, arranged to meet Petra in front of the hospital in twenty minutes. By the time Petra arrived, she was there.

Hard-body type, pretty, with very short dark hair tipped blond, wearing a pale blue dress, white socks, and tennies. Three filament hoops in one ear, a diamond chip and a gold stud in the other. Tattoo of a rose on her left ankle. Kind of punk for a woman of nearly forty—a woman with a gold wedding band on her ring finger—but Maria Murphy had an unlined face and an aerobic bounce in her step. Put her in the right duds and she could've passed for mid-twenties.

Her badge said *M. Murphy, MS, Registered Dietician.* Very hard body. Boyish hips. The benefits of vitamins?

She said, "Detective?" in a husky voice.

"Ms. Murphy."

"If you don't mind, I could use a little stretch. Been kind of cooped up."

They walked west on Sunset, past the hospital, fast-food joints, the prosthetic outfitters, after-care specialists, and linen suppliers that attach themselves to hospitals. Western Peds, where Sandra Leon had been treated for leukemia, was a couple of blocks east. What was with that doctor, Katzman.

Maria Murphy said, "I'm very grateful you're reopening my dad's case."

"It's not exactly like that, Ms. Murphy. I'm a Hollywood detective and I picked up a case that could conceivably bear some similarities to your father's. But it's not a dramatic match—we're talking small details, ma'am."

"Like what?"

"I'm not at liberty to say, ma'am. Sorry."

"I understand," Maria Murphy said. "I discovered Dad's body. I'll never forget it."

That fact had been in the file. Geraldo Solis had been found slumped over his food at one A.M. Petra asked Murphy why she'd dropped in so late.

"I didn't drop in. I lived there. On and off. Temporarily."

"Temporarily?"

"I was married at the time and my husband and I were having problems. I stayed with Dad, from time to time."

Petra glanced at Murphy's gold band.

Murphy smiled. "That's from my partner. Her name is Bella."

Petra sensed Murphy sizing her up, assessing her tolerance level. "So you and your husband were having marital problems."

"I changed the rules, midstream," said Murphy. "Dave, my husband, was a good guy. I was the one who initiated the breakup. Back then, I was pretty moody."

"How'd Dave react to that?"

"He wasn't happy," said Murphy.

"He get mad?"

Without missing a step, Murphy turned sharply toward Petra. "It wasn't like that, don't even think that. Dave and Dad got along great. You want to know the truth, Dave and Dad had more in common with each other than with me. Any time we had a fight, Dad took Dave's side. He couldn't believe what I was doing and why I was doing it. My whole family was in pretty strong denial."

"Big family?" said Petra.

"Two brothers, two sisters. Mom's been gone for a while. When she was alive, I suppressed myself. Not wanting to hurt her. After I came out, they all ganged up on me, wanted me to see a shrink. Which was exactly what I'd been doing for two years, unbeknownst to them."

"You didn't want to hurt your mother, but your father . . ."

"You get to a point," said Murphy. "And Dad and I were never close. He was always working, always too busy. I didn't resent it, he did what he had to do, we just weren't close. Even after I started living with him, we had very little to say to each other."

She flinched, sucked in a breath, quickened her step.

"How long did you live with him?"

"On and off," Murphy reiterated. "A month or so. I kept most of my stuff at my house, would bring a few changes to Dad's. The story I gave him was I was working a double shift and didn't want to drive home tired. Dad's place was a lot closer to the hospital."

Covina to Hollywood was an hour drive, minimum, a lot hairier with traffic. The trip from Solis's house on Ogden near Olympic was a lark in comparison, so that much rang true.

"When did you tell your father the truth?" said Petra.

"I didn't. My sibs did. A few days before the murder."

"What about Dave?"

"Dave already knew. He wasn't angry, he was sad. Depressed. Don't go there. Really."

Petra decided she'd be talking to Dave Murphy, sooner rather than later. She nodded at Murphy, tried to look reassuring. "So is there anything about your father's murder that you've thought about since the first detectives spoke to you?"

"I only talked to one detective," said Murphy. "Big, heavyset kind of Scandinavian guy."

"Detective Hustaad."

"Yes, that's him. He seemed nice. Had a real bad cough. Later, he called me to tell me he had cancer, was going in for treatment. He promised to make sure Dad's case got transferred to someone else. I felt terrible for him. That cough, it didn't sound good."

"The case was transferred to Detective Weber. He never talked to you?"

"Someone did call me," said Murphy. "Once. But a long time . . . years after Hustaad got sick. I'd called the police station a few times—honestly, not a lot, I was dealing with my own stuff. When no one called me back, I let it go . . . I guess . . ."

"What did Detective Weber tell you?"

"He said he was taking over Dad's case, but I never heard from him again. I guess I should've followed through. I guess I figured after no clues came up right away, it would be hard to solve. Being a stranger and all that."

"A stranger?"

"A burglar," said Murphy. "That's what Hustaad figured."

"Did Detective Weber ask you anything?"

"Not really—oh, yeah, he did ask about Dad expecting the cable guy. Which I'd already told Detective Hustaad. It was the only thing I did tell Detective Hustaad that I thought might be relevant. Mostly, I was a basketcase. At the time, I mean . . . finding Dad."

Nothing hysterical about her now. Talkative woman, calm. Resigned to the fact that her father's murder would probably never be solved.

Petra kept walking, waited for more.

Half a block later, Murphy said, "Detective Hustaad didn't seem to have much energy."

"You're wondering if he worked the case as hard as it should've been worked."

"I don't know. Maybe. I guess I'm a pretty factual person."

"What do you mean?"

"I can accept facts, even if they're tough. If Dad had been killed by a burglar, the only way they'd solve it was if the same criminal did it again, right? That's kind of what Detective Hustaad implied." She turned to Petra. "Is your case a burglar, someone pretending to be a cable guy?"

"Everything's preliminary, ma'am."

"So I shouldn't get my hopes up."

"It's a long process."

"What was weird to me, if it was a burglar," said Murphy, "was that the only thing taken was food. A fresh head of lettuce, some whole wheat bread, and two cartons of lemon yogurt. That's a pretty strange burglar, no? But Detective Hustaad said they do that—eat food, mark their territory. He figured the guy got scared before he had time to steal anything."

She shrugged. "Maybe cash was taken, I don't know. I don't think so because the moment Dad had any extra cash, like from his military pension, he banked it."

Murphy slowed her pace and Petra adjusted. Traffic on Sunset was fast and thunderous and the two of them swerved to avoid some construction workers who'd blown a hole in the sidewalk and set up orange-and-white sawhorses.

Murphy looked at the hardhats. "Dad did that. Worked construction, after he left the Marines. Then he had his own business. A tire store in Culver City. When that went under, he was sixty-five, said he'd had enough. Mostly, he watched TV."

"You're pretty specific about which food was taken," said Petra.

"Because it was my food. I bought it the day before. Dad was more of a chorizo-and-fried-potatoes kind of guy. He made fun of the way I ate. Called it rabbit chow."

Pain in her eyes said there'd been more than dietary conflict between father and daughter.

"Your food was taken," said Petra.

"It couldn't mean anything. Could it?"

"Is there anyone who'd want to get back at you through your father?"

"No," said Murphy. "No one. Since the divorce, everything's been smooth. Dave and I are friendly, we talk all the time."

"Any kids?"

Murphy shook her head.

Petra said, "Tell me about the cable call and why you think it could've been phony."

"That day in the morning, when I left for work—Dad told me the cable company was sending someone out to work on the set."

"At what time?"

"Late afternoon, early evening, you know how they are," said Murphy. "Dad sometimes napped at that hour, wanted me to wake him by seven."

"Were you having transmission problems?"

"No, that's the thing," said Murphy. "Supposedly it was something to do with the neighborhood lines."

"He wanted you to wake him," said Petra. "So you were home by late afternoon?"

"No. I called at three, told Dad I'd be home late. He asked me to call again."

"At seven."

"Yes."

"Did you?"

"I did and he was up."

"How did your father sound?"

"Fine. Normal."

"Then you went back to work?"

Murphy touched her finger to her jaw. "Actually, I'd left work early. It had been a tough afternoon, shuttling back between Dave and Bella. When I hung up with Dad, I was in my car. I took off and went to see Bella. We had dinner, went to a club, did some drinking. Neither of us was in the mood to dance. She wanted me to come home with her but I wasn't ready for that, so she drove back to her place and I drove to Dad's. Walked into the house and smelled food—cooked food, bacon and eggs. Which was strange. Dad never ate late. He'd have a beer or two, maybe some chip-and-dip while watching TV, but never a hot meal at that hour. If he ate heavy food too late, he had indigestion."

Maria Murphy stopped walking. Her eyes were wet. "This is harder than I thought."

"Sorry for bringing it all back."

"I haven't thought about Dad for a while. I should think about him more." Murphy pulled a hankie out of a dress pocket, patted her eyes, blew her nose.

When they resumed walking, Petra said, "So someone had cooked."

"*Breakfast* food," said Murphy. "Which was also weird. Dad was a very disciplined person—ex-Marine, very regimented. You ate breakfast food in the morning, sandwiches at lunch, a main meal at supper."

"You don't think he cooked the food."

"Scrambled eggs?" said Maria Murphy. "Dad didn't like scrambled eggs, he always had his eggs fried or soft-boiled."

She burst into tears, walked faster, at a near-run.

Petra caught up. Murphy threw up her hands and ground her jaws.

"Ma-am—"

"His brains," Murphy blurted. "They were on the *plate.* Along with the eggs. Pilled on *top* of the eggs. Like someone had added lumpy *cheese* to the eggs. Gray cheese. Pink . . . can we please turn around, now? I need to get back to work."

Petra waited until they were back at Kaiser to ask her if there was anything else she remembered.

"Nothing," said Murphy. She turned to go and Petra touched her arm. Solid and sinewy. Maria Murphy tensed up. Rock-hard.

Looking at Petra's fingers on her sleeve.

Petra let go. "Just one more question, ma'am. The date of your father's murder, June 28. Did that have any significance to you, or to anyone in your family?"

"Why would you ask that?"

"Covering bases."

"June 28," said Murphy, weakly. "The only thing significant about that is Dad was murdered." She sagged. "It's coming up, isn't it? The anniversary. I think I'll go to the cemetery. I don't go very often. I really should go more."

Interesting woman. Going through major life-stress at the time of her father's murder. Not getting sympathy from the old man, quite the opposite. Pulled in all directions, having to return to the old man's house. A father with whom she'd never been close. An ex-Marine whose sensibilities she'd recently offended.

It had to have been a tense situation.

From the feel of that iron-arm, Murphy was a strong woman. More than enough strength to bring a stout piece of pipe down on an aged skull.

Murphy's food, taken. Healthy stuff that the old man ridiculed.

Maybe the old man had humiliated her one time too many. Dumped lesbian daughter's victuals in front of lesbian daughter and that had driven her over the edge.

Petra had seen people killed with a lot less provocation.

She pulled into the station parking lot, sat there imagining.

Murphy comes home from a self-described rough day—driving back and forth between hubbie and lover. Calls dad, allegedly to wake him from his nap, but he gives her flack. She hangs up, goes dining and clubbing, has too much to drink. Returns home, craving a one A.M. nosh, finds dad up, waiting for her.

They argue. About her alternative lifestyle.

Her rabbit chow.

Dad scoops up the nutritionally virtuous stash, tells her what he thinks about it.

Murphy was a dietician. The gesture would have been laced with extra symbolism.

An argument ensues.

He screams, she screams. She picks something up—maybe a spare pipe, who knows what. Brains the old guy, sits him at the table. Cooks up some of the high-fat crap *he* calls food.

Pushes his face in it. *Eat that!*

Then she makes up a phony cable story to distract the easily distracted Jack Hustaad.

Some melodrama. And no evidence.

And if Maria Murphy had murdered her old man, what did that say about Marta Doebbler and the other five June 28 killings?

She'd follow up on Solis, talk to Murphy's ex-husband, the long-suffering Dave. But something told her it would be a waste of time.

Kurt Doebbler for his wife, Maria Murphy for her dad.

Meaning no connection.

No, that felt wrong. If Isaac was right, and she was moving toward confidence that he was, this was something quite different from family passion gone bad.

A woman lured from the theater. A hustler pulverized in a back alley. A little girl brutalized in the park. A sailor on leave . . .

Eggs and brains on the plate.

This was calculated, manipulative.

Twisted.

CHAPTER

18

When she got back to the detectives' room, the place was bustling with phone talk and keyboard clacks. Isaac was at his corner desk, writing something in longhand, one hand cradling the side of his head.

He gave her a quick wave with his free hand and returned to his work.

Give me space?

Maybe last night's steak and beer had been too much for him. She'd offered to drive him home but he'd insisted on being dropped off blocks away.

Petra figured he was ashamed of his digs. She didn't argue and as he trudged away, lugging his briefcase, she thought he looked like a tired old man.

Give him his space, she could use some, too. She poured coffee and flipped through her message stack. Nothing but department memos. Six new e-mail messages on her computer: four canned department announcements, something from *SmallDot@il.netvision* she figured for spam, and Mac Dilbeck informing her that Homicide Special would most likely take over the Paradiso case by Tuesday if nothing broke.

She was about to delete the junk mail when her phone rang.

A recorded message from the Intramural Police Football team chirped in her ear: *"Big game with L.A. County Sheriffs coming up next month, all able-bodied, athletically inclined officers are urged to . . ."*

Her finger drifted to the Enter button and she opened the spam.

```
Dear Petra,

This is rerouted for security purposes, can't be an-
swered. Everything's okay. Hope the same, there. Miss
you. L, Eric.
```

She smiled. *I send my L, too.*

She saved the message, logged off. Began looking for David Murphy.

Common name but an easy trace. The five-year-old Covina address narrowed it right down to David Colvin Murphy, now forty-two. He'd moved to Mar Vista, on the west side. Had registered a Dodge Neon three years ago, a Chevy Suburban twenty months after that.

No wants or warrants, not even a parking ticket.

She found his number in the reverse directory. A woman answered.

"David Murphy, please."

"He's at work. Who's this?"

Petra recited her title and the woman said, "Police? Why?"

"It's about an old case. Are you familiar with Geraldo Solis, ma'am?"

"Dave's ex-father-in-law. He was . . . I'm Dave's wife."

"Where does your husband work, Mrs. Murphy?"

"HealthRite Pharmacy. He's a pharmacist." Saying it with some pride.

"Which branch, ma'am?"

"Santa Monica. Wilshire near Twenty-fifth. But I don't know what he could tell you, that was years ago."

Don't rub it in.

Petra thanked her and hung up, looked up the drugstore's number while glancing over at Isaac's desk. The kid was still poring over his papers but the hand against his face had dropped and Petra saw a bruise, reddish-purple, high up on the left side of his face, between the rounded tip of his cheekbone and his ear.

As if suddenly aware, he reclamped his hand over the spot.

Something had happened between last night and today.

Rough neighborhood. Walking alone.

Or worse—something domestic?

She realized how little she knew about his private life, considered going over to check out the bruise. But he looked as if the last thing he wanted was company.

She called the HealthRite Pharmacy, Santa Monica branch.

David Murphy had a pleasant phone voice. Not surprised by her call. The wife had prepared him.

He said, "Gerry was a good guy. I can't think of anyone who'd want to hurt him."

According to Maria, her father had taken Murphy's side in the divorce.

Petra said, "Well, someone sure did."

"Terrible," said Murphy. "So . . . what can I do for you?"

"Is there anything you remember about the day Mr. Solis was murdered, sir? Maybe something that didn't come up during the initial investigation?"

"Sorry, no," said Murphy.

"What do you recall?"

"It was a terrible day. Maria and I were in the midst of breaking up; she was driving back and forth between our home . . . between me and her . . . and Bella Kandinsky. She's her partner, now."

"Emotional day," said Petra.

"You bet. She'd come home, talk to me, get upset, run to Bella. Then back to me. I'm sure Maria was feeling like the rope in a tug of war. I was pretty stunned."

"Stunned?"

"My marriage, suddenly over. Over another woman." Murphy laughed. "Anyway, that was a long time ago. We've all moved on."

"At the time of the murder, Maria was living at her father's house."

"On and off," said Murphy.

"Because of marital problems."

"We'd been quarreling. I didn't understand why, at the time."

"You ever go over to Mr. Solis's house?"

"I used to be there all the time. Before things got rough in the marriage. Gerry and I got along. That made it kind of rough on Maria."

"How so?"

"Gerry took my side. He was pretty conservative. Maria's choice was hard for him to swallow."

"That must've caused conflict between them."

"Sure."

"Heavy-duty conflict?"

Murphy laughed again. "You can't be serious. No, no, that's totally out of the ballpark. Don't even go there."

Same phrase Maria had used.

"Go where?" said Petra.

"What you're implying. Listen, I'm kind of busy—"

"I wasn't implying, just asking," said Petra. "But as long as we're on the topic, how serious was the conflict between Maria and her dad?"

David Murphy said, "That's absurd. Maria's a terrific person. She and Gerry had your typical parent-child things. I had them with my folks, everyone does. No way could she have hurt him, she's absolutely a terrific person. No way."

She defends him, he defends her. And *they* got divorced. Depressing.

He said, "Believe me, Detective, I'm definitely right."

"Mr. Murphy, in the file there's a note about a cable-repair appointment. Did Maria mention that to you?"

"No, but Gerry did. In fact, the guy was right there when I called."

"You called Mr. Solis."

"Sure. I wanted to find out where Maria was. She left our house pretty upset and I assumed she went home. I wanted to smooth things out. Gerry answered and he was grumpy. Because the cable guy had come late."

"What time was this?"

"Wow," said Murphy. "This was what—five years ago? I remember it was dark, already. And I'd been working late . . . I'd say eight, nine. Maybe even nine-thirty. Gerry said something about the guy saying he'd show up by six, then calling to push it to seven, then still not making it on time. He was pretty annoyed. If I had to guess, I'd say between eight-thirty and nine."

"Mr. Solis was upset."

"Because of having to wait. When I asked to speak to Maria, he said she wasn't there, he had no idea where she was. . . . He was kind of abrupt. In general, he was a grumpy guy."

Meaning Geraldo Solis, already annoyed by delays, could've had a serious chip on that evening. Been primed for a confrontation.

She said, "Did Mr. Solis have a bad temper?"

"No, not really," said Murphy. "More like . . . a curmudgeon. He was a very disciplined guy, ex-Marine, expected the world to work on a tight schedule. When things didn't go that way, it bugged him."

"Like a late appointment." Or a lesbian daughter.

"Sure—oh, wow, you're not suggesting—"

"Just asking questions, Mr. Murphy."

"The cable guy?" said Murphy. "Whoa . . . but the police said Gerry was killed around midnight. . . . I guess he could've been left there for a few hours . . . wow."

A cable guy who shows up after dark. Whose company had no record of any scheduled service appointment. Which wasn't necessarily significant two years later. Paperwork screwups happened all the time and the cable companies that serviced L.A. were notoriously inept. Still . . .

She said, "Did he tell you the reason for the cable appointment?"

"That's another thing that bothered Gerry. He hadn't complained about anything. It was the company saying they needed to come by. General maintenance, something like that. My God . . . you really think—"

"Mr. Murphy, did you tell any of this to the original detective?"

"Hustaad? He never asked about it and I never really thought about it. What he wanted to know was how I got along with Gerry. How Maria got along. I got the feeling he was checking me out. Psychologically. He also asked where I was around midnight—that's why I figured it happened around midnight. Normally I'd be asleep at that time, but that night I was pretty upset and went out with a friend—a buddy from work. We went out drinking and I cried in my beer . . . so to speak."

"Can you remember anything else Mr. Solis said about the cable appointment?"

"Not really . . . I don't think he said anything other than how annoyed he was."

"And he definitely told you the man was there, in the house."

"Yes. I think . . . but maybe I assumed. He was talking softly, so I assumed someone was there. It's not anything I could swear to. In court, or something like that."

Court. From your mouth to God's ears.

Petra pressed him a bit more, learned nothing. Thanked him.

He said, "Sure. Good luck. Gerry really was a good guy."

A cable repairman, quite possibly phony, shows up after dark. Tinkers around and cases the place. Maybe leaves a rear door or a window unlocked for a return trip.

Or he does Solis right there, has the presence of mind to cook breakfast, stick the old man's face in it.

Takes some food for the road.

Healthy stuff; a killer who took care of himself.

What did any of that say about Kurt and Marta Doebbler?

Isaac was right; killing your wife and then moving on to strangers was unusual—she'd never heard of anything like that.

On the other hand, what if Kurt had dispatched Marta because of some personal motive, then found out he'd liked it?

Too twisted. She knew she was thinking that way because Doebbler was an eminently unlikable individual.

Then again, bashing six people over the head on the same date, same time, was pretty weird.

Across the room, Isaac continued to study his numbers. Hand on face, concealing the bruise.

The kid had complicated her life. Why couldn't he have chosen to do his thing at the sheriff's?

She took a bathroom break, risked more coffee, returned to the June 28 files. Putting Solis aside and reviewing the other non-Hollywood case.

The sailor, Darren Ares Hochenbrenner. On shore leave. According to two other sailors, they'd started out in Hollywood, but Darren had parted ways when they'd gone to a movie at the Egyptian.

The body had been found downtown, on Fourth Street, pockets emptied.

Far from the others, the only black victim, and the pockets made it a probable strong-arm street robbery taken to the extreme. She rechecked the wound dimensions. Perfect match to Marta Doebbler—down to the millimeter.

The listed detective was a DII named Ralph Seacrest. He was still working at Central, sounded tired.

"That one," he said. "Yeah, I remember it. Kid started off in your neighborhood, ended up in mine."

"Any idea how he got to yours?" said Petra.

Seacrest said, "I'm thinking he got picked up."

"By a john?"

"Could be."

"Hochenbrenner was gay?"

"That never came up," said Seacrest. "But sailors on leave? Or maybe he got lost. Kid was from the Midwest—Indiana, I think. First time in the city."

"He was stationed in Port Hueneme."

"That's not the city. Why're you asking about him?"

Petra spun him the usual yarn.

Seacrest said, "Another head-bashing? Your vic get robbed?"

"No."

"Mine got robbed. This was a kid, got lost, found himself in a real bad neighborhood. Also, he was stoned."

"On what?"

"Mari-joo-ana, some booze—don't hold me to that, it's been a while, but that's what I remember. Bottom line: He was partying. Probably partied too hardy, got picked up, the rest is history."

Petra hung up, checked Darren Hochenbrenner's tox screen, found a blood alcohol of .02 percent. At Hochenbrenner's body weight, that probably meant one beer. Traces of THC had been found, but minimal, possibly days old, according to the coroner.

Hardly "stoned." She wondered how hard Detective Ralph Seacrest had worked the case.

A shadow fell across the file and she looked up, expecting to see Isaac.

But the kid was gone from his desk. No briefcase. He'd left without saying a word.

A civilian receptionist from downstairs, a blond, cheerleader type named Kirsten Krebs, newly hired, who'd been hostile from the get-go, handed her a message slip.

Dr. Robert Katzman had returned her call. Half an hour ago.

Krebs was on her way toward the stairs. Petra said, "Why didn't you put him through?"

Krebs stopped. Turned. Glared. Clamped her hands to her hips. She wore a tight, powder-blue stretch top, tight black cotton pants. V-neck top, it offered a hint of tan, freckled cleave. Pushup bra. Long blond hair. Despite a face too hard to be pretty, a couple of D's had turned to take in her firm young ass. This was a sexual harassment suit waiting to happen.

"Your line was *busy*." Whiny.

Petra aimed a hollow-point smile straight at the girl's upturned nose. Krebs sniffed and turned on her heel. Eyed Isaac's desk as she left.

Not much older than Isaac. Half Isaac's I.Q., but she had other weapons in her armamentarium. Could eat the kid alive.

Listen to me—the surrogate mother.

She got on the phone and called Dr. Katzman. Got his mellow voice on message and left a message of her own.

Not so mellow.

CHAPTER
19

The joke: Richard Jaramillo was fat, so they called him Flaco.

That was back in fourth grade. Then Jaramillo grew up and got skinny and the nickname fit.

Little else about Jaramillo had worked out so neatly.

Isaac had known him back in public school: a jumpy, scared fat kid who wore old-fashioned clothes, sat at the back of the classroom, and never learned how to read. The teacher, faced with fifty kids, half of whom didn't speak English, assigned Isaac to tutor Flaco.

Flaco had reacted to the assignment distractedly. Isaac concluded, almost immediately, that Flaco's biggest problem was that he didn't pay attention. Not long after, he realized Flaco had real *problems* paying attention.

Flaco hated everything about school, so Isaac figured some kind of reward might work. Since Flaco was fat, he tried food. Mama was overjoyed when he asked her to pack extra sugar-tamales in his lunch bag. Finally, Isaac was starting to *eat*.

Isaac offered Flaco tamales and Flaco learned to read at the first-grade level. Flaco never got far beyond that. Even with tamales, it was never easy.

"Big deal anyway," he told Isaac. "I'm passing into fifth same as you."

Then Flaco Jaramillo's father went to prison on a manslaughter conviction and the boy stopped showing up at school, period. Isaac found that he missed being the teacher and now he had to figure out what to do with the extra tamales. He wanted to call Flaco, but Mama told him the Jaramillos had moved out of the city in shame.

Which turned out to be a lie; Mrs. Gomez had never liked Isaac hanging out with a bad boy from that family, such a rotten bunch. In truth, the Jaramillos had been evicted from their Union District flat and were crammed into a roach-ridden SRO hotel near Skid Row.

Five years later, the boys ran into each other.

It happened on a hot, polluted Friday, not far from the bus stop.

Half day at Burton because of teacher training seminars. Isaac had spent the afternoon at the Museum of Science and Industry, alone, was returning home, from the bus, when he saw two black-and-white police cars, parked at the corner in careless diagonals, lights flashing. Up on the sidewalk, a few feet away, a small, thin boy in a baggy T-shirt, sagging pants, and expensive running shoes was being rousted by four muscular officers.

They had him in the position: legs spread, arms up, palms pressed against the brick wall.

Isaac kept his distance but stopped to watch. The police questioned the boy, spun him around, got in his face and yelled.

The boy remained impassive.

Then Isaac recognized him. The baby fat was gone but the features were the same, and Isaac felt his own eyes stretch wide as the unspoken "huh?" resonated in his head.

He stepped even farther back, expecting the police to arrest Flaco Jaramillo. But they didn't, just wagged warning fingers, screamed some more, and shoved the boy around a bit. Then, as if summoned by a silent alarm, all four got in their cars and sped away.

Flaco stepped into the street and flipped off the cops. Noticed Isaac and flipped him off, too. As Isaac turned to leave, he shouted, "What the fuck you lookin' at, motherfucker?"

His voice had changed, too. Small boy with a deep baritone.

Isaac started walking.

"Yo, motherfucker, you hear me?"

Isaac stopped. The skinny boy was advancing on him. Face dark and scrunched and intent. All that pent-up anger and humiliation ready to blow. Ready to take it out on someone.

Isaac said, "It's me, Flaco."

Flaco came within inches. He smelled of weed. "Who the fuck are you?"

"Isaac Gomez."

Flaco's eyes became razor cuts. His skinny face was rodentine with the same oversized nose, weak chin, and bat ears that Isaac remembered. The ears looked even bigger, exhibited mercilessly by a shaved head. Flaco was short but broad-shouldered. Veins popped on his forearms like sculptural bas-relief. The clear intimation of muscle and the desire to use it.

Tattoos on his knuckles and the left side of his neck. The one on the neck was a nasty-looking snake, mouth open, fangs bared, as if about to close on Flaco Jaramillo's jaw line. The number "187" atop his right hand. The police code for "homicide." Some bangers were telling the truth when they advertised having done it.

"Who?"

"Isaac. Fourth grade—"

"Gomez. My fucking teacher. Man." Flaco shook his head. "So . . ."

"So how you been?" said Isaac.

"I been cool." Flaco smiled. Rotten teeth, several missing on top. The herbal reek of marijuana permeated his clothing. That had kept the police on him. But they'd found nothing, Flaco had dumped his dope in time.

"Fucking teacher," said Flaco. "So what's with you, why you dressed like a fag?"

"Private school."

"Private school. What the fuck's that?"

"Just a place," said Isaac.

"Why you go there?"

Isaac shrugged.

"They make you dress like a fag?"

"I'm not one."

Flaco looked him over some more. Grinned. "You fucked up as a teacher, man. I don't know shit."

Isaac shrugged again, working hard at casual-cool. "I was nine. I thought you were pretty smart."

Flaco's grin faltered. "Shows what you know."

He flexed the hand with the 187 tattoo. Reached out. Slapped Isaac on the back. Held his hand out for a soul shake. His skin was hard and dry and crusty, like poorly sanded wood. He laughed. His breath was bad.

Isaac said, "Good to see you, man. Guess I'll be shoving off."

"Shoving *off*? What's that, from a movie or somethin'?" Flaco turned pensive for a second. Brightened. "Let's go smoke up some weed, man. I got it where the motherfuckers can't find it."

"No thanks."

"No *thanks*?"

"Don't smoke."

"Man," said Flaco. "You fucked *up*."

He stepped back, reassessing Isaac. "Whatever."

"Thanks anyway."

Flaco waved that off. "Go, man. Go away."

As Isaac turned, Flaco said, "You tried to teach me, I remember that. You gave me some tamales, or some shit like that."

"Sugar tamales."

"Whatever, thought I was smart, huh?"

"I did."

Flaco bared his bad teeth. "Shows what you know. Hey man, check *this* out: How 'bout we shove *off* and I smoke and you watch and we like . . . talk, man. Like find out what's been happening all these years?"

Isaac thought about it, not for too long.

"Sure," he said. In the end, he'd ended up taking a couple of courtesy puffs.

They ran into each other once or twice a year, mostly the same kind of chance meetings on the street. Sometimes Flaco had no time for Isaac, other times he seemed to crave company. When they got together it was always Flaco smoking and talking, Isaac listening. Once, when they were sixteen, Isaac, in a bad mood for whatever reason, took deep hits of weed, hated the way the smoke burned his lungs, the popcorn lightness in his head, laughing too much, losing control. He walked home woozy, stayed in bed until dinner. Ate well. Mama looking on approvingly.

When they were seventeen, Flaco had Isaac decipher some probation papers because his reading had remained at the first-grade level.

"My P.O.'s a dumb motherfucker but I want to keep it real, man, show up at appointments, get past this bullshit."

The papers said Flaco had stolen cigarettes from a vending machine and been sentenced to a year's probation. Penal Code 466.3. That kind of thing you didn't tattoo on your hand.

The following year, Flaco showed Isaac his guns. A big, black automatic weighing down a pocket of his saggy khakis, a smaller chrome-plated six-shot thing taped to his ankle.

Ankle gun? He probably saw that in a movie.

Isaac said, "Cool." By that time he'd developed a solid fix on Flaco's temperament: jumpy, unstable, completely devoid of fear. The last trait made Flaco more dangerous than any fanged snake.

Flaco went on about the guns, what they could do, how you cleaned them, what a bargain he'd gotten on the purchase.

Isaac listened. When you listened, people stayed calm and thought you were smart and interesting.

Flaco liked to say, "That life you leading, man. You gonna be rich."

"Doubtful."

"Doubtful my dick, man. You gonna be a rich doctor and get close to all that dope." Wink wink. "We still gonna be friends, man."

Isaac laughed.

"Funny," said Flaco. "Very fuckin' funny." But he laughed, too.

Isaac got off the downtown bus and found his way to the bar on Fifth near Los Angeles Street. Not far, he realized, from the alley where one of the June 28 victims, the sailor Hochenbrenner, had breathed his last.

Bad neighborhood, even with Downtown getting rejuvenated.

Cantina Nueva was where Flaco hung out during the day, did whatever it was he did. Isaac avoided asking but Flaco was eager to brag. There were stories Isaac listened to. Others he allowed to pass right through his consciousness.

Sometimes Flaco got really quiet, didn't talk about anything. Both of them were young men, now. Knew it was in their mutual interest if some things remained unspoken.

Isaac had been to the bar twice this year, both times at Flaco's request. Once, Flaco had needed some papers deciphered: the deed to a house on 172nd. Flaco's real estate agent had assured him everything was cool but the dude was a slippery motherfucker and Flaco knew who he could trust.

Flaco, at twenty-three, would soon be a homeowner. Isaac was broke and the irony didn't escape him.

The second time Flaco claimed he just wanted to talk, but when Isaac got there, Flaco remained in his booth at the rear and it was one of those days when he said little. He kept ordering beer-and-shots for both of them and Isaac tried to nurse his to the max. He got drunk anyway, grew really tired, and sat there as people streamed in and out of the cantina, made their way over to Flaco. Exchanged glances. And cash. Shiny chromium things in paper bags. Powders in plastic baggies.

All I need is for the place to be busted right now. Bye-bye med school.

Flaco had seated Isaac on the inside of the booth, facing the pool table, back to the moldy wall. Then he'd gotten in, next to Isaac. Trapping Isaac.

Wanting Isaac to see everything. To *know.*

A couple of beer-and-shots later, Flaco said, "My old man died, got cut in the shower at Chino."

Isaac said, "Oh, man, I'm sorry."

Flaco laughed.

This afternoon the bar was overheated and dim and sweat-sour, mostly empty except for a couple of old Tio Tacos hunched at the bar and three young guys who looked like they'd just crossed the border, shooting pool at the solitary, warped table. *Snick snick snick* as cues impacted plastic balls. A disagreeable clang as the balls slid down the metal chute. The Doctors Lattimore had a pool table at their house—had a whole, paneled room set aside for billiards. No noisy chute on that one, leather mesh sacks caught the balls silently.

Clang. Spanish curses. Bad mariachi-rock fusion blared from the jukebox.

Flaco slumped in the booth, wearing a black denim jacket over a black T-shirt, empty beer and shot glasses in front of him. He'd grown his hair out, but in a weird style. Shaved on top with two black stripes running along the side and a short, tightly pleated braid dangling at the back like a reptilian tail. Mustache wisps at the corner of his mouth. All he could grow.

He looked, Isaac decided, like some Hollywood director's notion of an evil Chinese guy.

He looked up as Isaac approached. Sleepily, Isaac thought.

Isaac stood there until Flaco motioned him in.

Quick soul shake. "Bro."

"Hey." Isaac slid across from him. He'd stopped at a pharmacy, bought a tube of cover-up makeup, done his best to hide the bruise. A patchy job at best, but if you weren't looking for it, maybe you wouldn't notice.

Nothing could be done about the swelling, but between Flaco's short attention span and the bar's poor lighting, he hoped he wouldn't have to explain.

"Whussup?" Flaco's voice slurred. His long sleeves were buttoned at the wrist. Usually, he rolled them up. Hiding needle marks? Flaco always denied shooting, made a point of preferring inhalation, but who knew?

He'd always been restless; unable to leave well enough alone.

Isaac said, "The usual."

"The motherfuckin' *usual* but you're motherfuckin' *here.*"

Isaac shrugged.

"You always do that," said Flaco. "With the shoulders. You do that when you wanna hide something, man."

Isaac laughed.

"Yeah, it's funny, asshole." Flaco's head rolled.

"I need a gun," said Isaac.

Flaco's head rose. Slowly. "Say what?"

Isaac repeated it.

"A gun." Flaco snickered. "What, like to shoot down planes, you gonna be one of them terrorists?" His cheeks puffed as he tried to imitate cannon fire. Feeble puffs resulted. He coughed. Definitely on something.

"For protection," said Isaac. "The neighborhood."

"Someone fuck with you? Tell me who, I kill their ass."

"No, I'm cool," said Isaac. "But you know how it is. Things get better, then they get worse. Right now, it's worse."

"You having problems, man?"

"I'm cool. Want to keep it that way."

"A gun . . . you mama . . . those tamales." Flaco licked his lips. "Those were *fine.* Kin you get me some more?"

"Sure."

"Yeah?"

"No problem."

"When?"

"Whenever you want them."

"I come over knock on your door, you invite me in, introduce me to you mama, get me some of them sweet tamales?"

"Absolutely," said Isaac, knowing it would never happen.

Flaco knew it, too. "A gun," he said, suddenly reflective. "It's like a . . . you know a . . . responsibility."

"I can handle it."

"You know how to shoot?"

"Sure," Isaac lied.

"Bullshit, motherfucker."

"I can handle it."

"You end up shooting off your ass—you shoot your own *cojones off,* man, I ain't gonna cry."

"I'll be fine."

"Bang bang," said Flaco. "No, I don't think so, man. What for you need to mess with motherfucking *guns?*"

"I'm going to get one," said Isaac. "One way or the other."

"You stupid, man." Then Flaco realized what he'd said and cracked up.

Isaac started to get up. Flaco clamped a hand over his wrist. "Have a drink, bro."

"No, thanks."

"You turnin' me down?"

Isaac swung around in the booth, faced Flaco full-on. "The way I see it, you're doing the turning down."

Flaco's smile dropped. His hand remained clawed over Isaac's wrist. Another 187 tattoo. On the other hand. Larger, fresher. Black ink. A tiny grinning skull nested in the upper circle of the *8*. "You ain't gonna drink with me?"

"One drink," said Isaac. "Then I'm going. Got to take care of business."

Flaco slid out of the booth, teetered to the bar, returned with two beer-and-shots. As the two of them drank, he drew a white plastic shopping bag out of the black denim jacket and lowered it beneath the table.

Isaac glanced down. Jewelry Mart logo on the bag, a vendor called Diamond World.

"Happy birthday, motherfucker."

Isaac took the bag from Flaco. Heavy. At the bottom was something swaddled in toilet paper. Keeping his hands low, he unwrapped it partially.

A shiny little thing. Squat, square-barreled, perfectly malevolent.

CHAPTER
20

Petra left two additional messages with Dr. Robert Katzman, the last unmistakably cross.

Then she regretted her tone. Even if she finally reached the oncologist, big deal. He'd treated Sandra Leon for leukemia, what else could he tell her?

Then again, she was sure the Oncology clerk had gotten antsy talking about Sandra. But who said that related to the girl with the pink shoes or any other aspect of Paradiso?

She went downstairs, found Kirsten Krebs idling by the watercooler in a tank top and jeans, told Krebs to put Katzman through immediately if he called back.

Krebs stared at the floor and said, "Yeah, fine." When she thought Petra was out of earshot, she muttered, "What-*ever.*"

Petra returned to her desk feeling aimless. She'd slept fitfully, burdened with too much of nothing. Just two weeks until June 28. No sign of Isaac for a few days. Had the kid lost his youthful enthusiasm about the nefarious plot? Or was it something to do with that bruise?

Either way, who cared?

Unfortunately, she did. She turned to the file copies, reviewed the two she knew the best—Doebbler and Solis—for new insights and failed to come up with any.

It stayed that way until she reviewed the coroner's report on Coral Langdon, the dog walker, and found something she'd missed the first few times around. Stuck in the middle of a small-print hair-and-fiber list stapled under some lab results.

Two types of canine hair had been found on Langdon's clothing. No mention of that in the coroner's nonquantitative summary. The pathologist hadn't deemed it important. Maybe it wasn't.

The presence of cockapoo hair was self-explanatory. Little Brandy had been bludgeoned along with her mistress.

Stupid little bitch. The world is my toilet.

But along with the champagne-colored curls raked from Coral's purple, cashmere blend, size M, Robinsons-May cardigan and her black, size 8 poly-cotton Anne Klein pants, was a smaller, but substantial number of straight, coarse hairs.

Short, dark brown and white. Canine. No DNA had been analyzed to determine the breed.

No reason to get that fancy. There were plenty of reasonable explanations, including maybe Coral Langdon had owned two dogs. Except according to the file she hadn't. Detective Shirley Lenois might have missed the June 28 link, but Shirley had been a dog person, owned three Afghan hounds, would have been sure to note the presence of a second pet.

Perhaps little Brandy had hung with a canine buddy, picked up hairs, transferred them to Coral.

Or a stray dog had come upon both corpses, sniffed around.

Or, Coral Langdon, walking alone, at night, in the Hollywood Hills, in the company of a pint-sized pooch that provided zero protection, had encountered another dog walker.

The two of them stop to swap dog chat. Dog people were like that, being devoted to your pet was grounds for instant rapport.

Because of that, dogs could be a great ruse for bad guys. Petra recalled a case she'd worked early in her grand-theft-auto days. Pleasant-looking frat-boy-type thief—what was his name—who always took along a lumbering, seventy-pound bulldog . . . Monroe. She remembered the dog's moniker but not the guy's. What did that say?

Frat-boy's modus was to "chance" upon women pulling late-model luxury wheels into shopping center parking lots. As they got out of their cars, he'd saunter by, Monroe in tow. The women would get one look at the stubby dog's wrinkled frog face and melt. Chitchat would ensue, Frat-boy—Lewis something—was brilliant at putting on the wholesome dog guy act, though Monroe really belonged to his sister. The women would coo and pet the stoic, panting beast, then walk off happy. Fifty percent of the time they forgot to lock their cars and/or set the alarms.

Yup, canine companionship could definitely impart instant decency to a stranger.

Petra thought about how Langdon might've gone down. A guy with a dog—a white, middle-class-looking guy—someone who wouldn't seem out of place in Coral Langdon's Hollywood Hills neighborhood—shows up on the quiet, hillside road.

Coral with her fluffy pal, the guy with a larger pooch. Nothing scary, like a pit bull. Short, dark brown and white hairs—could be a pointer, a mixed-breed, whatever.

Something mellow and nonthreatening.

She stayed with the scenario, imagining Coral and Dog Guy stopping to talk. Maybe laughing as their furry buddies engaged in mutual squatting.

Exchanging cute little "aren't dogs almost human" stories.

Coral—single, fit, and youthful for her age—might have welcomed some male attention. A bit of flirtation ensued, maybe even a phone-number exchange. No number had been found on Coral's body, but that meant nothing. Dog Guy could've lifted it when his job was done.

His job.

Biding his time as he and Coral exchange amiable have-a-nice-evenings.

Coral and Brandy turn to go.

Boom.

Bashed from behind. Like all the others. A coward. A calculating, manipulative coward reluctant to face his victims.

Creative, Milo Sturgis would call it. His favorite euphemism when cases bogged down.

Petra wondered what he'd think about all this. Delaware, too.

She was pondering whether to call either of them when Kirsten Krebs stomped up to her desk and straight-armed a message slip right in her face.

"He hung up?" said Petra.

"It's not the one you *said* to put *through,*" said Krebs. "But seeing as you're so into your *messages* I brought it to you *personally.*"

Petra snatched the slip. Eric had phoned three minutes ago. No return number.

The message on the slip, in Krebs's cramped writing: *"Don't believe everything you see on the news."*

"Whatever that means," said Krebs. "He sounded kinda strange."

"He's a detective, here."

Krebs remained unimpressed.

Petra said, "You told him I wasn't here?"

"He wasn't the one you *said,*" Krebs insisted.

"Damn . . ." Petra reread the message. "Fine. Bye."

Krebs clamped her hands on her hips, cocked one leg, sucked in her cheeks. "If you're going to be choosy, you have to give me *detailed* instructions." She marched away.

Don't believe everything you see on the news.

Petra headed for the locker room, where the latest cast-off TV sat.

This one was a Zenith, static-plagued, with no cable hookup, perched on a windowsill. Petra switched it on, flipped channels until she found a local broadcast.

Regional news, nothing remotely related to the Middle East.

Was Eric even there?

Don't believe . . . okay, but he was fine, he'd called, nothing to worry about.

Why hadn't he insisted on speaking to her?

Because he didn't want to. Bad situation? Something he couldn't talk about?

Her heart pounded and her stomach hurt. She hurried back to the detectives' room. Barney Fleischer was at his desk, sports coat bunched up at his shoulders. Humming and stacking his paperwork neatly.

She said, "Does anyone around here get CNN?"

Barney said, "I prefer Fox News. Fair and balanced and all that."

"Either way."

"The closest place would be Shannons."

Petra had never been to the Irish pub, but she knew where it was. Up Wilcox, just south of the Boulevard, a brief walk.

Barney said, "They've got a nice flat screen, sometimes they keep the news on when there's no game."

She racewalked to Shannons, sat at the bar, ordered a Coke. The flat screen was a fifty-two-inch plasma set like a window into the wall above the booze-rack. Tuned to MSNBC.

Nothing about the Middle East for one complete news cycle and the running banner at the bottom of the screen was cut off. She asked the bartender if there was any way to fix that.

"We format it this way on purpose," he said. "You format the other way, it burns lines in the screen."

"How about for a few minutes? Or maybe we can try one of the other stations."

He frowned at her soft drink. No way that justified special treatment. But business was slow, no one else shared the bar, so he fooled with the remote and the banner appeared.

She endured financial news, a basketball finals recap, then the international stories: an earthquake in Algeria—the Middle East—but nothing Eric would call her about.

Why couldn't he have just come out and—

The anchorwoman's voice rose in pitch and Petra's ears opened. ". . . reports that American military personnel may have been at least partly responsible for reducing the death toll from a suicide bombing in Tel Aviv . . ."

A beachside café on a restaurant-chocked avenue that paralleled the Mediterranean. People trying to enjoy themselves on a hot, sunny day.

Israelis, a couple of German tourists, some foreign workers from Thailand. Unnamed American "security officers."

Scumbag with a bomb vest under his raincoat approaches from across the street.

Scumbag's black raincoat on a hot day would've tipped off anyone with the slightest powers of observation.

It had. He'd been wrestled to the ground, put out of commission before having a chance to yank the detonator cord on his plastique-and-ball-bearing-and-nail-stuffed vest.

Score one for the good guys.

Moments later, Scumbag Number Two saunters over, gets twenty feet away and pulls his plug. Turning himself to jihadburger. Taking two Israelis with him—a mother and her teenage daughter.

And: *"Scores are reported injured . . ."*

Two evil shit-heads. But for someone's sharp eyes, it could've been worse.

Someone.

Scores injured could cover a lot of territory.

Eric had to be in good enough shape to call.

Why hadn't he insisted on talking to her, dammit?

"Seen enough?" said the bartender. "Can I format it back?"

Petra tossed him a ten and left the bar.

CHAPTER
21

Back at the station, she ran upstairs to the locker room, flicked on the old Zenith, caught the four P.M. broadcast on KCBS. The Tel Aviv bombing was the third-ranked story, after the legislature's credibility problems and a new bank fraud scandal in Lynwood.

Same bare-bones facts, nearly identical wording. What had she expected?

She entered the detectives' room, nearly collided with Kirsten Krebs.

"*There* you are. He's on hold."

Petra ran to her desk and picked up. "Connor."

"The irate detective," said a mellow voice. Dr. Bob.

"Sorry about that, Dr. Katzman. It's been a tough week."

"I imagine you get plenty of those."

You, too, being a cancer doctor. "Thanks for returning. As I mentioned, Sandra Leon was a witness to a murder and we're having trouble tracking her down."

"Unfortunately, I can't help you with that," said Katzman. "She's no longer my patient. And I could never track her down either."

"Where's she getting her chemotherapy?"

"Hopefully nowhere, Detective. Sandra doesn't have leukemia. Though she wanted us to think she did."

"She lied about being sick?"

"Lying," said Katzman, "appears to be one of her primary skills. I guess I misspoke when I said she was no *longer* my patient. She never was under my care in the first place. That's why I have no problem talking to you."

"Talk away, doctor."

"She showed up last year with a letter from a physician in Oakland saying she'd been diagnosed with AML—acute myelogenous leukemia—was in remission and needed to be followed. The letter also stated that she was an emancipated minor living with some cousins and would require financial assistance. Our social worker sent her to all the right agencies and booked her for an appointment with me. Sandra kept her appointments with the agencies but was a no-show at Oncology Clinic."

"What kind of agencies are we talking about?"

"There are several county and state programs set up for kids with cancer. They offer medication, transportation and housing vouchers, wigs when the patients lose their hair. Co-payment for treatment."

"Ah," said Petra.

"You bet," said Katzman. "And once a child's registered, the family also gets hooked into the general welfare system. Which gets you access to food stamps, et cetera."

"So Sandra got goodies but didn't show up for her appointment."

"For the agencies it wasn't a problem, technically. All they require is that a patient be diagnosed, not actively undergoing treatment. I found out later that on some of the application forms, she *was* listed as an active patient."

"Forms Sandra filled out herself."

"You've got the picture."

"Did you ever see her?"

"Months after talking to the social worker. The first time she didn't show, we phoned the number she listed on her intake form, but it was disconnected. That concerned me but I figured she'd moved. Or changed her mind and went to another doc. Then some of her forms came in for me to sign off on and I went back and checked and wondered what was going on. I sent the social worker out on a home visit. The address Sandra gave us turned out to be a mail drop."

"Where?"

"I wouldn't know," said Katzman. "Maybe Loretta, the social worker, would."

"Last name, please," said Petra.

"Loretta Brainerd. So Sandra witnessed a murder?"

"Murders," said Petra. "The Paradiso shootings."

"I heard about that," said Katzman.

"In Baltimore?"

"I left the day before it happened."

"You finally saw her," said Petra. "How'd you find her?"

"I had CCS—Children's Cancer Services—send her a letter to the effect that she'd lose her benefits if she didn't show up for her checkup. She was there the next day, right on time. In tears, all apologetic. Going on and on about some family crisis, having to travel suddenly."

"Travel where?"

"If she said, I don't recall. To tell the truth I wasn't listening. I was annoyed because I felt she was jerking me around. Then, when she turned on the faucet, I wasn't sure. She's a pretty good actress. Most important, I wanted to check her out medically because I didn't like what I saw. Her complexion was yellow, especially the eyes. Jaundice can be a sign of relapse—infiltration of the disease into the liver. I ordered a full panel blood workup. Depending on what that turned up, I was ready to do a bone marrow aspiration and a lumbar puncture— more intrusive tests, even the most compliant patients don't like them. But when I mentioned that to Sandra, she stayed calm. That made me wonder if she'd ever been through them in the first place. I ordered the tests back stat, scheduled her for a five P.M. recheck that day. She said she was hungry so I gave her some money to get a hamburger in the cafeteria. She and her cousin."

"Her cousin?"

"Another girl, around the same age," said Katzman. "The two of them showed up with a man, some guy in his forties. He dropped them off at the clinic and left but the cousin stayed. The blood workup came back negative for leukemia but positive for Hepatitis A—viral hepatitis. Which isn't as bad as Hep C but it should be followed. I was ready to admit her for observation but she didn't show for the recheck. Big surprise. That's when I phoned the doctor from Oakland. He'd never heard of her. Wasn't even an oncologist—a family practitioner working out of some Medi-Cal clinic. She must've gotten hold of some stationery and forged the letter."

"Is she in danger from the hepatitis?"

"Not unless her resistance gets bad and something else hits her. Hep A is generally self-limiting. That's doctor-talk for goes away on its own."

"Her eyes are still yellow," said Petra.

"She came in . . . I'd guess four months ago. By six months, patients are usually better."

"How do you catch it?"

"Poor sanitation." Katzman paused. "Prostitutes and other promiscuous people are at risk if they engage in anal sex."

"You figure Sandra for promiscuous?"

"She was flirtatious, but that's all I can say."

"During the time she was in the system," said Petra, "how much money did she squeeze out?"

"I couldn't begin to tell you."

"The cousin," said Petra. "What do you remember about her?"

"Quiet girl. Sandra was more outgoing, nice-looking kid, despite the jaundice. The cousin just sat there."

"Was she about Sandra's age?"

"Maybe a little younger."

"Shorter than Sandra? Chubby? Curly reddish hair?"

Silence. "That sounds familiar."

"Did she happen to wear pink sneakers?"

"Yes," said Katzman. "Bright pink. I remember that." He sounded amazed that the memory had returned.

Petra said, "What else can you tell me about their relationship?"

"I wasn't noticing. I was concentrating on Sandra's jaundice."

Petra tensed; had she touched the girl that night in the parking lot?

"Would you consider her contagious, Doctor?"

"I wouldn't exchange body fluids with a Hep A, but you're not going to get it by shaking hands."

"What can you tell me about the adult male who came with the girls?"

"All I remember is his dropping them off in the waiting room and leaving. I noticed because I'd stepped out to see a patient off. I was planning to have a talk with him—responsible adult and all that—but he was gone before I could turn around."

"What'd he look like?" said Petra.

"All I really saw was his back."

"You noticed his age," said Petra. "In his forties."

"Amend that to 'middle aged.' From the way he carried himself. Thirty to fifty."

"What was he wearing?"

"Sorry," said Katzman. "I'd be getting into the realm of fantasy."

Lots of that going around. Petra said, "Would Loretta Brainerd know more about any of this?"

"I wouldn't think so, but feel free to ask her."

"Thanks, Doctor."

"There is one thing," said Katzman. "Sandra gave her age as fifteen, but my guess is she's older. Closer to eighteen or nineteen. I can't back that up scientifically; it's just something that came to me after I realized I'd been conned. There was a certain . . . I wouldn't say sophistication . . . a certain confidence." He laughed. "About her confidence game."

She called Brainerd. The social worker barely remembered Sandra Leon.

Hanging up, Petra thought back to the parking lot interview. The girl had just witnessed the violent death of her "cousin" but had displayed no shock, no grief, none of the emotionality you'd expect from a teenage girl confronted by tragedy. On the contrary, she'd been dry-eyed. Tapping her foot . . . impatient. As if Petra was taking up her precious time.

The only thing that had sparked anxiety in the girl's eyes had been initial eye contact with Petra.

Cool about the homicide but nervous about the cops.

Claiming to be fifteen when she faked her patient status, but that night she'd given her age as sixteen.

Her dress and makeup fit with Katzman's guess that she was older.

Dolled up fancier than the girl in the pink sneakers. Party garb, down to the appliqué mole. Celebrating what?

An adult male had accompanied both girls. Sandra had mentioned a convict brother, a car thief. Petra flipped through her notepad, found her hastily scrawled shorthand.

Bro. GTA. Lompoc.

She called the state prison, spoke to an assistant warden, learned that two "Leons" resided within the walls: Robert Leroy, age sixty-three, fraud and grand theft, and Rudolfo Sabino, age forty-five, manslaughter and mayhem. The warden was kind enough to check both inmates' visitors' lists. No one had been to see Rudolfo Leon for over three years. Sad case, he was HIV positive and suffering from dementia. The older man, Robert Leroy Leon, had a bevy of visitors but no Sandra, no one close to the girl in approximate age and appearance.

Another lie?

Sandra Leon had progressed, officially, from witness to Person of Interest.

Petra paged Mac Dilbeck and told him about the scam.

He said, "She knew the vic but wasn't upset. So maybe she knew it was going to happen."

"That's what I'm thinking."

"Good work, Petra. Nothing else on this adult male?"

"Not yet. I'm wondering about something else. Leon quoted me her rights and I asked her if she had experience with the law. She told me a story about a brother locked up at Lompoc. Turns out to be another load of b.s., but why would she volunteer the information when it would tie her in with a criminal? Why not just dummy up?"

"Maybe your question threw her off," said Mac. "She's a liar but still in training. So she blurted out a half-truth, covered with a phony detail."

"A relative in the system," said Petra, "but not a brother. Maybe even a brother but not at Lompoc. That cancer scam was sophisticated, not the kind of thing a virgin would try. This girl's had experience, I wonder if she's part of a criminal enterprise—a family thing."

"Some kind of gypsy thing? Like the Tinkers. Like those Somalians we busted last year. Yeah, why not? If there's an Inmate Leon some-where in the system for scamming, that would be really interesting."

"Robert Leon's locked up for fraud and theft but he's too old to be her brother."

"Interesting."

"Maybe the murder's related to some scam thing and the girl in the pink shoes was the intended victim," she said. "They set it up to look like some gang thing. Sandra wasn't freaked out because she knew."

"Cold," said Dilbeck. "Very cold. Okay, time to check the entire system, state and federal pens, even county jails."

"Who's going to do it?"

"You mind?"

"I'm doing it solo?"

"Well," said Mac, "Montoya's already been assigned a fresh case and the rest of my day is committed: meeting with the hotshots down-town. Gonna sit there while they explain why they're so much smarter than we are. Course, if you want to trade places . . ."

"No, thanks," said Petra. "I'll go fetch my magic wand."

She ran cons named Leon through NCIC and the rest of the data banks, came up with way too many hits. Time for a little logic. Sandra Leon had brought Katzman a letter from a clinic in Oakland, meaning she, or someone she knew, had spent some time there.

She focused on Bay Area Leons, which narrowed the search to twelve.

Two inmates—John B., twenty-five, Charles C., twenty-four—fit the brother age-range. Both were from Oakland and when she pulled up their stats, she knew she'd earned her share of the taxpayers' money.

John's middle name was "Barrymore," and Charles's was "Chap-lin."

Katzman's take on Sandra: *She's a pretty good actress.*

Then she learned that the men were brothers and allowed herself a grin.

A passing detective said, "You're sure happy."

Petra said, "Once in a while."

John Barrymore Leon was serving a five-year sentence at Norco for mail fraud and Charlie Chaplin Leon had earned himself two years at

Chino for theft—breaking into vending machines in an Oakland arcade.

The wardens at Norco were unavailable and the guard supervisor was new on the job. But his counterpart at Chino turned out to be a font of information. The Leons were members of an Oakland-based crime group called The Players, and several of their cousins had done penitentiary time. His estimate of their membership was fifty to sixty, most related by blood, but some who'd married in or had been informally adopted. The majority were Hispanic—Guatemalan Americans—but there were plenty of whites and blacks and at least two Asians.

Petra said, "Diversity in the workplace."

The Chino guard laughed.

"They use violence?" she asked him.

"Not that I've heard. They concentrate on scams, run a lot of welfare schemes. They like to think of themselves as actors because the boss tried to be one."

The boss was a failed actor with a forty-year history of property crimes. Robert Leroy Leon, sixty-three, aka The Director. Currently residing at Lompoc. Lots of visitors but no Sandra.

Mac had been dead-on: The girl had slipped, blurted out a partial truth.

Petra pressed the Chino guy for everything he knew about The Players. He gave her the names of some possible members but not much more. She wrote down copious notes and booted up her computer.

Logging on to Google, she plugged in "The Players" and came up with 1,640,000 hits. "Players scams" pulled up exactly one website, a protest against corporate malfeasance.

It was nearly seven P.M. and she was suddenly tired and overwhelmed. She was staring at the screen and wondering where to go next when Isaac's voice drew her away from all those zeros.

"Hi," he said.

Her eyes shot to the bruise on his cheek. Faded—no, covered up. He'd tried to mask it with makeup. The result was clumsy, a flaking splotch.

"Hey," she said. "I hope the other guy came out of it worse."

CHAPTER
22

Isaac blushed through the makeup.

"No big deal," he said, too casually. "The hallway was dark when I got home and I bumped into the wall."

"Oh," said Petra.

A few flakes of makeup had landed on the shoulder of his blue shirt. He saw her looking at them and flicked them away. "I was wondering if there was anything I could do for you."

It was seven thirty-two P.M. "Working late?" said Petra.

"I had obligations on campus all day, figured I'd come by here, see if you needed me."

One million six hundred forty thousand hits.

Petra smiled. "As a matter of fact . . ."

She gave him the info on Sandra Leon and The Players and watched him hurry over to his laptop.

Thrilled to be busy.

She was worn-out and hungry.

◆

She returned to Shannons, took the same stool at the bar and ordered a Bud and a corned beef sandwich. The flat screen was tuned to an infomercial. None of the boozers at the bar were interested in buying cubic zirconium mystical bracelets.

New bartender on shift, a woman, and she didn't squawk when Petra asked her to put on Fox News and format it so the running border was visible.

"Yeah, it's annoying," the woman said. "You want to read something and it cuts everything in half."

Three other boozers nodded agreement. Older guys, grizzled, in wrinkled work uniforms. The bar smelled of their sweat. The color in their faces said St. Patrick's Day had started early.

One looked at Petra and smiled. Not a lecherous leer, paternal. Crazily, she thought about her dad, the shockingly rapid Alzheimer's fade.

She chewed on her sandwich, drank her beer, ordered another, shot her eyes to the TV when she heard "Tel Aviv."

Charred and twisted outdoor furniture, ambulance howls, Hasidic types cleaning up body parts. The death toll had risen to three—one of the wounded had succumbed to "injuries suffered in the blast." The number of wounded was now precise: twenty-six.

Hamas and one of Arafat's groups were each claiming credit.

Credit.

Fuck them.

The sandwich steamed up at her. Her nose filled with brine and her stomach began churning. She threw money on the bar and left.

The female bartender called out, "Everything okay, honey?"

When Petra reached the door, the woman shouted: "Can I at least wrap it to go?"

She drove around the city, aimlessly, recklessly. Listening to the horn blares of those she'd offended and not giving a damn.

Spaced out, she pushed the Accord through traffic as if it was on tracks. Not looking at people the way she usually did. Off the job—a job that never really ended.

But tonight, it had. Tonight, she wanted nothing to do with cons, scumbags, felons, and miscreants. Had no patience to look for furtive glances, suspicious moves, the sudden popcorn-burst of violence that changed everything.

Twenty-six injured.

Eric had phoned her, so he had to be okay.

But Eric was stoic about pain. After the stabbing, when he'd come to, he'd refused analgesics. Perforated, and he claimed he didn't feel a thing. The doctors couldn't believe he could tolerate it.

Propped up in that hospital bed, so pale . . .

His parents and her and the bimbo waiting silently.

Bye bye blondie, I won.

What was the prize?

She made it home without causing a collision and painted like a demon for four hours straight, working till her eyes crossed. Just after midnight, without stopping to appraise her progress, she switched off the lights, stumbled to bed, stripped off her clothes while lying down. Asleep before she took three breaths.

At four-fourteen A.M., she was jolted awake by the phone.

"It's me," he said.

"Oh," she said, stupidly. Clearing her head. "How *are* you?"

"Fine."

"You're not hurt? Thank God—"

"It's minor—"

"You—oh, God—"

"Tiny piece of shrapnel in the calf. Your basic flesh wound."

"Oh, God, Eric—"

"In and out, it's really no big deal."

Now she was sitting up, heart racing, hands frigid. "Shrapnel in your leg is no big deal!"

"I was lucky," he said. "The first asshole had packed his vest with nuts and bolts and ragged sheet metal. The second used ball bearings and they passed straight through."

"They? More than one wound?"

"A couple of small punctures, I'm fine, Petra."

"A couple meaning two?"

Silence.

"Eric?"

"Three."

"Three ball bearings through your leg."

"No bone or tendon damage, just muscle. It feels like I worked out too hard."

"Where are you calling from?"

"The hospital."

"Which one? Where? Tel Aviv?"

Silence.

"Damn you," said Petra. "What, I'm going to phone the goddamn PLO and give away state secrets?"

"Tel Aviv," he said. "I can't talk long. It's an ongoing investigation."

"Like they don't know whodunit."

Silence.

Petra said, "You're the one who spotted the first one, right?"

He didn't answer.

"Right?" she demanded.

"It was pretty obvious, Petra. Ninety degrees outside he's wearing an overcoat and looking like he's about to throw up."

"A kid? They use kids for that, right?"

"Early twenties," said Eric. "A punk. An asshole."

"You were with Army guys and cops. Anyone else spot him?"

Silence.

"Answer me, Eric."

"They were distracted."

"So you're the hero."

"Bad word."

"Tough," she said. "You're the hero. I want you to be my hero."

He didn't respond.

Shut up, girl. You should be comforting him, not playing dependent diva.

"Sorry," she said. "I'm just . . . I didn't know . . . I was *worried.*"

"I can be *your* hero," he said. "It's the other people who bug me."

CHAPTER

23

Isaac was waiting for Petra when she arrived. She walked past him and continued to the ladies' room.

Needing to compose herself. Frazzled, despite the weekend.

Because of the weekend, all the dread she'd suffered solo.

Determined to put the bombing—and work—out of her mind, she'd sustained herself with catch-up chores and manic bouts of painting that were proving monumentally depressing. Her O'Keeffe copy was a gloomy mess. The old gal had been a genius, Petra knew she could never approach that level.

But simply copying shouldn't be *this* hard.

Impulsively, she'd slathered black paint all over the canvas, then regretted it and sat at her easel crying.

Long time since she'd cried. Not since rescuing Billy and giving him up to his new life. What the hell was happening to her?

She covered the black with white, then followed with a coat of magenta because she'd heard that someone—some famous artist—used that shade for primer.

With the reek of turpentine stinging her nose, she washed her brushes, took a long, too-hot bath that left her body red and stinging and tight.

Maybe a run would help. Or at least a walk. No, to hell with that, she'd eat ice cream.

She finished off Sunday with shopping and phone calls to her five brothers. And their wives and kids. Five happy families. Their complete, hectic, domesticated lives.

A brief call from Eric late Sunday night brought a glow to her cheeks but left her feeling abandoned when he hung up without saying he missed her.

He'd be staying longer in Israel than planned, was booked for some high-level embassy meetings and whatnot. Then maybe on to Morocco and Tunisia. Quiet places for the Mideast, but there were rumors, that's all he could say.

In his absence, she turned to the papers and the TV news, seeking vicarious contact. Nothing more about the bombing.

Geopolitical business as usual.

At some level, aren't we all statistics?

Now she stood at the ladies' room mirror, blew her nose, primped her hair.

Thirty years old and my face is starting to sag.

Arching her back in order to flaunt whatever bosom Fate had provided her, she batted her lashes, fluffed her hair, struck a vixen pose.

Hey sailor.

Then she thought of the dead sailor, Darren Hochenbrenner, brained and left in a skid-row alley.

The other June killings.

Eleven days until June 28 and she was no further along than when Isaac had presented her with his little gift.

The kid was out there, looking eager.

She straightened her posture, put on a businesslike expression, erased all traces of femme fatale—as if there'd been any to begin with.

◆

He stayed at his desk until she beckoned him over.

"What's up?"

"As far as I can tell, law enforcement doesn't know much about The Players. Currently, there are five alleged members in prison. Alleged, because all five deny membership in any group."

Petra took out her notepad.

Isaac said, "I've got it saved, can print it out for you."

She put the pad away. "Who's in prison?"

"The two you found—John and Charles—are grandsons of Robert Leon. A nonrelative named Anson Cruft was convicted of possession of false identification papers, and a woman named Susan Bianca who ran a legal brothel in Nevada then tried the same thing in San Luis Obispo is locked up for pandering. She's a younger sister of Robert Leon's second wife, Katherine Leon. Robert's kind of interesting. Forty years ago, he did some fashion modeling, then he got a few small parts on soap operas, here in Hollywood. But after that, nothing. Somewhere along the line, he turned to crime. How he started is unclear. He's Guatemalan but has lived here most of his life. His first wife was Mexican, the daughter of a Nuestra Familia gangster. She died of cancer and he doesn't seem to have ever hooked up with N.F. At least that's what the prison people say. He did manage a porno theater in San Francisco, as well as some strip clubs and adult bookstores. That's where he met Katherine, she was a dancer. I suppose any of those environments could've put him in contact with other criminal types, but maybe it's a gang thing." He shrugged. "That's all I know."

"That's all, huh?"

"Your best bet is probably to talk to local police."

"I was kidding, Isaac. You did great, that's more than I could've pulled up."

The compliment seemed to zip right past him and he remained grave.

She turned to her own computer, pulled up Robert Leon's file on NCIC. The most recent mug shot showed a lean, silver-haired guy with a long, seamed face. Thick wavy hair combed straight back, jet-black mustache.

Sixty-three but he looked younger. Good bone structure, she could see hints of the young male model. On soap operas he'd be cast as a Latin lover.

Leon had smirked for the booking officer. Despite the wise-guy quality to the smile, it managed to be engaging.

Above the smile, the hard eyes of a seasoned con.

"Did you come across any sibs for the brothers?" she asked.

"Not specifically," said Isaac, "but I did find a story in a free San Francisco weekly that said Robert Leon had lots of kids. Kind of a gypsy king situation, but they're not ethnic Gypsies."

"Anything else interesting in the article?"

"Not really. It wasn't very well written. Hippie prose—kind of a retro-sixties thing. I'll print it, too."

Petra, born in 1973, considered all the hippie stuff quaint history. What could it mean to him?

"Okay, thanks," she said. "You've given me something to work with."

"On June 28, I haven't come up with anything new." He hesitated. "What?"

"Maybe I made something out of nothing."

"You didn't," said Petra. "It's definitely something. Let me run with what you've given me on Leon and his gang, then let's get together later—say four or five—and brainstorm the June 28 stuff. If you're free."

"I am," he said. "Definitely. I've got some things to do on campus but I can be back by then."

His smile was big as the ocean.

Petra phoned Lompoc a second time and got the details on Robert Leon's visitors. Three names interested her. An eighteen-year-old female named Marcella Douquette with a Venice address on Brooks, and two guys in their forties who'd listed residences here in Hollywood: Albert Martin Leon, forty-five, Whitley Avenue; Lyle Mario Leon, forty-one, Sycamore Drive.

She tried all three phone numbers. Disconnected.

Back to NCIC. Albert and Lyle had both done time for nonviolent crimes, Albert in Nevada and Lyle in San Diego. Mug shots showed a clear resemblance to Robert Leon—the same leanness, the wavy hair.

Albert's was already gray and he wore it parted in the middle and down to his shoulders. No looker; his nose was mashed and off-center and his eyes crowded the misshapen cartilage. His stats said his body was full of scars. He was a bad-check artist.

Lyle Leon's hair was still dark. Clipped at the sides, bushy and squared-off on top—an eraserhead-do far too young for his age. An earring and a bristly soul patch said this guy thought himself quite the hipster. He'd been busted for peddling worthless cleaning solutions to old folk, had done less than a year in San Diego.

Smalltime hustler trying to look like the Big Dude?

There was no mention of the relationship between either man and Robert Leon. Given the age difference, the patriarch might've sired sons early. Or Albert and Lyle were Robert's cousins, whatever.

No criminal record for Marcella Douquette. The girl was young, give her time.

Maybe none of it meant a thing, but it was time to do some legwork.

Albert and Lyle Leon's addresses were bogus. Same setup as Sandra's: multiunit apartments, no record of either man ever living there. Neither con was on parole and neither had registered any motor vehicles, so there was no way to trace them.

Petra drove to Venice. The Brooks Avenue house was one of three clapboard single units on a dirt lot in definite gang territory. Teeny little shacky thing, sitting askew on a raised foundation. Tar-paper roof, ragged boards. The surrounding lot cordoned by chain link and full of litter: spare tires, an old washing machine, rolls of plastic tarp, soda bottles, beer cans, splintered parts of wooden pallets.

It was one P.M. and the shaved-head crowd was sleeping in. Petra could smell the ocean—a nice, salty fragrance with just the slightest undertone of rot. The shack was a total dive but only a quick hop to the beach. Venice Beach, where deviance was the norm and scamsters worked the tourists every Sunday.

Perfect for The Players and their ilk. Petra's chest twitched. Maybe she was finally on to something.

She got out of the car, looked up and down the block, let her fingers settle atop the spot on her hip where her gun rested. A platter of soupy, gray fog pressed down on the ocean—the usual June gloom—and the entire neighborhood was washed in newspaper-photo tones.

Maybe that's why the head-basher chose June to do his thing. Depressed over ugly weather.

She waited some more, took in Marcella Douquette's alleged residence from a distance and made sure no low-riders were cruising. The chain-link fence was locked and bolted but low, barely at waist level.

Petra approached the property, waited for the requisite pit bull to show. Nothing.

She checked out the street one more time, got a toehold in a chain-link diamond, and was over.

No doorbell, no answer to her assertive knocks. She was about to walk around behind the shack when the door to the neighboring unit opened and a man stepped out, squinting.

Hispanic, mid-twenties, bare-chested, wispy crew cut. Wispy mustache to match. Like that old actor . . . Cantinflas.

He wore baggy blue swim trunks and nothing else. His soft, hairless chest—all of him—was the color of mocha ice cream. Nicely burgeoning potbelly. Outsized outie navel that resembled a summer squash—sue *that* obstetrician.

No tattoos or scars that she could see. No macho-swagger either. Just a sleepy-looking, flabby guy getting up at 1:20 P.M.

She gave him a businesslike nod.

He nodded back, sniffed the air. Yawned.

She went up to him. "You live here for a while, sir?"

His reply was too soft to make out so Petra got closer and said, "Pardon?"

"Just for the summer."

"When did you start living here?"

The guy stared at her. She flashed the badge. He yawned again. Through the door to his shack she saw a gray-carpeted room with a blue couch and a pumpkin-colored beanbag. Outsized black leather case atop the couch. The window shades were drawn. Mildew from the carpet wafted out to the stagnant June air.

"I started May one," he said. "Why?"

"Why May?" said Petra.

"That's when school was over."

"College?"

"Cal State Northridge." He hitched his swim trunks. They slid back down. "What's up?"

Petra evaded the question with a smile. "What're you studying?"

"Photography. Photojournalism. I live in the Valley, figured Venice would be a good place to get shots for my portfolio." He frowned. "What's going on?"

Petra looked up at the sky. "How does the fog affect your photography?"

"With the right filters you can do cool stuff." Another frown. "Are there problems? 'Cause I didn't realize how sketchy the neighborhood was but now I see where it's at."

"Problems?"

"I wouldn't leave my equipment in the house, alone."

"Bad neighbors?"

"The whole neighbor*hood*. I don't go out much at night. Probably, I'll leave at the end of the month."

"No lease?"

"Month to month."

"Who's the landlord?"

"Some corporation. I got it from an ad at the C-SUN bulletin board."

"Cheap?" said Petra.

"Real cheap."

Petra said, "I'm trying to track down a young woman named Marcella Douquette."

"She the one next door?"

"There's a girl living next door?"

"Used to be. Haven't seen her for a while."

"How long's a while?"

He scratched his chin. "Maybe a couple of weeks ago."

Right around the time of the Paradiso shootings.

Petra said, "Could I have your name please, sir?"

"Mine?"

"Yes."

"Ovid Arnaz."

"Mr. Arnaz, I've got a photo here. Not the kind of thing you'd take. From the Coroner's Office. You up for looking at it?"

"I've been to the coroner's," said Ovid Arnaz. "For a class. We met with crime photographers."

"Strong stuff."

Arnaz stretched his neck. "It was interesting." He glanced at the shack next door. "What, she's dead?"

Petra showed him the least disturbing postmortem of the girl in the pink sneakers.

Ovid Arnaz regarded it without a trace of emotion. "Yup," he said. "That's her."

Petra phoned Pacific Division, explained the situation to an amiable sergeant, and within five minutes three patrol cars had sped to the scene. The tech van took another twenty minutes to arrive, during which the uniforms stood around and Petra talked more to Ovid Arnaz.

On the quiet side, but he turned out to be a first-rate source. Photographer's memory, keen eye for details.

He remembered Marcella Douquette's pink shoes—she always wore them—and described her face and body to a T. More important, he reported that she'd lived with two other people. Another girl, pretty, slender, blond, who had to be Sandra. And an older guy with a weird, bushy haircut and a soul patch.

Lyle the Dude Leon.

Petra showed Arnaz Lyle's mug shot to be sure.

"That's him. Dressed like a pirate."

"What do you mean?"

"Silk shirts with those big sleeves. Like pirates used to wear."

He was less helpful when it came to describing behavior or emotion. No, he'd never seen any conflict among the three of them. No, he had no idea how they got along or how they spent their free time.

None of the three had spoken to him much. They went their way, he went his.

"During the day I'm mostly out shooting film. When I go out at night, it's in the Valley, 'cause that's where my friends live. Sometimes I spend the night there."

"At your friends."

Arnaz looked away briefly. "Yeah, or my folks."

Scared by the neighborhood, he returns to mom and dad at night.

He said, "They don't like me living out here. I tell them it's cool."

Petra said, "Makes total sense, though. Long as you're out there, avoid the drive back."

"Yeah," said Ovid Arnaz. "And I know my equipment's safe."

CHAPTER

24

Mac Dilbeck looked at the photo of Marcella Douquette. "Our victim."

Petra said, "Maybe our main victim. She's got no record but was living with a member of a known criminal enterprise. Could be the other kids just happened to be in the parking lot at the wrong time."

The two of them were having coffee at Musso and Frank, the front room, one of the stiff-backed booths. Hollywood oldsters and retro types Petra's age loped in and out. Petra was having apple pie and Mac had chosen rhubarb with vanilla ice cream. Luc Montoya, occupied with his new case, a Selma Avenue stabbing, was off the Paradiso case permanently.

Mac forked loose an equilateral triangle of pie and guided it smoothly into his mouth. It was five P.M. and he'd been on for a day and a half, but his gray sharkskin suit was immaculate and his white shirt looked freshly pressed. Petra had left a message with Isaac at USC, canceling their P.M. meet. She felt exhilarated by the I.D. on Douquette but on the verge of letdown because of all the whodunit that remained.

Eleven days till June 28, but this was more important, this was *now*.

Mac said, "You did great work." He wiped an already clean mouth with a linen napkin. "Out of nowhere you pull an I.D."

"Abracadabra," said Petra. She waved an imaginary wand.

Mac smiled. "So, you're thinking this Lyle character's the one."

"He and Sandra Leon lived with Marcella in Venice. The landlord said Leon paid six months rent in advance, hard cash. Gave the name Lewis Tiger."

"Leon means 'lion' in Spanish right?" said Mac. "Lion, Tiger. Cute."

"If he did this he's a damned snake," said Petra. "The Players have no rep for violence but maybe internally it's different. Maybe Robert Leon rules with an iron fist from his cell in Lompoc. Sandra never visited him but Marcella did, last year. And guess what, she's the only female who did."

"You're thinking she offended the boss."

"The coroner said she'd had a recent abortion. Maybe that broke some kind of rule."

"Getting pregnant or having the abortion?"

"Could be either," said Petra. "Maybe the father was an outsider. Or Lyle. He was living with both girls in a very small house, anything could've happened. For all we know, getting pregnant was the ideal— the females' role in the group is to breed—and by terminating she committed a big-time no-no."

"Providing young'uns for the clan," said Mac. "Sounds like a cult. What about Sandra?"

"Sandra's sick. Hepatitis A. That could've prevented her from conceiving, or Lyle knew about it and stayed away. Or he was the one who gave it to her." She repeated what Katzman had told her about unsanitary sex.

Mac excised and ate a smaller triangle of pie. "Kind of ironic, her trying to fake out like she had cancer and she's sick with something else."

"Maybe the group knew all along she was sick and has been taking advantage of it to pull off medical scams."

"Dangerous game, no? I assume viral hepatitis is pretty serious."

"Type A goes away by itself, usually by six months."

Mac put his fork down and ran his index finger along the border of the postmortem photo. "Assuming Marcella was hit by Lyle or another Player, you think Sandra knew about it?"

"When I interviewed her she wasn't shocked. She *was* edgy, that's why I noticed her. Maybe she's learned to keep things to herself."

"The Players," said Mac. "Never heard of them."

"They mostly work the north end of the state and Nevada."

"Isaac got you all this?"

Petra nodded.

"The Genius," said Mac. He pushed his plate away, the pie a half-eaten polygon. "It's progress, but I'm not sure it's good enough to keep the downtown boys at bay."

"We hand them the I.D. and the probable cause and they chase it down?"

"You know how it works, Petra. Maybe it's best that way. D'Ambrosio's their captain. He wants five guys, he gets five. He asks for ten, he gets ten. That kind of coverage could be what the case needs."

"Fine," said Petra.

"It isn't, but . . ." Mac folded his napkin into a rectangle. "I'll do my best to see you get credit for developing the lead."

"Don't worry about it," she said.

"Fair is fair."

"On what planet?"

"Sorry," he said. "Wish there was a choice."

"I understand," she said. But she was thinking: *Maybe there is a choice.*

25

The gun didn't weigh that much, but Isaac felt the difference in his briefcase.

He'd swaddled the twenty-two in a cheap blue bandanna purchased at a ninety-nine-cent outlet a few blocks from Cantina Nueva, stuffed the package in the bottom of the case, under his laptop.

Tools of the trade.

USC was a short bus ride from the bar and he made it on time for his appointment with Dr. Leibowitz.

Avuncular Dr. Leibowitz. At their first meeting, Isaac had thought, "Too good to be true." Later, he'd seen that Leibowitz was supportive of all his students. A year from retirement, a man at peace.

The meeting went well, as always, Leibowitz smiling and fooling with an empty briar pipe. He'd been off tobacco for years but kept the pipes and a collection of smoking accoutrements as props. "How're those multivariates coming along?"

"Some of my initial hypotheses seem to be panning out. Though the process seems to be infinite. Each new finding engenders another hypothesis."

In truth, he hadn't looked at his calculations for over a week.

Caught up with June 28. The rhythm of the detectives' room, all that noise and anger and frustration.

Petra.

Leibowitz nodded sagely. "Such is science."

Fortified by Leibowitz's strong tea, Isaac headed straight for a seldom-used men's room at the end of the hall. Pressing his back against the door, he placed the briefcase on the floor, removed the gun, unwrapped it. Hefted it.

Pointed it at the mirror and scowled.

Tough guy.

Ludicrous.

Footsteps in the hallway caused him to panic. He dropped the gun and the bandanna back in the case. The weapon landed with a thud.

The footsteps continued on and he stooped and rewrapped the twenty-two. Added another layer of concealment—the brown paper bag from the lunch Mama had fixed him today.

If anyone looked inside, they'd see a grease-specked care package redolent of chili and cornmeal.

Mother love.

Getting the gun into the station was no problem. Since nine-eleven, front security at the Wilcox Station had been tighter but inconsistent. On most days, eyeball scrutiny of incoming traffic sufficed. When the terror alert rose to a warm color, a portable metal detector was wheeled in and all the cops entered through the rear door on the south side of the building.

Isaac's political connection had gotten him an official-looking clip-on LAPD badge and a 999 key that unlocked the rear door. He rarely needed to use the key. The station was old, with an inefficient cooling system, and the door was generally left open for circulation.

He climbed the stairs filled with pleasant expectations of his meeting with Petra.

Four male detectives were there but she wasn't.

An hour later, he finally accepted the fact she wasn't going to show.

Packing up, he descended to the ground floor, made his way to the rear door. Closed, now. He opened it on the overly lit expanse of asphalt. All those black-and-whites and unmarked sedans.

Warm night. He wondered why she'd stood him up. She'd seemed to be taking June 28 seriously.

It's not a stand-up, stupid. She's a working detective, something came up.

He'd go home, arrive in time for dinner, make Mama happy. Tomorrow morning, he'd head straight to campus. Hide away at his corner table in the far reaches of Doheny Library's third subbasement. Cosseted by yellow walls, red floors, dusty stacks of old botany books.

He'd sit. Think.

Needing to produce.

Needing something to show Petra.

CHAPTER

26

When the bastard called Petra in, she was ready. Knowing full well what she'd done and ready to take the heat.

The approved way to get what she wanted would've been to notify the shift lieutenant, receive his permission to talk to the captain, obtain *his* permission to contact the department's public affairs office, make a phone request to the P.A. desk jockeys, follow up with a tedious written application that gave away too many facts of the case, and then wait for approval.

Her way had been to call up five reporters she knew—newshounds with whom she'd accumulated brownie points by trading "anonymous" info for discretion.

Patricia Glass at the *Times* and four TV field correspondents. No radio folk because they were of no use to her on this.

All five were interested and she faxed the cleanest photo she had of Marcella Douquette along with Lyle Leon's mug shot. Spicing up the package with intimations of mysterious "crime cabals" and pleas not to "say too much."

"A cabal, huh? Kind of like Manson?" said Leticia Gomez from Channel Five.

Burt Knutsen from *On The Spot News* made an almost identical comment.

The recent college grad who worked for ABC said, "Kabbalah like Madonna's into?"

Petra hedged, didn't deny. At this point, whatever got the photos on the air was good.

All four local news broadcasts aired them at eleven P.M., repeated it on today's morning broadcast. Nothing in the *Times,* but that was a massive bureaucracy so maybe tomorrow.

At two P.M., Schoelkopf ordered her into his office.

She expected hell, got only lackluster purgatory. Schoelkopf leaning back in his Naugahyde desk chair, tossing out all the appropriately hostile utterances. But not with his usual vitriol, more of a formal recitation. Distracted, as if none of this really mattered.

She kind of missed the old way. Was he feeling all right?

When he paused to take a breath, she actually said, "Are you okay, sir?"

He sprang forward, glared, smoothed his gelled black hair. "Why wouldn't I be?"

"You look a little . . . fatigued."

"I'm in training for the marathon, never felt better. Cut the bullshit, Connor. Stop trying to change the subject. The facts are you fucked up by not going through channels and wasted everyone's time and quite probably fucked up a case."

"I admit I was a little hasty, sir, but in terms of wasted—"

"Wasted," he reiterated. "HOMSPEC's taking it off your hands."

"First I've heard about that," she lied. "Is—"

He cut her off with a wave. His nails, usually manicured and buffed, were too long. His beige designer imitation suit was wrinkled and his shirt collar looked too large. Weight loss due to marathon training?

He *definitely* looked tired.

Then Petra noticed another discrepancy. The framed photo of him and his third wife vacationing in Mazatlan was gone from his desk. Empty space where the picture had sat.

Problems at home?

She said, "I'm sorry, sir—"

Another wave. "Don't fuck up again or there'll be repercussions. There's a limit to how far your status can carry you."

"My status?"

Schoelkopf smirked. "Speaking of special treatment, what's your pet genius doing?"

"His research."

"Meaning?"

"He works on his doctoral dissertation and keeps out of trouble."

Schoelkopf's eyes hyphened. "No problems on that end?"

"None, sir. Why?"

"I don't need a 'why,' Connor."

"That's true, sir."

"Are you keeping a close eye on Alberto Einstein?"

"I didn't know I was suppo—"

"You're on *babysitting* duty, Connor. Get it? Don't fuck *that* up." Schoelkopf adjusted himself in his chair. "So what did all your media hype accomplish?"

"We've had calls—"

"Cut the crap."

"Nothing yet, sir, but the calls are still—"

To Petra's astonishment, Schoelkopf nodded, said, "Who the hell knows, maybe something'll actually happen because of your fuckup. If not, you just fucked up."

By four P.M., she'd fielded thirty-five messages resulting from the broadcasts, all duds. At four thirty-two, Patricia Glass from the *Times* phoned and said, "You obviously don't need us anymore."

Petra said, "We need all the help we can get."

"Then you should've waited," snapped Glass. "I had the article all written up and ready to go. Then my editor saw it last night on Four and killed it. We don't rehash old stories."

Petra thought: *Have you actually read your own paper?* She said, "It's not old, Patricia, the case is still unsolved."

"Once the airheads get it, it's old. Next time, let me know if you're going to them. Don't waste my time."

"I'm sorry if it put you in a position, but—"

"It did," said Glass.

Click.

By five-thirty, twenty additional calls came in, five from alleged psychics, three from obvious psychotics, the rest from well-meaning citizens who had nothing to offer.

She'd messed up and gotten nothing in return.

She felt bad for a minute, then thought: *In a world where fanatical idiots blow themselves up, big deal.*

But she had trouble rationalizing it away. Feeling low, she was about to call the day to a close when her phone rang and Eric's voice said, "I'm at Kennedy, scheduled for an eight o'clock back to L.A. If it's on time, I should be in by eleven."

"Back for good?" said Petra. "Or are you en route somewhere?"

"No other plans."

"What happened to Morocco and Tunisia?"

"Canceled."

"Are you all right?"

"Yes."

"You're okay to travel? With your leg?"

"I considered leaving the leg behind but decided to take it along."

"Funny," she said. Then she realized it was. Also, the first time he'd ever tried to joke with her. And she'd killed it. Lord . . .

She said, "I'll pick you up. What airline?"

"I'll catch a cab."

"No," she said. "I'll pick you up. What airline?"

Eric hesitated.

"Want me to circle the airport?" she said.

"American."

She hung up with her heart pounding—what was *that* all about?—filed what needed to be filed, shut down her computer, collected her stuff, and left the dectectives' room.

Time to do something for herself before heading for LAX. A light dinner somewhere casual and quiet—that storefront Mongolian place on La Brea, the family that ran it always treated her like royalty. Followed by a soak in the tub, some of that girlie-stuff bath lotion one of her brothers had sent her for her birthday that she'd never used. Then, careful application of makeup—even mascara, which she detested because she could never apply it without getting grit in her eyes. A little blush—her cheekbones were still good. Her best feature, she'd always thought.

Nick had always made a big deal about her cheekbones during the first years of their marriage, when he was still noticing things.

Eric had never remarked upon them, or any other of her physical features. Never really complimented her except when they were making love and all sorts of utterances flew out of his mouth like little birds.

Afterward, sweat-coated and panting, they shared mutual silence . . .

She never complimented him either.

Would he notice the little touches? No matter, she'd feel the difference.

Mascara and blush and a change into something feminine and— dare she say it—sexy?

After a day like this, could she muster up sexy?

We'll just have to see about that.

She took the stairs down to the rear exit, nearly bumped into Isaac in the stairwell. He'd just shoved the door open and was heading up.

The kid didn't drive. Why was he entering through the parking lot?

Probably because that's where she took him when they exited. He recovered from the surprise and said "Hi." His back was erect, his shoulders high. Grinning at her with . . . bravado?

"Hi," she said.

"I hoped I'd catch you," he said. "You were working pretty late last night."

Last night? Their meeting. Oh, crap.

"I'm sorry. Something just came up."

"On the Paradiso shootings?"

"Yup," she lied.

He waited for elaboration. When none followed, he started swinging his briefcase against his leg. Little boy, disappointed. No more bravado.

"And I've got to leave now," she said.

"Sure," he said. "Whenever you have time."

The decent thing would be to go back upstairs and shmooze with him. She was just too tired.

He said, "I've got someone, a librarian at Doheny, the university library, checking out historical references."

"What kind of references?"

"Old crime stories, out-of-print books, papers. Anything related to June 28."

"You think someone's studying history and reliving it?"

"It's all I could come up with," he said, sounding anything but confident.

Petra thought about that. Isaac must have taken it for skepticism because he blushed. "I didn't tell her why I was asking, just asked her to focus on the date. She has access to the rare-book section, so if something bypassed the Internet, she'd be the one to find it."

"I thought the Net swept up everything," said Petra.

"That's exactly what the Net does—sweep. It's a big cyber–vacuum cleaner that sucks up everything in its path indiscriminately. But corners get overlooked. For all the garbage that gets ingested, you can find arcane—obscure references—that never make it to any website. I had one situation, in a graduate anthropology course, where we were looking into tribal matchmaking rituals and you'd think there'd be absolutely nothing not already covered in the primary and secondary sources, but—"

He cut himself off. Kicked one foot with the other. "I also spooled some microfiche of the main L.A. papers but all I got through was the last thirty years. If I have time, I'll do some more. Of course, if the source isn't local, that would be a problem."

Petra said, "I appreciate all the time you're putting in on this."

"It'll probably end up being futile."

"Now you're starting to sound like me," she said.

His smile was weak. "Anyway, have a nice evening." He began to move past her.

"You're sticking around?" she said.

"Seeing as I've got a desk, I might as well do some work." He chewed his lip. "Of course, if you're free for dinner or something . . ."

"I wish I was, Isaac. Unfortunately, I've really got to run—catch you tomorrow?"

"Probably," he said. Tight voice. "I'm not sure when I can make it over. I've got a couple of meetings, then I was planning to go back and do more microfiche."

"Don't exhaust yourself," she said. Sounding nothing but maternal.

"I'm okay," he said. Sounding nothing but adolescent.

She smiled in his general direction but he was looking away again. Without another word, she shoved at the door and hurried out to the parking lot.

The night was warm and sweaty. Two detectives she didn't recognize slouched toward the far end, laughing, chatting. One pivoted to look at her, then returned his attention to his partner's banter.

She hurried to her car, putting Isaac's discomfiture out of her mind.

Time to focus: *me, me me.* Mongolian hot pot, they treat me well, I deserve to be treated well.

Maybe she'd pick up a magazine and read while she ate. Something not too challenging.

Playing with her chopsticks. Pretending to be content.

Then she'd go get Eric.

*S*tupid!

Isaac hunched at his desk, faced a grubby wall. Hot and sandy-eyed and abashed, alone in the detectives' room except for that old guy, Barney Fleischer, who always seemed to be around but never seemed to be really working.

Fleischer had a radio on at low volume, some sort of easy-listening instrumental, didn't even look up when Isaac entered. By now, no one in the detectives' room noticed his comings and goings. He was a fixture to all of them.

Including Petra.

Asking her to dinner when she's rushing out on a case! *What had he been thinking?*

Unlike Fleischer, Petra worked. The job mattered to her. Despite all the frustration, chasing down leads that failed to materialize.

A woman like that needed to parcel out her time carefully. Why in the world would she even contemplate stopping for dinner?

With *him.*

To her, he was an assignment, nothing more.

And yet, she'd been generous with her time. Letting him ride along, sharing details of cases.

That skin, those eyes. The way her black hair just floated into place. *Stop it, stupid.*

He started to wonder again about the June 28 murders. Was his hypothesis all part of an inane infatuation?

He'd been so *certain.* The thrill of discovery when he first came across the pattern had nearly blown him out of his seat.

Eureka!

Ha.

At the time, he thought he'd been careful not to leap into conjecture without calculating and recalculating, subjecting his hypotheses to multiple tests of significance. The data had seemed clear. This was *something.*

But what if he'd convinced himself a mathematical quirk was meaningful because he'd been blinded by his own bullshit?

Because he'd wanted to *produce* for Petra.

Did it all boil down to preening, the ludicrous mating rituals of an absurd little game bird?

God, he hoped not.

No, it had to be real. Petra was an expert and she believed it.

Because he'd worn her down?

All his life—his academic life—he'd been told he was built for success. That the combination of brains and perseverance couldn't miss.

But perseverance could be pathological, couldn't it?

He had that in him: the blindered compulsiveness, the irrational relentlessness.

Barney Fleischer looked over his shoulder and stared and said, "Hey, there."

"Hey, Detective Fleischer."

"Burning the midnight oil?"

"A few hours left till then."

"She's out, you know. Left a few minutes ago."

"I know," said Isaac.

Fleischer studied him and Isaac could see cold, hard appraisal in the old guy's eyes. Once a detective . . .

"Anything I can do for you, son?"

"No, thanks," said Isaac. "I thought I'd do some paperwork. On my research."

"Oh," said Fleischer. He turned his music up louder, resumed whatever he'd been doing.

Isaac took out his laptop, booted up, called up a page of numbers, pretended to be concentrating. Instead, he flashed back to the agony of self-doubt.

Step back, be objective.

Six victims, nothing in common but the date. His calculations said it *had* to be meaningful, but could he be trusted to think straight?

No, no, however dorky his motives, this was real. He'd run the numbers too many times for it to be anything but real.

June 28. Today was the eighteenth.

If he was right, someone, some unsuspecting, innocent, *random* person would step out into a night full of expectations only to experience the crushing pain of a cranium pulverized to pulp.

Then nothing.

Suddenly, he wanted to be wrong. That had never happened before.

CHAPTER

28

The flight's arrival had been delayed for two hours and the baggage claim area stank of uncertainty.

All those weary loved ones sitting, pacing, peering at the board, shaking their heads, sometimes cursing, as the numbers got worse.

Petra spent the time sitting and rereading a copy of *People* magazine.

The bath she'd taken three hours ago had been okay, but she'd been too hyped up to enjoy it.

Jumping out, toweling off, spending a lot of time on her makeup and clothes, finally selecting a tight black top over gray linen slacks. The smooth, black Wonderbra gave her a lift nature hadn't.

She drove quickly to the airport, found parking after two go-rounds and still arrived early.

Then she waited.

When the arrival time was finally announced—an hour away—she left the terminal to take a walk along the dim, mostly deserted walkways of the airport's lower level.

A woman walking alone. Her gun was in her purse. No metal detectors anywhere near the baggage claim. A clear lapse of security that she welcomed tonight.

When she got back, passengers from a Mexico City flight had clogged the area. When they finally cleared, the "Landed" sign was flashing for Eric's flight and she stationed herself near the swinging doors that bottomed the arrival ramp, and peered through the glass.

Sparse flight, just a trickle of zombies bumping down the ramp. Eric was among the last passengers to appear and she spotted him well before he got to the doors.

Dark blue sweatshirt, faded jeans, sneakers, his little olive-green, Swiss mountain-climber's backpack slung over one shoulder.

Light wood cane in his left hand.

A limp.

When he saw her he straightened and waved the cane as if it were superfluous.

He came through the doors, she rushed him, hugged him, felt bones and sinew and tension. The cane bumped against her leg.

"Excuse me!" Annoyed female voice.

They were blocking the exit. Stepping aside, Petra caught a murderous glance from an all-in-black harridan who tried to engage her in extended ocular warfare. She smiled and hugged Eric again.

He said, "One suitcase." They walked toward the carousel. Petra reached for his backpack.

He held on to it. "I'm fine." Handing her the cane, to prove it.

They stood there, silent, as bags bumped through the chute.

Boy, this is romantic.

She got between him and the revolving luggage, kissed him hard.

On the ride home, he said, "Thanks for picking me up."

"It was a tough decision."

He touched her knee, withdrew.

"It's good to see you," she said.

"Good to see you."

"How's your leg? Really."

"It's okay. Really."

"How long do you have to use that thing?"

"I could probably ditch it now."

She took Century to the 405 North. Not much traffic on the freeway. Good time to challenge the speed limits.

"Your place?" she said. Thinking she really didn't want to drive to Studio City.

"We could go to your place."

"We could."

When they arrived, he pronounced himself "rancid," and took a shower. She ran the water and as it warmed, fixed him coffee. When he slipped off his sweatshirt, she saw white flesh and bones, the thin sheath of muscle that rescued him from downright scrawny. A bandage on his shoulder.

He saw her eyeing it. "A fragment nicked me. It's nothing." He stepped out of his jeans and removed his jockeys. His left calf was encased in thick bandages.

She said, "You can get it wet?"

"There's inflammation but no infection. In a couple of days I'll find a doctor and have the dressings changed."

He headed for the bathroom and Petra followed at a distance. Stood in the door as he hobbled into the shower, got a hard spray going, water bulleting the pebbled glass door.

Petra watched his fuzzy reflection.

To heck with this.

She stripped down and joined him.

Cruel and inconsiderate, the positions she got him into. A wounded man, no less. He cried out in gratitude and when they were done and lying naked and moist on her bed, he said, "I missed you."

Touching her breast. Her nipple sprang erect.

"Missed you, too."

They kissed and he got hard again. Had he really craved her? Or was it just *this* he'd desired?

Was there a difference?

She broke a long clinch. "Hungry?"

He thought about that. "Maybe I'll scrounge in your fridge."

She placed a hand on his flat, warm chest. "Don't move. I'll fix you something."

He made his way through the turkey sandwich, potato chips, and hastily assembled, almost-fresh salad she prepared. Eating the usual Eric way: silent, deliberate. Chewing slowly, the politely closed mouth. Not a single errant crumb, nary a grease stain on his lips.

She studied the turn of his wrists. Thin, for a man. Long, delicate fingers. He should've played an instrument. She realized she'd never heard him hum, or sing or express any interest in music.

The shower had loosened his shoulder bandage and he'd redressed the wound with ointment from his backpack, then popped an antibiotic. Petra thought the three-inch gash a lot more than "nothing." Ragged and puffy, surrounded by puckered, reddened flesh. Horrible. What would his leg look like?

She said, "Why'd you cut the trip short?"

"To see you."

"I wish."

"It's true," he said.

"Maybe partially true. Tell me the whole thing."

It had gone down this way: Eric, an Israeli security officer, and three other foreign cops—an Englishman, an Australian, and a Belgian—sitting at the café on Hayarkon Street with iced coffees and soft drinks and, in the Englishman's case, lots of beer. Ninety degrees in Tel Aviv, with equivalent humidity. You showered, dried off, were drenched moments later.

The five of them had been training all day, watching footage, reviewing Interpol data, scanning partially declassified documents. The other cops were miserable, hated Tel Aviv.

Eric didn't mind the city. He'd been there twice before, a few years ago, running errands for the American embassy. Courier service from Riyadh to Israel via Amman, Jordan. Tight little packages, no idea what they were, but he got through Customs everywhere with no explanation. Later, he'd explored this very street, taking in the cheap beach hotels, the bars and clubs and restaurants, Thai and Romanian hookers doing the stroll.

Lots of embassies nearby. Prostitutes and diplomats, there was a match for you.

When the Israeli went off to fetch more drinks, the other policemen started in again about how much they despised the entire damn country. Too noisy, too humid, the food was too spicy, Israelis were rude.

"Too you-know-what," said the Belgian. Obnoxious by nature, anti-Semitic by choice, he was ready to display his biases the moment the Israeli security guy's head was turned. Smirks, grimaces, tugs at the nose. Sotto voce comments about Arabs and Jews all being sand-jockeys, why not just let them blow each other to smithereens.

This was the guy Brussels had sent to work on international security cooperation. Back home, he'd been a police bureaucrat, before that an Army officer.

Belgian Army officer, when was the last time the Belgians had fought anyone? Probably back in the fifties when they were slaughtering Congolese.

Yesterday, when the Belgian and Eric were alone, both of them urinating in a men's room at police headquarters on French Hill in Jerusalem, the Belgian aimed his wienie away from the urinal and began spraying the floor. Laughing and saying, "I piss on all of them."

When the first bomber showed up, the Israeli officer was still off ordering refills. Eric would forever swear he'd smelled the asshole before he actually saw him. *Felt* his fear, an instant flick of some primeval nerve filament.

Whatever the reason, he'd been the first to catch on.

Turning and watching the guy wend his way through the tables. Young, pudgy, hair spiked up and blond-tipped to look like an Israeli beach bum.

But *wrong*. The long, black coat in ninety-degree weather. The sweating, the warp-speed eyes.

Eric said, "We've got trouble," and cocked his head and prepared to move.

The Belgian said, "This whole fucking country is troub—"

Eric got up. Slowly, casually. Taking his empty glass in hand, as if ready for replenishment.

The asshole in the coat got closer.

The Australian and the Belgian were oblivious but the Englishman followed Eric's sidelong glance and caught on right away. He started to rise, the unspoken message: flank him, take him down together.

Alcohol had dulled his responses and his foot caught in the leg of his chair and he lurched forward.

The Belgian laughed, said something in French.

Eric swiveled slowly, careful not to make eye contact with the bomber.

Ten feet between them, five. Eric knew what the bastard was doing: positioning himself in the middle of the crowd, wanting to maximize the slaughter.

Now they were brushing elbows. Now he really could smell the guy, putrid with anticipation.

Wild eyes. Lips moving, some sort of silent prayer.

Acne on his forehead and chin, dirt creases in his neck. A kid, twenty, tops.

The Belgian said something else. Louder. Eric knew enough French to make it out. "Hot as hell and the idiots dress like Polish refugees."

The guy in the coat might've caught the disdain in the comment because he stopped. Glared at the Belgian. Reached inside his coat.

The Belgian started to catch on. Turned white. Blinked and stared and peed his pants.

Eric sprang, hit Black Coat hard in the throat with his right hand, used his left to twist the asshole's arm. Up and back. Way back, hard. He heard bones snap. The guy's eyes bugged and he screamed.

Fell.

His coat flapped open. Big, thick, black vest around his torso. Tug-wire at the bottom.

Trying to reach it, Eric ripped the asshole's shoulder joint, stomped on the free hand and broke it. Stomped on the guy's chest, too, hearing ribs snap.

The bomber's eyes rolled back.

Someone said, "What's going on?"

The tail end of the question was drowned out by screaming.

Scattering, upending chairs and tables. Glass shattered. Plates of food slid to the ground as people bolted in panic.

The bomber wasn't moving.

Thank God it was over.

Then the Englishman said "Shit," and this time it was Eric's turn to follow his eyes.

To the periphery of the fleeing crowd. Another long-coated figure, same approximate age, smaller, thinner, dark-haired. Olive-drab coat, Israeli Army surplus.

Too many people between them to do anything.

Number Two shouted and reached into *his* coat.

Eric threw himself to the ground.

Hell arrived.

29

E ric had told the story quickly, in the flat voice that Petra had once considered weird.

He got out of bed, went to the kitchen, came back with two glasses of water, handed her one.

Her head was still full of horror. "Sorry if I pushed you—"

"As far as the department knows I'm on my way to Morocco. The whole thing was a fraud—security cooperation. The Europeans were clowns, it was just a p.r. exercise. After the bombing, we were all called into the U.S. embassy. A bunch of envoys, each of our countries, wearing expensive suits and shit-eating grins, presenting us with citations. The American was an Ivy League twerp who informed us the takedown was going to be spun as a collaborative effort. The smoothly oiled international team working in concert."

"Including the Belgian," said Petra.

"The Belgian was already wearing a medal his envoy had given him. Velvet box and all. They must keep them in stock."

He rolled toward Petra. "I left before they got to me. Packed up and found a flight and here I am."

"When will you tell the department?"

"Don't know if I need to."

She stared at him.

He said, "I've been thinking about leaving for a while. Except for you, I'm not happy. For a long time I figured I never would be happy but now I'm thinking there's a chance."

He kissed her lips very lightly.

She swung her arm over his shoulder, pressed his head down onto her breasts.

"There's more than a chance," she said.

"My quitting," he said. "You wouldn't mind?"

"Why would I mind? Who better than me to know what you mean about the job?"

He thought about that.

She said, "Any idea what you want to do?"

"Maybe private work."

"Security?"

"Don't know," he said. "Maybe basic p.i. stuff. I've had enough of politics."

"Don't blame you."

"Think I'm crazy?"

"Of course not," she said, but she was still reeling. The contingencies. No more partnering. Not seeing him every day at work.

Was there more to his discontent than the job?

He said, "If I made a living at it, I could buy a house."

"That would be cool," she said.

"More space wouldn't be bad."

"Not bad at all."

"The Valley's probably all I could afford," he said. "But maybe I could find a place with good natural light. I could set up a room for you. To paint?"

"I'd love that."

"You've got major talent—have I ever told you that?"

He hadn't.

She said, "Many times, my dear."

She pressed down gently and he nuzzled between her jaw and her collarbone. Her nightstand clock said 3:18 A.M. She'd feel dead tomorrow.

"Maybe it's stupid," he said.

"Do what makes you happy, Eric."

"I want to."

"Good night, sweetie," she said.

He was already asleep.

When the phone rang, she bolted up and was surprised to find Eric in her bed. Oh, yeah, the airport, bringing him here, the horror . . .

The damn thing continued to blare and Eric's eyes opened and he propped himself on his elbows.

Wide awake; his training. Petra was still woozy.

5:15 A.M.

She snatched up the receiver. *"What!"*

"Oh, man, I woke you, sorry. It's Gil, Petra."

Gilberto Morales, one of the night detectives, a guy she liked. She didn't like him now.

He said, "I figured I'd get a machine."

She grunted.

Gil said, "I feel shitty, Petra. Normally I wouldn't even bug you to leave a message but the desk guy was all hyped up. He came up here expecting to find you—you're still on nights, right?"

"The Paradiso thing's been carrying me over to days and nights."

"And I screwed up your biorhythm. Sorry, go back to sleep."

She was up now. "What's the desk guy have his shorts all bunched about?"

"The Paradiso thing," said Gil.

When he told her the specifics of the message, she thanked him. Really meant it.

Lyle Mario Leon, scamster of old people, last known roommate of Marcella Douquette and Sandra Leon and the prime suspect for multiple murder had phoned her three times.

Every hour on the hour between two and four A.M. *Needing* to talk to her. Refusing to tell the desk officer why but insisting it was crucial.

Finally, during his five o'clock call Leon mentioned Paradiso and

Mr. Desk intercommed Petra's extension, got no answer, went looking for her in the detectives' room. Told Gil to try her at home.

Eric said, "What's up?"

Too tired to answer, she stared at the cell number Leon had left. Probably a nontraceable rental. She punched the phone, got a recorded message:

"This is A-1 auction services. Our offices are closed now, but . . ."

Real urgent. Dammit! Probably some crank-yanker fueled by the news coverage . . .

Or maybe she'd reached a wrong number.

She tried again, got the same message, waited until it was finished and said, "This is Detective Connor—"

"Good, it's you," a man's voice broke in. "Thanks for calling back." Smooth voice but not like Dr. Katzman's. This guy sounded *coached* in Smooth, as if he'd taken voice lessons. Young-sounding, too. Lyle Leon was forty-one.

Tensing with distrust, Petra said, "Who is this?"

"Lyle Leon. You ran my picture all over TV so now we need to meet, Detective."

"Now?"

"You nearly killed me."

"You sound pretty alive to me, sir."

"I'm not kidding," said Leon. "You don't understand."

"Educate me."

"I know who killed Marcella. Killed everyone."

He wouldn't give details, insisted on a face-to-face, got progressively edgier as the conversation stretched. She told him to meet her at the station in an hour.

"No way, too public. I can't take the chance."

"Of what?"

"Being the next victim."

"Of who?"

"It's complicated. Now that they know who I am, I'm a target. I'm scared shitless, not ashamed to admit it. I've done some things in my life but this . . . it's a whole new game. I'll meet you somewhere off the beaten path. With lots of space all around—how about a park?"

"Oh, sure," said Petra. "I just waltz into some dark park at this hour because you claim to be someone with information."

"I've got more than information, Detective. I've got all the answers."

"Give me a hint."

"I can't risk that. I need to know you'll protect me."

"From who?"

Long pause. "Detective, I can solve your case, but we have to do this my way. How about Rancho Park—a relatively open area, right off Motor—"

"Not possible, sir."

"Okay, okay," said Leon. "Somewhere else, then. You make a suggestion. Bring other detectives with you, I don't care about that. I just don't want to be seen at the Wilcox station because for all I know they're watching the place."

"Who's they, sir?"

Silence.

"Your fellow Players?" said Petra.

Laughter. "I wish. Them I could deal with."

"Who, then?"

"Okay, not a park. But nowhere in Hollywood or in Venice."

"Why not Venice?"

Leon ignored the question. "Would the Valley be okay?"

"There's an all-night coffee shop at Ventura near Lankershim."

"Too public . . . how about Encino?"

"If you told me exactly what you are afraid of, sir, I could—"

"You were there. In the parking lot, after the shooting. All those bodies. And you're asking me that?"

"Give me a name, sir. I'll make sure that whoever—"

"This is my final offer: There's a Jaguar–Land Rover dealer in Encino, on Ventura, west of Sepulveda. Nearby is a felafel joint. It's closed right now but they keep their benches out, chained to the ground. The car lot keeps its lights on so some of the benches are illuminated. I'll wait on a dark one. When I see you approach I'll step out with my arms up, so you can make sure this isn't an ambush."

"Sounds pretty theatrical," said Petra.

"Life is theater, Detective. Say in an hour?"

Petra knew the exact spot, she'd eaten there. No back alley approach, even with backup there'd be limits to how careful she could be.

Sidewalk café. The similarities to Tel Aviv were creepy. But this was too good to lose. She'd figure out a way.

She said, "An hour it is."

Eric said, "Sure it could be an ambush."

"I call for uniform backup at this hour," said Petra, "everything goes crazy."

"Maybe it needs to."

He'd watched her get dressed, hadn't commented until she asked him what he thought about the call. Now he got out of bed, limped to the chair, and reached for his own clothes.

"What are you doing?"

"Backing you up."

"How long's it been since you slept?"

"Once I'm up, I'm up." He turned his dark eyes on her.

"It's not necessary," she said. "Mac Dilbeck's the primary. I'll call, let him decide."

"You're the one the guy's expecting."

"That's only because my name was attached to the news story." The story she'd provided.

Eric finished dressing. "Where's your extra gun?"

"Stay here and rest. I can get plenty of backup."

"Like who?"

"How about the Belgian?" she said.

He laughed. Headed for her closet. Knowing where she kept her spare nine millimeter.

She said, "I really am calling Mac." Reached for the phone to prove it.

"Mac's a good man." He found the automatic on an upper shelf, nestled in its hard-shell case, between two black sweaters. Found the black nylon holster she favored, adjusted the strap and set himself up.

Petra said, "You really don't need to do this."

"Yeah, but it's fun."

She dialed Mac's number.

Ventura Boulevard at five forty-three A.M. was a dark and ghostly stretch buzzed by intermittent traffic. The Jaguars and SUVs in the fenced lot were gray mounds. Some grace time until the sun rose, but not that much. Which could be good or bad, depending on how this shook out.

Mac Dilbeck arrived in his old Cadillac DeVille, parked two blocks west, as arranged, near a dormant medical building. He wore a navy sweatshirt, black slacks, dark shoes. First time Petra had seen him without a suit and tie. His hair was parted and brushed but white stubble clouded his chin. Luc Montoya arrived in a company car, an unmarked he'd taken home. Off the case, but this morning he was on it. Tense but smiling; this was more fun than yet another dummy-homicide.

Eric's presence elicited raised eyebrows from the two of them but no comment.

Protocol called for blues, but this was the whole team. Four detectives, a quartet who rarely fired their weapons, filled their days mostly talking on the phone and filing paper. The Paradiso shooting had been a vicious drive-by. If this was a serious ambush, it could go beyond ugly.

But Petra, having cruised by the felafel stand twice from the north side of the boulevard, was feeling relaxed. Neither she nor Eric had spotted anyone at or near the little kiosk. And Eric was a spotter.

If the man claiming to be Lyle Leon was righteous and really scared, there'd be only one place to hide: behind the stand. No easy escape from there: a high block wall rose to the south, at least twelve feet of impediment. Beyond that, another half-acre of British car storage.

No cars parked nearby, so if Leon was waiting for her, he had no simple flight plan.

Mac reviewed strategy. Clipped, businesslike, that combat-sergeant manner of his. Petra would cross Ventura on rubber-soled shoes, approaching the stand from the north, her gun out but keeping it close to her body so as not to attract attention from the occasional motorist. Once at the building, she'd press herself up against the white stucco walls before announcing herself. Anyone behind the stand would have to slip around, show himself at least partially. The three other detectives, approaching simultaneously from east and west would be ready for trouble.

No rescue word. There'd be no time to scream.

The big question mark, as she saw it, was a drive-by from Ventura. Eric knew that and she could tell it bothered him. He kept quiet. She felt better knowing he'd be scoping out the boulevard.

"You okay?" Mac asked her.

"Let's do it."

Feeling cool and competent, she walked briskly toward the kiosk. Before she got there a man stepped out from behind the building, arms in the air, fingers wiggling. Spreading his legs, he leaned against an outdoor table.

Mac and Montoya swarmed him and Eric did the initial pat down.

The guy said "A welcoming party" in that same smooth phone voice. "It's so nice to be appreciated."

After the guy was cuffed, Eric patted him down again. That was Eric.

Same long, craggy face as the mug shot.

She said, "It's him."

Lyle Leon wore a maroon Jacquard silk shirt tucked into baggy, cinch-waisted, black nylon cargo pants and lace-up boots with healthy heels. Like pirates used to wear . . .

The eraserhead coif had been mowed down to a conservative bristle. No more soul patch and a little dark hole centered his right earlobe where the earring had once sparkled.

The shirt was a work of art. Petra checked the label. Stefano Ricci. She'd spotted one of those in a Melrose vintage boutique. Five hundred bucks used.

Leon smiled at her. Well-built and relatively clean cut. Bereft of cosmetic affectations, a good-looking guy.

Eric handed her the fat wallet he'd found in a pocket of the cargo pants. Inside was a Cal driver's license that looked real and fifteen hundred dollars, in fifties and twenties. The address on the license was a Hollywood Boulevard number Petra knew to be a mail drop.

Leon said, "Can we talk now?"

31

The five of them piled into Mac's Caddy and drove around the corner, to a residential side street. Nice, well-kept houses, a hint of daylight turned everything lilac-gray, almost pretty.

Petra imagined some citizen spotting the old car, phoning it in, Hollywood D's having to explain to a nervous Valley uniform.

Lyle Leon sat sandwiched in back, between her and Luc. Good cologne—clean, laced with cinnamon. Trying to smile but his mouth wasn't buying it.

Definitely scared.

Motivation. She liked that. "Tell us your story, Mr. Leon."

"Marcella was my niece. Sandra's my third cousin. I was supposed to take care of both of them but it got out of control."

"Where are their parents?" said Petra.

"Marcella's father died years ago and her mother left."

"Left the Players?"

Lyle said, "Can we keep them out of it?"

"That depends on how the story goes."

"It doesn't go *there*," said Leon. "We're thieves but we don't hurt anyone."

Petra said, "Why'd Marcella's mother leave?"

"She said she needed space, ended up hooking in Vegas. Marcella was the youngest of four kids. One of my cousins took them all in. Later, it got to be too much and I got Marcella."

"What Sandra's story?"

"Sandra's father's in jail in Utah for another couple of years and her mother's got mental problems. What's the difference? I was put in charge of them and it got out of control. The problem was Venice. We went there last summer, then again this year. The deal was we'd be working Ocean Front walk a couple of hours a day, have the rest of the day to enjoy the beach. The girls loved it."

"Working how?"

"Selling merchandise. Sunglasses, hats, tourist stuff."

From the front, Mac said, "You sell tourist junk while they pick pockets?"

Petra felt Leon tense up against her shoulder. Mac was a vet but he was approaching this wrong. Challenging the guy. Leon was a con, maybe worse, but let him talk.

She said, "So you moved to Venice last summer?"

Leon stayed tight. "Picking pockets is crude, sir. We practiced a time-honored American tradition. Buy low, sell high."

He'd been busted for selling useless house products to old people. Petra pictured fake gold chains that disintegrated into dust, sunglasses that melted in the summer heat.

She said, "The girls loved Venice but it turned out to be a problem."

"Marcella met a person." A beat later: "She got pregnant."

"And had an abortion," said Petra.

"You know about that."

"The autopsy showed it."

"I didn't know an autopsy could do that . . . okay, so you know I'm telling the truth."

"About Marcella getting pregnant? Sure."

"The abortion," said Leon, "was what started the problem. Supposedly. That's not what he said the first time around. Just the opposite, he was furious she hadn't taken precautions. I had to pay him off, he seemed fine with that. Then he showed up this summer, wanting to know where the baby is. I told him there was no baby and he went nuts."

"Who are we talking about?"

"Omar Selden. A seriously bad person. Gangbanger, though you wouldn't know to look at him. Half white, half Mexican, something like that. You'll have him in your records, he did some time for robbery. But never for what he really did."

"Which was?"

"Killing people," said Leon. "Lots of them, according to what he told Marcella. Even if half true, he's a monster."

"He bragged about killing to Marcella?"

"It impressed her," said Leon. "Stupid girl."

"Who'd this Selden kill?"

"He claimed to be the head hit man for his gang—VVO. Said he'd also done freelance work in prison. A hundred bucks and he'd hit someone. I told Marcella it was bullshit 'cause that's what I thought at the time. I was wrong."

VVO was Venice Vatos Oakwood. Tight band of low-grade psychopaths, supposedly inactive until last year when they'd resumed shooting people in broad daylight.

Petra remembered one case Milo Sturgis had worked. Family man, clerk at a Good Guys store, mistaken for a VVO dropout and hit while strolling his two-year-old near Ocean Park. The baby spattered with blood, wide-eyed, mute. The shooter, a fourteen-year-old turned out to be learning disabled. Nearsighted, never taken in for a damn eye checkup.

Lyle Leon said, "Once I paid him off, I thought we were free of him. The whole year I never heard from him again so I figured it was okay to return to Venice—the girls had really enjoyed the summer. Then stupid Marcella spots Selden on the walkway. I turn my head for a second and she's winking at him. And he's winking back, soon they're off on the sand, talking. Couple of days later—couple of nights later— he drops by."

Leon shook his head. "You saw Marcella. Fat, dumpy, those stupid shoes she insisted on wearing. Sandra's a hard-body, put her in a thong bikini, some Rollerblades, she'd turn heads. So who does Selden develop a thing for? Marcella. And Marcella falls for it."

Teenagers, thought Petra. Even scam artists couldn't control them.

Then she flashed on Leon's leering description of Sandra and wondered where his head was at. Hepatitis A. Unhealthy sexual practices.

Tension filled the car. Mac and the others wondered, too.

"Sandra's a hard-body," she said.

"Hey," said Leon. "I'm being objective. Sandra could attract attention if she wanted to."

If *he* wanted her to. Using the girl as a distraction while he and Marcella pulled the scam of the moment. But Marcella had picked up an unwelcome admirer.

She said, "Sandra has hepatitis."

Leon was silent.

"You knew, Mr. Leon. You showed up with her at the clinic. Did you ever get her any serious medical help?"

"It's self-limiting. That's medical talk for it goes away by itself."

"You're a doctor, too," said Petra.

"Listen," said Leon, "I took good care of those girls. For ten years, on and off, they lived with me and ate well and learned to read and I never touched them. Not once."

Petra recalled the cramped quarters of the Brooks Avenue shack. A grown man and two hormone-suffused girls.

And the blue ribbon for fatherhood goes to . . .

She said, "So Omar Selden and Marcella reignited their affair."

"It wasn't an affair," said Leon. "The first summer she snuck away to be with him and he fucked her silly. Idiot doesn't use a condom and he's amazed when she gets knocked up. For all I know, he shared her with his friends, wasn't even the father. One thing he made painfully clear: He wasn't going to *be* a father. He threatened me until I paid him off and promised to finance the abortion. Thousand bucks, out of my pocket. A year later, Marcella winks at him and he's back. The week before the murder, I'm alone in the house 'cause I let the girls go to a concert, some new band at the Troubador. I dropped them off at ten, was supposed to pick them up at two A.M. By eleven I'm back in Venice, mellowing out. At eleven-thirty, the door explodes and Selden is standing over me. He kicked it in, is standing over me, saying where's my son? Idiot assumed it was a son, all that macho bullshit. I told him there was no baby, I'd done exactly what he wanted. He says 'No way, man, I never said that.' I try to reason with him."

Leon sucked in his breath. His cheek twitched.

"First I think he's listening, then suddenly, he *swells* up—I swear you could see him *inflate,* like he's hooked up to a bicycle pump. All red in the face, veins bulging, screaming that I'm a murderer."

A longer tremor, snakelike, coursed from Leon's brow down to his chin. His lips trembled.

"That's when I realize he's nuts. Last summer he was freaking out because she was pregnant, couldn't wait for her to get rid of it. Now he's screaming for his kid. I try to calm him down, he grabs my hair, yanks my head back, suddenly he's got a gun out and he's jamming it against my throat, *grinding.* It hurt like hell. He starts talking in this insane whisper about how he's going to blow my tongue out for lying. Finally, I manage to talk him down."

"What deal did you make with him?" said Petra.

Leon didn't answer.

"I'm sure you're a persuasive fellow, Lyle, but charm alone wouldn't talk a guy like Selden down."

Leon stared straight ahead.

Mac said, "You did something you're ashamed of. We can all live with that if this sad story leads somewhere."

Leon tightened up again.

"The deal was," he said, "that I'd let him have another go at Marcella. So he could knock her up again. Have his fucking baby."

No one spoke. The Caddy felt hot and close. Leon's cinnamon cologne had turned sour, polluted by fear-sweat.

He said, "I never intended to follow through. We made an appointment, for the following night, and the idiot left looking happy. The moment I was sure he was really gone, I packed all our stuff out of there, picked up the girls at the Troubador, and left."

"Where'd you go?" said Petra.

"Another place."

"Where?"

"We have places," said Leon.

"What kind of places?"

"Houses, apartments, short-term rentals."

"Give us an address, Mr. Leon, or face a Hindering an Investigation charge."

Leon twisted to face her. "I call *you* and I'm hindering?"

"You call us and tell us a self-aggrandizing story."

"I tell you how I screwed up and it's self-aggrandizing?"

"Stop echoing."

Leon said, "That's what shrinks do and it works."

Petra got in his face. "You're not a shrink! Give us an address *now!*"

"Okay, okay . . . I took them to a place in Hollywood." He recited an address on North McCadden. "If you go there, it'll be vacant. I'm scared as hell, living out of my car."

The sympathy ploy. She said, "Then I guess you shouldn't drive too far."

"Listen to me—" He touched her wrist. She glared and he pulled back. "Selden won't let go of this. You saw what he did to Marcella. To those other kids. On top of that, I don't know where Sandy is. The day after Marcella was killed, she disappeared. All she had to do was stay put in the apartment for one day, but when I got back she was gone."

"Back from where?"

"I had business to take care of."

"What kind of business?"

"Getting some cash together, what's the difference? The plan was for Sandy to wait and then we'd leave L.A. Instead, she split on her own." Leon's eyes shut. "I'm thinking, somehow she got spotted by Selden or one of his homeboys."

"Selden's everywhere?"

"He's like a mad dog on scent. The thing that scares me is I don't know how much Marcella told him. About where we stay, what we do."

"Maybe Sandra figured it was smarter not to stick around with you."

"No," said Leon. "No way. She didn't take anything with her. Not her clothes or her frog—she's got a stuffed frog she sleeps with every night. I got it for her when she was little, told her it came from her mother. No way would she leave without it."

"She have any money?"

"I always let her keep some in her purse. But not much. A hundred bucks, a hundred fifty."

Enough for a bus ticket.

Leon said, "I'm scared she left for a short while, got abducted."

"Left for what?"

Leon hesitated. "Sandra had gotten into stuff."

"Drug stuff?"

He nodded. Downcast, every bit the failed parent. Then Petra remembered: The Players saw themselves as performers.

"Which drugs?"

"Weed, pills."

Petra said, "So you're figuring she went somewhere to score dope, got spotted by Selden."

"Had to be. For all I know her source was someone who knew Selden and tipped him off."

"You're making him sound like the Godfather."

"It had to go down that way," Leon insisted. "There's no other explanation."

"Unless you killed Marcella. Sandra, too."

The accusation didn't ruffle Leon. "Why," he said quietly, "would I do that?"

"Maybe there's more to your relationship with the girls than you've told us."

"Ask anyone," he said. "Anyone who knows."

"Should I ask Robert Leon?"

"You can try."

"Meaning he won't talk to me."

"Robert will talk, but he won't tell you anything."

"You visited him six weeks ago," said Petra. "Was that to give him a report on the state of the business? How well you were taking care of the girls?"

"We're family. I visit."

"What does Robert think about Marcella's murder?"

"He's not happy," said Leon. "No one is."

"That put you in additional danger?"

Leon shook his head. "Not physically. I told you, we're not violent."

"Not physically, but . . ."

Leon gazed at the Caddy's dome light. "Financially. I'm screwed. I'm going to have to leave."

"The Players."

"I messed up too severely to be allowed to stay. That's why I'm living out of my car. I can't stay in any of their properties anymore. Which is fine, it's time for a change. I don't even want to be in California. Too crowded."

Mac said, "You're very much going to be in California. Right here in L.A., friend. Material witness."

Leon nodded, dropped his head. "I knew this might happen but I had to come forward."

"In the interests of justice," said Petra.

"In the interest of getting the monster who murdered my niece and probably my cousin."

Before he gets to you.

Leon said, "If you ever catch him and need a live witness, don't lock me up."

"Stop being so dramatic," said Petra. "We'll put you somewhere safe." Winging that one, movie stuff. She had no authority to make the promise.

"Sure," said Leon. "Sure, that makes me feel so comforted."

Mac said, "Cut to the chase. Where can we find Selden?"

"Marcella told me he lived in the Valley. Panorama City. Went back and forth between there and Venice. If your gang people don't have their heads totally up their asses, they'll have files on him."

The Valley to Venice route, and something else Leon had said early, tweaked something in Petra's consciousness.

"Selden doesn't look like a gangbanger. How so?"

"No tattoos and he's a fat-boy—soft. He told Marcella he went to college for at least a year, some government-funded gang-rehab thing. Maybe he did, when you first meet him he comes across not-stupid."

"He into photography?" said Petra.

Leon tensed up tighter than ever. Struggled to make eye contact with Petra. "You've got him?"

"Tell me about the photography."

Leon licked his lips. "That's him. Carries around a camera, claims to be taking pictures. That's how he hooked up with Marcella in the first place. Told her she was beautiful, wanted her to model. If she'd had any self-awareness, she'd have known he was bullshitting her. Sandy, that would've been a different story. She's got great bones. And with black and white you couldn't see the yellow in her eyes."

◆

They took Leon back to the station, put him in a holding cell and found the mug books.

One look confirmed it.

Omar Arthur Selden aka Omar Ancho aka Oliver Arturo Rudolph. Gang monikers: Zippy, Heavy O, Shutterbug. Longtime VVO member.

Petra had an aka that wasn't in the files.

Ovid Arnaz.

The quiet young man she'd encountered on Brooks. In his four-year-old arrest photo for robbery he looked nondescript. The charge had been pled down to larceny and Selden had done three years.

A year after his release, he'd met Marcella Douquette on Ocean Front Walk.

Petra's jaw ached as she recalled how smoothly he'd spun the story about renting the shack for a summer photography project. Claiming he'd been afraid to go out at night in a "sketchy" neighborhood.

Knowing the name of the landlord. She'd verified Leon and the girls' residency but not Arnaz/Selden's.

Meaning maybe he'd never even lived there.

Meaning he'd watched her arrive from next door. Had probably been staying in the neighboring unit—an empty, moldering unit—so he could stake out Marcella's digs. Hoping to spot Lyle Leon so he could finish the job.

She'd had the bastard, right *there.*

She remembered Selden's reaction to Marcella's postmortem shot. Not a trace of emotion.

Claiming he'd seen it before. Visiting the coroner's as part of a photojournalism class.

She'd swallowed it whole, had barely glanced at his I.D., the Valley address he'd given her. The numbers matched a vacant storefront not far from the revitalized NoHo arts district. Plenty of galleries there, so maybe he really was into photography. The possibility didn't make her feel one bit better.

Mac said, "You couldn't be expected to know."

But she'd seen happier faces at funerals.

CHAPTER

32

It would help," said Klara Distenfield, "if you could be a bit more specific about what you're after and why."

Isaac, smiling up at her from his worktable, said, "Sorry, that's all I can say."

"Boy," said Klara. "Talk about high intrigue."

She was a senior research librarian, forty-one years old, bright and sophisticated, with thick calves, a soft, heavy bosom, long, wavy, flaming red hair that she barretted at the sides, and a peach-blush complexion.

Klara had a soft spot for graduate students. Isaac's reputation had preceded him, and the divorced mother of two gifted kids had made sure to be available when he had reference questions.

Isaac had fantasized wildly about her, on and off, since the first time they met.

Lately, Petra's faced had nudged Klara's out. Still, when he spotted her, filling out one of those flowered dresses . . .

Today's dress was pale green printed with white peonies and yellow butterflies, some sort of clingy material, not silk, trying to be silk . . .

Klara said, "Earth to Isaac," and flashed a generous mouthful of white teeth.

"Sorry," he said. "I know it sounds oblique, but I really can't say more."

"Official police business, huh?"

Did she just wink?

He said, "Nothing exciting."

"Do they treat you well over there?"

"Very well."

"Still," she said, "it must be quite a contrast to here." She motioned with one soft arm, taking in the book-lined stacks.

"It's different," he said.

Klara leaned against the table and nibbled on the eraser of her pencil. Her breasts swung, luxuriant, barely fettered.

Older women, he just loved the way they . . . what was *wrong* with him?

What was wrong was he was a sexual retardate. But for a couple of unfortunate encounters with hookers set up by Flaco Jaramillo, he was a damned virgin.

Klara said, "Are you okay, Isaac? You look kind of fatigued."

"I'm fine."

"If you say so." She rolled the pencil against one hip. "Well, that's all I've managed to come up with, so far."

She aimed her gold-green eyes at the computer printout she'd laid on his work surface. Hundreds of historical events tied in with June 28. Nothing he hadn't seen already.

Perhaps the clue was in here, among all that history, but if it was he was missing it.

"I really appreciate the time, Klara."

"My pleasure." She shifted even closer and his nose filled with the sweet scent of soap and water. Concern widened her eyes and smoothed out her laugh lines. "You really do look *tired*. Especially there." A pale hand indicated the skin beneath his eyes. A fingertip grazed his right cheek and electric current sizzled along his thighs. He crossed his legs, hoping Klara hadn't noticed his erection.

She smiled. *Had she?*

"I'm at the top of my game," he told her. "Energy-wise."

"Well, that's good. It's refreshing to hear some confidence from you. You grad students fall into two groups: slackers and slaves. You're the latter, Isaac. You're here all the time. Alone."

His spot was in the remotest corner of the subbasement, surrounded by old and ancient books on botany. Since Leavey Library had opened, all the undergrads studied there. Doheny—huge, grand, restored magnificently—served grad students and faculty but everyone did their research on-line.

Once in a while someone wandered up there looking for an obscure text. Mostly he had the place to himself. So different from home, sharing that cell of a room with his brothers, the street noise . . .

"I enjoy the solitude," he said.

"I know you do." Klara pushed a wave of copper hair away from her face. Not a beautiful face, not by a long shot. More . . . pleasant. Clean-looking.

"My daughter, Amy, wants to be a physician. A surgeon, no less. She's smart enough, but I tell her, 'You're twelve, there's time to decide.' She is a straight-A student, though. So maybe."

"You must be proud of her," said Isaac.

"I am. Proud of her brother, too." A new kind of smile. Open, maternal. Suddenly Isaac couldn't banish the vision of nursing at those pendulous . . . and then there they were, blocking his vision as she leaned down.

Presented her mouth to him.

Like stepping off a precipice, he moved in. Her tongue tasted lemony, the sweet lemon of hard candies. Had she schemed to do this? That possibility excited him further and he felt he'd burst out of his pants.

Now she was in his lap, a soft, substantive weight, arms curling around him. His hands found her back, her breasts, reached under her dress, touched smooth flesh. Smooth thighs, warm and moist lifted and she was allowing him, she wasn't stopping him.

Then she took hold of his hand, placed it over the silky material. Butterflies jumped. Even as she pushed him down, she said, "Oh, Isaac, I'm sorry. This is wrong."

He tried to pull away but she held his hand fast. Sandwiched the other between her legs. Looked him straight in the eye and said, "This won't happen again."

With a clumsy shifting of haunches, her eyes aimed at the ceiling, she rolled off her panties.

CHAPTER
33

No TGIF end of week joy for Petra. She sat at her desk, wondered why Isaac hadn't shown up today or yesterday.

She asked Barney Fleischer if he'd seen the kid.

"Wednesday," he said. "Last night. He was here until around eight."

"All by himself?"

"I was here," said Barney. "Have you heard about Schoelkopf?"

"No, what?"

"Split from his wife, the third one." The old man smiled serenely.

"It's L.A." said Petra.

"Always has been."

She sat back down. Exhausted from the meeting.

Such fun, detecting.

With Omar Selden I.D.'d as the prime suspect for Paradiso, the logical step would've been running an immediate search for the mass killer. Instead, Petra had been ordered to clear paper, specifying how she'd come up with Lyle Leon as a witness. Then: sit tight until notified further by the Homicide Special Squad.

The call came on Thursday. Big-time meeting tomorrow at two P.M.

They'd adjourned an hour ago, at three. She and Mac Dilbeck and three golden downtown boys. The agenda, actually written on the whiteboard: *"intradivisional interfacing."*

The three H-S detectives had turned out to be relaxed types, nothing but praise for the way Hollywood had come up with Selden. Petra figured it for total b.s. but smiled prettily. The confab ended up being Petra and Mac fact-sharing and the hotshots reciting everything they knew about VVO and other Westside/Valley gangs. They'd brought props—an easel, charts, statistics. The last sheet on the easel was a crater-pored blowup of Omar Selden's soft, glaring face.

Seeing him like that, there was no other way to think of Selden but as a Seriously Bad Guy. Petra realized how close she'd been to evil and fought not to shiver.

At two fifty-eight, the head Downtown guy announced the plan, obviously preordained: The new San Fernando Valley Gang Unit would search for Omar Selden because, even if Selden was the shooter, he'd been accompanied by other bangers and the takedown required specialists. H-S would handle "formal liaisoning" with the gang squad and get back to Mac about a follow-up meeting for the entire "apprehension team."

Don't call us, we'll call you.

Petra raised the issue of the missing Sandra Leon. The head Downtown guy said, "Wouldn't you say she's probably dead? We bring Selden in alive, maybe we'll find out the details. That's why it's important to do it right."

She left the conference room more worn-out than if she'd driven all over town looking for Omar.

Now she sat at her desk, thinking about the June brainings because there was nothing left to think about on Paradiso. The kill-date was seven days away and she and Isaac hadn't sat down for a while.

She'd dropped the ball. But Paradiso had been the here and now, she could be forgiven.

Seven days; Lord help the next victim. Unless Isaac was wrong.

How could he be? The wound-stats were nearly identical.

That old gnawing feeling surfaced under her breastbone. Retrieving the June 28 files, she reviewed the cases yet again.

Concentrating on Marta Doebbler, lured out of the theater. Because she'd met Kurt Doebbler and he was weird.

Then: old man Solis and the phony cable guy. Coral Langdon, the dead dog. The more Petra thought about her dog-walking-killer scenario, the better it felt.

Nothing in common between the victims except a calculating, psychopathic flavor to the killings. Someone extremely clever, calculating, willing to shift his approach . . . chameleonlike.

Heterogeneous victims. Not a sexual thing? Or an ambisexual killer.

Or did it have to do with the challenge? Fun of the hunt?

Even so, there had to be *something* that tied the six dead people together.

She strained to come up with a unifying factor.

Half an hour later, it was killer six, detective zero.

Seven more days. Had the creep selected his quarry? What criteria did he use? What was it that *marked* them?

Why crack their skulls? A lot riskier than shooting or stabbing. That had to mean something.

Alex Delaware had told her about cannibals eating their victims' brains in order to capture their souls. Was this some new-age cannibal thing?

Or was the killer boasting: *I'm the brain.*

A self-styled genius? Lots of psychos had inflated self-esteem. This one had gotten away with it for years, maybe he really was smart.

If so, her best weapon was a Big Brain on her side. Which she already had. But where was he?

All that youthful exuberance, the way Isaac had latched on to her like a puppy, why keep his distance now? Because she'd put him off? Or was it something to do with that facial bruise? No way did she buy his story about walking into a wall.

Some babysitter I am.

Was Isaac in trouble? She imagined a host of worst-case scenarios, pictured headlines, stories, her name paired with "neglectful cop."

Councilman Reyes demanding her badge.

Now her stomach was a sloshing sack of acid.

Stop it, he's fine. Working on his dissertation, gonna be a double-doctor one day. Why hang around here? You've given him no reason.

Or was Isaac making himself scarce because he couldn't figure out June 28? If a genius couldn't untangle the pattern, how could she hope to?

She placed the six files back in a drawer. Tried to rationalize away the stress-ache by reminding herself that she *had* produced Omar Selden.

The old-fashioned way. That would be useless for June 28. . . .

She shifted her thoughts to Eric.

She hadn't seen him since early Wednesday morning when he'd slipped away—limped away—from the station as Lyle Leon was being booked. Drawing Petra into the stairwell, kissing her briefly, then hurrying off.

One call since then. The message slip had greeted her when she arrived this morning.

I'll be in touch soon. E.

Off doing his thing, whatever that was. Did that mean a prolonged retreat into one of those long, dark silences of his?

She tried to retrieve the taste of his lips on hers. Failed. Satisfaction over Selden began to tarnish. Because collaring the bastard wouldn't bring back Marcella Douquette and the other Paradiso victims.

She phoned the Biostatistics Department at USC, was told Isaac was rarely in, but she could leave a message.

To heck with it, she'd kill the next hour driving the streets and pretending to be observing her turf. No, better to walk, bleed off nervous energy.

Collecting her purse, she left the station. Out in the parking lot, she saw two guys loitering by her car.

A pair of suits she didn't recognize. Dark suits, badges on their breast pockets. Then she realized she had seen them before. The pair that had been shmoozing and laughing in the lot a couple of nights ago.

That time, they'd ignored her.

Now, they were waiting for her.

She walked straight up to them. Two mustachioed guys, one fair-skinned, one swarthy. Blue tie, blue tie.

The light one said, "Detective Connor? Lew Rodman, the gang squad."

All business, no smile. The 'stache above his bloodless lips was the color of summer weeds. His partner's was a black pencil line so thin it could've been grease pencil.

Gang guys wanting to talk to her directly about Selden instead of going through Metro? She *had* come up with the I.D. Nice to be appreciated.

She smiled. "Good to meet you guys. So what's the plan on Omar?"

Rodman and Grease Pencil exchanged glances.

Pencil said, "Who's Omar?"

Nothing appreciative in their eyes.

Petra said, "What's this about?"

Rodman said, "Can we talk somewhere private?"

"If you tell me what it's about."

Rodman looked at Pencil. The dark-skinned man said, "It's about an intern you supervise named Isaac Gomez."

"Isaac? Is he okay?"

"That," said Pencil, "is what we're trying to find out."

Their bronze Crown Victoria was parked at the far end of the lot. The car was stifling, meaning they'd been here for a while. Petra got in the back and Rodman and Pencil, identified as Detective II Bobby Lucido, sat in front and cracked their windows. Petra's was inoperative and they made no effort to give her air.

She said, "It's sweltering, push the release." Rodman moved, a click sounded and now she could breathe.

Lucido looked over the seat, checked her out. His hair was gelled and thinning, runways of scalp alternating with thick, black strands. "So what can you tell us about Gomez?"

"Nothing," said Petra, "until you tell me why you want to know."

Lucido gave a disgusted look and showed her the back of his head. She heard him breathe. He made eye contact again.

"You're his babysitter."

Petra didn't answer.

Lucido smiled at her, a mustachioed gecko. "Here's the situation: Gomez has been spotted consorting with a known drug dealer and all-around very bad guy."

The facial bruise. The kid really was in trouble.

Lucido said, "You don't seem surprised."

Petra said, "Of course I am. You're kidding."

"Yeah, we're a stand-up team," said Rodman. "Doing the Laugh Factory tonight, the Ice House tomorrow."

Petra said, "Who's the alleged bad guy?"

"You don't know?"

She felt her face go hot. "I'm his babysitter for official police stuff. Meaning he hangs around, rides along, plays with his computer at his desk. What I *know* is he's a genius, accepted to med school, going to get a Ph.D. at twenty-two for fun. You want to tell me what's going on, fine. You want drama, go take acting lessons."

The black line bisecting Lucido's face dipped, then rose. "A Ph.D. for fun."

Rodman said, "No telling."

Petra stared at both of them.

"Well," said Lucido, "maybe he likes all kinds of fun."

He turned away from her again and Petra heard paper shuffling. Something passed over the seat.

Eight-by-eleven black-and-white glossy of Isaac and a skinny guy sitting together. Really skinny guy, the sunken cheeks and droopy eyes of a junkie. The two of them huddled in what looked to be a restaurant booth. Plywood booth, no food in front of them. Maybe a cheap bar. The junkie wore black clothes and had a pathetic bit of fuzz over his top lip. Aggressively bizarre haircut: skinned on top, skunk stripes at the side, a very long, eely braid hanging over his right shoulder.

Isaac looked like Isaac: neat, clean, button-down shirt. But different around the eyes.

More intense than she'd ever seen him. Angry?

He and Junkie sat close together. The camera had caught them in the middle of something serious.

Petra said, "Who's the skinny one?"

"Flaco Jaramillo," said Bobby Lucido. "That's 'skinny' in Spanish. Flaco Jaramillo aka Mousy aka Kung Fu—'cause of the braid. His real name's Ricardo Isador Jaramillo. Known dope dealer and there's talk he kills people for money though he never got called up for that."

"Which gang?"

"He's not a banger," said Rodman. "But he deals with bangers from East L.A. and Central."

Omar Selden had bragged to Marcella about doing odd-jobs for various gangs. Could there be some connection?

Petra studied the photo some more. "Where was it taken?"

"All these questions," said Bobby Lucido.

"If it's answers you want, you came to the wrong place."

"How'd you come to work with Gomez?"

"He was assigned to me by my captain. Who got his orders from Deputy Chief Randy Diaz, who got his from Councilman Reyes."

"Yeah, yeah, we read all the p.r. bullshit. What we want to know is his connection to a sack-of-scum like Flaco Jaramillo."

"Then ask him," said Petra. "The only side of him that I've seen is a well-behaved graduate student, Detective Lucido."

"Call me Bobby. This is Lew. The place we got the photo is on Fifth near L.A. Cantina Nueva. Dealers, border *coyotes,* freelance scum, your basic bottom-feeding dive."

Petra flicked the edge of the photo with her fingernail. "You have an undercover guy there?"

"Let's just say we're in a position to take pictures," said Lew Rodman. "And Flaco's the subject of lots of them. So when your boy showed up, looking all preppy, he got noticed. Especially when he slides right into Flaco's booth, is clearly a k.a. of Flaco. We got curious and followed him, figuring to run his tags. Turns out he has no car, takes the bus. We did a nice slow MTA tail, that was fun. Got Gomez's home address, traced it to Gomez's father, finally I.D.'d the kid yesterday but didn't know he was connected. Then someone in our detail was looking at the picture, recognized Gomez's name from a story in the paper. Reyes giving him some kind of award for being smart."

Petra said, "Obviously, he knows Jaramillo but that's a long way from being a k.a."

"They associate, they're known associates," said Rodman. "We're *not* getting Ph.D.'s but we do know how to add. Your boy's palling around with Bad News Boy in a back booth at Cantina Nueva."

"Any evidence Gomez is engaged in criminal activity?"

Bobby Lucido said, "He talked to Flaco, Flaco got up and went behind the bar, sat back down. A few minutes later, Gomez left with a briefcase."

"He always carries a briefcase."

"Bet he does," said Bobby Lucido.

Petra's gut churned. "So what do you want from me?"

"Nothing yet. Just continue to do what you've been doing. But keep an eye out for anything sketchy. The situation changes, we'll let you know."

"All of a sudden I'm working for you?"

Lucido said, "You're working for the department. Same as us. You got a problem with any of this, feel free to complain."

Petra felt an urge to bolt and twisted the door handle. It didn't budge. Why would it? She was in the suspect seat.

Before she could say anything, Lew Rodman laughed and pushed another release button.

As she got out, Lucido said, "So who's Omar?"

Petra leaned into his window. He drew away and she stuck her head in the car.

"You guys from the Valley?"

Lucido shook his head. "Central Gang."

"Then you don't need to know."

34

Petra watched the Crown Victoria drive off the parking lot.
Isaac into something *really* bad.

She changed her mind about walking, decided to get her stuff, play hooky. As she reached the station's back door, someone called her name.

She turned.

And there he was, Mr. Double Life, waving with the hand that wasn't gripping his briefcase. Wearing what appeared to be the same clothes he'd had on in Nueva Cantina.

Had he been watching her chat with the Gang D's? Could the kid be that savvy?

He trotted up to her. The bruise was paler but still swollen and covered with pancake makeup.

"Hey," she said. "Been a while."

"Sorry, I've been burning the midnight oil."

Bet you have. "Dissertation stuff?"

"Mostly. Some June 28 research. Nothing to show on that, unfortunately. The librarian's still looking." He frowned. "To be honest, I've been wondering if I was wrong. Maybe I made too big a deal out of what was actually a statistical artifact."

"You didn't," said Petra. She eyed the bruise conspicuously.

Isaac's hand rose toward the spot, dropped back down. "You're convinced it's genuine."

"Seems that way." She showed him her watch. Tiny black numerals in the calendar window declared 21.

"I know," he said. He shifted the briefcase to his left hand. His shoulders drooped.

Petra said, "You look a little beat."

"The buses were running late so I took an alternate route, ended up walking a few extra blocks."

Did you, indeed?

Petra said, "Must be hard, without a car."

"You get used to it. I heard one of the Leons' face was on TV. My father saw it on the news. I'd mentioned to my parents that you were working the case. I hope that wasn't indiscreet."

"Nope," said Petra. "My name was on the broadcast."

"So is Leon the shooter?"

She shook her head, unsure how much to tell him—now.

Engine noise made her look over his shoulder. A black SUV had entered the lot and it nosed aggressively into the first empty slot. At the wheel was one of the Downtown hotshots. Square-shouldered and confident as a movie cop. His buddy rode shotgun, same demeanor. Reflective sunglasses on both of them. The motor gunned, then turned off. Petra said, "Let's talk later," and held the door open for Isaac.

Reverse chivalry, he thought, as he entered the station. To her I'm nothing but a kid.

Hotshot I said, "Hi, ready for the meeting?"

"What meeting?"

"In five. We called."

"When?"

"Fifteen minutes ago."

While she'd been sitting in Rodman and Lucido's car. Short notice, like she was their handservant.

She said, "What's up?"

Hotshot II said, "Let's meet and find out."

♦

Isaac set up his computer at his corner desk. Two other detectives were in the room, Barney Fleischer and a heavy man he didn't know, wearing an X-shaped, leather gun harness that bit into a tight green polo shirt.

He plugged in, logged on to the Doheny Library database, pretended to have something to do.

Pretended nothing had happened with Klara.

But it had and now he'd fouled things up personally and professionally.

Taking advantage of a vulnerable woman, which by itself was sleazy. The bigger issue was mixing business with . . . pleasure and the risk of a screwup on the June 28 investigation.

He tried to rationalize it away by telling himself that Klara had taken advantage of him. The impressionable student wanting only peace and quiet and musty books, not the clashing of thighs, the moaning . . .

It had been great. The second time, not the first. The first had been over before he could digest the fact that his head throbbed with surprise and orgasm. Klara had kept moving and he'd stayed hard. Cupping his face in both her hands, she'd whispered, "Yes, keep going, keep it going."

Which, of course, had only charged him up further.

The second time had felt fantastic. For Klara, too, if writhing and mewling and having to muffle her own cries with her hand counted for anything. Afterward, she remained in place, straddling him, trapping his detumescence. Kissing his neck, scratching the back of his shirt with her fingernails, loose strands of red hair tickling his face until he could no longer stand it and he turned his head and she took it for fatigue and said, "You poor guy. All my weight on you, I'm so fat."

She was smiling but looked about to cry, so he said, "Not at all," and kissed her and grabbed hold of her pillowy hips through the butterfly dress.

"God, I'm still tingling," she said. Then the tears came. "I'm so sorry, Isaac. What do you need with a fat, hysterical old woman?"

That led to his reassuring her, caressing her. Kissing her some more, though by that time his emotions had shriveled along with his penis and body contact was the last thing he craved.

She *did* feel heavy.

"You're so sweet," she said. "But this really can't happen again. Right?"

"Right," he said.

"You agreed pretty fast."

At a loss, he said, "I just want what you want."

"Do you?" she said. "Well, if it were up to me, we'd fuck a hundred more times. But cooler heads must prevail."

She kissed his chin. "It's a shame, isn't it? The way life gets so complicated. I'm old enough to be your mother."

She frowned at the thought. A blade of shame cut through Isaac's brain. He fought to banish it, focused on butterflies and flowers. Shifted his weight to let her know he was uncomfortable.

"But," she said, finally getting off him, stepping high, as if to avoid touching him. Avoiding his eyes, too, as she rolled up her panties and put on her shoes and fluffed her fiery hair.

Isaac fixed his khakis and zipped up his fly and sat there, waiting for the rest of her sentence. Got only a weak smile. Tremulous lips.

"But what?" he said.

"But what?"

"You said 'but' and then nothing."

"Oh," she said, dropping her hand and grazing his groin with her fingernails. "*But* it was still fantastic. Even *though* I'm old enough to be your mother. We can be friends, can't we?"

"Of course," said Isaac, not sure what he was agreeing to.

Klara's grin was crooked and complex. "So can we go out for coffee? As friends."

"Sure," he said.

"Now?"

"Now?"

"Right now."

They left the library together and walked to a coffee shop on Figueroa, across the street from the campus's eastern border. Passing students and faculty, people walking with people their own age.

Klara's hips swayed and touched him from time to time. Isaac tried to put some space between them—enough to dispel any image of intimacy but not so much that she'd catch on. She kept bumping into his flank.

At the restaurant, she led him to a booth and ordered mint tea and a mixed green salad, Thousand Island on the side. Isaac, suddenly parched, asked for a Coke.

When the waitress left, Klara confided, "I always get hungry." Her neck turned rosy. *"After."*

For the next hour she proceeded to tell him about her schooling, her childhood, the young marriage she'd once thought eternal, her two gifted children, her wonderful mother who could be controlling but only with the best of intentions, her corporate-attorney father, retired only for a year before he died of prostate cancer.

When she was through, she said, "You're a great listener. My ex was terrible about listening. Have you ever thought about becoming a psychiatrist?"

He shook his head.

"How come?"

"I haven't thought about any specialties yet. Too far off in the distance."

She reached over and touched the tips of his fingers. "You're a beautiful boy, Isaac Gomez. One day you'll be famous. I hope you think of me kindly when you are."

He laughed.

Klara said, "I'm not being funny."

He walked her back to her desk in the reference section and turned away as she began chatting with her assistant, Mary Zoltan, a mole-faced woman ten years younger than Klara but somehow more crone-like. When Klara saw he was leaving, she ran after him, caught him by the door, touched his shoulder and whispered fiercely that he *was* beautiful, *it* had been beautiful, too bad it could never happen again.

Mary Zoltan was staring. No warmth in her rodent eyes.

Klara squeezed his shoulder. "Okay?"

"Okay." He moved out of her grasp and left the library. Too wound up to concentrate on his doctoral research or June 28 or anything else. As he stepped out into the open air, the bulk between his legs throbbed, and Klara's scent adhered to his skin, his throat, his nasal passages. He stopped in a men's room in the neighboring building and washed his face. To no avail; he *stank* of semen and Klara.

No way could he face Petra.

He had nothing to offer her, anyway.

Why was he feeling as if he'd been unfaithful to her?

He walked back to Figueroa, caught the Metro 81 bus to Hill and Ord, picked up the 2 at Cesar Chavez and Broadway, and bypassed the Sunset/Wilcox exit for the station house. Continuing to La Brea, he got off and walked all the way to Pico Boulevard. There, he caught a Santa Monica Blue Line 7 to the beach.

It was nearly six by the time he arrived at the pier, where he bought a chewy corn dog, crisp fries, and another Coke, walked a while, checked out the few old Japanese guys fishing from the far end. Then he just hung out. His grad-student clothes and briefcase drew stares from tourists and tough-faced teens and vendors.

Or were they seeing something else?

The person who never fit in, never would.

If they only knew what bounced at the bottom of the case.

Leaving the pier, he walked down to the beach, got sand under his socks and didn't care as he continued to the shoreline where he rolled up his khakis and got barefoot and waded out into the cold surf.

Standing there until his feet grew numb, he thought about nothing.

That felt great.

Then he flashed back to June 28.

Petra thinks I'm right, but I could still be wrong. It would be good to be wrong once in a while.

He walked back onto the sand, put his socks and shoes back on without bothering to dry his feet.

By the time he got back home it was close to ten and his mother was sulking because he'd missed the dinner she'd prepared. *Albondigas* soup teeming with meatballs and herbs, beef tamales, a big pot of black beans with salt pork. As Mama hovered and counted every forkful, he ate as much as he could stomach. When his guts were about to burst, he wiped his chin, told her it was great, kissed her cheek, and headed for his room.

Isaiah was already asleep in the upper bunk, lying on his back snoring rhythmically, his left arm flung across his eyes. For the past year, Isaiah, an apprentice roofer, had bounced from one construction job to another, working for barely above minimum wage, acquiring a permanent reek of tar. Generally, Isaac was used to it, but tonight the tiny space smelled like a freshly asphalted freeway.

His older brother snuffled and rolled over and returned to his original position. The job demanded rising at five A.M. in order to be in place at the pickup spot when the shift boss drove by in his panel truck and collected day laborers.

Isaac removed his shoes and placed them down on the floor quietly. His younger brother Joel's rollaway cot was empty, still made-up from the morning. A part-time city college student when he wasn't clerking at the Solario Spanish Market on Alvarado, Joel had taken to staying out late without explanation. The same transgression committed by the older Gomez boys would've brewed a parental storm. But Joel, good-looking, with a Tom Cruise smile, got away with everything.

Isaiah snuffled again, louder. Muttered something in his sleep. Went silent. Isaac disrobed carefully, folded his clothes over a chair, and slipped into the lower bunk.

A slurred "Hmmm" came from above and the bed frame squeaked. "That you, bro?"

"It's me."

"Where you been? Mom's pissed."

"Working."

Isaiah laughed.

"What's funny?" said Isaac.

"I can smell it all the way up here."

"What are you talking about?"

"You smell like heavy-duty fucking, man. Yo, little bro. Right *on*."

The following day, he returned to the library, determined to meet Klara's eyes forthrightly.

We're all adults here.

She wasn't at her desk.

"Sick," said Mary Zoltan.

"Nothing serious, I hope."

"When she called in this morning, she sounded pretty bad."

"A cold?" said Isaac.

"No, more like . . ." Mary stared at him and Isaac felt his face catch fire. He'd showered for a long time but if Isaiah, half-asleep, could smell it . . .

"Whatever," said Mary. "Is there something I can help you with?"

"No, thanks."

She smirked.

Sick. More than a cold.

A woman on the edge and he'd driven her over.

Bad enough on its own, but there goes June 28.

As he made his way down to the third subbasement, nightmare scenes tumbled out of his brain like a payoff of slot-machine quarters.

Klara, having convinced herself she'd been sexually exploited—by a young, ambitious man—had plunged into a deep, dark depression.

And dealt with it by self-medicating.

Overdosing.

Or, she'd drowned her sorrows in pills and alcohol—pills and white wine.

Yes, that fit: tranqs and chardonnay. Besotted, she staggers to her minivan. Another car heads her way but it's too late.

Two gifted children left orphaned.

A police investigation ensues: What had led a middle-aged librarian to engage in such rash behavior?

Who was the last person she'd been with?

Mary knew. From the way she'd looked at him, Mary *knew*.

He stopped midway down the second flight. *What if the two of them hadn't been as discreet as they'd believed and someone, some botany scholar, some damned chlorophiliac, lured to Isaac's quiet, dark corner by a crumbling, antiquarian text on molds or marigolds or whatever, had seen everything?*

Career-killing publicity.

Bye bye med school.

Bye-bye Ph.D., for that matter. He'd be standing with Isaiah at five-thirty A.M., waiting for roofing jobs.

The shame. His parents . . . the Doctors Lattimore. Everyone at Burton Academy. The university.

Councilman Gilbert Reyes.

By the time he reached his corner, he'd conjured a vivid image of Reyes calling a press conference in order to distance himself from his prodigal project.

He looked around. No one in the Botany section. As usual. But what did that mean? During the whole thing—the entire damned orgiastic fifteen minutes or however long it had taken—his eyes had been shut.

He shut them now, as if to bring back the moment. Opened and saw high library stacks. Dim, empty corridors.

But everything felt wrong; the *air* smelled reproachful.

He turned face and ran back to the stairs. Tripped and nearly tumbled but managed to maintain balance.

Or something that passed for it.

He couldn't be here today. Back to the beach, the beach had been good. He'd return, stuff his face with junk food, play video games like an everyday bonehead, numb his feet, and whatever else demanded numbing, in the vast, relentless Pacific.

He did it. But by noon, he craved the police station.

35

The second meeting was worse for Petra.

Five minutes after it started a Valley Gang Unit rep arrived, a uniformed three-striper, a huge man with a shaved bullet-head, ice eyes, and all the charm of a virus. He kept inspecting his nails as Hotshot I gave more speeches about gang behavior.

The search for Omar Selden and associates was now an official task force.

Schoelkopf had decided to sit in.

Not that the captain said much. For the most part he looked sleepy and small, and Petra, knowing about his third wife, felt sorry for him. She started nodding off as Honcho droned on. Finally, the guy slapped his notepad shut and motioned for his buddy to collapse the easel.

"So," he said, tightening the knot of his tie, "we're all on the same page."

Petra looked at the big gang sergeant and said, "One thing you might want to check out: Our boy Omar took college courses in photography and when I saw him in Venice he had camera equipment with him. He listed a phony address in NoHo, so maybe he's got some kind of connection there."

"It was a *phony* address," Schoelkopf cut in. "That was the point of lying, Detective Connor. To throw you off."

Which was utter nonsense. Criminals lacked imagination, made stupid mistakes all the time. If they didn't, police work would be an exercise in futility.

No one backed her up.

She said, "Still, sir—"

The gang guy stood to his full six-four and broke in: "Never seen any bangers in NoHo, except for a few straggling in when there's a street fair. No street fairs till next month."

He left the room.

The head Downtown guy said, "Onward."

When Petra returned to the detectives' room, Isaac was waiting for her. Now she did need to walk and she told him so. They left the station and headed south on Wilcox. Isaac was smart enough not to talk as she stomped her way toward Santa Monica. Eventually, she cooled down and noticed that he was keeping his distance from her. She was probably scaring him. Time to force a smile.

"So," she said. "June 28. The date has to mean something—a birthday, an anniversary, something personal to the bad guy. Or some historical event that turns him on. I checked DMV stats on all the principals in the files. None of the vics were born that day. So maybe our boy *is* a history freak."

She waited for him to comment. He didn't.

"Any ideas?"

"Everything you're saying sounds reasonable."

Was he losing interest? Distracted by his other life?

"What keeps coming to me," she said, "is an extremely seductive killer. Someone subtle, really careful about the way he sets things up. Marta Doebbler being called out of the theater, Geraldo Solis possibly being conned by a phony cable appointment. If the cable guy is our suspect, he was canny enough to case the house and come back later. Maybe he was also canny enough to use a dog as a lure."

She told him about the two kinds of canine hair found on Coral Langdon, recounted her friendly neighborhood dog-walker scenario.

"The setups," she said, "could be as much a turn-on as the kill."

"A choreographer," he said.

"That's a good way to put it. So what do you think?"

"You're right about the subtlety."

"Until he blitz-attacks the victims from behind and bashes their brains out. That's anything but subtle, Isaac. To me that says (a) cowardice—he's afraid to look them in the eye so he avoids the usual sex-psycho strangulation thing—and (b) he's got lots of rage beneath the surface that he's able to control in everyday life. More than control. He functions well until he's triggered. We know the date is one trigger, but there has to be something about the victims."

They walked for a while before she said, "Anything you want to add is okay."

He shook his head.

"You okay?"

He startled. She'd shaken him out of some sort of reverie. "Sure."

"You seem a bit spacey."

"Sorry," he said.

"No apology necessary. I just want to make sure you're okay." She smiled. "As your mentor—not that I've mented much. Is that a verb?"

Isaac smiled back. "Nope. Mentored."

"Feel free to speculate about what I just said."

"Everything you're saying makes sense. I wish I had something to add, but I don't."

A half-block later, he said, "One thing does occur to me. There's a discrepancy between Marta Doebbler and the others. If the killer was able to disguise himself as a cable repairman to get into Mr. Solis's place, Mr. Solis obviously didn't know him. If the dog theory's true, the same could go for Coral Langdon: She met a man walking his dog in her neighborhood, chatted, turned to go, and got bludgeoned. The killer could've rehearsed the scene by dog-walking previously in order to familiarize himself with the surroundings. But he still could've been a relative stranger. That *can't* be true of Marta Doebbler. She wouldn't have left the theater in the middle of the show unless she knew who had called her. Plus, a stranger wouldn't have known Marta was *going* to the theater."

"Someone she trusted," said Petra. "Back to the husband." Weird

Kurt. "There's another discrepancy between Marta and the others. She was killed on the street but then placed in her car. You could look at that as her being treated with a bit more respect. Which would also fit with a killer who knew her well."

He grimaced. "I should've thought of that."

Distracted. By Klara. Self-doubt. Flaco's gun . . . my gun . . . would I ever really use it?

"That's why it's good to brainstorm," said Petra. They reached Santa Monica Boulevard. Traffic, noise, pedestrians, gay hustlers loitering on corners.

Petra said, "Here's yet another distinction for Doebbler: She was the first. When Detective Ballou told me he thought Kurt Doebbler's reaction was off, and then after I met Kurt, it got me thinking: What if the bad guy never set out to commit a string of murders? What if he killed Marta for a personal reason and found out he *liked* it? Got himself a hobby. Which brings us back to Kurt."

"A-once-a-year hobby," said Isaac.

"An anniversary," she said. "What if June 28 is significant to Kurt because he happened to kill Marta on that day? So he relives it."

He stared at her. "That's brilliant."

Return of the youthful exuberance. Oddly, it deflated Petra's enthusiasm and she said, "Hardly. It's a theory. But at least we're focusing."

"On Marta Doebbler?"

"For lack of anyone better."

"Maybe," he said, touching his bruise absently, "we should find out who knew she was at the theater. She went with friends, right?"

Staring at her with that unlined, precocious, innocent face. She wanted to kiss it.

They returned to the station and Petra pulled the Doebbler file. Marta had gone out with three friends and Detective Conrad Ballou had listed their names dutifully along with the fact that he'd contacted two, Melanie Jaeger and Sarah Casagrande, "telephonically." The third, Emily Pastern, had been out of town.

According to Ballou's notes, neither Jaeger nor Casagrande knew for certain who'd called Marta out of the theater.

"Witness Casagrande reports that Victim Doebbler appeared agitated by telephonic interruption and that Vic Doebbler reacted quickly to said interruption, 'jumped out of her seat and just left. Like it was an emergency, she didn't even apologize for having her cell phone on. Which wasn't like Marta, she was always considerate.' Likewise Witness Jaeger, interviewed independently.

Vic's husband, Kurt Doebbler, denies calling Vic at any time that night, denies owning cellular phone. K. Doebbler agreed to immediate inspection of home telephonic records, which was accomplished this morning at 11:14 a.m. per Pacific Bell, confirming said denials."

Ballou's next notation identified the origin of the call as the pay phone around the corner from the theater.

Isaac, reading over Petra's shoulder, said, "Doebbler could've driven from the Valley to Hollywood, called Marta from the booth, and waited by her car. What if he agreed to have his phone records inspected because he knew they wouldn't incriminate him?"

Petra said, "I wonder if Mr. Doebbler has ever owned a dog."

She called Valley SPCA. No dog registrations at the Doebbler household, but plenty of people didn't register their pets.

Next, she phoned the numbers Ballou had listed for Marta's friends, Melanie Jaeger and Sarah Casagrande. Both were now owned by new parties.

Transitory L.A.

DMV records showed no listings for Jaeger anywhere in California, but a Sarah Rebecca Casagrande was listed on J Street, in Sacramento. Petra got her number from the Sacramento directory and phoned it.

The receptionist at a family medicine clinic answered. *Doctor* Casagrande was with a patient.

"What kind of doctor is she?"

"Psychologist. Actually, she's a psych assistant."

"Is that like a nurse?"

"No, Dr. Casagrande is a new Ph.D. She's supervised by Dr. Ellis and Dr. Goldstein. If you'd like an appointment—"

"This is Detective Connor, Los Angeles Police. Would you please have her call me?" Petra recited her number.

"The police?"

"Nothing to worry about," said Petra. "An old case."

◆

Next, she tried Emily Pastern, the sole friend Ballou hadn't reached.

A machine picked up on the fifth ring and a perky female voice said, "This is Emily and Gary Daisy's place. We're not in now, but if you'll leave . . ."

Petra sat through the message. Blocking out the words because the background noise had captured her attention.

Running canine commentary as Emily Pastern chirped away.

A dog barking.

As she hung up, Mac Dilbeck passed her desk, shot her a long, unhappy look, and kept going toward the men's room.

She followed, waited in the hallway, was there when he exited the lav. He was only mildly surprised to see her.

"Something up, Mac?"

"For the record," he said, "I thought your point about photography was good."

"Thanks," she said.

"It's at least something, Petra. Which was more than those yahoos had to offer." His eyes glinted. "I just got a call from one of the victims' mother. The Dalkin kid, that freckled boy trying to look punk. Poor lady was sobbing. Begged me to say we've made some progress. So what could I tell her?"

He slapped his hands together hard. The sound, as sharp as a gunshot, nearly made Petra jump.

"You know what's happening, don't you, Petra? We hand them their prime suspect on a silver platter, they take over but don't have the smarts to move their sorry butts and find him." He looked around, as if seeking somewhere to spit. "*Task force.* All they're going to do is keep taking meetings, with their easels and their diagrams. Like it's a football play. They'll probably give themselves a sweet little name. 'Operation Alligator,' some garbage like that." He shook his head. Brylcreemed hair didn't budge but his eyelids fluttered like crepe banners.

"Taking their sweet time," he went on, "until word gets out to Selden that they're coming for him and he rabbits. If he hasn't already."

He looked old, tired, miserable. Petra didn't console him. A man like Mac wouldn't take well to consolation.

"It's a drag," she said.

"It's a super-drag. Regular *Cagé au Follies.*" His smile was nervous, fleeting. His neck tendons flexed and lumps formed under his ears. "That was a joke. By the way."

Petra smiled.

Mac said, "I crack wise like that at home, everyone tells me I'm inappropriate. Believe it or not, I used to be a funny guy. Back in the service, I was part of this theater review, we had this little stage set up—in Guam—I'm talking bare-bones but we got some laughs."

"Musical review?" she said.

"We had ukuleles, whatever we could come up with." He colored. "No one dressed up as women, nothing like that, that's not what I'm getting at. Just that I used to know my way around a joke. Now? I'm a humorless geezer. *Inappropriate.*"

His discomfiture made Petra edgy. She laughed, more for herself than him. "Come over and joke any time, Mac."

"Sure," he said, walking off. "We call that police work, right?"

Petra watched him vanish around a corner. People. They could always surprise you.

Returning to her desk, she saw Isaac hunched over his laptop.

She returned to the Doebbler file, studied it as if it was the Bible.

By five-thirty Friday, neither Dr. Sarah Casagrande nor Emily Pastern had returned her calls. She tried again with no success. Everyone gone for the weekend.

Suddenly all the energy generated by her brainstorm with Isaac was gone. She walked over to his desk. He stopped typing, cleared his screen. An Albert Einstein screensaver popped up. Genius in a funny bow tie. Wild hair. But ol' Albie's eyes . . .

Isaac closed the laptop. Something he didn't want her to see?

She said, "Want some dinner?"

"Thanks, but I can't." He looked down at the linoleum and Petra prepared herself for a lie. "Promised my mother I'd spend some time at home."

"That's nice."

"She cooks these enormous meals and gets deeply hurt if no one's around to eat them. My father does his bit but it's not enough, she wants all of us. My younger brother tends to stays out late and sometimes my older brother eats on the job, comes home and goes straight to sleep."

"Leaving you," said Petra.

He shrugged. "It's the weekend."

"I really do think it's nice, Isaac. Mothers are important."

He frowned. *Klara, her kids . . .*

"You okay?" said Petra.

"Tired."

"You're too young for that."

"Sometimes," he said, "I don't feel very young."

Petra watched him tramp off, lugging the laptop and his briefcase. Something was definitely weighing him down. That junkie, Jaramillo, putting on some kind of pressure? Maybe she'd disobey the Downtown gang guys and confront the kid.

No, that would be a *really* bad idea.

Still, they'd put her in a bad position. Drafting her into the unpaid job of keeping an eye on the kid with no authority to do anything.

Babysitting, just as it had been all along.

Could she let Isaac go down without a warning? Could she afford not to?

Meanwhile, she'd use him on the June 28 killings.

The mess he'd foisted on her in the first place.

Her head hurt. Time for dinner. Another solitary night. Maybe Eric would call sometime during the weekend.

As she cleared her desk, he phoned, as if she'd conjured him. "Free?"

"Just about. What's up?"

"Doing things," he said. "I'd like to tell you about them."

"I'd like to hear about them."

They met just after six at a Thai café on Melrose near Gardner, a place favored by faux-depressed hipsters and wannabe performers. But the food was good enough to override the self-conscious atmosphere.

Petra figured she and Eric fit in, at least superficially. He was wearing a white V-neck T-shirt, black jeans that drooped on his skinny frame, the crepe-soled black oxfords he favored on stakeout, his oversized, multizone military wristwatch.

Eric was as far as you could get from hip. But add up the clothes, the close-cropped haircut, the indoor complexion, the deep-set eyes and emotionless face and he looked every bit the misunderstood *artiste.*

With her black Donna Karan pantsuit and matching loafers, she figured she'd be taken for a stylish career woman. Maybe someone in the entertainment biz.

Hah!

The place was already starting to fill but they got seated immediately, served quickly, ate their papaya salads and *panang* curry with silent enthusiasm.

"So," said Petra, "what you been doing?"

Eric put down his fork. "Looking seriously into private work. The licensing requirements don't seem too tough."

"Don't imagine they would be." He'd done military special op work, spent a tour as an M.P. detective before signing on with LAPD. All that had taught him endless patience for surveillance. Perfect for private work.

"The question," he said, "is do I go out on my own or hook up with an established p.i."

"So you're definitely doing it."

"Don't know."

"Whatever you decide is okay," she said.

He rolled the fork's handle.

Petra's warning system, already primed by too much frustration at work, went on full alert. "Something else on your mind?"

The frost in her voice made him look up.

"Not really."

"Not really?"

He said, "Are you upset?"

"Why would I be?"

"At me. For quitting."

She laughed. "No way. Maybe I'll join you."

"Bad day?"

One eye started to itch and she rubbed it.

He said, "Paradiso?"

"That, other stuff."

He waited.

She was in no mood to talk. Then she was, pouring it out: shunted aside on Paradiso, Schoelkopf dissing her in front of the others. Zero progress on the June 28 killings, with the target date a week away.

"Someone's going to die, Eric, and I can't do a thing about it."

He nodded.

"Any ideas?" she said.

"Not about that. As far as Selden, you're right about the photography angle."

"Think so?"

"Definitely."

"You'd pursue it?"

"If it was my case."

"Well," she said, "go and tell the geniuses in charge."

"Geniuses are rarely in charge." His eyes slitted and he picked at his salad. Petra wondered if he was thinking about Saudi Arabia. Or a sidewalk café in Tel Aviv.

An uneasy expression slithered onto his face.

"What?" she said.

He looked at her blankly.

"You're holding back, Eric."

He rolled the fork some more and she braced herself for yet another put off.

He said, "If I go out on my own, it'll mean less money. Until I build up a clientele. I haven't been LAPD long enough to get a city pension, all I have is my military pension."

"That's decent money."

"It pays the bills but I couldn't buy a house." He returned to his food, chewed slowly—excruciatingly slowly, the way he always did. Petra, a rapid eater, table habits borne of growing up with five ravenous brothers, typically sat idly as he finished. Most of the time it amused her. Or she rationalized that she should learn to emulate him. Now she wanted to flip his switch onto High, squeeze some emotion out of him.

She said, "A house would be nice but it's not necessary."

He placed the fork on the table. Shoved his plate away. Wiped his mouth. "Your place is small. So's mine. I thought . . . if the two of us . . ." His shoulders rose and fell.

Petra's chest grew warm. She touched his wrist. "You want to move in together?"

"No," he said. "Not the right time."

"Why not?" she said.

"Don't know," he said, looking about twelve years old.

She thought about the magnitude of his loss. What it took for him to express himself emotionally even at this level. Heard herself saying, "I don't know either."

CHAPTER

36

FRIDAY, JUNE 21, 8:23 P.M., THE GOMEZ APARTMENT, UNION DISTRICT

The kitchen was hot and fragrant, not even a trace of Isaiah's asphalt leaking through the savory steam.

His mother washed dishes, pivoted to accept Isaac's cheek peck. "You're early." Not true; it sounded like an accusation. "No more work?"

"It's the weekend, Ma."

"You're not too busy to eat with us?"

"I smelled your food from miles away."

"This? It's not fancy, just tamales and soup."

"Still smells great."

"A new kind of beans, black ones but bigger. I saw them in the market, the Korean said they would be good." She shrugged. "Maybe he's right."

"Sounds pretty fancy to me."

"When someone gets married, I'll make a real meal." She began puttering at the stove. "Also rice with onions and a little chicken. This time I added more chicken stock and some carrots. I do that for

Dr. Marilyn and it comes out good. I cooked a fresh whole chicken to get the stock and put the white meat in the tamales. Whatever's left is in the refrigerator. Mostly skin, but you can snack on it now if you're hungry."

"I'll wait. Where's Dad?"

"On the way home. The Toyota acted up again, he had to take it to Montalvo. Hopefully he won't get robbed blind."

"Anything serious?"

"Montalvo *claims* some kind of filter, I don't know that kind of thing." She scurried to the refrigerator, poured him a glass of lemonade. "Here, drink."

He sipped the cool, overly sweet liquid.

"Have another glass."

He complied.

"Joel's not coming home," said his mother. "A night class. On Friday. Can you believe that?"

Isaac figured Joel was lying. If it kept going like this, maybe he'd talk to him. He drained the second glass of lemonade, headed for his room.

"Isaiah's sleeping, so go in quiet."

"Did he eat already?"

"He ate some but he'll come to the table for more." Small smile. "He loves my tamales. Especially with raisins."

"I do, too, Mom."

She stopped, turned. Her mouth was set tartly and Isaac prepared himself for a guilt trip.

She said, "It's nice you're here, my doctor." Returning to the stove. "For a change."

He removed his shoes and cracked the bedroom door carefully but Isaiah sat up in the top bunk.

"Man . . ." Rubbing his forehead, as if trying to restore focus. "It's you."

"Sorry," said Isaac. "Go back to sleep."

Isaiah sank down on two elbows, glanced at the brittle shade that yellowed the solitary window. Air shaft light glared through. The security bulb, yellow-gray. The asphalt smell was strong in here.

Isaiah said, "You're here, bro."

"Got out early," said Isaac.

Isaiah laughed wetly. Coughed, wiped his mouth with the back of his hand. Isaac wondered about his lungs, the alveoli clogged with all that . . .

"Got out early?" said Isaiah. "Sounds like probation or something."

Isaac stashed his briefcase well under the bed, took off his shirt, and put on a fresh T. He lifted the shade and stared down the air shaft. Stories below, garbage flecked the pavement.

Isaiah shielded his eyes. "Cut that out, man."

Isaac dropped the shade.

"I stink bad. Can you smell it?"

"No."

"You lie, bro."

"Go back to sleep."

When Isaac reached the door, his brother called out: "You got a call. Some *lay-dee.*"

"Detective Connor?"

"I said a lady."

"Detective Connor's female."

"Yeah? She cute?"

"Who called?"

"Wasn't no detective." Isaiah grinned.

"Who?"

"You getting excited?"

"Why would I?"

" 'Cause *she* sounded excited, bro."

"Who?" said Isaac. Knowing. Dreading.

"Wanna guess?"

Isaac stood there.

Isaiah's eyebrows bounced. "Someone named *Klara.*"

He'd never given her his home number. She'd probably gotten it from the BioStat office. Or Graduate Records. Now, it starts . . .

He forced his voice calm. "What'd she want?"

"To *talk* to you, bro." Isaiah snickered. "I stuck her number under your pillow. Eight one eight—you messin' with a *Valley* girl?"

Isaac retrieved the scrap of paper, made a second attempt to leave.

"She cute? She white? She sounded *real* white."

"Thanks for taking the message," said Isaac.

"You *better* thank me, man. She was hot to go." Isaiah sat up again. New clarity in his eyes. "She the one you did that other night, right? She sounded like she could be fun. She give good head?"

"Don't be stupid," said Isaac.

Isaiah's mouth hung open and his face turned old. He sank down hard, flat on his back, staring up at the ceiling. One hand drooped over the side. Blackened with tar, the fingernails cracked, filthy beyond redemption.

"Yeah, I'm stupid."

Isaac said, "Sorry, man. I'm just tired."

Isaiah rolled over. Faced the wall.

CHAPTER

37

No more talk of moving in together. Friday night, after dinner, Petra and Eric had driven to the Jazz Bakery in Venice. Separate cars.

A moody quartet was the main act, sleepy-eyed guys stretching old standards with an ear toward atonality. By eleven, Petra was bushed. The two of them returned to her place—her *small* place—and fell asleep in each other's arms.

Saturday morning, they awoke feeling fresh and horny.

The next few hours had been lovely. Now they were checking out the NoHo galleries for some connection to Omar Selden.

Eric's suggestion.

"You sure?" she'd said.

"Why not?"

Why not, indeed. Doing police work—even unauthorized, probably futile police work—was easier than thinking about the *other* stuff.

The square mile encompassing Lankershim just south of Magnolia had been a breeding ground for board-ups and petty crime for years. Transformed by creative types and obliging developers into an arts district, the area was an amalgam of pretty and seedy. Petra had been there several times for the street fair and to browse galleries. The fair had great ethnic food and crappy tourist trinkets. The galleries were an interesting mix of talent and self-delusion.

On a nonfair Sunday, NoHo was peaceful and gray, livened in spots by the colorful signage of clubs and cafés and exhibitions. Foot traffic was moderate, for the most part people looked happy.

They took Petra's car, parked on a side street, and went hunting. Eight galleries featured photography and five were closed. Of the remaining three, one was showing hand-manipulated Polaroid landscapes—dreadful stuff—by a Latvian émigré. Another combined photocollages of Asian women with woodblocklike oil paintings.

Flash Image, a half-width storefront next to a defunct theater academy, was all black-and-white camera work. The bright, pencil-thin room had warped wood floors. Water marks browned the acoustical ceiling. Very good lighting and hand-lettered partitions showed a real attempt to spruce up what had obviously been a dump. The smell of mildew interfered.

This month's exhibit was: "i-mage: local artists do l.a."

An alphabetical list of half a dozen photographers was posted on the front partition.

First on the list: ovid arnaz.

The multiple murderer was good with a camera.

His contribution to the show: half a dozen street scenes, unframed and mounted on board. Buildings and sidewalks and sky and bare trees, no people. From the cool light and chopped shadows, probably winter. The lack of activity said early morning.

Night owl prowling empty city streets with a Nikon?

Good use of structure, Omar. Decent composition.

The photos were dated and signed OA, the initials graffiti-square. Dated six months ago; she'd been right about winter. The posted prices ranged from a hundred-fifty to three hundred dollars. The two best prints—a long shot of the Sepulveda Basin and a fisheye up-shot view of the Carnation Building on Wilshire—were red-dotted.

In order to look casual, they moved on to the other pictures in the exhibit—all throwaway pretense—and returned to Selden's work.

Petra's black hair was tucked under a white-blond wig she'd used for undercover jobs back in her auto-theft days. Posing as a shady maybe-hooker type, out to buy a Mercedes cheap. Real hair, nice quality, courtesy LAPD. She'd found it tucked in her closet, under a pile of winter clothes, had to shake out the dust and comb out the tangles.

Her duds were a long-sleeved black jersey top under a black denim jacket, tight black jeans, loafers, and big-framed Ray-Bans. The shades were leftovers from her marriage—one of Nick's twenty pairs. She'd ripped up the clothes he'd left behind, always wondered why she hadn't stepped on the sunglasses.

Karma; a purpose for everything.

Eric wore mirrored ski shades, yesterday's black jeans, and soft shoes, had traded his white T-shirt for a black V-neck and put on his black nylon baseball jacket with the custom gun pocket.

His limp had subsided a bit but his gait was still a bit off. No need for the cane, he insisted. Only a few more days of antibiotics.

The pink-haired girl who worked at the gallery had smiled at him more than once from behind the scratched metal desk she used as a work station. Petra hooked her arm around his as they both stared at the same photo.

The parking lot of the Paradiso.

Flat stretch of blacktop, devoid of cars, bounded by posts and chains.

Different light. Longer shadows than the others.

Dated a week before the murder.

The title: *Club*.

Take it home for only two hundred bucks.

Pink Hair came up to them. She wore a short green dress that did little for her hair—how could anything go with bubble-gum? Clearly a wig, cheaper than Petra's blond tresses, probably Darnel. For some reason that made her feel smug.

Pink said, "Ovid is acute, isn't he?"

"Perfect aim," said Petra. "Where's he from?"

"Ovid? He's from here."

"L.A.?"

"Right here in the Valley."

"How'd you find him?"

"He was part of a student class at Northridge," said Pink. "But he's the only one we took on. Way better than anyone else."

Eric leaned in closer to the photo, studied the details.

Pink Hair said, "Are you guys interested?"

Petra said, "Are we, honey?"

Eric said, "Hmm."

"What I like," said Pink Hair, "is that it's pure line and shadow, no clutter of humanity."

"Who needs people?" said Petra.

"Exactly." The girl smiled, hoping for a shared ethos.

Eric wandered over to the next print. Full-on shot of a theater on Broadway, downtown. One of the old ornate dowagers. Its marquee now read *Jewelry! Gold! Wholesale!*

Selden had an eye.

Petra eyed the Paradiso photo. "I really like this one, honey."

Eric shrugged. Stepped backward and positioned himself midway between the two photos.

Pink Hair said, "Everything's priced good."

Petra said, "We need personalized signatures."

Pink Hair's smooth little brow mustered up a shallow furrow. "Pardon?"

"These just have generic initials. We want it signed to us personally," Petra explained. "After we *meet* the artist. We do that with everything we collect." She favored the girl with a cool smile. "Art's more than buying and selling. It's about chemistry."

"Sure—"

Eric said, "Maybe I like this better." Pointing to the theater.

"I like *this* one, honey."

Pink Hair said, "You could take both."

Silence.

"I guess I could ask Ovid. About signing it to you. Especially if you buy two."

"We begin any collection with a single piece," said Petra. "Take our time to see how we live with it. After that . . ."

She looked Pink up and down.

Pink said, "Well, sure . . . so which one—"

Petra said, "I assume you've got some stretch on the price."

"Well . . . we could give ten percent courtesy."

"We always get twenty percent courtesy. On this, we were thinking more like twenty-five."

"I'm not the gallery owner," said Pink. "Twenty-five off would be . . ."

"One-fifty," said Eric, keeping his back to them.

Pink said, "What I meant is it would be a lot. More than we usually give."

"Whatever," said Petra. She began to walk away.

Pink Hair said, "I guess I could call the owner."

"If that works for you." Petra continued toward the exit. "We'll check out the other galleries, maybe come back if—"

"Hold on . . . I mean, the owner's my boyfriend, I'm sure he won't mind." Big smile. A sprig of fake hair protruded above one ear, haloed by artful gallery lighting. "You guys look like serious collectors, it'll be okay."

Eric swiveled. Turned robot eyes on her. Petra thought the girl would swoon.

"One-fifty," he said.

"Sure, great."

Petra said, "When can we meet the artist?"

"Um, that's the thing, I don't know . . . let me try to arrange it. If you leave a deposit—"

"We'll leave you fifty," said Eric, producing two twenties and a ten.

Pink took the money. "Great. I'll take your number and let you know . . . I'm Xenia?"

Turning it into a question, as if unsure of her own identity.

"Vera," said Petra, arching an eyebrow as she scrawled her cell number. "This is Al."

"Vera and Al, great," said Pink Hair. "You won't regret it. I think one day Ovid's going to be famous."

Back on Lankershim, strolling north along with the Saturday throng, Eric said, "Al and Vera."

" 'Cause we're silky smooth."

He smiled.

Petra said, "You're very good."

"At what?"

"Acting."

"Then I can get a job as a waiter." A beat. "Provide us some income."

She gripped his arm harder. "You've got the military cushion and once you get going privately, you'll probably double your income."

"If I get going."

"Why wouldn't you?"

He didn't answer.

"Eric?"

"Private clients means kissing butt," he said. "Charm."

"You can be charming."

He stared straight ahead, kept walking.

"When you want to," said Petra.

Suddenly, he veered out of the pedestrian stream, guided her toward the facade of a vintage boutique. Placed his hands on her shoulders. Something new in his eyes.

"Sometimes I feel like I'm running on empty," he said. "You make me feel . . . fuller."

"Baby," she said, hugging his waist.

He pressed his cheek to hers, touched the back of her neck softly.

She said, "You're good for me, too."

They stood there as people moved past them, drawing a few stares, a few smiles, mostly apathy. Clanking sunglasses. Then weapons, as their gun pockets brushed.

The percussion made them break the embrace.

Petra smoothed down her jacket, fooled with her wig. "If Pinkie actually phones for a meet with Omar, I'll have to notify the task force. Which will cause all kinds of complications."

Eric said, "The task force should be grateful."

"And I should be rich and famous." She frowned. "This whole thing's nuts. I get them their suspect, hand them everything, and they're futzing around. The rationale is they've got to proceed cautiously in order to get Selden's associates. But if we had Omar in custody, we'd have a better chance of doing that."

"True."

"Sandra's probably dead, right?"

He said, "That's where I'd put my money."

"Stupid kid," said Petra. "Stupid case."

From inside her purse, her cell phone squawked.

"Vera? This is Xenia, from the gallery. Guess what? I managed to find Ovid and he's real close by. He can be there in a half hour to meet you and sign your print."

"Great," said Petra, her mind racing.

"Do you think you might like two? Al really liked *Theater*, didn't he? Personally, it's my favorite. My— The owner says you can have it for the same price as *Club*."

"Sounds like a deal."

"It's an awesome deal."

"I'll ask Al. Let you know when we show up."

"Okay," said Xenia. "But I'd seriously think about both of them. Ovid's a seriously talented artist."

38

With a pounding heart, trying not to look panicked, Petra scanned Lankershim, found a Mexican café across the boulevard that had a clear diagonal view of the gallery's entrance. They lucked out by scoring a window booth, ordered food they'd never touch, coffee they would.

Rummaging through her purse, she found the head Downtown hotshot's number and tried to reach him. Machine at his desk number, no answer on his cell. She waited out the tape, recited clearly and slowly, hoped her fear didn't seep into the message. A call to Parker Center trying to reach the guy was no more helpful, even after she convinced the desk that she was legit. Out, no forwarding.

Same for his cohorts; all three hotshots were checked out for the weekend.

The big, aloof gang sergeant was gone, too. Yet another tape answered at the Valley gang unit's main extension.

Multiple murderer on his way and all the experts were mellowing for the weekend. Some task force. If Joe Taxpayer only knew . . .

She phoned Mac Dilbeck's house and his wife, Louise, said, "Aw, honey, he took the grandkids to Disneyland, didn't take a phone. Something you want me to tell him?"

"Not important," said Petra. "We'll talk tomorrow."

What next . . . informing Schoelkopf was proper procedure but out of the question. He'd kill the whole deal, discipline her for insubordination, and Omar would get away. Worse: A no-show at the gallery might make Omar suspicious and motivate a serious rabbit.

Upon arriving at NoHo, she'd spotted three uniforms: a black-and-white one block east, near a chained parking lot, the officers shmoozing, and a single female cop on foot patrol up near Chandler Boulevard. The woman had clipped hair, thin lips, shorts that exposed dimpled knees. An LAPD T-shirt above her equipment-laden belt, the whole blend-in thing.

Calling in any of them was too risky. With twenty-five minutes to go, there wasn't even time to explain the basics and she couldn't risk having Omar spot blue and bolt.

Besides, nothing was more dangerous than a poorly designed operation.

That left her and Eric. He sat across from her, looking calm. Serene, even. She pressed *End* on her cell, pocketed the little contraption.

Tried to take his example and *calm down.*

Any way you cut it, she was in trouble. Might as well catch a bad guy.

They planned it this way: Omar Selden had never met Eric, so Eric would be the inside guy, returning to the gallery alone, pretending to browse, not talking much. Petra would remain across the street in the café, her eyes fixed on Flash Image's front door. As soon as she spotted Selden, she'd connect with Eric's cell, ring twice, hang up.

After that, it would all be improvisation.

Twenty minutes after Xenia's call, Eric left his breakfast burrito minus two bites on the table, drained his coffee cup, and walked out.

Petra watched him ease his way across Lankershim. Gliding. A graceful man. In another world, he'd have been great at ballet.

Eric in leotards. That made her smile. She *needed* to smile because her gut was churning, her temples were pounding, and her hands had gone cold.

She rubbed them together. Her fingers felt fuzzy. Slipping her right hand down into her gun pocket, she traced the outlines of her Glock.

Their waitress, matronly, smiling, Latina, came over, saw her nearly untouched food. "Everything okay?"

"Great," said Petra, cutting into her own burrito. "My boyfriend got called away. I'll take the check."

"Nice girlfriend."

My boyfriend.

Alone again, Petra pushed rice and beans and chicken enchilada around her plate. Closed her eyes and took a deep breath.

Opened them to see Omar Selden's stocky frame approaching the gallery from the south end of the boulevard.

Twenty yards away. With a girl. Her frame was blocked by Omar's.

She autodialed Eric, beeped twice. Kept her eye on Omar. He had a rolling, flat-footed walk, appeared loose, casual, not a care in the world.

Fresh haircut—a skin job—made him look like a banger. His baggy brown T-shirt was marked "XXXXL" in big white letters on the back. Under it were even baggier knee-length khaki shorts and brown sneakers.

Color-coordinated killer.

Petra could see the girl's legs but she remained mostly out of view. Damn, a complication.

She squinted, kept her eyes on both of them. Then Omar stepped ahead momentarily and she got a partial look at his companion.

Petite, long blond hair, nice figure. A black halter top with a shoelace back exposed smooth bronze skin. Ultralow, tight jeans showcased slim but curvy hips, denim lifting and cupping ass cheeks too firm to be anything but young.

Spiky, open-backed shoes. Hot Little Mama on a Sunday morning stroll.

The girl's skinny arm snaked around Omar's torso, reached midway across his broad waistline.

Petra watched as the two of them nearly reached the gallery and the girl turned.

Tossing her hair and laughing at something Omar had said.

Sandra Leon.

Petra got the check, tossed money on the table, stuck her hand in her gun pocket and left the café.

Someone called after her and her chest constricted.

The waitress stood in the café's doorway, holding a white bag. "You hardly ate anything. I packed it for you to-go!"

Rushing back, Petra snatched the food.

"Thanks, you're a doll."

"Sure. Have a real nice day."

When the woman returned to the café, Petra placed the bag by the curb and made her way toward the gallery. Thinking how funny it would be if that female foot officer happened by and tried to bust her for littering.

It was time to stop thinking about anything else but the job she had to do.

Omar Selden was bent over the metal desk, signing *Club*. Flanked by a stoic Eric and a grinning Xenia.

No sign of Sandra. Probably in the ladies' room. Good, maybe this could go smoothly.

Petra walked toward them. Omar looked up.

Eric said, "I decided to buy both of them."

Omar smiled. Barely glanced at Petra. No sign of recognition.

Not good, pal. An artist should be more discerning.

"Okay," he said. "Signed." Trying to be casual, but pleased at the celebrity.

"Cool," said Xenia. "I love your signature, Omar."

Petra was a few feet away when a voice behind her said, "Hey!"

Sandra Leon. Stepping out from behind one of the partitions. Staring right into Petra's face.

Less yellow in her eyes, but still jaundiced.

Up close, way too much makeup. The things you noticed.

Petra held up a pacifying hand.

Sandra screamed, *"Cops, Omar! They're cops!"*

Selden dropped his pen, looked up, stupefied for less than a second. Then a foxy gleam brightened his eyes and he reached under the baggy brown T-shirt.

Petra had her gun out. Sandra was pounding her back, still screaming. She shoved the girl hard with one hand, concentrated on keeping
her Glock steady.

"Easy, Omar."

Selden cursed. More screaming: Xenia's horror-flick shrieks.

Omar got his hand out of his shirt. Aimed a black matte gun, a
Glock, too, plastic, one of those fool-the-metal detector deals.

Pointed straight at Petra's face.

Eric had moved directly behind Omar. Expressionless.

Petra saw his shoulder twitch, but no other sign of movement.

Eric's arm jumped, ever so slightly.

Still expressionless.

Pop pop pop.

Omar stiffened. His face scrunched with pain and surprise and his
mouth made a little stunned O. Then blood began seeping out of his
nose, his ears. Gushed from his mouth as he toppled over.

Facedown on the desk. Pinning his artwork.

Color on the photos, now.

Xenia had backed away and stood against the wall. Her hand covered her mouth but that did little to squelch the pitch and volume of
her shrieks. A golden puddle of urine settled and pooled at her feet.
She sat down heavily in her own water.

Sandra Leon had rebounded from the shove and was up on her
feet, flailing at Petra. Long sharp nails, jet-black, caught in Petra's
jacket sleeve.

When Sandra tried to head-butt Petra, Petra slapped the girl hard
across the face. The blow stunned her, gave Petra time to spin her
around, bend an arm back, and kick her behind the knees. Easy, no
weight to her. She pushed the girl down on the floor, kept a knee in the
small of that smooth, shoelaced back, and got her cuffs out. Making
sure she was nowhere near Sandra's teeth, all that saliva teeming with
virus.

"Bitch cunt murderer!" Sandra was screaming. "Murdering cunt!"

Xenia, sounding half-comatose, said, "I'm calling the police."

CHAPTER

39

A slew of black-and-whites arrived with sirens blaring. Then crime-scene techs, the coroners.

The usual, but this felt different to Petra. This was *hers.*

And Eric's. He hadn't blinked during the shooting or since. Someone you could depend upon.

Still, it threw her off.

In charge was a Valley lieutenant, soon supplanted by a captain. Both started off treating Petra and Eric like criminals but eventually eased up.

Last to show up was the officer-involved shooting team. Two Internal Affairs detectives with all the emotional resonance of statuary. Questioning Eric and Petra separately, Eric first.

Petra watched from ten feet away, knew the story he was telling, the one they'd prepared. It had been *his* idea to go looking for Selden; he'd had to overcome Petra's reluctance. Once the meet had been set up, she'd made multiple attempts to call for backup, finally decided there was no choice but to go ahead.

The fact that Eric had done all the shooting backed that up.

Clear and present danger, protecting a sister officer.

In the best of circumstances, he'd be suspended with pay, for as long as it took to sort out the paperwork. If the media got hold of it—some P.C. moron at the *Times* or one of the throwaway weeklies trying to manufacture a racial thing or a police brutality thing—it could get ugly and go on longer. That would mean lawyers, the police union, maybe suspension without pay.

Petra had tried to talk him out of being the scapegoat.

He said, "That's the way I'm telling it. Back me up." Gave her arm a short, hard squeeze and left to face the turmoil.

She stood by as the shooting investigators double-teamed him. Watched as they came up against his stoicism and started passing glances between them.

She knew what they were thinking. *This is weird.*

Cops, even hardened vets, usually reacted to blowing out the back of someone's head with a modicum of emotion. For all the feeling he was displaying, Eric might've just filed his nails.

Because he had to. Because he was protecting her. She couldn't remember the last time someone had protected her.

At three-forty P.M., with the scene still cordoned and active, the head Downtown hotshot showed up, wearing a freshly pressed suit and tie. Meaning he'd been out by the pool or playing golf or whatever, had finally been reached, rushed home to dress for the occasion.

Before he stepped into the mess, he looked around. At the media vans congregated outside the yellow tape.

Hoping to be noticed. When it didn't happen, he frowned, spotted Petra, came toward her.

She told him the story. He said, "Messy," left, conferred with the techies.

Sandra Leon had been on the scene for hours, mostly stashed in a rear storage room of the gallery under guard. Petra ached to interview her, knew it would never happen.

Now, two uniforms escorted Sandra to a cruiser and put her in the back. Downtown strode over, opened the door, said something, stepped back with a stunned, angry expression. The girl had dissed him, probably with the foulest language possible.

He told the driver to leave, and the black-and-white rolled away.

Glided past Petra. Through the side window, Sandra Leon glared at her, twisting her body so she could maintain eye contact through the rear glass.

Petra stared back. Received a clearly enunciated "Fuck you" as the girl diminished. Disappeared.

CHAPTER

40

Finally released for duty by the shooting team, Petra arrived at work to find Kirsten Krebs's little butt perched on a corner of her desk. Right atop Petra's blotter. She'd wrinkled some papers.

From across the room, Barney Fleischer shot her a sympathetic smile. Did the old guy ever leave?

Krebs arched her back, as if posing for a boudoir shot. One of her fingers twirled blond hair. What was she doing up here on the second floor?

When she saw Petra, she smirked. Nicotine teeth. "Captain Schoelkopf wants you."

"When?"

"Now."

Petra sat down at her desk. Krebs's thigh was inches away.

"Did you hear what I just said?"

"Comfortable, Kirsten?"

Krebs got off the desk and left, pissed off. Then she flashed a knowing smile. Like she was in on some private joke.

Why was a downstairs receptionist delivering Schoelkopf's message personally? Did Krebs have some special rapport with the captain?

Were she and Schoelkopf . . . could it be?

Why not? Two misanthropes finding common ground.

Schoelkopf's third marriage kaput. Because of a woman even younger than the latest wife?

The captain and Krebs, wouldn't that be great. . . . She glanced over at Barney Fleischer. The old guy's back was to her. Punching the phone with a pencil eraser. He misdialed, hung up, started again.

Petra cleared her throat. Barney didn't acknowledge her.

Time for fun.

Schoelkopf sat back in his tufted, leatheroid desk throne. The two side chairs usually positioned for visitors had been shoved into the corner. The room smelled of pineapple juice but there was no sign of the liquid anywhere. Freaky.

When Petra made a move for one of the chairs, Schoelkopf said, "Leave it alone."

She drew back. Stayed standing.

"You fucked up," he said, without preamble. His desktop was clear. No photos, no papers, just a blotter and pens and a digital clock that displayed time and date on both sides.

He removed a plastic-wrapped cigar from a drawer and held it suspended between his index fingers.

No smoking in the building but he played with it for a while. She'd never known him to smoke. Kirsten sucked cigarettes. A nicotine-fiend's gift?

"You fucked *up*, Connor."

"What can I say, sir?"

"You can say 'I. Fucked. Up.' "

"Is this confession time, sir?"

Schoelkopf bared his teeth. "Confession's good for the soul, Connor. If you had one, you'd understand."

Anger tightened her throat.

He said, "You're amoral, aren't you?"

Petra's hands clenched. *Keep your mouth shut, girl.*

Schoelkopf gave an airy wave, as if her control didn't impress him.

"You contravened direct orders and fucked up a well-thought-out task force agenda."

"Sorry," she said.

"Don't think you're going to get any credit for Paradiso. Or publicity."

"Publicity?"

"TV interviews, all that shit."

"That's fine with me."

"Sure it is. You and I both know that's what floats your boat."

"Getting on TV?"

"Any kind of attention. You're an attention junkie, a media hound, Connor. You learned it from Bishop—Mr. Hair-Dye Screen Actor's Guild. You and him, Ken and Barbie. Big fashion show, huh? The big pity is you messed up a good detective like Stahl. He's in deep shit because of you."

Stu Bishop had been her first Homicide partner, a brilliant, photogenic DIII widely rumored to be in line for a deputy chief promotion. He'd trained her well. Did have a SAG card because he played occasional bit parts on cop shows.

He'd retired to take care of a wife with cancer and a slew of kids, and bringing him up now felt like sacrilege. Petra's face burned like a habanero pepper, her eyes were gritty and dry. But her heartbeat had slowed. Going into attack mode, her body marshaling its reserves.

She was prepared, ready, to spring for the bastard's throat but kept all the rage in a tiny little zone of her prefrontal lobes.

Eric had it right. *Say nothing, show nothing.*

But she couldn't resist. "Detective Bishop's hair color was natural, sir."

"Right," said Schoelkopf. "You're amoral and sneaky, Connor. First you sneak to the media with that picture of Leon instead of doing it the right way. Then you ignore task force instructions and sneak in your own little grandstand play. You're *toast,* get it? Suspended. Without pay, if it's up to me. Leave your gun and badge with Sergeant Montoya."

Petra tried to stare him down. He wasn't biting, had opened another desk drawer, busied himself with shuffling whatever was inside.

She said, "This isn't fair, sir."

"Yadda yadda. Go."

As she turned to leave, she noticed the date numerals on his desk clock: 24.

Four days until June 28 and she was being cut off. From her files, her phone, access to data banks.

From Isaac.

Fine, she'd adapt. Call the phone company and have her calls forwarded to her home number. Take what she needed from her desk and work from home.

Petra Connor, Private Eye. Absurd. Then she thought of Eric, going out on his own.

"Bye," she told the captain.

The lilt in her voice made him look up. "Something funny?"

"Nothing, sir. Enjoy your cigar."

When she returned to her desk, the top was cleared—even the blotter Krebs had sat on was gone.

She tried a drawer. Locked.

Her key didn't fit.

Then she saw it. Brand-new lock, shiny brass. "What the—"

Barney Fleischer said, "Schoelkopf had a locksmith in while you were in his office."

"Bastard."

The old guy stood up, looked around, came over. "Meet me downstairs, near the back door. Couple of minutes."

He returned to his desk. Petra left the detectives' room, descended the stairs to the ground floor. Less than a minute later, slow, plodding footsteps sounded and Barney came into view, wearing an oversized tweedy sports coat and draping a longer garment over one arm.

A raincoat, a wrinkled gray thing that he usually stashed in his locker. Once in a while, she'd seen it draped over his chair. Had never actually witnessed him wearing it. Not today, that was for sure. The heat had burned through the marine layer this morning, temperatures rising to the high eighties.

The old man looked as if he was ready for winter.

He paused three steps from the bottom, eyed the top of the stairwell, descended all the way. Unfurling the raincoat, he produced half a dozen blue folders.

Doebbler, Solis, Langdon, Hochenbrenner . . . all six.

"Thought you might need this."

Petra took the files. Kissed Barney full on parched lips. He smelled of onion rolls. "You're a saint."

"So they tell me," he said. Then he climbed back up the stairs, whistling.

Back home, she cleared away her easel and paints and set up a workstation on her dinette table.

Stacking the files, laying out her notepad, a fresh legal tablet and pens.

Eric had left her a note on the kitchen counter:

P,
Appts. at Parker until ???
Love, E.

Love . . . that started all kinds of gears grinding.

Time to concentrate on something she could control. She started with the phone company, put in the forwarding request. The operator started off friendly, came back a few seconds later with a whole different attitude.

"The number you're forwarding from is a police extension. We can't do that."

"I'm an LAPD detective," said Petra, rattling off her badge number.

"I'm sorry, ma'am."

"Is there anyone else I can talk to?"

"Here's my supervisor."

A steely-voiced, older-sounding woman came on, with a manner so rigid Petra wondered if she was really a department plant.

Same message, no give.

Petra hung up, wondering if she'd done herself even more harm.

Maybe the Fates were telling her something. Even so, she'd work June 28. To do otherwise would drive her crazy.

She got herself a can of Coke, sipped and flipped through her notes. The calls she'd put in Friday.

Marta Doebbler's friends. Dr. Sarah Casagrande in Sacramento, Emily Pastern in the Valley.

Emily, with the barking dog.

This time the woman answered. No noise in the background. Still perky, until Petra told her what it was all about.

"Marta? It's been . . . years."

"Six years, ma'am. We're taking a fresh look at the case."

"Like that show on TV—*Cold Case* whatever."

"Something like that, ma'am."

"Well," said Pastern. "No one talked to me when it happened. How'd you get my name?"

"You were listed in the file as someone Ms. Doebbler had gone out with that night."

"I see . . . what was your name again?"

Petra repeated it. Cited her credentials again, as well. Committing yet another breach of regulations.

Impersonating an active officer of the law . . .

Emily Pastern said, "So what do you want from me now?"

"Just to talk about the case."

"I don't see what I could tell you."

"You never know, ma'am," said Petra. "If we could just meet for a few minutes—at your convenience." Working up her own perkiness. *Praying* Pastern wouldn't call the station and check her bona fides.

"I guess."

"Thanks very much, Ms. Pastern."

"When?"

"Sooner the better."

"I've got to go out at three to pick up my kids. How about in an hour?"

"That would be perfect," said Petra. "Name the place."

"My house," said Pastern. "No, let's make it at Rita's—it's a little coffee place. Ventura Boulevard, south side, two blocks west of Reseda. They've got an outdoor patio. I'll be there."

Wanting distance from her home. Somewhere out in the open, well within her comfort zone.

Petra said, "See you there." *Don't be the suspicious type, Emily.*

She got out of the morning's black pantsuit and searched her closet for something more . . . welcoming.

Her first try was one of the few dresses she owned, a short-sleeved, gray silk A-line patterned with nearly invisible lavender squiggles. Too clingy, way too *party.* The black Max Mara jersey affair with the cap sleeves and the price tag still attached was even less appropriate.

Back to basics. A slate-blue pantsuit, free of lapels, some cute reverse stitching along the hems. Tiny hyphens of celluloid laced into the stitches. When she'd bought it at the Neiman's summer sale two seasons ago, she'd thought it way too frou-frou. But on her it looked subtle, a bit dressy.

Maybe Emily Pastern would be impressed.

She made it to the Valley with time to spare, drove around a bit, pulled up in front of Rita's Coffees and Sweets right on time.

The place was a pair of cute, tile-roofed bungalows combined into one establishment. One of a group of little Spanish-style structures assembled around a small patch of foliage, several steps up from the sidewalk. At the center of the green patch was a gurgling fountain. Older buildings, from the twenties or earlier.

Tarzana had been farmland back then, and Petra wondered if the houses had been built for migrant workers. Now they housed teeny, trendy retail businesses.

Giovanna Beauty, Leather and Lace Boutique, Optical Allusions. Even the premises of Zoë, Psychic Adviser looked cute.

The outdoor patio was off to the right of the coffee house, surrounded by low wooden fencing with a latched gate. One woman sat there, visible from her bosom up.

Pretty strawberry blonde, hair pinned loosely, mid- to late thirties, wearing a long, gauzy sleeveless smock the color of daybreak.

Behind her, through open French doors, Petra spied groupings of well-put-together women sitting indoors, laughing, sipping. The West Valley was ten degrees hotter than the city. Torrid. But Emily Pastern wanted an al fresco meet.

Petra climbed the stairs and the woman watched her as she un-latched the gate.

"Ms. Pastern?"

Pastern nodded, gave a small wave.

So far, so good.

As Petra made it to the gate, she saw that Pastern had chosen the table farthest from the restaurant. The pale blue top was worn over fashionable jeans and white clogs. Pastern had milky skin, lots of freckles, eyes the color of the iced tea or whatever it was that filled her brandy snifter.

Lying at her feet was why she wanted the patio. Needed the patio.

The biggest hunk of canine flesh Petra had ever seen. Blue-brindle and massively boned in repose, ears clipped to nubs. Body and face a mass of loose skin and acromegalic bone. Head shaped like that of a hippo, resting on the flagstone floor.

Big as a hippo.

She stopped as the dog glanced up. Drooled. Checked Petra out with tiny, red-rimmed eyes. Intelligent eyes. Lord, the thing was huge. An upper lip flapped. Teeth fit for a shark.

Emily Pastern bent in her chair and whispered something to the dog. The beast's eyes closed and it returned to sleep or whatever it was protective dogs did during their downtime.

Petra hadn't budged.

"It's okay," said Pastern. "Just sit down on this side." Indicating the seat farthest from the dog. "She's fine if you don't try to get too friendly with her too fast."

The dog cocked an eyelid.

"Really," said Pastern. "It's okay."

Giving wide berth to the behemoth, Petra settled in a chair.

"Good girl," Pastern whispered to the dog.

Petra held out a hand. "Petra Connor."

"Emily." Pastern's fingers were long, cool, limp.

The dog remained inert. Making sure her foot was nowhere near its mouth, Petra tried to get comfortable. "Is that Daisy?"

"No, Daisy's home."

You've got two of these?

"How do you know about Daisy—oh, my phone tape. No, this is Sophia, Daisy's little sister."

"Little?" said Petra.

"Figuratively speaking," said Pastern. "Birth-order-wise. Daisy's a ten-year-old Cavalier King Charles Spaniel. She weighs fifteen pounds."

"A little lighter than Sophia."

Pastern smiled. "Sophia likes her food."

"What breed is she?"

"Mastino. Neopolitan Mastiff."

"All the way from Italy."

Pastern nodded. "We imported her. She's great protection."

"Does Daisy get to ride her?"

"No, but my kids do."

Doggy chitchat relaxed the woman. Time for business. "Thanks for agreeing to meet with me, Emily."

"Sure." Pastern looked over at the French doors. A slim, androgynous waiter came over and Petra ordered coffee.

"The daily blend?"

"Sure."

He left looking puzzled. Pastern said, "They're not used to that. No interrogation. Most people who come here are picky about their coffee."

"Half-caf, seventeen drams of soy foam, one-fifth Kenyan, four-fifths Jamaican, and a sprinkle of Zanzibar allspice."

Pastern displayed pretty teeth. "Exactly."

"I don't care as long as there's octane in it," said Petra. An oversized mug of something dark and hot came and the waiter took a few seconds balancing it on the table. Bit of a challenge; the top was fashioned of hand-laid mosaic tiles. Blue and yellow and green shards arranged in graceful florets and grouted carefully. Petra ran her fingers over the contours. Nice work, but impractical.

"Like it?" said Pastern. "The tiles."

"Very nice," said Petra.

"My work."

"Really? It's lovely."

"I don't do much art anymore," said Pastern. "Three kids, my husband's an orthodontist."

The first fact seemed to explain things, the second didn't.

Petra said, "Busy."

"You bet . . . would you tell me this, Detective: How come no one talked to me six years ago? My friends, the other women who were at the theater, were interviewed."

Because the D who worked the case was an alkie burnout who didn't follow through when he didn't reach you the first time.

Petra said, "Ms. Jaeger and Dr. Casagrande?"

Pastern's penciled brows arched. "Sarah's a doctor?"

"She's a psychologist in Sacramento."

"Isn't *that* something?" said Emily Pastern. "She always talked about becoming a therapist, but I never thought she'd actually do it. Guess Sacramento was good to her."

"How long's she been there?"

"She and her husband moved up there a while back—not long after Marta was killed. Alan's a lobbyist and they wanted him full-time at the capital. How's Sarah doing?"

"Haven't spoken to her yet. Haven't been able to reach Melanie Jaeger either."

"Mel's in France," said Pastern. "Got divorced and moved there a couple of years ago. Finding herself." She stirred her tea some more. "No kids, she's got mobility."

"Finding herself how?" said Petra.

Pastern pushed fine, ginger hair away from her face. "She thinks she's an artist. A painter."

"No talent, huh?" Petra's palm caressed the tabletop. Trying to communicate: *as opposed to you, Emily.*

"I don't want to bad-mouth, we were all friends, but . . . guess I'm the only one still in the Valley . . . so why wasn't I talked to?"

"From what I could tell, the detective couldn't reach you."

"He called when I was out and left his number," said Pastern. "I called him back."

Petra shrugged.

"Six years," said Pastern. "Is there some reason it's been re-opened?"

"No dramatic evidence, I'm afraid. We're just trying to be thorough."

Pastern frowned. "Are you from here?"

"Originally, Arizona," said Petra. This was getting personal. Lonely woman? Or was Pastern resisting?

"I've got cousins in Scottsdale—" Pastern stopped herself. "You don't care about any of that. This is about Marta. Do you have any theories who killed her?"

"Not yet. How about you?" said Petra.

"Sure do. I always thought it was Kurt. But no one asked my opinion."

Petra's hand clamped around her coffee mug. The ceramic was scalding and she freed her tingling fingers. "Why do you think that, Emily?"

"I'm not saying I *know* he did it, it's just my feeling," said Pastern. "Marta and Kurt's marriage had always seemed off."

"In what way?"

"Remote. Platonic, even. Like they never went through that initial passion stage most people start out with. Know what I mean?"

"Sure," said Petra.

"Everything cools down eventually, but with Marta and Kurt you just felt there'd never been any heat in the first place. Not that Marta ever said anything. She was German, had that European reserve."

"Remote," said Petra, remembering Kurt Doebbler's flat affect. Two cool people. One had ended up beaten to a pulp.

"I never saw them kiss," said Pastern. "Or touch, for that matter. Then again, I've never seen Kurt display anything in the way of emotion. Even after Marta died." She bent toward Sophia, kneaded the dog's neck folds. "He still lives there, you know. In the same house. Seven blocks from mine. After we heard about Marta, I brought over food, offered to help any way I could. Kurt took the plate at the door, never invited me in, never thanked me."

"Charming fellow."

"Have you met him?"

Petra nodded.

"So you know. I can't prove he did it, I just feel it. Always have. We all did—Sarah and Mel and I. Not just because Kurt's strange. Because of the way it happened. That night in the theater, when Marta's phone rang, she bolted up so quickly she nearly tripped over my legs. Then she hurried out, without explanation, as if her life depended on it." Pastern smiled queasily. "That came out wrong."

Petra said, "Did she slip the phone open and read the sender's number?"

Pastern thought. "I don't think so . . . no, I'm sure she didn't. I don't think her phone even had a lid to flip—six years ago mine didn't. No, she just switched it off and got up and ran out. We were pretty taken aback. Generally, Marta was super-polite. Sarah wanted to go out and check immediately but Melanie told her it might be a private family affair, she should give Marta her privacy. Marta *was* a private person. You never really knew where she was coming from. The three of us were making too much noise discussing it and people started to shush us, so we shut up and waited until intermission."

"How long was that?"

"Maybe ten minutes," said Pastern. "Maybe fifteen. When Marta didn't return in a couple, I remember not being able to concentrate on the show. Then I figured she didn't want to cause any more disruption by coming back for such a short interval, was probably waiting for us in the lobby. The moment the curtain dropped, we hurried out to find her but she wasn't there. We immediately called her cell but no one answered and that's when we started to get worried. We decided to split up to look for her in the theater. Which wasn't easy, the Pantages is a big place, all those people streaming out."

She frowned. "I got the job of checking the ladies' room. Kneeling down and checking the shoes in the stalls. Marta wasn't there. Wasn't anywhere. We tried to figure out what to do. The consensus was that she'd been called out on a personal matter, probably by Kurt. Maybe something to do with Katya, it had to be serious for her not to return, not to even tell us. Maybe she needed to keep her line clear so we decided not to try to call her again and went back in, saw the rest of the show. I didn't really enjoy it."

"Worried about Marta."

"At that time, I was more worried about what had caused her to leave so impulsively," said Pastern. "Do you have kids?"

Petra shook her head.

"It's a lifetime of anxiety, Detective. Anyway, after the show, the three of us walked to my car—I'd driven. Everyone except Marta, she came in her own car."

"Why?"

"She had an appointment in the city, didn't want to bother coming back to the Valley then back again. She arrived when we did, parked right near my car. When we looked, her car was gone. That made sense to us—given what we figured."

"Where was the lot?"

"Right across the street from the theater."

Marta's vehicle had been found around the corner from the theater and two blocks down. Ballou had made no mention of it being moved from the parking lot.

She'd left with the killer. Lured to a dark, quiet spot. Bludgeoned on the sidewalk, then propped behind the wheel of her own vehicle.

Petra said, "What kind of appointment did Marta have in the city?"

"She didn't say." Pastern shifted. Looked down at her own tile-work. "Marta went into the city a lot. My initial take was that the Valley bored her. She grew up in Hamburg, which is supposed to be a pretty sophisticated city. Back in Germany, she'd been some sort of mathematician or engineer. That's where she met Kurt, he's a rocket designer or something like that—he was doing something for the government at one of the military bases. They got married there, had Katya in Germany, moved to the States soon after."

Long answer to a short question and now Pastern was stirring her tea rapidly, as if willing the liquid to evaporate. Talking about Marta's errands had made her jumpy.

"Your initial take was boredom," said Petra. "Any other reason for her to come into the city frequently?"

The spaces between Pastern's freckles pinkened. "I don't want to say when I don't know."

"Say what, Emily?"

"Are you married, Detective?"

"Used to be."

"Oh. Sorry for prying."

"No prob."

"It's funny," said Pastern. "The way we're talking, as if this was just two girls. . . . I'm glad the police let women do important jobs now."

Down below, Sophia stirred. Pastern dipped a finger in her snifter, rubbed liquid over the dog's nose and mouth. "The heat's not great for her, but she's pretty robust. Back in Italy, they live outdoors, guard estates."

"Did the Doebblers own a dog?"

"Never," said Pastern. "At one point, Marta wanted one. For Katya. She said Kurt wouldn't allow it. I think that's abusive, don't you? Animals are great for kids. They teach them a lot about giving and sharing."

"Absolutely," said Petra. "So Kurt doesn't like animals."

"He told Marta they were too messy." Pastern fiddled with her hair. "What I said before—that I always thought Kurt did it. That won't get back to him, right? Because it's not an accusation, just a feeling. And he does live close."

"It will absolutely not get back to him, Emily."

"I'm going to believe you on that. I guess that's about it."

Petra said, "Could we talk more about Marta's errands in the city?"

Pastern answered quickly. "She liked to shop—discount clothing places, that kind of thing."

Let it ride. "Okay . . . can you think of any reason Kurt might have to murder Marta?"

"So you do suspect him?"

"At this point I don't know enough to suspect anyone, Emily. That's why it's important for you to tell me everything you know."

"I have." Pastern's smile was shaky.

Petra smiled back. Tasted her designer coffee. Dreadful. She'd give Pastern one more try and if the woman continued to resist, follow up with a phone call tomorrow. Tonight.

Emily Pastern untied her hair and shook it loose. She had knotted it up tight, created an austere little bun that gave her face an ascetic cast.

"The errands," said Petra.

"Okay. I might as well tell you because you've taken the trouble after all these years and you do seem like someone who cares."

She moistened the dog's snout again. Breathed in deeply.

Dramatic type; Petra wondered how much of what she said could be taken seriously.

"Okay," Pastern repeated. "I'm pretty sure Marta was having an affair."

Petra waited for the woman's breathing to slow. "With who?"

"I don't know, Detective. But she gave off all the signs."

Petra held out an expectant palm.

Emily Pastern said, "Dressing better, walking bouncier—sexier. Color in her cheeks. She was still reserved, but there was something going on beneath the surface. A glow. A fire."

The color in Pastern's cheeks heightened. Ah, suburbia.

Petra said, "Happier than usual."

"More than happier. *Alive.* It wasn't because of Kurt, believe me. He was the same old dull Kurt."

"But Marta changed."

"Anyone who knew her could tell she had. Suddenly she was gone all the time. Rushing here, rushing there. Which wasn't like Marta at all. It was true what I said about her being bored. She told me she found the Valley too slow. But her way of coping had been stay-at-home stuff. Being a PTA mom, collecting—glass figurines, samplers, little Japanese teapots. She used to hit the flea markets regularly. Then all that stopped and she boxed up her collections and started driving into the city regularly."

"Around the same time she started to dress and walk sexier?"

"Exactly the same time," said Pastern. "You're a woman. You know I'm right."

"You're making a good case, Emily."

"Maybe Kurt found out. Maybe that's why he did it. It sure wasn't for any romantic reasons of his own. He's never remarried and if he's been hooked up with another woman, I haven't heard."

"Would you have heard?" said Petra. "With his being distant and all that?"

"Oh, yeah," said Pastern. "Our kids still go to the same school. West Valley Prep. It's still suburbia, Petra."

Petra watched as she wiped her lips daintily. Drama queen or not, Pastern had given her something to work with. She asked her if there was anything else she wanted to say and when Pastern shook her head, thanked her, fished a ten out of her purse and stood.

Sophia grumbled.

Pastern patted her calm and reached for her own purse. "No, it's on me."

"Against regulations," said Petra, smiling. Little Miss By-the-Book. Ha.

"You're sure? Okay, then, nice to meet you, hope you get him."

As Petra started to leave, Pastern said, "Why'd you ask me if Kurt and Marta had a dog?"

"Just curious," said Petra. "Trying to get a feel for them as people."

"*He's* a cold person," said Pastern. "*She* was a nice person. I'll tell you who did love dogs: Katya. She was always over playing with Daisy. Her needs were so obvious. But Kurt wouldn't hear of it."

"Too messy."

"He's compulsive." Pastern frowned. "Real life isn't like that."

"Sure isn't," said Petra. "What color is Daisy?"

"A deep beautiful mahogany red. She's show-quality."

No match to the hairs on Coral Langdon. So much for the complex transfer scenario Petra had formulated. From daughter to dad to . . .

She said, "I'll bet she is. Any idea how Katya's doing?"

"My daughter, who's in the same grade but not the same class, says she's very quiet, keeps to herself. What else would you expect? Growing up with someone like *that*. Besides that, a girl needs a *mother*. It's basic psychology, right?"

Petra flashed a plastic smile, muttered something. Escaped.

CHAPTER
41

Petra drove east on Ventura Boulevard to Laurel Canyon, took
that winding, leafy route back to the city. She loved Laurel,
with its mix of ramshackle, radical, and royal. Great place to live in the
unlikely event she ever had money.

She zipped past what was left of the old Houdini estate. Some
magic would be nice right around now. Something to help her figure
out if Emily Pastern's suspicions were righteous.

Marta's infidelity, Kurt a revenge murderer.

If so, he'd planned meticulously, lured his wife out of the theater,
maybe using Katya as the bait. Then he'd exploited his daughter again
for an alibi.

From everything she'd seen, now buttressed by Pastern's comments, Kurt was a cold fish. One of those technically minded guys who
saw everything as an equation.

You humiliate me, I kill you?

No reason it *couldn't* have happened that way. She ran the scenario
through her head: Kurt calls Marta from the phone booth, then heads
over to the theater parking lot to wait. Marta shows up, they drive off—
he drives. Then he pulls over around the block. Tells her the real reason
he's there. He knows about all those trips to the city.

Maybe there's a confrontation, right there. Or perhaps Marta, caught off-guard, tries to smooth things out. Kurt's beyond appeasement; he's brought a weapon.

Or perhaps he'd planted it in the trunk of Marta's car. Or had used something already there—a jack, a tire iron.

No, the coroner's report said something wider, smoother.

Marta tries to escape, runs from the car. He grabs her.

Spins her, gets behind her. A tall guy like Kurt would have had plenty of leverage for a crushing occipital blow.

She goes down, he continues bashing her brains out. Doing it on the street. *You act like a slut, you die like a slut.*

Had he intended on leaving her there, remembered that the bleeding thing on the sidewalk had once been his wife and relented? Propped her back in the car? Or had that just been an attempt to conceal the body in order to give him more time to get home, crawl into bed, and enjoy murderer's dreams?

Marta hadn't been found until morning. Kurt, getting Katya ready for school, would've had plenty of time to be "surprised."

As she passed the Canyon Market, Petra thought of a third possibility. Positioning Marta behind the wheel had been a different kind of message: *You drove into the city to meet your lover. Now sit in the driver's seat in that same damn car with your brains leaking out.*

Destroying her humanity, her soul. Would a tech type like Kurt Doebbler believe in the soul? Or would he view people as nothing more than the sum of their cells?

I pulverize your gray matter, I reduce you to nothing.

Pastern had called Kurt compulsive. Maybe that cold, flat demeanor masked volcanic rage.

He does Marta, gets away with it. Decides he likes it.

Decides to commemorate the date.

What were anniversaries but time souvenirs? And psycho killers loved to keep mementos.

Nice little profile she was developing. The only problem was, lots of stuff didn't fit. Like the dog hairs on Coral Langdon when Kurt hated animals. And Kurt, as charmless a man as Petra had ever encountered, seemed the last guy Coral would have stopped to have a pooch chat with.

Did he have acting skills no one knew about?

She decided she'd made too much out of the hairs. Langdon was a dog person, ran into other dog people, picked up foreign hairs.

But what of the phony cable visit to Geraldo Solis's house? How did Doebbler synch with that?

Maybe Kurt had worked in the cable business before becoming a missile designer—some sort of student job? Even so, if he'd wanted to commemorate his wife's murder, why not choose a victim similar to Marta? At the very least a woman, not a grumpy old ex-Marine like Solis.

Unless Solis had somehow been *involved* with the Doebblers . . . could *he* have been Marta's lover in the city? Then why wait a year to get him?

Solis was a cantankerous old loner, thirty years Marta's senior. People made strange choices but it just didn't fit.

She ran through the rest of the victim list. Langdon, Hochenbrenner, the young black sailor. Jewell Blank and Curtis Hoffey, two street kids.

What was the damned *pattern*?

By the time she made it to Sunset, her head throbbed and she decided she'd been fixing air sandwiches.

As she reached Fairfax and Sixth, her phone beeped. Mac Dilbeck's mobile.

"Just heard, Petra. Sorry."

"I really couldn't expect different, Mac."

"Only because they've got their heads tucked so tightly up their posteriors they can't see the light of wisdom."

"Thanks, Mac."

"I should be thanking you," he said. "For clearing the case. Saving us the paperwork and the city a trial. Some types deserve killing and he fit the bill, right?"

"Right."

"What's Eric's situation?"

"Meetings at Parker."

"When the dust clears, he'll be okay. It was righteous."

"It sure was."

"I'm also calling to fill you in on Sandra Leon. The gods from Olympus allowed me to sit in on her interview. She wouldn't talk to them no matter what they did so finally they left to *confer*." He snorted.

"So while they're gone, I do the old grandfatherly bit and guess what? She starts to open up."

"Oh, yeah," said Petra, smiling.

"Oh, yeah, indeed," said Mac. "I made sure the tape was running. By the time they got back with a plan, with a big old *task force* plan, she's talking and at least they're smart enough to keep their mouths shut and back off. Sandra's story is she and cousin Marcella didn't get along too well. Big-time jealousy, going way back. That scumbag Lyle Leon was messing with both of them for years and they ended up competing for his attention. When Marcella got involved with Omar Selden, Sandra figured that was wrong, she was the pretty one. So she moved in on Marcella's territory. Also—get this—there was bad feeling because once, when Sandra was waiting to see a doctor for her hepatitis, Marcella left her alone, found an arcade on the boulevard, and played games for two hours. That really frosted Sandra."

"Sounds like a motive for murder to me."

"You should've heard the kid, Petra. Cold. She was the one told Omar that Marcella had aborted his baby. Told him Marcella had joked about it, called the baby garbage."

"Lord," said Petra. "She set Marcella up."

"She did more than that. She told Omar the two of them would be at the Paradiso, pinpointed where and when Marcella would be coming out."

"Omar photographed the parking lot a full week before the concert. The whole thing was well planned."

"Oh, boy," he said.

"That's why Sandra was so cool after the shooting. She stuck around to gloat, got a little nervous when I tried to interview her. But no grief, she was digging the scene. That is one sick kid. What's she being charged with?"

"D.A.'s not sure yet. I'm pushing for a full one eighty-seven, but the only evidence is what Sandra said on tape, so maybe they'll plea it down to something juvie. She's pretty smug, seems to think she'll get away scot-free because she's seventeen. For all I know, she will. Some slick private attorney showed up this afternoon. He wouldn't tell me who hired him, but I'm sure he's being paid by The Players. He's already making noises about dismissing the confession because I didn't give Sandra her rights right before she talked. The Downtown guys Mirandized her at the beginning and I was in the room, so the ADA's claiming I was part of the 'interrogatory team,' the first warning was enough."

"Here goes the system," said Petra.

"So what else is new?"

"What about Lyle? He's open to a big fat pedophilia charge."

"Lyle rabbited right after we let him out of the holding cell. Which would've posed some problems if Omar had gone to trial. So it's pretty nice that he won't be needed. For that I thank you again."

"You're welcome," said Petra.

"You all right?"

"Taking some downtime. How about you?"

"I'm off to play putt-putt golf with my grandson. Don't let them grind you down, kid. You're a solid girl."

Shrinks kept forty-five-minute hours, so at four forty-five Petra tried the clinic where Dr. Sarah Casagrande worked, was transferred to voice mail, left a forceful message. No return. She repeated the process at five forty-five and this time a woman's voice broke in.

"This is Sarah." Soft, breathy, hesitant. "I was just about to call you."

"Thanks," said Petra. "As I said in my message, Doctor, this is about Marta Doebbler."

"All these years," said Casagrande. "Has something changed?"

"In terms of . . ."

"The detective I spoke to led me to believe the case was unlikely to be solved."

"Did he?"

"Oh, yes," said Casagrande. "I suppose he was being honest, but at the time it was hard to hear."

"Do you remember what reason he gave?"

"He said there was no evidence. He had suspicions, but nothing more."

"Suspicions of who?"

"Kurt. I felt the same way. All three of us did."

"You told him that?"

"Of course."

Something Ballou had neglected to tell her. Or write down.

"Why did you suspect Kurt?"

"He made me uneasy. Sometimes he made me feel uncomfortable."

"Lecherous?" said Petra.

"No, I couldn't say that. Couldn't say he was actually projecting any interest in me. It was just the opposite, a lack of emotion. I'd see him looking at me, during a barbecue or some other social thing, and then I'd realize he wasn't, he was looking *through* me. I told my husband and he said he'd noticed that, too, all the guys thought Kurt was strange, no one invited him to play poker."

"You're a psychologist. Care to diagnose?"

"I'm a psychological assistant," said Casagrande. "A year away from taking the licensing exam."

"Still," said Petra. "You know more than the average person. How would you classify Kurt Doebbler?"

"I hate to do that. Long-distance analysis isn't worth much."

"Off the record, Doctor."

"Off the record, if I had to bet, I'd say Kurt displays schizoid tendencies. That doesn't mean he's crazy. It refers to an asocial personality. Flat emotion, a lack of connection to other people."

"Can that lead to murder?"

"Now," said Casagrande, "you're really asking me to step outside the bounds of my—"

"Off the *record,* Doctor."

"Most asocial types aren't violent, but when they do act out—when schizoid tendencies are combined with aggressive impulses—it can be pretty horrendous."

Meticulous planning followed by stunning violence . . .

"The Unabomber comes to mind," said Sarah Casagrande. "A life-long loner who hated people. He constructed an ecological excuse for murder, but all he wanted to do was destroy."

The bomber had been a tech type, too. Math Ph.D., meticulous, scheming. And how many years had it taken to bring *him* down . . .

"I'm not saying Kurt's like the Unabomber," said Casagrande. "That was serial murder. We're talking about someone killing his wife."

If you only knew. "If Kurt did murder Marta, what do you think his motive was?"

Casagrande laughed nervously. "All this speculation."

"Detective Ballou thought the case was hopeless and maybe he was right, Doctor. But I'm trying to prove otherwise and I need all the help I can get."

"I hear what you're saying . . . a motive. I'd have to say jealousy."

"Of who?"

"It's possible—and this is real speculation—that Marta was seeing someone."

"So I've been told."

"You have?"

"By Emily Pastern."

"Emily," said Casagrande. "Yes, it was Emily who raised the possibility in the first place, but I'd been thinking the same thing. We all had, because of changes in Marta's behavior. She seemed happier. There was more . . . physicality to her. The way she carried herself, the way she dressed."

"Sexier wardrobe?" said Petra.

"No, Marta was a very restrained person, even after the changes she was a long way from sexy. But she did start wearing more feminine clothing—dresses, stockings, perfume. She had a lovely figure but always used to cover it up under baggy sweats. She had great bone structure. Fixed up, with just the smallest touches, she was a very attractive woman."

"How long before she was murdered did she start to change?"

"I'd say . . . months. Four, five months. I suppose there could've been other reasons for it."

"Such as?"

"Trying to breathe new passion into her marriage. But I never saw any change in the way Marta and Kurt related."

"Which was?"

"Platonic."

The exact same word Emily Pastern had used. Which could be nothing more than consensus born of girl-chat. On the other hand, these were smart, perceptive women who'd known Marta Doebbler a lot better than Petra could ever hope to.

She pressed Casagrande more on the affair, got nothing but a polite denial of details. Running Casagrande through the events at the theater produced an account consistent with Pastern's.

"Thanks, Doctor."

"I hope you succeed in getting him," said Casagrande. "If it is him . . . have you considered his job, what he does for a living?"

"Missile designer," said Petra. "Guidance systems."

"Think about that," said Casagrande. "He figures out ways to destroy things."

CHAPTER

42

Isaac's eyes had blurred twenty minutes ago, but he waited to take a break until he'd finished the *Herald Examiner* files.

His self-assigned task of today: going back to the birth of as many L.A. newspapers as he could find and reading every June 28 issue. In the case of the *Herald,* cross-referencing to the photomorgue when something interesting came up.

Lots of duplication among the papers, but all that history added up to hundreds of felonies, mostly robberies, thefts, burglaries, assaults, and, as the automobile took control of the city, drunk-driving arrests.

He whittled down the homicides to those that weren't bar killings or family disputes or related to robberies. Some of what remained was distinctively psychopathic: a series of Chinatown prostitutes slashed at the turn of the century, unsolved drownings and shootings, even some bludgeonings. But nothing matched the modus or the flavor of the six cases.

No huge surprise; when he'd first come across the pattern—before he'd gone to Petra, before running his statistical tests of significance—he'd covered some of the same ground in the *L.A. Times* files. Still, it paid to be careful, maybe he'd missed something.

Three days to go until June 28, and after nearly seven hours of tedious, back-cramping, eyestraining work, he'd come up with nothing. Yesterday had been just as futile, spent on the third floor of the Goodhue Building, in the Rare Books Department, where he'd showed up full of purpose only to be informed that he needed an appointment. Which was logical, these were collector's items, what had he been thinking?

He'd flashed his grad student I.D., made up some story about thinking the BioStat Department had already made an appointment, and the librarian, a thin older man with a bristly white mustache, had taken pity.

"What is it you're looking for?"

When Isaac explained—keeping it ambiguous but you couldn't get away from the word *murder*—the librarian looked at him differently. But he'd been helpful, anyway, handing Isaac a written application form, then guiding him through the holdings.

California History, Mexican Bullfighting, Ornithology, Pacific Voyages . . .

"I suppose it's the first that would concern you, Mr. Gomez, seeing as bulls and birds don't commit murder."

"Actually, they do," said Isaac and he'd delivered a little treatise on violent animal behavior. The odd member of the herd or flock who turned out to be antisocial. It was something he thought about from time to time.

"Hmm," said the librarian, and directed him to the history catalog. Five hours later, he'd left the room exhausted and unfulfilled. No shortage of human beings turning murderously antisocial during California's bloody history, but nothing that could be construed as relating to his cases.

His. As if there was pride of ownership.

Let's face it, there is. Coming across the pattern thrilled you.

Now he was more than willing to relinquish ownership. . . . Petra was probably right. The date was personal, not historical. Leaving him with nothing to offer her.

He hadn't heard from her since Friday, had shown up at the station Monday morning, earlier than usual, ready to brainstorm again. She wasn't there and her desk was clear. Totally clear.

Three other detectives were in the room. Fleischer, Montoya, and a man at the bulletin board.

"Any idea where Detective Connor is?" he'd said to no one in particular.

Fleischer's shoulders rose but he didn't speak. Montoya frowned and left. What was that all about?

Then the man at the board said "She's out," and turned. Dark suit, thinning black hair, pencil mustache. Kind of pimpish—Vice?

Isaac said, "Any idea when she's coming in?" and the man stepped closer. Detective II Robert Lucido, Central Division.

Why had *he* answered the question?

Lucido said, "I'm looking for her myself. You're . . ."

"An intern. I work with Detective Connor doing research."

"Research?" Lucido peered at Isaac's badge. "Well, she's out, Isaac."

He winked, exited.

Leaving Fleischer, who sat there with the phone receiver in his hand but not dialing. What did he *do* here all day?

Isaac scribbled a note for Petra and left it on the bare desk, was headed for his own seat in the corner when Fleischer put the phone down and waved him over.

"Don't waste your time."

"What do you mean?"

"She's not coming in. Suspended."

"Suspended? For God's sake, why?"

"Shootout, North Hollywood, Saturday." Fleischer's bushy eyebrows turned into croquet wickets. "It was on the news, son."

Isaac hadn't watched the news. Too busy.

"But she's okay."

Fleischer nodded.

"What happened?"

"Petra and another detective were staking a suspect, there was a confrontation and the bad guy didn't respond appropriately."

"Dead?" said Isaac.

"Extremely."

"The suspect on the Paradiso case?"

"That's the one."

"For that she got suspended?"

"It's a procedural thing, son."

"Meaning what?"

"Rules were broken."

"How long will the suspension last?"

"Haven't heard."

"Where is she, now?"

"Anywhere but here," said Fleischer.

"I don't have her home number."

Fleischer shrugged.

"Detective Fleischer," said Isaac, "it's important that I get in touch with her."

"She have your number?"

"Yes."

"Then I don't see any problem, son."

She hadn't called and now it was Tuesday.

Caught up in her own problems, she'd probably forgotten about June 28.

Not that he had anything for her.

He missed . . . being at the station.

Suddenly, his neck kinked painfully and he got up from his computer terminal in the history and geneology catalog room and stretched.

Being left out in the cold was poetic justice. Over the past few days, he'd ignored half a dozen phone messages from Klara. Had stayed away from campus and made the public library his work station expressly to avoid her.

The decision to break communication had been rationalized as kindness: Given Klara's fragile emotional state, wouldn't contact do her more harm than good? Though, what had happened down in the sub-basement was regrettable, but not a felony. Two adults doing what adults did, one of those odd confluences of time and place. And hormones.

Thinking about it now, he couldn't believe what he'd done. The impulsiveness . . .

Klara, whatever her emotional complexities might be, needed to realize that he—

"Sir?" said a wispy voice behind him.

He looked over his shoulder, then down several inches, saw an elderly black woman smiling up at him. Oversized purse in one hand, big, green reference volume tucked under her other arm. Tiny and stooped, she looked to be ninety, had beautiful skin the color of prunes. A too-heavy wool coat bulked her meager frame. A green felt hat sat atop marcelled hair the color of fresh snow.

"Are you through, sir?" she said and Isaac realized his was the only free computer in the room. All those geneology addicts clicking away. The fire in the old woman's eyes said she was probably one of them.

He had a few more years of *Herald* to cover, but said "Sure," and stepped aside.

"Thank you, young Latin gentleman." She enunciated clearly, some kind of Island lilt. Scurrying past him, she plopped down in front of the terminal, cleared the screen of newspaper references, clicked, found what she was looking for, and began rolling through databases.

Ellis Island Immigration records, 1911.

She must've felt Isaac looking over her shoulder, turned and smiled again. "Tracing your roots, sir? Mexico?"

"Yup," Isaac lied, too tired to get into details.

"It's marvelous fun, isn't it? The past is delicious!"

"It's great," he said. The deadness in his voice killed the old woman's glee.

She blinked and he left the room. Quickly, before he ruined someone else's day.

CHAPTER

43

Petra spent a good deal of Monday trying to locate Melanie Jaeger, the fourth member of Marta Doebbler's theater party. Living somewhere in the South of France.

She recontacted Emily Pastern, who now seemed reluctant to talk, but pushed and got the woman to specify "somewhere near Nice, I think." Using the Internet, she pulled up maps and phoned every listed hotel and pension in that region.

Slow, painful process. Being cut off from official data banks, the ability to use the reverse directory, any clout with the airlines, reminded her that she was just another civilian.

She spoke to a lot of baffled/bored French desk clerks, lied, tried charm, finally struck gold at a place called La Mer where a concierge who spoke beautiful English put her through to Madame Jaeger's room.

After all that, Jaeger had nothing new to tell her. She, too, was certain Kurt Doebbler had brained Marta.

Why?

"Because he's a spooky creep who never smiled. Hope you catch him and cut off his balls."

◆

By eleven P.M. she still hadn't heard from Eric. Popping a couple of Benadryl, she sank into ten hours of drugged-out sleep and awoke Tuesday, ready to work.

Back to the computer. Experienced private eyes had their own methods, could sometimes tread where cops couldn't. Her ignorance of all that bugged her. Eric was a fast learner. Soon he'd be in touch with all that good stuff.

If he really made the move.

She allowed herself a fantasy: the two of them working together, partners in a high-end p.i. firm. Beautiful office suite on Wilshire or Sunset or maybe even out near the beach. Cool, deco furnishings, rich clients . . .

You write the screenplay and I'll pitch it to the networks.

He called at noon, just as she was finishing a quick lunch of toast, a green apple, and strong coffee. She chewed fast, swallowed. "Where are you?"

"Downtown."

"Second day, running?"

"Maybe the last day," he said.

"How's it going?"

"They're being . . . thorough."

"You can't talk freely."

"I can listen."

"Okay," she said. "I'm really sorry, Eric."

"For what?"

"Your having to go through this because of—"

"No sweat. Got to go." In a softer voice: "Honey."

Google pulled up zero on Kurt Doebbler—an achievement in itself because the search engine was a monstrous cyber–vacuum cleaner.

She supposed the absence of a personal website was consistent with Doebbler's asocial personality. But his name did come up on the Pacific Dynamics homepage. One of many names on a roster of the company's "Senior Staff."

Kurt was listed as senior engineer and technical designer on something called Project Advent. No details on what that was. The bio did note that Doebbler had "interfaced" with the 40th Engineering Battalion at Baumholden Army Base, in Germany. Having spent his high school years as an Army brat near Hamburg, and speaking fluent German, "Kurt was a natural for the assignment."

That seemed odd. American Army engineers would speak English.

Was Kurt into hush-hush stuff?

Something else to make her life more difficult?

She read on: B.S. from Cal Tech, M.S. from USC—Isaac's alma mater.

Speaking of which, she hadn't talked to Isaac since Friday. With nothing to show there was no sense bothering the kid. According to the bio, Kurt Doebbler was well-regarded as a systems designer who'd worked at Pacific Dynamics for fifteen years. Meaning soon after grad school. No listing of prior employment as a cable dude. But why would there be?

She printed the info, reread it. The German connection got her going in a whole new direction, and she spent the afternoon making international calls until she reached the right person at the Hamburg Police Department.

Chief Inspector Klaus Bandorffer. It was the early morning hours in Germany, still dark, and she wondered what kind of chief inspector kept those hours. But Bandorffer sounded chipper, a professional but amiable fellow, intrigued by a call from an American detective.

Adding yet another potential infraction to her departmental jacket, she told him the June 28 cases were being actively and officially investigated and that she was the lead detective.

"Another one," said Bandorffer.

"Another what, Chief Inspector?"

"Serial killer, Detective—is it Connor?"

"Yes, sir. You've got a lot of serials in Hamburg?"

"Nothing active, right now, but we have our share," said Bandorffer. "You Americans and we Germans seem proficient at growing such sociopaths."

A spooky thought. "Maybe we're just good at detecting patterns."

Bandorffer chuckled. "Efficiency and intelligence—I like that explanation. So you believe you have a suspect who may have lived in Hamburg?"

"It's possible."

"Hmm. During what time period?"

Kurt Doebbler was forty. "High school years" meant twenty-two to twenty-five years ago. She gave Bandorffer those parameters and the details of the head-bashing.

"We had such a murder last year," he said. "Two drunks in a beer hall, brains knocked clear out of the skull. Our killer's an illiterate carpenter, never been to the United States . . . Your suspect's family name is Doebbler, Christian name Curtis?"

"Just Kurt. With a *K.*"

Click click click. "I find nothing under that name in my current files but I will check retrospectively. It may take a day or so."

Petra gave him her home number and her cell and thanked him profusely.

Bandorffer chuckled again. "Times like these, we efficient, intelligent law officers must cooperate."

She tried every cable outfit in L.A., Orange, Ventura, San Diego, and Santa Barbara Counties, dealing with paper-pushers at Human Resource Departments, lying when she needed to.

No record of Kurt Doebbler ever working as an installer or any other type of employee. Which didn't mean much; she hadn't expected them to keep records that old.

And that was it.

Still, Doebbler was all she had. Especially for his wife's killing.

Worse came to worst, she could stake out his house June 28. Hope for a miracle and prepare herself for disappointment.

Maybe it *was* time to try Isaac. He'd had a few days to mull. Perhaps a high I.Q. could accomplish what her average little brain couldn't.

He'd probably been by the station yesterday and learned about her suspension. Whatever his issues were with that Jaramillo loser, she knew that hearing about her plight would upset him. In her self-obsession, she'd neglected to consider that. Some babysitter she'd turned out to be.

It was six-fifteen P.M. and all the university departments were closed. She phoned the Gomez residence and Isaac picked up, sounding sleepy. Dozing in the middle of the afternoon?

"Isaac, it's—"

A loud, flapping yawn drowned her out. Like a horse's neighing, kind of gross. This was a side of Isaac she hadn't seen.

He said, "You, again?"

"Again?"

"This is Klara, right? Listen, my brother's—"

"This is Detective Petra Connor. You're Isaac's brother?"

Silence. "Hey, sorry, I was sleeping, yeah, I'm his brother."

"Sorry for waking you. Is Isaac there?"

Another yawn, then a throat clearing. The guy's vocal tones were a lot like Isaac's. But deeper, slower. Like Isaac on downers.

"He ain't here."

"Still at school?"

"Don't know."

"Please tell him I called."

"Sure."

"Go back to sleep, Isaac's brother."

"Isaiah . . . yeah, I will."

At eight P.M. she fought the urge to throw together a lonely gal, out-of-cans dinner and went out. If she was forced to live like a civilian, she might as well reap the benefits.

She drove around the Fairfax District for a while, considering the Grove or one of the places on Melrose. Ended up at a little kosher fish restaurant on Beverly where she and Stu Bishop had lunched from time to time. The owner's father, a doctor, was a colleague of Stu's ophthalmologist dad. Petra had returned by herself because the place was close to her apartment, had sawdust floors, fresh, tasty, cheap food, and a counter pickup policy that avoided chitchat with the waitstaff.

Tonight, the owner was out and two Hispanic guys in baseball caps were running the place. Lots of people and noise. Good.

She ordered grilled baby salmon with a baked potato and slaw, snagged the last vacant table, and sat next to a Hasidic family with five tiny, rambunctious kids. The black-suited, bearded father pretended not to notice her, but when she caught the eye of the pretty bewigged mother, the woman smiled shyly and said, "Sorry for the noise."

As if her progeny were responsible for all the din.

Petra smiled back. "They're cute."

Bigger smile. "Thank you . . . stop it, Shmuel Yakov! Leave Yisroel Tzvi alone!"

◆

By nine forty-five she was back at her place. Eric's Jeep was parked on Detroit and when she cracked her door, he got up from her living room couch and hugged her. He had on a tan suit, blue shirt, yellow tie. She'd never seen him in light colors and it gave his skin a little earth tone.

"It wasn't necessary to dress for me, big boy."

He smiled and removed the jacket.

"Aw," she said.

They kissed briefly. He said, "You eat yet?"

"Just finished. You were figuring on going out?"

"Out or in, doesn't matter." He moved his mouth toward hers again. She turned her head to the side. "My breath smells of fish."

He took her face in his hands, touched lips gently, then pressed his tongue forward and got her to open up. "Hmm . . . trout?"

"Salmon. I can still go out. Have coffee and stare while you eat."

He moved to the kitchen, opened the fridge. "I'll forage."

"Let me fix you something."

By the time she reached him, he'd taken out eggs and milk and pulled a loaf out of the bread box.

"French toast," she said. "I do that real well."

She cracked eggs and sliced bread. He poured milk and said, "You haven't heard about Schoelkopf."

"What about him?"

"It was on the news."

"I haven't watched TV in two days. What's going on?"

"Dead," said Eric. "Three hours ago. His wife killed him."

She left the kitchen and sat down at the dinette table. "My God . . . which wife?"

"The current one. How many did he have?"

"She was number three. What, she left him and then decided to kill him?"

"From what I hear," said Eric, "he left her."

No one from the station had thought to call her. "What happened?"

"Schoelkopf moved out of the house a few weeks ago, rented an apartment near the station—one of the high-rises on Hollywood Boulevard west of La Brea. He was up there with his girlfriend, some civilian clerk. They headed out for lunch, went down in the sub parking lot to get his car. The wife stepped out and started shooting. Schoelkopf caught three in the arm and one right here." He tapped the center of his brow. "The girlfriend got shot, too, but she was alive when the ambulances arrived. Then the wife turned the gun on herself."

"Is the girlfriend named Kirsten Krebs? Blond, mid-twenties, worked downstairs?"

Eric nodded. "You knew about it?"

"I guessed about it. Krebs always had an attitude with me. The day Schoelkopf called me in, she was the messenger. I found her sitting on my desk liked she owned it. Where's the wife?"

"On a respirator, not expected to live. Krebs is in bad shape, too."

She got up, flicked on the TV, found news on Channel Five. A cheerful Latina in a mock-Chanel suit delivered bad news:

". . . investigating this evening's murder of an LAPD police captain. Edward Schoelkopf, forty-seven, a twenty-year veteran, was allegedly gunned down by his estranged wife, Meagan Schoelkopf, thirty-two, who shot herself fatally in what investigators believe was a love-triangle murder-suicide. Also wounded was a yet-unidentified young woman . . ."

The backdrop shifted from a ragged, white "Homicide" header over a chalked body outline to a wedding photo of the couple in happier times. ". . . that left this quiet residential area of Hollywood shocked and Schoelkopf's colleagues at the police department stunned. Now on to other local news . . ."

Petra switched the set off. "I couldn't stand him and Lord knows he despised me—why I'll never know—but this . . ."

"He hated women," said Eric.

"You say that as if you know for a fact."

"When he first interviewed me, he tried to sound me out. About minorities, women. Mostly women, it was clear he didn't like them. He thought he was being subtle, wanted to see if I agreed."

"What'd you do?"

"Kept my mouth shut. That made him assume it was okay to talk freely and he told some really nasty antifemale jokes."

"You never told me."

"What was the point?"

"None, I guess." She sat down. Eric walked behind her and massaged her shoulders.

"I've found," he said, "that in most situations, the less said, the better."

But not all situations, my dear. "Schoelkopf dead. . . . What will it mean for us—in terms of our suspensions?"

"Before it happened, I was led to believe they weren't going to be too hard on either of us. It'll probably delay our dispositions."

"No matter to you. You're leaving."

His hand stopped working. "Maybe."

She twisted around, looked up.

"I'm still thinking," he said.

"Big decision, makes sense."

"Disappointed?"

"Of course not. It's your life."

"We could still get a house," he said. "With both of us working, we could probably get a decent place sooner rather than later."

"Sure," she said. Surprised by the coolness in her own voice.

"Is there a problem?"

"I'm a little overwhelmed right now. Dangling. And all because I helped get rid of a really bad guy."

She broke free, stood, marched into the kitchen. "Plus, there's the June 28 stuff. Three days to go and I've got squat."

"What about that husband—Doebbler?"

"Everyone's sure he killed his wife, but there's no evidence. He fits in some ways but not in others."

"Like what?"

She elaborated. He listened. Petra saw the eggs and bread and milk sitting on the counter. Time to be *useful.* Scooping butter into a pan, she turned on the gas, soaked the bread in milk, and, when the butter was bubbling and barely brown, dropped in two slices.

Nice sound, the sizzle. There was something to be said for mindless work.

Eric said, "You could surveil Doebbler on the twenty-eighth. He moves, he's your guy."

"And if he doesn't, someone dies."

He shrugged.

"*Mister* Blasé."

He didn't answer.

The French toast was ready. She plated it, set it in front of him.

He didn't move.

"Sorry for snapping," she said.

"I didn't mean to be glib," he said.

"You didn't do anything wrong."

"I didn't take you seriously," he said. "You're up to your eyeballs in junk."

Gazing up at her. Eyes softer than she'd ever seen.

She cradled his head. Picked up a fork and slipped it between his fingers. "Eat. Before it gets cold."

WEDNESDAY, JUNE 26, 10:00 A.M., NUMBER SEVEN BUS, SANTA MONICA LINE, PICO
AND OVERLAND

Isaac almost left home without taking the paper bag.

Plagued by restlessness all night, he'd slept until eight-forty.
His parents and his brothers were gone and he admitted, with some
shame, that the resultant silence was wonderful.

With the bathroom all to himself, he took his time showering, shaving, walked around naked, slid his briefcase out from under the bunk
bed. Checked under his papers to make sure the gun was all right.

Why wouldn't it be?

He pulled it out, aimed it at the mirror.

"Bang."

Stupid idea, the gun. What had he been thinking? He rewrapped
it, put it back in the bottom of the case, touched the bruise on his
cheek. No swelling, slightly tender. Those kids had been stupid little
punks, he'd overreacted.

Maybe he'd return the gun to Flaco.

Running his hands over his body, he lifted an edge of window shade, looked out, and caught a blade of sky above the air shaft. Blue streaked with white.

He put on fresh khakis and a short-sleeved yellow shirt. The heat that had already permeated the apartment said this would be a short-sleeves day.

Even at the beach, where the air was always cooler.

Was he growing addicted to sand and ocean?

There were worse vices.

Last night, unable to sleep, he'd allowed himself fantasies of living there one day. Rich doctor, beautiful wife, brilliant kids, set up in one of those big houses on the Palisades.

Or, if fate really steered things his way, a place right on the sand.

Surf, gulls, pelicans, dolphins. Waking every morning to the sound of the ocean . . . about as likely as waking up naturally blond.

But he could while away another day at the pier.

He'd worked hard, was entitled.

Spoiled brat. Deservedness has nothing to do with it.

The key to success wasn't virtue, it was knowledge, knowledge was power.

The old familiar mantra filled his head: *stay on target, get educated.* The Ph.D, then the M.D. Acquire a specialty, get an academic appointment, publish like a demon, earn early tenure, build a reputation that can be parlayed into lucrative consultantships.

Maybe even an M.B.A., a position at some pharmaceutical company . . .

One day he'd be Dr. Gomez. Meanwhile, he'd gotten himself into a fix with Klara.

She kept calling. How long could that go on?

He'd have to deal with it, sooner rather than later. But today . . . the beach.

He went into the kitchen, put his briefcase on the counter, and poured a glass of milk. Changed his mind. He'd return to the public library, use the tools he'd come to believe in: thorough data collection, deductive and inductive reasoning, hard work. Problems were solvable; there had to be an answer.

He gulped the milk and headed for the door. Saw the bag on the tiny mail table to the right of the door.

Brown paper, neatly folded—his mother's trademark. His name

printed in red crayon. Shaky letters because she'd never been confident about her literacy.

The exact same way she'd printed his lunches when he was at Burton. All the other kids eating in the school cafeteria—a wonderful place, those steam tables, the hairnetted women, jewel-green and sun-yellow vegetables, slabs of pink meat and white turkey, things he'd never seen—succotash? Welsh rarebit?

His mother had been afraid of the strange food. Or so she'd claimed. Later, he'd found out that scholarship students didn't qualify for the caf, the school's generosity only went so far.

He'd been ashamed of his sack lunches, until some of the other kids had thought his tamales and black beans cool. There'd been a few snickers—this *was* middle school, after all. But the Burton student body had been well-drilled in the virtues of diversity and, for the most part, had seemed impressed by Irma Gomez's cooking.

That made it easy for Isaac to trade his homemade fare for the contents of the rich kids' caf trays. Chewing away with forced aplomb, pretending to like the bland stuff, because he desperately wanted to blend in.

It had been a while since Mama had packed him a lunch. Maybe he'd ditch it, get himself a fried sausage from a street vendor near the library.

No way, the guilt would overwhelm him. He stuffed the bag in his briefcase, left, and hurried down the stairs.

Guilt was a big part of his makeup. So scratch the M.B.A. and the drug companies.

There goes the house on the beach.

As he hit the street, he changed his mind again. Two days of library work had produced nothing. What could he hope to find? He walked to Pico, caught the number seven bus, and rode all the way to Overland when the aroma of his mother's food, seeping through the brown paper, got his gastric juices going and he unfolded the flap and looked inside.

Atop the foil-wrapped morsels was a scrap of paper, folded over. He fished it out, read "BRO," in large, clumsy capitals. Isaiah's writing.

He unfolded the note.

THE LADY COP CALLED LAST NIGHT.

Just that, no number.

He got up from his seat, rang the buzzer. Exited at the next stop.

The station's rear door was locked. Since he'd been coming here that had only happened twice, because someone had forgotten to open it. He found his 999 key.

It didn't come close to fitting. Change of locks? Then he noticed the closed-circuit camera above the door. Flaking paint where the device had been installed. The lens was focused right on him. It made him feel like a suspect and he turned his back.

New security measures because of some terrorism alert?

He was thinking about that when he saw an older silver Cadillac drive into the lot and park. That old drill-sergeant type, Detective Dilbeck.

Isaac approached the car and Dilbeck rolled down his window.

"Morning, Detective."

"Morning, Mr. Gomez."

"The door's locked and my key doesn't work."

"Mine neither," said Dilbeck. "Everyone comes in through the front until things calm down."

"Calm down from what?"

Dilbeck bared his teeth. "Captain Schoelkopf was murdered yesterday."

"Oh no."

"For the time being, they're being extra careful. Not that what happened to the captain applies to anyone else. He cheated on his wife, hell has no fury and all that. You haven't annoyed any feisty females lately, have you, Mr. Gomez?"

Isaac smiled. His stomach churned.

Dilbeck got out of his car and began walking toward the lot's entrance. Isaac stayed in place.

"No work today, Mr. Gomez?"

Isaac half heard him. Thinking: heightened security probably means a metal detector. The gun . . .

"Actually, I'm on my way to school, just dropped by to get Detective Connor's number. She phoned me last night but my brother neglected to write down her number."

"She's home," said Dilbeck. "You know what happened to her?"

"Yes, sir. It's kind of important that I talk to her. She was trying to reach me about a case we're—she's working on."

"Well, she's not working on anything now, Mr. Gomez."

"Still, I think I should return her—"

Dilbeck clapped his shoulder and stared into his eyes. "You're a nice young fellow, but we're sticklers for privacy around here. How about I call Detective Connor and tell her you stopped by. Give me a number where you can be reached."

Isaac gave him the BioStatistics office number. Now he *had* to return to campus. *What a tangled web we weave.*

He reached USC forty minutes later, took an indirect route to BioStat that circumvented Doheny, and headed straight for his mailbox. It had been days since he'd checked and the box was stuffed. Circulars, departmental memos, junk mail.

Five messages from Klara, all in the same curvy handwriting. The last three were dated yesterday. Exclamation points.

Sandwiched between those was a single slip listing Petra's name and a number to call. A 933 prefix that had to be her home.

He asked the secretary if he could use a department phone to make a local call.

She said, "Haven't you been a stranger."

He shrugged. "Working on the dissertation."

"Poor baby. Don't tie up this one, use the extension in the Xerox room. You know the drill: eight for an outside line and no phoning Europe."

The door to the photocopy room was open. He'd nearly made it over there when a hand landed on his upper back.

Light touch, the barest contact. He wheeled and faced Klara Distenfield. She wore a royal blue dress printed with tiny yellow fish, fresh lipstick, mascara, perfume—the same perfume. Her hand remained near the side of his neck.

She smiled and said, "Finally."

◆

He ushered her into the room.

"What an elusive fellow."

"Klara, I'm sorry—"

"You should be." No rancor in her voice. That made him *really* anxious. He found himself looking her up and down, stopped, but not before the images had registered. Red hair pinned, soft hairs escaping. The blue dress, tight over round belly and meaty hips. The breasts. The perfume. Oh, shit, he was hard.

Her gold-green eyes narrowed. "Do you know how many times I've tried to reach you?"

"I've been out. Family issues—"

"Everyone's got a family." Her lips pursed and tiny wrinkles formed above the gloss. "Whatever the family issue was, it couldn't be too grave. I talked to your brother and he didn't say anything. He sounds like you, by the way."

The prospect of constructing another lie exhausted him. He said, "Nothing grave, it just took time."

"So you're okay?"

"I'm fine. What about you?"

"Me?" She laughed. "I'm great. Why?"

"I thought you were upset."

"About what?"

"What happened."

"Me?" She placed a dainty hand over one commodious breast. "I was a little . . . thrown. But then we had coffee, remember? And I was fine. Didn't I seem fine?"

"The next day," he said, "you weren't at work. Mary Zoltan said you were sick. She implied it was more than a cold." He shook his head. "Maybe I misread the whole thing."

"Mary's an idiot. I wasn't the least bit sick. I missed two days be-cause my *daughter* was ill. High fever, stiff neck. We were worried about—"

"Meningitis. Is she okay?"

"She's fine, just a virus. But I was pretty frantic." She sidled closer to him. "You were worried I had some big old neurotic reaction to our little tumble? That's kind of touching." Her smile was wry. "Except that you dealt with it by *avoiding* me."

"Not neurotic," he said. "I thought I . . ." He shook his head.

"You thought you'd traumatized the poor sex-starved librarian and she was going to make your life miserable." She threw back her head and laughed. Soft laugh. Sexy. Her hand moved down to his crotch. "You're not *that* worried."

"Klara, what happened—"

"Was great. Don't see it any other way." She squeezed him, released him. Winked.

"Klara—"

"Chemistry is chemistry, Isaac. One can never explain it rationally. That doesn't mean we have to give in to our impulses." Sly grin. "Though I can think of worse things." She stroked his face. "You're really a beautiful young man. I admire your brain and I adore your body, but it could never be anything more than an erotic tumble. Which isn't half-bad, right? You've got the potential to be a fantastic lover and I'm a pretty good teacher."

Another downward glance. "Don't worry, that's not an invitation for Episode Two. Because right now there are more important things to discuss. And that's why I've been trying to reach you for days, silly lad. First of all, a cop has been nosing around, asking about you. He just left the library, as a matter of fact. Which is why I came *here* to leave you yet *another* message."

"A cop?" he said. "What's his name?"

"Detective Robert Lucido."

The guy who'd been hanging near the bulletin board. "Pencil mustache?"

"That's the one," said Klara. "I didn't know anyone but John Waters wore those anymore."

"What did Lucido want?"

"He said he was carrying out a routine security investigation of LAPD volunteers because of some new September 11 regulations. Wanted to know what kind of person you are, who you hang out with. Then he got downright unconstitutional: what books you checked out. Of course, I declined."

"How'd he get to you?"

She eyed the door. "He came to BioStat first and they told him you spent most of your time doing research in the stacks. His story—a routine investigation—is it baloney?"

"Probably."

"What's really going on, Isaac?"

"I don't know," he said. "That's the truth. I was just over at the station and they changed the locks. Maybe it's because their captain got murdered—"

"I heard about that—"

"Or it really is terrorism-related."

"That," said Klara, "would scare me. You know how open our campus is. Are you sad about the captain?"

"I didn't know him well."

"Cheating on his wife," said Klara. "One must be careful who one fucks. And who one fucks *with.*"

She dropped one hand and Isaac readied himself for another goose. Instead, she held his hand. He felt leaden. So many unanswered questions, but his erection hadn't flagged. *Down, you little bastard!*

"And Lucido just left?"

"Maybe ten minutes ago," said Klara. "I made sure he didn't follow me when I came here."

"Thanks," said Isaac.

"Thank me with a kiss."

He complied.

She said, "Yum. You've got serious potential, but first things first. The *main* reason I've been trying to reach you isn't Lucido. It's because I finally came up with something on those June murders."

"What?"

She pressed herself against him, positioned his hands on her rear. Pressed down and made him squeeze. When she spoke, they were so close her lips grazed his.

"I do think I may have solved your mystery, Isaac."

Klara left first, exiting the building to make sure Lucido was gone. Isaac waited in the hallway and moments later she stuck her head in and gave him the thumbs-up sign. Enjoying the adventure.

They walked back to Doheny, blending with student traffic. A girl in shorts and bikini top lay on the lawn of the five-story building reading philosophy. A couple of male students hurried by wearing sweatshirts that read "LSU Sucks, Tenn. Swallows."

Klara wore a beatific smile.

Once they were inside, instead of descending to the subbasement, they climbed two floors.

The Rare Book Room. A series of locked chambers and brief, hushed corridors. Klara had all the right keys.

Inside, the central reception area was cozy, hushed, paneled in new, beautiful oak stained oxblood, discreetly lit by milk-glass lamps and chandeliers that hung from a white, coffered ceiling bordered with turquoise. Green leather chairs, oak tables. Off to the left side, a few administrative offices.

No one in sight. Lunch hour?

Klara led him to a room marked "Reading." Inside was a medium-sized conference table, a photocopy machine, a small desk sided by an armchair.

"That's for the student monitor," she explained. "Someone sits and watches when you read the really rare material. I told her to take an early lunch."

"I spent some time here," said Isaac. "Researching Lewis Carroll for an English class. Pencils, no pens, white linen gloves when necessary."

"We have a *wonderful* Carroll collection. Sit. We've got an hour."

He pulled up to the table, expecting her to leave and return with something. Instead, she settled next to him. Unclasped her purse.

Out came a book—a booklet—brown-paper cover printed in rough black lettering. Wrapped in a zip-sealed plastic bag.

She said, "I was a very bad girl, taking it out of here. I did it just in case that Lucido person was still skulking around and we were unable to return."

He took her hand and kissed it.

She laughed, smoothed out the plastic, removed the booklet carefully. "Talk about esoteric. I found it in the Graham Collection. It wasn't even cataloged in the main collection. It was in one of the appendices."

Out of her purse came a pair of soft, white gloves. "Speaking of which," she said, rotating the booklet so the title faced Isaac.

He gloved up. Read.

THE SINS OF THE MAD ARTIST
AN ACCOUNT OF THE HORRIBLE DEEDS
OF
OTTO RETZAK
RECOUNTED BY
T. W. JOSEPH TELLER, ESQ.
FORMER SUPERINTENDENT OF THE MISSOURI STATE
PENITENTIARY
AND PUBLISHED BY HIM IN ST. LOUIS
A.D. MCMX

The brown cover was cardboard, acid-burned brown at the borders, brittle. Isaac lifted it gingerly, flipped, began reading.

After covering a single paragraph, he turned to Klara. "You're brilliant."

She beamed. "So I've been told."

Otto Retzak was the son of Bavarian immigrant farmers who'd come to America in 1888 and ended up on a scratchy patch of rock-strewn land in the southern Illinois region known as Little Egypt. The sixth of nine children and the youngest son, Otto had been born on American soil.

Born June 28, 1897.

One hundred years to the day, before Marta Doebbler's murder.

Isaac's hands started to shake. He steadied them and hunched over the crudely printed text.

Retzak was eight when his drunkard father abandoned the family. Considered extremely bright but uneducable due to "a frightfully overactive and heated temperament," Otto displayed a precocious ability to "wield charcoal stubs in a way that created faithful images." His artistic talent went unappreciated by Otto's drunkard mother, who routinely beat him with switches and kitchen implements and left him to the mercies of his older brothers. With great enthusiasm and teamwork, the elder siblings sexually abused the boy.

At age nine, the illiterate Otto burgled a neighboring farm of twenty-nine cents hidden in a flour jar and a "plump laying hen." The money was traded to another farm boy for a rusty clasp knife. The bird was found off the pitted dirt path that led to the decrepit Retzak homestead, gutted, its eyes scooped out, its head yanked off manually.

When confronted, Otto admitted his guilt "with no sense of childish shame, on the contrary, he boasted." Beaten by his mother with special severity, he was turned over to the neighbors, who added their own lash-work to his tender back and worked him as a barn-hand for a month of fourteen-hour days.

The day after returning home, Otto stabbed his younger sister in the face without apparent provocation. As Superintendent T. W. Joseph Teller recounted: "A cold eye, even a sly smile, he did present to all those in attendance as the girl shrieked and wept and bled."

The local sheriff was called in and Otto was locked in a cell with adult miscreants. Two months later, the boy, bruised and limping, was brought before an itinerant magistrate who warned him about "substantial characterological degeneracy" and sentenced him to five years in a state reform school. There, Otto claimed to have learned that *"mankind is not glorious nor good nor fashioned in God's image. Rather it is a dung-heap of stink and sin and hypocrisy. The hatred that was to drive me for the entirety of my accursed life took hold and was fed in that dark place. The outrages that were done to my person and mind in the name of spiritual cure were of benefit to me in a manner that could not be predicted. They turned my belly to iron and my mind toward revenge."*

Bound over for two extra years because of chronic disciplinary problems, sixteen-year-old Otto, now strapping and hard-muscled, was released. "Of a surprising pleasant countenance when not enraged, Retzak presented the thoughtful mien and demeanor of a man in his twenties. Yet all that could change in a trice."

During his stay in the reformatory, the boy had been befriended by the wife of one of the guards, a woman named Bessie Arbogast. Impressed by Otto's drawings, she brought him paper and charcoal sticks and it was to her house that he headed on his initial day of freedom.

"Once free of his bonds, the incorrigible repaid Mrs. Arbogast's kindnesses by entering her bedroom through an open window."

What commenced was described in Retzak's alleged words, though the flowery language made Isaac wonder if Teller had taken substantial literary liberties.

"In the chamber of her common little snuggery, enriched by the pleasure of violating her worm of a husband, as well as her flabby person and dewy-eyed soul, I used a wooden hairbrush in plain sight to bash him energetically about the head. Feeling quite fond of myself, then had my way with her in manners all the more pleasurable to me for their unspeakability."

William Arbogast survived the beating as a cripple. His wife's trauma rendered her "virtually mute."

Retzak escaped on foot and avoided capture. Traveling the country by hopping freight trains, he survived by eating pilfered domestic animals and produce, and meals donated by kindhearted housewives. Often, he repaid them by doing odd jobs before moving on. Sometimes he left them drawings that were "universally appreciated. The young man was capable of capturing garden scenes and furniture with utmost accuracy. It was only the portrayal of the human figure that posed technical problems for him."

"Interestingly," Teller went on, "during this period, Retzak did not choose to inflict similar punishments upon these altruistic women as he had upon Mrs. Arbogast. When I inquired as to the cause of this discrepancy, Retzak seemed genuinely puzzled.

"I do not know why I do what I do. Sometimes I have the urge and other times I don't. Sometimes my brain remains cool and other times it boils like a cauldron of lard. I am not controlled in my impulses as are most men and I do not regret the lack of restraint in my soul. I have been anointed by Satan or howsoever you recognize The Dark Angel to behave in the way that I do and I have obeyed my Master with the same mechanic idiocy as the fools and worms who squander their wretched little lives kneeling before the altar of some blabbering lying Diety."

It was, Teller concluded, "a great puzzle of medicine and characterology, in that Retzak's entire anatomy, including his brain, has been examined by learned physicians and found unremarkable. This has included detailed measurement of his cranium by practitioners of the discipline called phrenology, now considered of questionable scientific merit by some, but employed in the hope of ascertaining basic truths about the fiend. That analysis deciphered nothing out of the ordinary, as did all other analyses. One can only hope that exposure to the twisted workings of this monster's soul as put forth by this humble tract will benefit mankind. That is, in fact, the purpose of The Author."

At the age of eighteen, Retzak made his way to San Francisco, where he was hired as a deckhand aboard the steamer *Grand Tripoli* bound for the Orient. The ship made a stop in Hawaii, where Retzak took shore leave and abandoned his post.

"In Honolulu, Retzak embarked on a course of drunkenness and debauchery with numerous women of ill repute. Soon, he was living in common law with a prostitute, a fallen Alsatian girl named Ilette Flam, spectral and pasty as such types tend to be, and an opium addict. Retzak appointed himself Ilette's procurer and for a period of nearly one year, sustained himself with her ill-gotten earnings."

On Retzak's nineteenth birthday, Ilette threw a party for him at a waterfront dive. During that celebration, she made an offhand remark that annoyed Retzak and when the two of them returned to their flat, an argument ensued. Retzak claimed not to recall the precise manner in which Ilette Flam had offended his sensibilities. However, when challenged by myself on this point, he owned up that *"it was something about my being lazy. The sow was hazy with dope and booze and believed my intake of rum would dull my thinking and allow her to insult me with no consequence. Just the opposite! My senses were heightened and every stupid remark from her flapping sow lips served to inflame me further! When she uttered another taunt—perhaps it was something that challenged my intelligence—a definite thought crossed my field of vision like a beacon: your sow brain is that of a mindless animal."*

Waiting until Ilette had fallen into a drugged stupor *"because she'd earned me a fair bit of money and for the most part she wasn't all-bad,"* Retzak put her to bed, turned her on her stomach, picked up an iron pry bar and bashed the back of her head.

"The skull cracked like an egg and gobbets of brains seeped out, accompanied by a clearish liquid, then some blood. The sight of it thrilled me as nothing had thrilled me before. New feelings took hold of my mind and I maintained a focused wielding of bar against bone. Specks of the tissue sprayed out like the finest mist and adhered to the walls. When a large brainy clot slipped down the back of her dress, I stared at it, amazed that this ugly grayish pink gelatin might very well house what Christian fools considered the seat of the soul. Could there be anything more hideous? Just one look at the cloudy mucus would inform any logical man that religion is rot. Suddenly, I was awash in calm and sat gazing at my handiwork with rapture. It was a new feeling and I quite liked it. I fetched my tablet of drawing paper and some pens I'd stolen from Berringer's Department Store in Waikiki. As the sow lay there, leaking and seeping and Demonstrably Dead, I drew her. For the first time I was able to capture the human form with a degree of accuracy."

It was, Retzak concluded, *"a fine birthday present."*

Isaac's throat had gone dry. His hairline ached. Swallowing and gulping, he tried to stimulate saliva.

Klara said, "This has to be it." Her voice was thick.

He nodded. But he was thinking something else:

June 28 had been a double anniversary for Otto Retzak. Commemoration of his birth and the date of his first murder.

His first victim, a common-law wife.

The L.A. killer had begun in 1997. Commemorating the centenary of Retzak's birth.

His first victim, a wife.

Marta's friends were sure Kurt Doebbler had killed her. Sometimes things were just as they seemed.

Isaac turned the page.

Upon finishing the drawing of Ilette Flam's mangled corpse, Retzak wrapped it in a bloody sheeting, packed a duffle, walked to Honolulu Harbor, and got himself a job on an oil tanker bound for Venezuela.

"All the way there, the memory of what I'd done to the sow burned in my brain like a sacrament. The ability to extinguish the flame, the power. As I swabbed decks and emptied slop buckets, I barely thought of anything else. I was much more than a deckhand. I had danced a dance few men can hope to know. At night, as I lay in a bunk surrounded by snoring swine, it was all I could do not to bash them all. But cunning prevented me from such rashness for the ship was a prison at sea, with no chance of escape. It was on shore in Caracas, months later, that I allowed myself the next delicious indulgence. The proprietor of a beer-house, a foul-mouthed old Mestizo, got on my wrong side and I decided he'd be the one. Waiting until he'd closed for the night and retired upstairs to his personal lodgings, I snapped the latch on the rear door of his establishment and surprised myself to find him awake and eating a late supper of pork and rice and some such swill. As he started to curse, I picked up a frypan resting atop the stove. A lovely cast-iron implement it was, with agreeable heft and a stout handle. Within seconds, gray half-breed gelatin had leaked into that Hispanical dinner. No different did it look from the sow's and as I sketched the scene, I got to thinking that all persons are but pathetic sacks of flesh and gristle and disgusting fluids. Our delusions of cleanliness and nobility are the basest of lies, the world teems with hypocrisy and falsehood and loosing the pitcocks of humanity in order to free the fluids is the greatest honesty of all. It was my destiny, I decided, to bring about Truth."

Once again, Retzak jumped ship and hid out in South America for several months. Eventually making his way back to the States, he tramped across the country stealing and doing odd jobs, finding employment as a menial laborer, a short-order cook, or a night clerk at shabby hotels. His off-hours were spent brawling, overindulging in alcohol, opium, marijuana, and patent medicines, seducing and raping prostitutes, sneak-thieving, butchering wild and domestic animals at whim.

Murdering five more human beings.

The third victim: a matron walking her dog in Le Doux, Missouri, an affluent suburb of St. Louis. Nocturnal walk; she'd been surprised by a handsome, strapping fellow with a mutt in tow.

"I'd watched this one for days, a sturdy sow she was, and I admired her form and her walk, believed her someone I'd enjoy knowing in the biblical sense. But then the urge came over me to go beyond that merest intrusion and I stole an old yellow cur from a front-yard in her neighborhood, a wretched mongrel so old and blind that he put up no resistance when I lifted him over the fence. Fashioning a leash from a length of rope, I set out to see if he'd cooperate and he did, though in a clumsy, halting manner. I offered him a slab of meat and he regarded me as a religious fool might regard a Savior. That night, I stationed myself outside the sow's house and she emerged, as always, at nine p.m. with her fluffy little annoyance tethered by a satin cord. As she strolled from her house, she began humming a jaunty tune and that inflamed me further. I followed her at a distance until she entered a dark section of her street, then hurried after her, carrying my borrowed mongrel. When I was sufficiently close, I set the dog down, walked past her, stopped several yards ahead and pretended to be tending to the cur. My possession of a canine companion caused her to see me as trustworthy and she approached without hesitation. Within moments we were chatting idiotically and I sensed that she found me gentlemanly. After an exchange of polite utterances, she turned to leave and down came the ax handle I'd secreted in my coat. The gelatin! Her little fluffy thing began whimpering and for dessert, I stomped it. Its gelatin appeared no different to my eye than hers and I found that quite amusing. When I was finished recording the scene in my tablet, I picked up the yellow mongrel, carried it a half mile away, to a wooded place. It looked up at me with affection as I twisted its neck. After inspecting its vitals, I kicked it under a tree."

Isaac exhaled. Klara's breathing was audible and minty. He hesitated before turning the page, knowing what would follow.

Number four: A "nigger sailor" stalked, accosted, and bludgeoned in a Chicago back alley.

Five: *"An insolent prostitute, skinny as a young girl but syphilitic and insolent,"* brutalized in a New Orleans park.

Six: *"An abominable Nancy Boy living in the same hotel as myself in San Francisco pursed his lips at me in a disgusting manner and repeated the insult the following day. I pretended to enjoy his attentions, waited until a moonless night and followed him when he went out to prowl the streets in order to accomplish what that ilk accomplishes. Accosting him in a quiet alley, I agreed to grant his request. He bent and looked up at me, much as the yellow dog had. I told him to close his eyes and proceeded to dispense the Sodomite with energy and efficiency using the handle of an ax I'd stolen that very morning. Visiting ministrations of my unique design to his perversity-filled cranium was a special joy. His brain resembled that of a normal man in every way."*

Perfect match.

But Retzak hadn't stopped at six.

Hitchhiking from San Francisco to Los Angeles, the itinerant killer decided he was now capable of drawing the human figure and face. Setting up an easel near the central railway station, he tried to earn a living drawing caricatures of tourists.

"However," wrote Superintendent Teller, "whatever technical ability he did have was over-ridden by a tendency to depict others as leering, saturnine creatures. His rendering of the eyes, especially, was upsetting to those who sat for him and payment was often refused. Retzak kept the unsold drawings and these works have provided much fodder for analysis by alienists of both the Boston and the Vienna Schools."

When his artist's career failed to materialize, Retzak resumed his pattern of thievery and transitory labor, working as a ditchdigger, a cook, a janitor at a school, even a foot-courier for a small independent bank. Careful never to pilfer from the money satchels, he was found stealing paper and pens from the financial institution and dismissed. It was summertime, and rather than pay for lodgings, Retzak began sleeping outdoors, near railyards and in parks. His wanderings took him to Elysian Park, where "a sanitorium for tubercular war orphans and other sick children had existed for decades in that tree-shaded and verdant place. Retzak, always careful to present himself in a clean and acceptable manner, attracted the attention of the staff by sitting on a bench near the children's rest area and drawing. Curiosity brought the young ones and their caretakers over and soon Retzak was creating pictures for them. They began regarding him as a friendly, wholesome young man. That, of course, was the falsest of false impressions."

"*I was able to impersonate the character of a sound, conventional, stupidly amiable man with laughable ease. All the time, even as I smiled and nattered and sketched the wheezing piglets, the fire burned in my brain. I contemplated luring one of them away from the trough, dashing its little brains upon hard ground, then watching the gelatin seep into the sand. It had been some months since I'd indulged myself in my favorite game, for there were periods when I did try to abstain. During those arid days, memories of my exploits served to amuse me. But of late, I had grown weary of mere nostalgia and knew that something new and fresh—a fine challenge—was called for. I'd learned what I could about brain-jelly and decided that nothing short of a complete medical exploration, from cranium down to the toes would suffice. A composite of humours, a veritable flood of release would elevate me to new heights of devilry. Not piglet humours, something mature.*

"*It was then that my eyes settled upon the smiley, chanting starchy-white nurses who attended to the little gaspers. My favorite was one sow, in particular, a Dago-looking type, of fine form and dark eyes. Of apparent cold nature, she had not joined the others in inspecting my sketch-work. Quite the opposite, she maintained a careful distance, gazed at me with impudence, seemed to harbor a disdain for Fine Art.*

"*Such rudeness could not be countenanced. I was determined to teach her a hard lesson.*"

Klara stretched. "It's dreadful stuff, no?"

"When was the book donated?" said Isaac.

"Thirty years ago. Dr. Graham was a forensic psychiatrist. He died in 1971. His sons were wealthy bankers and they gave us his books as a tax deduction."

"I need to know everyone who checked this out."

"That would be a violation of constitutional rights."

"Unless the F.B.I.'s looking for terrorists."

She didn't answer.

"Please," said Isaac. "It's essential."

"Finish reading."

When he did, she made him a copy of the booklet, then led him out of the reading room. He followed her down to her desk at the reference counter. One middle-aged woman spooled microfilm, her back to the desk. No sign of Mary or any other librarians.

Klara said, "Walk away. Over there." Pointing to a stack of periodicals.

Isaac obeyed, pulled out a copy of *The New Republic,* and pretended to read as Klara sat down at her computer, put on half glasses. Typed. Brought something to the screen.

Pursing her lips, she touched her right temple. Looked around. Returned to Isaac.

"Oh, dear," she said. "I've just gotten the worst headache. Time to find myself an aspirin before it gets out of hand."

She left, wiggling prettily.

Isaac stepped forward.

CHAPTER

46

A nurse," she said.

"Maria Giacometti," said Isaac. "Her murder was different from the others. A lot more violent. More intrusive." Instinctively, he closed his eyes, remembering the butchery. Opened them quickly, not wanting to come across squeamish.

"Escalation is typical," said Petra. "What turns them on in the beginning stops working so they get nastier."

Isaac knew that intellectually; he'd learned a term for it—sensory saturation—but saw no reason to mention that. He sat at Petra's dinette table as she leafed through the photocopy of the booklet.

Such a neat, clean, compact apartment, a faint feminine smell. Exactly what he'd imagined.

She turned a page, said, "Oh my."

At seven, she'd gone out for dinner with Eric. Then he drove up to Camarillo to visit his parents, said he'd be back in the morning. When she returned home just before nine a message from Barney Fleischer was on her machine. Isaac Gomez had been by the station, had seemed anxious to talk to her, kind of nervous. Also, Barney added, some clown from Central Gang Control was asking around about the kid.

She called the Gomez home, more out of some sort of hazy maternal obligation than expectation.

As the phone rang, she wondered if she'd wake the poor brother again. But Isaac picked up and when he learned it was her, he began talking, shouting, at warp speed. "Thank God! I've been trying to get you all day!"

"Detective Fleischer told me you—"

"I've got the *answer,* Petra. To June 28, the pattern, the motivation. Who and why, everything. Who his next victim will be."

"Who's *he?*"

Silence. "Doebbler!"

Breathing hard, almost panting.

She said, "Start at the beginning."

She picked him up in front of his building at nine-forty. He was pacing the curb, swinging his briefcase, jumped into the car before her tires stopped rolling. His eyes shot back reflected streetlight. Bright. Jumpy. She had to remind him to fasten his seat belt.

As he chattered, she drove back to her place. Initially, she'd figured on a restaurant meeting, then decided they needed total privacy. Bringing Isaac home was something she'd have considered out of the question an hour ago. Now things were different. Forget all the personal stuff; this was the job.

She finished the booklet. "Where's the list?"

Isaac pulled a folded slip of paper from the case. Computer printout from Klara's workstation.

```
Teller, T.W.J.
The Sins of the Mad Artist
Subjs: crime, U.S. history, Retzak, O.
Graham Coll. Catal. # 4211-3
```

Below that, a list of everyone who'd requested a peek at the booklet. Short list.

September 4, 1978: Professor A. R. Ritchey, Pitzer College

May 15, 1997. K. Doebbler, using an alumnus library card

Kurt Doebbler had imbibed these horrors one month and thirteen days before murdering his wife.

Seeking inspiration? Or had the bastard come across the booklet by chance and decided to emulate Otto Retzak?

She asked Isaac what he thought.

He said, "My guess would be he already knew about Retzak. He could even have read the book somewhere else and wanted to refresh his memory."

"Where else could Doebbler have gotten hold of something this obscure?"

"It's esoteric but not really that obscure. Once I had Retzak's name as a keyword, I went back on the Internet. He's been discussed in a few true-crime chat rooms and the booklet's in the holdings of at least twenty campus libraries. Also, soon after it was published initially, it was translated into French, Italian, and German. Doebbler lived in Germany as an adolescent."

"Makes sense," she said. "He could've stumbled across it, gotten stimulated, decided to take a second look." She got up and paced her small living room. Isaac watched her, then stopped abruptly and stared at the carpet.

She noticed, became aware of his maleness. Her clothing. Baggy chocolate sweater over black leggings. Skintight leggings. Revealing more thigh than she would've liked, but no one could accuse her of being seductive.

She caught Isaac's eye. He just sat there, looking like an abashed schoolboy.

She said, "Okay, let's lay it out: Marta cheated on Kurt, he found out, built up some serious anger. He'd always been a cold, controlled man, but now his control was slipping. He stewed, started to obsess, re-membered the Retzak book from his impressionable teen years. Or, he was a true-crime buff, lots of serials are—any clues from those chat rooms?"

"I skimmed them searching for some indication Doebbler was chatting. If he was, I didn't catch it."

"Let's pull them up, see if there's something traceable."

He shook his head. "Chats can't be traced because they occur in real time, aren't stored on the hard drive. I double-checked with a guy I know who's a real computer wizard and he confirmed it."

"Damn," she said, cracking her knuckles. "Okay, back on track . . . one way or the other Doebbler read about Retzak and Retzak's first murder stuck in his head: a common-law wife who ticked the guy off. Suddenly, Doebbler finds himself to be a ticked-off husband and Retzak's adventures take on a whole new meaning. That turned killing Marta into more than revenge. He was reliving history, assuming the persona of a big-time monster . . ." She shook her head. "Doebbler wanted to be Otto the Second, so seven innocent people died. It's beyond twisted but it makes sense . . . feels right."

"Victims with no apparent link gave him confidence," said Isaac. "Why would he even imagine getting caught?"

Petra smiled. "He wasn't figuring on you."

"I was lucky." Eyes back to the floor. Blushing. Cute, when he did that. She wished she could find him a genius girlfriend.

Seven innocent people.

She sat back down and reread the booklet. Despite Superintendent Teller's delicacy in dancing around the details, Maria Giacometti's murder was stomach-churning.

Retzak had been found sitting under a California oak, not far from the Elysian Park sanitarium, with the young woman's entrails around his neck. Peaceful expression on his face, knees crossed, like some homicidal yogi. Humming softly, seemingly entranced.

A hobo crossing the park spotted the horror and ran terrified to the nearest police officer. No big detective work necessary; Retzak had left a blood trail snaking from the playground kill-spot to his tree.

"Sounds like he lost it," said Petra.

"Thank God," said Isaac. "Can you imagine the next one?"

She put the booklet aside. Her head felt swollen and her heart raced.

"Seven for Mr. Retzak. Six, so far, for Mr. Doebbler," she said. "And we're going to make sure it stays that way."

◆

She fixed coffee for both of them, gave the booklet's final chapter yet another scan. Otto Retzak's final days; his arrest, trial, and execution had taken all of three weeks. The good old days.

Retzak had gone defiantly to the gallows. Proclaiming his hatred for God, humanity, and "all that you brainless sheep deem sacred. Give me a chance to leave this room and I'll brain every one of you, chew on your guts, have myself a blood and gelatin party."

Petra said, "I wonder how many Italian-American pediatric nurses are out there."

"If Doebbler's really a stickler," said Isaac, "we should be looking at an Italian-American pediatric nurse who takes care of respiratory patients."

"That would narrow it down. Not that it matters. Prevention's worth a whole lot of cure. We're going to be surveilling Doebbler starting tomorrow morning. He's not going to get close to number seven."

"Just tell me what you want me to do."

He'd scooted forward on the couch. All eagerness, misinterpreting "we."

Uh-oh.

She said, "By 'we,' I meant police officers. I can't afford to involve you in this, Isaac."

His face fell. He tried to recover with a confident nod. "Oh. Sure, I can see that. No active involvement, I'll just ride along and observe. In case you need a free set of hands or there's some function I can fill."

She shook her head. "Sorry. You're absolutely the hero of this story, without you nothing would've happened. But having civilians along on high-risk operations is a big-time no-no. Especially now. I'm in enough trouble, can't afford more."

"It's beyond absurd," he said, with sudden adamance. "Your suspension, I mean. Selden slaughters all those kids and the department's worried about picayune procedure."

"The department is a paramilitary organization. I obey, therefore I am." Putting on the calm, wise mentor persona while her mind raced: Who *did* I mean by "we"?

It would have to be her and Eric. Sorry Reverend Bob and Mary, right now I need your son more than you do.

Eric would be a major asset. He was great on surveillance, had the patience, the low resting heart rate. But a two-person surveillance was bare-bones, fine for a low-stakes, stationary watch. What if Doebbler's house provided some kind of rear escape? Or the bastard took a complicated route and they got snarled in heavy traffic?

Losing him was out of the question. No way, it just couldn't happen.

Three would be a whole lot better than two. Three pros . . .

She glanced over at Isaac. Crestfallen and trying to hide it. Could she risk it? No way. Especially not with Gang Control surveilling *him*.

Maybe she should break *that* wide open.

No, not a good idea.

Why *not*?

She said, "So, how's Flaco Jaramillo?"

He turned white. Nearly fell off the couch.

Several moments passed. "Why do you ask?"

"You tell me, Isaac."

"Tell you what?"

"Your connection to Flaco Jaramillo."

He stayed calm but his face got hard. Hawkish, a little scary. His hands tightened into fists and as he rolled them, forearms bunched, veins popping like miniature pylons. Thick arms. Some serious muscles she'd never noticed. All that brain power had made her forget this was a healthy, young man in his prime.

Now she'd tapped into something that evoked his physicality. She wondered how much of himself he'd kept from her.

"So that's it," he said.

"That's what?"

"Someone from the department's been asking about me over on campus. Some detective named Lucido."

"Bobby Lucido. He and his partner spoke to me a few days ago."

Isaac's eyes flashed with anger. "You didn't think to tell me."

"I didn't even consider it, my friend. Because I didn't know what you were up to. Still don't."

"Idiots," he mumbled. His laughter was coarse, staccato, free of amusement. "Not you. But you work with a bunch of really stupid people."

"We can't all be geniuses."

"I didn't mean it that way, Jesus." He knuckled the spot between his eyebrows, raised a rosy spot.

"They've got pictures, Isaac."

His shoulders stiffened. "Of what?"

Now I've buried myself. "Of you and a low-life dope dealer slash possible triggerman shmoozing it up in a low-life bar."

She folded her arms across her chest.

He tried to force relaxation.

His body cooperated but his eyes were way too jumpy. Just like a suspect. The kid had broken the case and now she was breaking him. Did life have to be this hard?

He said, "I can see why that might lead to a mistaken impression."

"Don't bullshit me," she said.

He blinked hard. No more hard guy, scared kid. What was real, what wasn't?

"I'm not bullshitting you," he insisted. "But there's nothing ominous going on. Flaco and I go back. We grew up together, I tutored him in grade school. In public school, before I got into Burton. We run into each other from time to time. I know he's been in trouble, but I've never been involved in any of that. A few days ago, he called me up and asked me to meet him. To help him out with a family matter."

"What kind of family matter?"

"His mother's sick. Cancer. She's illegal, can't qualify for Medi-Cal. He was under the impression I was already in medical school, figured I could help her get free medical care. He's always about that, getting an angle. I went to see him because he used to stick up for me when we were kids. I explained that I wasn't in the system. He didn't want to hear that, got persistent. I told him I'd look into it. When I got back to campus, I made a few calls. Couldn't do a thing. Told him. That's it."

"Is it?"

"Yes, dammit."

"You're not a dope courier?"

His eyes got wide. "Are you insane?"

Petra didn't answer.

"I promise, Petra. I swear. I've never had anything to do with dope. *Never.* And growing up the way I did there was no lack of opportunity. Flaco's a psychopath and a felon but we don't hang together. This was about doing a favor, that's all, and I think it's crazy that I'm being persecuted for it. I guess you couldn't tell me earlier, but if you had, I could've cleared it up."

"Sick mother," she said.

"Yes."

"That can be verified pretty easily."

"Verify away." His dark eyes met hers and held the gaze. His fists had uncurled. He looked tired.

Petra said, "There was some curiosity about your briefcase. Flaco going up to the bar, maybe getting something to give you under the table."

He laughed. "The briefcase? Have you ever seen me without it? Here, want to check?" He picked up the case, offered it to her.

Praying.

"It's okay," she said.

"I've never sold dope and I'm certainly no mule. Jesus, Petra, can you imagine what would happen to my med school career if I got caught doing something like that?" He frowned. "What *still* might happen if your idiot colleagues keep harassing me?" He gnawed his lip. "Maybe it's time for me to get an attorney."

"Do what you need to do. But I can't imagine that any kind of publicity could help you."

"True, true." He shook his head. "What a mess."

"If nothing happened, there won't be a problem."

"How can I prove a negative?" he said.

"Take a polygraph. If it comes to that. Once this is resolved I'll do what I can to run interference for you. So it's important for *your* sake that I don't lose any more department brownie points. Is there anything else you haven't told me?"

"No. Your suspension, that didn't have anything to do with me, did it?"

"No, that I did all by my little lonesome."

She got up, poured yet more coffee for herself, offered him a refill.

"No, thanks."

"Any more insights on Doebbler?"

He shook his head.

She said, "I'll drive you home."

"I can take the bus."

"No way," she said. "Not at this hour. By the way, that bruise you were sporting. What really happened?"

"My brother and I had a little scuffle," he said. "Nothing serious, you know what it's like with siblings."

"You guys are a little old for roughhousing."

"Isaiah's a good guy, Petra, but life's hard for him. He works like a dog, doesn't get enough sleep."

"Last time I called you, I woke him, poor guy."

Isaac smiled. "He told me." He got to his feet, lifted the briefcase.

Petra said, "All right, I'm glad we cleared the air."

"Me, too."

They left her apartment, stepped out into the warm June air. Twenty-five hours until the killing hour.

"I meant what I said before, Isaac. You really are the hero."

"On the other hand, if I hadn't spotted the pattern, you never would have had to worry about it."

"Yeah, ignorance can be bliss," she said. "But I like it better this way."

CHAPTER

47

The plastics fabricator, a massive, white, windowless hatbox, two miles north of the freeway, was ringed by an open, un-guarded asphalt lot. The space was half-filled with cars and trucks and vans. Lots of empty slots in random places. The first few rows provided a nice clear diagonal view of the smaller brick structure across the street.

Sand-colored brick. Mirrored windows, cursory landscaping, black block lettering above the mirrored front door. *Pacific Dynamics.*

Kurt Doebbler's workplace was less welcoming than its looming neighbor. Wrought-iron fencing surrounded the property. A slot-key parking arm bisected the entry. You could walk under, but no drive-through. No front parking either. A driveway snaked down to the left of the building and continued around to the west side. Once Doeb-bler's Infiniti made the turn, no visual access. Damn.

Petra was wondering about rear entry to the building when Doeb-bler's tall, angular form appeared at the top of the drive, walking slowly, almost tentatively, on long, thin legs. He wore a short-sleeved, pale-green shirt, brown slacks, white running shoes. Dunkin' Donuts bag in one hand, steel attaché case in the other. With his black-framed glasses and loose-limbed shamble, the guy was a walking promo for the Nerd Channel.

Nothing humorously quirky about this nerd. She watched as Doebbler strode over to Pacific Dynamics' front door and walked in.

That was at nine-thirty A.M. It was five hours later and nothing had happened and Petra and Eric remained at opposite ends of the Plexi-Tech lot, drinking coffee, chewing on the dry sandwiches she'd packed. Communication was cell phone speed-dials.

A couple of those nifty, hard-to-jam, two-way radios the department had just stocked up on would've been nice.

An officially sanctioned departmental investigation of Kurt Doebbler would've been nice.

Hot, sunny day this far west. Chemical smell in the air, and despite the heat, the sky was sheathed by a sickly gray cloud cover. She'd phoned Eric at his folks' home last night, just before midnight, after dropping Isaac at home. The kid was clearly dejected about being excluded from the stakeout but pulled it off with grace. Once this was over, she'd fix the misunderstanding over Flaco Jaramillo.

At first, Eric didn't pick up and she wondered if he'd gone to sleep early. Normally he was a night owl, but the Reverend Bob and Mrs. Stahl retired early, so maybe he'd conformed.

Sleeping in his boyhood room in the modest, Camarillo ranch house. The pennants and poster and athletic trophies his parents had held on to. The military medals he'd wanted to throw out, arranged on a corkboard by mom.

Just as she was about to hang up, he said, "Hi."

"Did I wake you?"

"No, I'm up."

"Sorry to pull you away, but June 28 seems to have clicked." She told him about Otto Retzak, Doebbler's reenacting hundred-year-old murders.

He said, "When do you need me?"

◆

The next day the two of them met up at six forty-five A.M. at a taco stand on Reseda Boulevard one mile north of Ventura. A five-minute drive to Doebbler's house on Rosita.

Eric, a stranger to the quarry, was the obvious choice as the up close. He headed north in his Jeep, found the pale-gray traditional, continued up the street, and U-turned into a tree-shaded watch-spot. Sitting low at the wheel, shielded by windows tinted way darker than the legal limit.

Quiet block; a few sleek women jogged by and late-model foreign sedans pulled out of driveways as men in suits left for work. The Jeep was black, unobtrusive, a perfect match for the neighborhood. If anyone asked, Eric had several alternative stories ready. Police I.D. if it came to that.

It didn't.

Petra was stationed just south of Ventura, pulled over to the east curb, ready to tail Doebbler if he headed for the 101 or turned either way onto the boulevard. A left turn was most likely; Pacific Dynamics was sixteen miles west.

At eight-fifteen, Eric called in. "Doebbler and the daughter are getting into the Infiniti. . . . He's backing out, driving east. Unless her school is somewhere up in the hills, he should be passing you soon. I'll have a quick look around the back of the house and catch up with you."

Minutes later, Doebbler's champagne-colored sedan cruised through a green light at Ventura. Petra let two more cars pass before she pulled out and followed. Doebbler bypassed the freeway, continued north until Riverside, turned left, drove four blocks, then hung a right. Three more blocks and the Infiniti was pulling into a line of cars facing West Valley Comprehensive Preparatory Academy. A rent-a-cop directed the slow-moving motor queue. No sign of Eric. She'd call and let him know where she was. But just as she started to punch in the speed-code, she spotted a black Jeep in her rearview. Someone else's? No, the blackout windows and the dusty grille meant Eric. He passed her without acknowledgment, drove past the motor queue, faded from view.

Petra parked and kept her eye on Doebbler. The Infiniti was easy to spot: lone sedan in a stop-and-go parade of four-wheelers. Trim, well-coiffed moms in too-big motorized behemoths dropped off well-fed kids in school uniforms as they talked into cell phones. White shirts for the student body. Olive pants for the boys, olive-plaid skirts for the girls.

A strawberry blonde in a blue Volvo C-70 drove past. Emily Pastern at the wheel. Two kids in the back of the convertible. Petra sank lower.

The rent-a-cop waved. Doebbler inched forward.

West Valley Comprehensive Prep was a small place with a big name, what looked to be four fifties-era apartments converted into a school. A stingy grassy area in the center, the whole thing behind high iron fencing. The kids hunched under oversized backpacks were all white, with a high proportion of blonds. The Infiniti made it to the gate and Katya Doebbler, tall for her age, her straight, dark hair pulled into a ponytail, got out and walked through the school's gates without a word or a backward glance at her father.

Sad-looking kid. Soon, she'd be a lot sadder.

Doebbler pulled into the street and continued up the block. A second later, Eric called. "It's a cul-de-sac, I'm going to hang back."

"I'll pick him up," said Petra.

Emily Pastern unloaded her brood and got out to talk to another mother. Petra shifted into Drive, ready for Doebbler. She caught a glimpse of the bastard as he sailed by, oblivious. Sitting tall, staring straight ahead, bespectacled, sharp-jawed. Expressionless.

Both hands on the wheel. The perfect ten-three driving position.

Law-abiding citizen.

Back on Reseda. A commuter rush curdled the two blocks just north of Ventura Boulevard, but Eric managed to regain the number-one position and when Doebbler made his westward turn, the Jeep was three cars behind.

Both vehicles rolling along in the slow lane. From the center lane, five cars back, Petra watched as Eric maintained a steady tail, unobtrusive to the point of invisible. His style was silky, effortless, a surveillance ballet that never lost sight of the quarry. Her man had grace.

Her man.

She laughed out loud. Didn't like the sound of that and said, "Oh, shut up."

◆

Doebbler turned the trip to Westlake Village into a leisurely, slow-lane cruise. Staying on Ventura, giving every amber light the benefit of the doubt, allowing other motorists to cut in and pass, making full stops for pedestrians.

Getting busted for a traffic violation wouldn't do. Not when you had big plans for tonight.

Half a mile short of his work address, Doebbler pulled into a Dunkin' Donuts, got out and ordered, emerged with a bag.

Junk-food breakfast? Who'da thunk?

He returned to his car with that same robot-face.

Scary; did it all come down to weird wiring?

Doebbler looked around briefly, got back in the Infiniti, resumed his leisurely exploration of the broad, sun-washed western tip of the Valley.

Five hours, eighteen minutes of boredom.

In all that time, two interruptions.

At ten-forty, Eric crossed the street to Pacific Dynamics and walked under the parking arm. Retracing the Infiniti's path, he walked down the westside driveway and was gone for ten minutes.

When he popped back up at Petra's window, he said, "Loading dock, bolted from the outside, doesn't appear to be in active use. The lot's aboveground, one level's interior, the top's out in the open. Doebbler's parked on top. If he drives out, he'll have to come back the way he went in."

"What about on foot?"

"Fifteen-and-a-half-foot block wall at the back. On the other side's some kind of warehouse. Unless he's a rock-climber, there's no alternative exit. He leaves, we see him."

At eleven-fifty, Petra left for a much-needed bathroom break, driving all the way back to Ventura before she found an accommodating Denny's. Picking up some fries for fortification, as long as she was at it.

Some for Eric, too, and she hazarded a sprint to the Jeep to give it to him.

Moments later, right after she'd settled back in her own car, thirty-three people exited Pacific Dynamics in small, chatty groups, got into their cars, and drove away. Twenty-five men, mostly in shirtsleeves, like Doebbler. Eight woman, equally casual.

Lunchtime. No sign of the quarry.

"Maybe he's eating donuts," said Petra. "Carbo-loading for his big night." Eric's voice through the phone was soft. "Working at his desk would fit a compulsive personality."

Which could apply to Eric. And her.

She glanced two aisles up, where the Jeep was parked. "Kind of weird, having to talk to you this way. How about some phone sex?"

"Sure," he said. "But only as prep for the real thing."

By three-twenty, Doebbler still hadn't appeared. Just to be sure they hadn't missed something, Eric called his work number. Doebbler picked up and Eric said, "Mr. Doebbler?"

"Yes."

"This is Dwayne Hickham from New Jersey Life. Have you considered term—"

Click.

"Friendly fellow," said Petra.

Eric didn't answer.

At three fifty-three, her phone squawked. Her butt was sore, she had a hunger-headache, and her bladder was bursting. The scene through her windshield was a damned oil painting. What could Eric have to say?

She pressed Talk. "What's up?"

A cheerful voice said "Detective Connor?" Teutonic accent.

"Chief Inspector Bandorffer."

"Yes, this is Klaus. I thought this might be a good hour to reach you."

"It is, sir. What's up?"

"What's up," said Bandorffer, "is that I came across something intriguing in our records. Not a serial homicide, not a homicide at all. An assault. But it occurred on June 28 and the details are provocative."

"What year?" said Petra.

"Nineteen seventy-nine. A young woman named Gudrun Wiegeland, a cake-icer at one of our finest bakeries, was attacked while walking home. She'd been decorating an elaborate wedding cake, left work shortly before midnight. Two blocks from her destination, someone hooked an arm around her neck, pulled her down onto the street, turned her over onto her stomach, and began kicking at her ribs. Then she experienced crushing pain at the back of her head. The attacker remained behind her so unfortunately she never saw him. Her injuries were serious. Three broken ribs, bruised internal organs, and a fractured skull. She was unconscious for two days, woke up and had nothing of value to tell the police. I paid her a visit today. She's a frightened, middle-aged woman, lives with her elderly mother and collects public assistance. She rarely ventures out of her apartment."

"Poor thing."

"Fraulein Wiegeland had a reputation as a wild girl, and our men suspected a former lover, a pastry baker with a drinking problem. The two of them had engaged in public arguments. But the man was able to account for his whereabouts and the crime was never solved. I have confirmed that your Mr. Doebbler and his family were living at the Army base during that time period."

"How many blows were delivered to the head?" said Petra.

"One," said Bandorffer.

"Our boy bashes his victims repeatedly," said Petra.

"Perhaps he panicked. Being young and inexperienced. If it was your boy."

Twenty-four years ago, Kurt Doebbler had been eighteen.

The creepo *had* come across the Teller book as an adolescent and something had twisted up inside him.

Raging hormones. Sexual confusion.

A kink in some nerve fiber, Lord knew what else.

Plotting and planning but unable to pull off his virgin murder. Had he dealt with failure by pulling back until eighteen years later?

Or just the opposite?

Other cities, other Junes. The thought was sickening. Either way, Marta's cheating had been a catalyst. Stoking—or restoking—the fires.

She said, "Thank you, Inspector."

"My pleasure, Detective. Please let me know if you come up with a solution."

Bandorffer hung up.

Petra thought: Isaac had nailed it again.

CHAPTER

48

This is lovely," said Klara. She rolled the bedcovers down to her waist, ran her hands over soft, white, spreading breasts, pinched her own pink nipple and watched with satisfaction as it inflated. Reaching over to the chipped nightstand, she lifted her wineglass and sipped.

Fifteen-dollar bottle of chardonnay; she'd insisted on paying.

Isaac lay on his back, next to her, staring up at cottage cheese plaster-spray. Studying the brown stain where the air-conditioning vent had leaked. Brown inkblot, like a Rorschach . . .

"Isn't it?" said Klara, wetting her finger with wine and tracing it along his upper lip. "Lovely?"

He nodded. In his position, that meant bobbing at the ceiling.

She leaned over and chewed his earlobe. "You were a bit more enthusiastic five minutes ago, my dear. You were *more* than enthusiastic. *Volcanic,* I'd say."

Isaac smiled. The brown stain had a definite shape. Two bears, a large one and a small one, facing off. Or dancing. What did that say about his unconscious?

"My personal Vesuvius," said Klara. She reached down. "Ready for another eruption?"

Isaac's member was sore and his neck ached, but Klara had all kinds of skills, and the second time ended up being fine. Afterward, she said, "Shower time," and sashayed into the tiny motel bathroom, flaunting the fullness of her body, unfazed by slackness of waist, drooping bosom, the occasional clot of cellulite. He liked her better for that and when she yelled, "Come on in," he complied. And when she pulled him under the spray for a deep kiss, he didn't mind at all.

The shower stall was prefab fiberglass, just like the one at home but not as clean. Klara soaped him with enthusiasm, positioned his hands all over her slick, dolphin softness, threw back her head and laughed into the water.

"Pretend it's a waterfall," she said. "Somewhere exotic, just the two of us."

She shampooed her hair with a travel bottle she'd brought, rinsed, squeezed her red hair dry and wrapped it in a towel. They returned to the queen-sized bed with its coin-slotted "Electric Fingers" gadget bolted to the fake wood headboard.

Tawdry. Isaac was surprised at how much he liked that.

Somehow, he wasn't sure when the transition had occurred, he'd turned into someone else. The person he imagined when he made love to her.

Horny Latin stud bunking down with a willing, flame-haired woman. Trysting in a cheesy, claustrophobic room with cigarette burns along the curtain hems, the odors of sin and beer and instant coffee rising from the thin, worn carpet.

Casa Figueroa. Two stories of mud-colored, spray-stucco under a fake tile roof. Thirty-two AAA-sanctioned rooms looking down on a kidney-shaped swimming pool, individual entrances for each unit. Klara had paid with her Discover card, taken the key from the clerk with panache, swung her rear as she led Isaac up the stairs.

Not a trace of shame. That made it easier for him. Still, if his mother, or anyone from church, had seen him . . .

She'd done all the planning. Arranged a babysitter for her gifted daughter and son, brought the wine and condoms and a roll of quarters for the vibrating bed.

And a Hershey bar that she broke in half. "Dessert, m'dear?"

They both ate candy.

"Fattening," said Klara, licking chocolate from her lips. "But loaded with good stuff, too, like antioxidants. We deserve some fun. Solving a big case like that."

She'd found him at six P.M., down in the stacks, working on his data and trying not to think of what Petra was doing. Marching right up to him, she took his hand and slipped it under her dress.

No panties.

Isaac's face got hot. She knew she had him and grinned. "Pack your books, sir, we're out of here."

They watched twenty minutes of an atrocious show on USA Network as Klara combed out her hair. At the commercial break, she said, "Time to go home, sweetie. Domestic obligations and all that. We'll do this again." Her tongue thrust between his lips, sweet with chocolate. "Sooner rather than later."

As Isaac walked her to her car, she said, "It really is fantastic. The way we solved all those murders. I mean, just think of it, Isaac. People like us—book people—turning out to be the real detectives."

"You're the master sleuth, Klara."

She slapped his shoulder lightly. "Of course I'm *not*! I was merely the tool of *your* intellect."

They reached her car and she rested her head on his shoulder. Sensing that she needed more praise, he said, "Klara, I couldn't have done anything without you."

She stood there pressed against him in the dim, tacky motel parking lot. Finally, she straightened and unlocked her car. "I read it again," she said. "That horrible little book." She shuddered. "How could anyone be so evil?"

Isaac shrugged.

"I mean it," she said. "How do you explain something like that?"

"Retzak claimed he was abused."

"Lots of people are abused, but they don't end up like that."

"True."

She took his hand, played with his fingers. "I know you need to be discreet and all, but was that guy, the one the police are focusing on, abused? Because there'd have to be parallels, right? Between him and Retzak. Otherwise why imitate Retzak and not just do his own thing?"

"I don't know," he said. "Don't know much about him."

"Well," she said, "one thing we do know: He's evil. And you've made a major contribution to getting him off the streets."

"The police will do that."

"Hopefully, they'll be competent," she said. "Because I have to tell you, I haven't always found that to be the case. One time, years ago, there was a burglary in my neighborhood—one of my neighbors, a woman living alone—and all the police did was fill out reports."

"The detective on this case is great," said Isaac. Sounding defensive.

Klara said, "I hope he is. Anyway, when you can tell me more, please do, the whole thing fascinates me. I was a history major at Smith, but I've always been curious about psychology. About what transforms people. It's the greatest mystery of all, right?" She touched his cheek. "One day, you'll be a physician. Not a psychiatrist, but who knows, maybe you'll get closer to figuring it out."

"Right now I'd be satisfied finishing my dissertation."

"You'll finish. You've got character and people with character finish what they begin."

She opened her car door, took his face in both her hands. "I believe in you, Isaac Gomez. I don't love you, never will. But I sure like you a lot. Can we be friends?"

"We already are."

Her eyes moistened. Then the right one winked. "Time to go home and be a mom. But I'll be thinking about volcanoes."

CHAPTER

49

THURSDAY, JUNE 27, 9:21 P.M., THE DOEBBLER RESIDENCE, ROSITA AVENUE, TARZANA

He's here." Eric's whisper barely filtered through the phone.

"Doing what?" said Petra.

"Reading a magazine and doing hand exercises."

"Hand exercises?"

"With a spring-grip. While he reads."

"Getting in shape for his big night. Any weapon in sight?"

"No."

"He probably keeps it in one of the cars," she said. "What about Katya?"

"Not here."

"She's probably upstairs. The day I interviewed him she stayed up there the whole time. He look tense?"

"Not really."

"Normal demeanor?"

"Expressionless," said Eric.

"That's normal for him."

She clicked off and her cell phone went dark. Two lines on the gizmo, but only one was open on vibrator mode. And only for Eric. After too many interruptions by telemarketers, she and Eric had decided to have all calls but theirs forwarded to their land phones. It took a bit of doing, but they shared the same cellular carrier and by eight-thirty, they were functionally locked in. Every half hour, each of them checked for messages to make sure they didn't miss anything. The last time had been ten minutes ago: a couple of junkers and a call from her brother Brad. Nothing urgent, he just wanted to say hi. She'd deal with that tomorrow.

After all this was over.

Shifting in the driver's seat, she drank bottled water, popped a couple of Skittles, maintained her visual fix on the gray house. Determined, this time, to spot Eric as he emerged from the backyard and returned to his Jeep.

She was fifteen yards from Doebbler's front door, facing west. The Jeep was a ways up, just out of view, aimed east. No matter which direction Doebbler took, someone would be ready to pick him up.

A few trees, but good visibility on the dark street. And fences prevented escape from one property to the next.

Doebbler would have to show himself.

Ten plus hours of nothing. Petra's brain was starting to crumble from disuse.

At four-thirty P.M., Kurt Doebbler had left Pacific Dynamics along with a slew of other employees. After picking up a Domino's pizza, he drove to Katya's school, made it just before five. At that hour, West Valley Comprehensive Prep looked closed, but Doebbler's bell-ring brought a sullen Katya to the gate, accompanied by a gray-haired, female teacher-type who let the girl out.

Some kind of after-school day-care thing. The teacher smiled and said something to Doebbler who left without responding. No conversation between father and daughter as they headed for the Infiniti. Katya's backpack looked stuffed. Doebbler made no attempt to carry it for her.

The Infiniti headed straight home, arrived at five twenty-six. Doebbler walked to the door with that dorky stride of his, stayed several feet ahead of Katya, remote-locked the vehicle without glancing back. The girl hurried to catch up and he did hold the door for her as she entered the house.

He collected his mail from the box bolted next to the door, stood outside shuffling through envelopes. Not a glance up the street as he stepped inside and closed the door.

Why would he be nervous? He'd pulled it off six years in a row.

Since then, no sign of him or the girl and both of Doebbler's cars remained in the driveway. At nine o'clock, Petra and Eric agreed that someone should have a look from the backyard, just to make sure the quarry hadn't managed to sneak out on foot.

Someone was Eric.

Petra's watch read 9:28. He'd been back there eight minutes, still hadn't emerged. Had something engaged him?

Her phone vibrated.

"Me again."

"Where are you?"

"Back in the car."

"I was looking for you. How the hell do you *do* that?"

"Do what?"

"Mr. Invisible."

"I just walked."

"Sure you did, Master Ninja." Making light of it but failing to spot him bugged her. Despite her determination to focus, had her mind wandered? God, she hated stakeouts, the erosion of I.Q.

"What kept you there so long?"

"Watching."

"Anything new?"

"No."

Hell would be an *infinity* of stakeouts.

They cut the connection and Petra ate more candy. Brain-death and tooth decay. A minimum of two and half hours to kill-time and Doebbler was sitting in his easy chair, reading a magazine and flexing his hands.

What, the latest edition of *Modern Murderer*?

Working on his grip strength. Maybe that meant he *was* getting edgy.

Two and a half hours; had he planned so well that there was no need to leave any earlier?

Preselecting the prey. A nurse. Someone who took care of children. Maybe with lung disease. Maybe an Italian girl, if he was imitating Retzak that closely.

She'd already confirmed that no hospital remained in Elysian Park. When it came to kids, the first thing you thought of was Western Pediatrics Medical Center, back in Hollywood. Not that far from the park, she could see it appealing to Doebbler.

At this hour, Western Peds was at least a half-hour freeway ride from Tarzana, probably longer, so Doebbler was really cutting it close.

Petra knew the hospital's shift schedule because Billy Straight had been taken there and she'd spent plenty of time at his bedside. Afternoons: three to eleven. Meaning day nurses would be heading for their cars between eleven and eleven-thirty as the night shift arrived. Lots of women walking to and from the outdoor lots.

Shabby side streets, East Hollywood. Not the greatest area and security was lax, but in all her time at Hollywood Division, she hadn't heard of any serious problems.

With all those women, how would Doebbler pick a victim?

He'd picked already.

Five minutes passed. Ten, fifteen, still no movement from the gray house. A trip to Hollywood seemed increasingly unlikely, so she was probably wrong about Western Peds. Okay, there had to be lots of pediatric units all over the city.

With the time ticking away, Doebbler had probably aimed closer to home. Somewhere right here in the Valley.

Northridge Hospital was a fifteen-minute drive, even less with no traffic. Did Northridge nurses follow the same schedule as the Western Peds staff?

Speed-dialing Eric, she let him know her line would be busy for a few minutes and made the call. The Northridge night clerk confirmed it: three to eleven.

More than enough time for Doebbler to get over there. She had no idea how the parking was laid out at Northridge.

No confidence the site would *be* Northridge.

The Valley was a big place. When Doebbler made his move, she'd have to improvise.

Didn't it always come down to that?

CHAPTER

50

From the upper bunk came the sound of Isaiah's snoring, loud and intrusive as a leaf blower. The eldest Gomez brother had come home late and exhausted, in a foul mood that silenced the rest of the family. Flinging his work clothes on the floor, he'd lurched straight to bed.

Tar reek bittered the room. Along with alcohol. Isaac would keep that to himself, no reason to upset Mama.

On the other side of the cell-like space, Joel slept on his air mattress, eyes closed, chest rising and falling slowly, a smile on his almost-pretty face. A maddeningly cheerful bundle of libido and superficiality, Joel would always be happy.

Isaac, sapped from his motel time with Klara, had eaten lightly and fallen asleep quickly. His dream cycle was frantic and ambiguous. In the midst of an abstract expressionist nightmare, he woke drenched with sweat and disoriented. The din from the top bunk told him where he was. God bless Isaiah's deviated septum.

Now he was wide awake, trying not to think about Klara but, of course, thinking of nothing else.

Not the things she'd done. Something she'd said.

There would have to be parallels . . . otherwise why imitate Retzak.

An eccentric woman, probably neurotic woman, but smart. Too smart to be ignored and now Isaac was sweating for another reason.

A big fat balloon of denial punctured.

It's out of your hands. Petra knows what she's doing.

Reaching out for the wooden crate that served as his nightstand, he got hold of his watch: 11:02.

Less than an hour to showdown. Soon it would be over.

Would it?

He closed his eyes and the facts loomed larger. Discrepancies impossible to ignore. Sliding out of the bunk, he found his briefcase, tiptoed across the closet-sized space.

Isaiah moved and bedsprings squeaked. A mumbled: "Whu?"

Isaac left the bedroom, closing the door silently, and went into the kitchen, hoping his parents in the neighboring room wouldn't hear him. His mother, in particular, had the sleep rhythms of a Chihuahua.

Switching on the dim light under the stove, he sat and thought. Decided he wasn't being psychotic.

Pulling his laptop out of the case and plugging it in—shifting the rag-wrapped gun in the process—he rummaged some more and finally came up with his seldom-used modem. Connecting the box to the corner phone jack behind the table, he booted up and hoped for the best. He'd set up the modem years ago but rarely used it. No reason to, given high-speed access on campus. The apartment's phone wires were eroded and chancy. Even if he got a line, making it to the Internet would be an infuriatingly slow ordeal.

Neanderthal dial-up. What a joke.

Spoiled boy.

Scared boy.

The modem squawked. Stopped. Made more noise.

His mother padded in, rubbing her eyes. "What're you doing?"

"Studying."

"At this hour?"

"I thought of something."

"What?"

"My research, it's not important, Ma."

"If it's not important, you should go back to sleep." She blinked, couldn't focus. "Go back to sleep. You don't sleep enough."

"In a few minutes, Ma. It's my doctoral research."

"It can't wait until tomorrow?"

"No, Ma. Go back to sleep."

The modem buzzed and hummed and beeped, kept chirping its little modem song. Interminable!

"What's that?" said his mother.

"The thing that connects to the Internet."

"Why's it plugged in there?"

"I'm using our phone line."

"What if someone calls?"

"No one's going to call, Mama."

She looked at the stove. "I'll fix you something to eat."

"No." He raised his voice and she gave a start. He got up and placed an arm around her shoulder. "No, thank you, Ma. Really, I'm fine."

"I . . ." She looked around the kitchen.

He guided her back to her room. Wasn't sure she'd really been awake.

When he returned to the kitchen table, the connection had been completed and he logged on to his university server. Scanning his bookmarks, he found the chat room text he'd saved, began retracing cyber-steps.

Five minutes later, his heart was pounding so hard, it felt as if it would rip through his rib cage.

```
Online Host:  *****You are in BloodnGutsChat*****
CrimeGirl: The way i see it OttoR was = to Manson or
    anyone.
BulldogD: U shouldn't glarify him he was just anther
    semi organize serial
CrimeGirl: It's not glorifying (spell-boy!!) It's tell-
    ing it like it is.
```

```
BulldogD: I can spell I just don't bothe
CrimeGirl: Yeah right. I still think OR was interest-
    ing maybe unique for his time.
P-Kasso: You're both missing the point.
Mephisto: Hey look! There's always some guy with a
    point.
CrimeGirl: I for one want to hear an intellegient
    point. Speak, P.
P-Kasso: Retzak stands above the others because of his
    artistic integrity. His motivation is far more ele-
    vated than manson, bundy, JTR, anyone of that ilk.
    For him it was all about art, he captured the scene,
    I'd put him more like Van Gogh
Mephisto: Did he cut off his ear haha
CrimeGirl: Funny. Not.
BulldogD: Pee-Kasso. What U're one of those artsty
    fartsies, too that's why U see it that way???
Mephisto: No asnwer?
P-Kasso: I've been known to wield a brush.
BulldogD: How about a stout cudgel?
Mephisto: No answer now?
CrimeGirl: Guess he left.
Mephisto: Chickenshit.
CrimeGirl: There's no need for that kind of la
P-Kasso: I'm still here. But now I'm leaving. You peo-
    ple are brainless.
Mephisto: Arrogant asshole.
CrimeGirl: Im still waiting for intelligence in a y
    chromosomer.
BulldogD: What about John Gacey? Buddies with Jimmy
    Carter And all the time he's burying bodies
Mephisto: It was Rosmarie Carter
CrimeGirl: Rosalyn, fact-boy
```

P-Kasso: a self-styled artist. Retzak's biggest fan.

Isaac rescrolled the chat, read it again. Felt his fingers go cold. Logging off, he unplugged the modem, hurried to the wall phone, punched in Petra's cell.

It connected to her land line. Her machine; he talked to it, trying not to sound weak or scared or frantic, guessing that he'd failed.

Would she call home for messages? Why would she? Busy on stake-out.

Thinking she knew.

The clock on the stove said: 11:11.

P-Kasso.

Rushing back to his room, he looked for his shoes, couldn't find them, felt around under the bunk, finally got hold of the right loafer, then its mate. He'd gone to sleep in a T-shirt and sweatpants, no socks. That would have to do. Shoes in hand, he ran toward the door.

Isaiah sat up. "What the . . ."

"Sweet dreams, bro."

"Where . . . goin'?"

"Out."

Down on the floor Joel rolled to the wall. Rolled back. Smiled.

Isaiah said, "Goin' out for more pussy?"

Isaac closed the door on both of them.

Isaiah owned a pickup truck that needed an engine. The sole operating Gomez vehicle was the intermittently operant Toyota Corolla Papa chanced driving to work. Papa's keys dangled from a plastic frog screwed to the wall next to the fridge.

The car was just back from the shop, new filters of some sort. Isaac slipped the ignition key off his father's ring, began sneaking across the kitchen, feeling like a burglar, before he stopped.

Minor omission.

He corrected that. Left.

CHAPTER

51

You're sure?" said Petra.

Eric had just returned from another look behind the house. This time she'd seen him emerge, the faintest black smudge against the indigo Valley night. He'd probably showed himself on purpose, to make her feel good.

"No more magazine, he was watching TV. I couldn't get an angle to see the screen. At eleven sharp, he got up, turned off the light, went upstairs."

Less than an hour to go. Both of Doebbler's cars were in place.

"You're sure there's no way he can leave from behind?"

"Steep hillside up to the neighbor's property, then wrought-iron fencing. Anything's possible but—"

"If it's *possible* we need to *worry* about it." Little Miss Shrew. Before she could apologize, Eric said, "Want me to go back there and stay?"

"That would mean no two-way view of the street, but maybe . . ."

"Just tell me."

"What do you think?"

"Tough call," he said.

"This doesn't feel right, Eric. Even if the kill-spot's some close-by clinic, he's cutting it too close. He's compulsive. Would take his time setting it up."

"Maybe he's preparing right now. In his head."

"Maybe," she said. "Okay, look, go back there. If nothing happens within ten . . . fifteen minutes, I'm marching up to the front and ringing the bell."

No response.

"You think it's a bad idea?"

"No," he said. "I'm on my way right now."

CHAPTER

52

The Toyota stalled again.

Third time in a mile. Isaac shifted into neutral, coasted into the right lane as cars sped around him. Depressing the clutch, then releasing as he gassed, he tried to revive the ignition. A sputter, a nanosecond of panic, and the puny engine was chugging again. Pausing on the brink of death . . . resuscitating.

Barely.

Freakin' piece of junk. So much for Montalvo, his father's friend, the alleged mechanic.

Or maybe it was his own fault—poor stick-shift skills. It had been a long time since he'd gotten behind the wheel.

He snail-crawled north on Vermont, struggling to keep the gas flow even, anticipating lights and working at minimizing unnecessary stops and starts.

Half-moon night, pebbled lunar light filtering through neon and smog and humidity. No shortage of activity on Vermont at this hour. Rainbows of neon in Spanish, then Korean, then Spanish again. The car wheezed steadily past darkened buildings that alternated with the flash and buzz of bars and liquor stores and clubs.

Asian kids milling around the better-looking clubs. Nice clothing, souped up wheels that worked. The confident smiles of affluent youth.

Then back to the working-class Mexican and Salvadoran joints.

Vamos a bailar . . .

English was his language, his passport to some suburban Xanadu, but sometimes he dreamed in Spanish. Mostly, he didn't dream.

Music poured out of a raunchy-looking dance-place as he putt-putted by.

The gaiety didn't seem right for killing time.

Neither did the weather; warm night, a pleasant breeze.

Maybe this *wasn't* killing time.

Had to be. No, it didn't. Look how *wrong* he'd been.

P-Kasso.

Even if something was going to happen tonight, he'd almost certainly embarked on a fool's mission.

Heading for a destination based on theory and the cold, flat religion that was logic.

The single best deduction, given the facts. But what did facts mean?

Chances were he was wrong, yet again. Dreadfully, tragically wrong.

At Third Street, the Toyota sputtered and threatened to die once more. Holding his breath he pressed down gently on the accelerator and the damn thing relented.

He made it to Fourth, Beverly . . .

Idiotic and quixotic, but what else could he do? Petra's cell was still transferred—some police thing, for sure, what the cops called a tactical line. And contacting anyone else at the department was out of the question. Would bring the cops looking for *him.*

Four-fifteen mental case, male Hispanic, heading north on Vermont in a moribund clunker.

He passed Melrose. Just another couple of miles . . .

And then what?

He'd park at a safe distance, proceed on foot. Check out the layout and find some kind of vantage point.

Playing detective.

The object of his guess: Western Pediatrics Hospital. The one place you could count on a slew of nurses who took care of children.

He'd rotated through Western Peds as a pre-med sophomore. Introduced by a bio professor who wanted aspiring physicians to see what health care was really like.

Isaac had found the hospital a wonderful, terrifying place, brimming with compassion, frantic activity, the saddest stories of all.

The big-eyed stares of very sick kids. Bald heads, waxy skin, stick-limbs tethered to I.V. lines.

He'd decided, then and there, that pediatrics wasn't for him.

Now he was headed back there on a return trip so terribly asinine it made him tremble.

The car made a retching noise. Isaac's body lurched backward as the vehicle accelerated spontaneously. He maintained shaky control, rolled through an intersection just south of Santa Monica. Violated a boulevard stop and narrowly avoided being pulverized by a house-sized supermarket truck.

The trucker's klaxon rage filled his ears as he kept going.

Two seconds later, the Toyota gave up.

On foot.

Jogging the half-mile to Sunset, staying in the darkness, close to buildings so as not to attract attention.

Male mental case running north . . .

He reached his destination by eleven forty-three, slowed his pace, and stayed on the south side of the boulevard as he ambled toward the big, blocky buildings of the hospital complex.

Most of the structures were dark. The Western Peds logo—a pair of blue-and-white clasped hands—glowed from the top of the main building.

He remained in the shadows as women, mostly young women, in white and pale pink and pastel blue and canary yellow uniforms, streamed out of several doors and crossed Sunset.

Only twenty or so nurses, stragglers at the end of the day shift. If through some miracle he was right, the bastard would be watching.

But from *where*?

Isaac watched the nurses arrive at a sign that said "Staff Parking." Arrows pointed both ways and the group split into two. Most of the women headed west, a few east.

Two lots. Which way?

He thought it out. If Doebbler were here, he'd want things as quiet as possible.

East.

He followed five distant, female shapes down a surprisingly dim street. Shabby apartment buildings, not unlike his own, lined the journey. Half a block north sat a two-level parking structure.

Dark. The nurses walked right past the cement tiers and as Isaac got close to the structure, he saw the chained entrance. The sign hanging from the mesh gate.

"Earthquake Retrofitting, Due for Completion, August 2003."

The nurses kept going. Twenty more feet, thirty, fifty. Nearly to the end of the block. Another sign, too distant to read, but Isaac made out cars in dirt.

He sped up.

"Temporary Staff Parking."

High-intensity lights bleached the rear right-hand corner of the outdoor lot. The left fixture was out and half the space was a belt of black.

Poor maintenance or a predator's move?

The slim chance of the latter gave Isaac hope he'd guessed right.

Stupid hope. The city was filled with scores of other health facilities, many of which treated children. How many treated lung diseases? He had no idea.

This was worse than angels-on-a-pinhead academic theorizing. This was wild guesswork primed for the worst kind of error.

He crossed the street and slipped between two apartment buildings, feeling the softness of weeds beneath his feet. Smelling the stink of dog shit.

Home sweet home.

He stepped back another foot, made sure he had a long but clear view of the dirt lot. For all he knew, Doebbler was watching from a nearby spot, could hear his raspy breathing.

He silenced himself. Watched the five nurses head for their cars, some highlighted by the functioning light fixture, others slipping into invisibility.

The dark side would have to be it. If . . .

11:54.

Ififififififif.

CHAPTER

53

JUNE 27, 11:46 P.M., THE DOEBBLER RESIDENCE, TARZANA

Petra said, "I'm going to the front."

"Want me to stay back here?" said Eric.

"Yeah."

Removing her gun from her purse, she got out of her car, paused for a moment to steady her breathing, crossed to Doebbler's front door.

Hand on the Glock, ready for anything.

The queasy feeling in her bowels told her anything could happen. This was wrong. How could she have been that off?

She rang the bell. Nothing. A repeat ring elicited silence, too. Maybe Doebbler had somehow managed to get out without Eric or her seeing him.

Fooling *her*, she could see. But Eric?

She rang a third time. Nothing. She called him. "No response here."

"Same . . . scratch that, he's coming down the stairs . . . switching on the landing light. Bathrobe and pajamas. Looks like you woke him. He's pissed."

"Weapon?"

"Not that I see. Okay, he's headed to the front, I'm coming around."

Kurt Doebbler's voice behind the door demanded: "Who is it?"

"Police. Detective Connor." Petra had backed a few feet away. Behind her, concealed by bushes, Eric waited. She could smell him. Such a good smell.

No answer from Doebbler. Petra repeated her name.

"I heard you."

"Could you please open up, sir?"

"Why?"

"Please open."

"Why?"

"Police business."

"What kind of business?"

"Homicide."

The door swung open and Doebbler stared down at her, long arms crossed over a white terry bathrobe. Sleeves too short for his big, bony hands. Huge hands. Under the robe were striped pajamas. Big bare, veiny feet. His gray hair was mussed. Without his glasses, he was less nerdy, not that bad-looking, in a cold-eyed, angular way.

Petra's eyes were level with the robe's shawl lapel. She noticed a small sienna spot on the right side that could be dried blood. Her eyes climbed and she saw the shaving nick on Doebbler's neck. Three nicks, scabbed.

Old Kurt a little nervous this morning? Planning for something that he'd decided to cancel because he knew he was being watched?

How had he known?

"Sir," she said. "May I come in?"

"You," he said. More contempt in that single word than Petra had believed possible.

He blocked the doorway.

Petra said, "In for the evening, sir?"

Doebbler pushed hair away from his forehead. Sweaty forehead. Shadows under his eyes. His arms twitched and for a second, Petra thought he'd close the door on her. She moved forward, ready to block him.

He watched her and frowned.

She repeated the question.

"In for the evening?" he said. "As opposed to?"

"Going out."

"Why would I be going out?"

"Well," she said, "in a few minutes, it'll be June 28."

Doebbler went white. "You're sick." He braced himself against the doorpost with one hand. Tall enough that the contact was inches from the top.

"I'm not going out," he said. "Some of us work and take care of children. Some of us do our job with minimal competence." Muttering something Petra was nearly certain was "imbecile."

"May I come in, sir?"

"Come *in*?"

"To your house. To talk."

"For a little *social* visit?" said Doebbler. He managed a smile, detached, all mouth, no eyes. Knitted his big hands and cracked his knuckles and stared down at her.

Past her—through her—the way he had the first time. The way Emily Pastern and Sarah Casagrande had been stared through. A cool, dry snake slithered down Petra's spine and she was glad Eric was backing her up.

She smiled back at Doebbler.

He slammed the door in her face.

CHAPTER

54

Isaac watched the digital numerals of his watch click into place.
12:07.

The ultimate numerical reproach.

All the day shift nurses, gone.

Unlike another nurse, somewhere, a dark-haired girl, maybe Italian . . .

He imagined what was being done to her and the starch went out of his spine and he hunched like an old man.

He stayed in place, not knowing what else to do. Kept staring at the dirt lot. Three cars on the illuminated side, two, maybe three, parked in darkness, it was hard to tell.

Probably night-shifters who'd arrived early.

But if that was the case, why so few?

No big puzzle: The staff obviously preferred the western lot. Probably better lighting, anyone who arrived early nabbed a space there.

12:08.

He'd give it another five minutes, then he'd return to where he'd left his father's Toyota parked along Vermont. He'd forgotten to lock it. What had Dad left inside . . . not much, Dad was neat.

A set of work clothes folded on the backseat. Probably some papers in the glove compartment. Hopefully, nothing worth stealing.

Would the car even be there?

If it wasn't, how would he explain it to his parents?

The five minutes passed. Reluctant to face reality, he lingered.

At twelve-nineteen, feeling like the idiot he was, he slipped out from his hiding spot and began walking south.

Voices from Sunset made him stop. Female voices.

Three women . . . small women, young-sounding women, passed the chained cement parking structure and entered the dirt lot.

Isaac hurried back to his spot, watched them.

White uniforms, dark hair pulled into ponytails. Tiny women . . . Filipinas? They chattered gaily. Paused ten feet into the lot. One nurse veered into the light, the other two crossed into the darkened area.

No danger there. Doebbler wouldn't go for a pair, would want his prey alone.

The lit-up nurse started up her minivan and drove away. A set of headlights went on in the dark side and a zippy little sports car—a yellow Mazda RX—sped out, making that distinctive rotary sound.

Leaving one nurse.

He waited for more headlights.

Darkness.

Silence.

Had he missed something—a rear exit? As he stepped closer to the sidewalk, a low, mulish sound cut into the night.

The futile whine of an engine refusing to turn over.

A car door opened. Shut.

Then: a scream.

Reaching into his pocket, Isaac ran. The gun caught in the generous fleece of his sweatpants and refused to pull free.

He picked up his pace, shouted "Stop!" Screamed it louder.

Ripped frantically at his pocket. The gun was hopelessly tangled.

He reached the lot, sprinted across black dirt. Unable to see anything, homing in on the site of the scream.

Then he saw.

A man—a very tall man, wearing a long white coat, a doctor's coat—standing over a tiny, prone woman.

She lay on her stomach. One of the man's feet pressed down in the center of her back. Pinning her like a butterfly on a board.

She struggled in the dirt, arms and legs effecting an earthbound breaststroke. Cried out again.

The man reached into his coat, drew out something the size and girth of a baseball bat. Not wood . . . translucent.

A thick rod of clear plastic.

Slick, dense. That would explain the lack of fibers in the wounds. *Stop analyzing idiot, and* do *something!*

Isaac raced toward the tall man. Out of his mouth came a strange voice, hoarse, bellowing. *"Stop motherfucker or I'll shoot your ass!"*

The man in the white coat maintained his foothold on the tiny, dark-haired woman. Pretty woman, Isaac could see her terrified face now. Young, maybe even younger than him. Not Filipina, Latina.

Or maybe she was Italian—*stop!*

He was three feet away, still struggling with the gun.

The tall man must've pressed down harder on the girl's cheek, because her features compressed and her mouth was forced shut. Eating dust; she choked, coughed.

Isaac *ripped* at the pocket *fuckingidiotfuckingclown*

The man faced him, translucent truncheon held diagonally across his chest. Very tall, broad-shouldered, powerful. Plaid shirt and jeans and sneakers under the white coat.

Those shoes would leave marks in the dirt but Thad Doebbler was a careful man, an artist; he would be sure to clean them up when he was through.

Handsome man, with the confidence that tall, handsome men acquire easily. Undeterred by Isaac's goofy presence. He knew he could handle a fool like this.

"Hey," he said.

Isaac said, "P-Kasso."

Doebbler's grin died. The cudgel caught filmy moonlight and gleamed.

Isaac's battle with his pocket continued. All told, seconds of struggle, but it felt like years.

Suppressing panic, he stopped. Analyzed. Felt around. Some metal piece on the gun, maybe a rough spot on the barrel, was snagged on fleece threads, the key was to free it with a circular movement rather than fight and twist it tighter.

Thad Doebbler, his foot still on the girl's back, stepped forward with his free leg. Long leg, big stride, the motion brought him within two feet of Isaac's head. Striking distance.

He lifted the weapon and Isaac danced back, while yanking his pants upward. Tight around the crotch. He'd given himself a fucking wedgie and Thad Doebbler laughed.

See me now, Petra. Idiotclownidiotclown.

The little dark girl moaned in pain.

Thad Doebbler closed another few inches of the space between him and Isaac.

Isaac said, "Let her go or I'll shoot you. I mean it."

Thad Doebbler regarded Isaac with amusement. "With what? Your little dick?"

Isaac yanked the gun free. Stepped within the downward arc of Thad Doebbler's murderous arm. Dodged the crushing blow by inches and managed to maintain his balance as he aimed upward.

For the handsome face.

He pressed the trigger.

Shut his eyes involuntarily and kept pressing.

CHAPTER

55

A historian, Thad.

A renaissance man, of sorts. Website designer, graphic artist, alternative comix illustrator, computer animator.

Sculptor in Lucite and polymer resins and space-age plastics.

Abstract stuff, not to Petra's taste. But she was forced to admit that his work showed talent. Serpentine twists of translucent rods imbedded with polychrome fiber-optic filaments, good eye for balance and composition.

Last year he'd exhibited across the bay in San Francisco, at a Post Street gallery. Two to three grand per piece and three had sold.

P-Kasso.

Him and Omar. Her year for artists.

Bundles of spare Lucite rods in various sizes were stacked neatly in Doebbler's garage.

The largest size conformed to the June 28 skull compressions.

When she'd met him at his brother's, he'd claimed his home base as

San Francisco. But his digs were in Oakland, nice part of town, a cute little mock Tudor on a hill, landscaped prettily. No bay view, but a tree-framed rectangle of the Oakland hills was visible from the second-floor bedroom.

Nothing in the bedroom but clothing, a few true-crime paperbacks, and a TV on a card table. The rest of the house was similarly spartan.

Attached to the garage, out back, was a four-hundred-square-foot windowless cinder-block add-on secured by a bolted steel door. Thad Doebbler's track-lit studio.

Thad Doebbler's museum.

A man of parts, Thad. More useful to Petra, a damned egomaniac and compulsive chronicler of his own dark side.

Twenty-four years of dark side.

The guy had kept every playbill, airline ticket, and receipt cataloged compulsively. Within moments, Petra was able to verify his quarterly flights to L.A. But Petra already knew that Uncle Thad stayed with older brother Kurt and niece Katya in the house on Rosita.

Bunking down in a spare bedroom next to Katya's, where he kept a few pairs of pants, three shirts, a leather jacket, and a black Italian sports coat. Nothing of obvious forensic value, until the techies managed to scrape tiny little stains from two of the shirts and a jeans leg that had somehow managed to survive laundering and pressing.

Maybe it was Kurt Doebbler's inefficient, balky Kenmore washing machine, a contraption characterized by solemn-eyed Katya as: "Crap. It leaks all the time and never really cleans stuff the way you want it."

Dagger eyes at dad.

Kurt had flinched—finally some emotion. "I'll get a new one, Katie."

"You *always* say that."

Three of the stains were too degraded for DNA analysis. One was a perfect match to Marta Doebbler, another fit Coral Langdon's genetic makeup, a third matched that of Navy Ensign Darren Ares Hochenbrenner.

Petra had made it to the scene after hearing about it on her scanner. Hearing it during the debacle at Kurt Doebbler's house.

When she got there, Isaac was being treated like a suspect by two Hollywood D's who didn't know him well enough. He'd dropped Councilman Gilbert Reyes's name and that of Deputy Chief Randy

Diaz. Finally, someone called Diaz, who drove up in a Corvette dressed in black velvet sweats and two-hundred-dollar running shoes. Just in time for Petra to grab him and brief him.

"The kid solved it, sir." She spat out details.

Diaz said, "Impressive. Think he'll share credit with the department?"

"I don't think credit matters to him," said Petra. "He's a good kid, a great kid. I vouch for him absolutely."

Diaz smiled. Probably thinking she was in no shape to vouch for anyone.

"That's big of you, Detective."

"He earned it."

Isaac using an illegal gun to kill Thad could be a problem, they agreed.

Diaz said, "It can be dealt with." Long, searching look of Petra's face. "So can *your* issues, Detective. If everyone's discreet. There're going to be some changes in your division. I'd like them to be smooth."

"What changes?"

Diaz put a finger over his lips. Walked over to Isaac.

The following night, Petra flew to Oakland, and Sunday morning, accompanied by a friendly Oakland D named Arvin Ludd, she began the first of two solid days in the cinder-block trove.

Finding the best stuff in a double-wide black filing cabinet, a folder marked "Travel."

Beautiful penmanship, ol' Thad. He'd filled three muslin-bound, made-in-France notebooks with detailed accounts of murderous fantasies initiated at age twelve.

The melding of sex and violence and power, solidified by a chance encounter with a copy of the Teller booklet, found in a Hamburg antiques store.

"Retzak is me and I am him. I don't know why people like us are what we are. We just are. I like it."

After that: a lifetime of converting fantasy to reality.

Thad described his failure to murder the German cake-icer, Gudrun Wiegeland, as *"an understandable lapse, given my youth and inexperience, plus a modicum—but only that—of anxiety."* At the time of the

Wiegeland bludgeoning *"with a crowbar borrowed from the base auto-shop,"* he'd been a sixteen-year-old Army brat. Two years younger than "Ever Pedestrian Kurt."

Perhaps Thad's anxiety had been higher than he was willing to admit. By his own account, it took another eight years for him to try another murder.

After a two-year stint in the Army, most of it spent as a layout editor for a military newspaper in Manila, Thad moved to Pittsburgh and enrolled in Carnegie-Mellon as an art and design major. *("Andy Warhol's alma mater. They told me he drew shoes for newspapers ads. I am a good deal more conceptual.")* Soon after graduation, he waylaid an eighteen-year-old co-ed named Randi Corey as she enjoyed a late-night campus jog.

June 28, 1987. The spring semester had ended but Corey had remained for the summer to practice with a gymnastic coach.

Thad Doebbler had stayed in town to murder her.

The girl incurred three crushing blows to the back of her skull, and according to a newspaper clipping Thad had mounted in Volume 1 of his chronicles, was "likely to remain in a persistent vegetative state."

"When I cracked her open, I did manage to get a look at the gelatin. But not much, the bones wouldn't give when I tried to pry them apart. Then I heard someone coming and skedaddled. It was two days later that I learned I'd, once again, inexplicably, failed to exert enough pressure to snuff the soul candle. I will not repeat that transgression."

Two months later, a fifty-two-year-old university maintenance man, Herbert Lincoln, succumbed to a fatal braining as he walked to his car in an off-campus lot. From what Petra could tell, no connection had been made between the homicide and the attack on Randi Corey.

Young woman, older man. Some accordance with Otto Retzak's pattern, but Doebbler had veered from the June 28 routine.

Still in training. The deviation hadn't muted his feelings of triumph.

"I studied him as he leaked, watched the spark leave his eyes and sketched the phases. A wholer sense of completion can't be imagined."

Sandwiched into the book were the drawings.

Horrible because the bastard really *could* draw.

End of Volume 1.

As Petra put it aside and picked up the next notebook, she made a mental note to try to locate the Pittsburgh detectives who'd worked Corey and Lincoln. Find out if the girl was still alive; her family and Lincoln's would want to know.

She flipped the next book open. Arvin Ludd said, "Interesting?"

"If you like that kind of thing."

He smiled, crossed his legs. While Petra worked, he'd mostly mellowed out in Thad Doebbler's original, mint-condition Eames chair. Now he got up and stretched. "I'm about ready for a coffee fix. Want a latte or something?"

"Double espresso if they have it."

"You got it." Ludd was boyish, dark, blue-eyed. Well-dressed and laid-back almost to a fault and probably gay. Swinging his car keys, he left the block building.

Left alone, Petra was hit by the stillness of the room. Silent, cold. Perfect kill-spot. Perfect dungeon.

Had Doebbler ever brought any victims home? Preliminary luminol tests had found no blood. But she wondered. She'd suggested to Ludd that Oakland P.D. bring cadaver dogs and sonar for the backyard. He'd listened, nodded, hadn't said yes or no. Hard to read the guy. Maybe he wasn't gay . . .

Volume 2.

Here we go.

After murdering Herbert Lincoln, Thad had adhered to the June 28 pattern. But not with yearly regularity. Being a salaried employee had constrained him; the crimes had depended upon his travel schedule.

June 28, 1989: A computer seminar in Los Gatos, California. Thad had flown in from Philadelphia, where'd he'd been temping as a bank teller while seeking employment in the computer animation biz. Shortly after midnight, Barbara Bohannon, the secretary to an Intel executive, was brained in the subterranean parking lot of her hotel. Bohannon's missing purse led investigators to suspect robbery as a motive.

Doebbler had emptied the purse and tossed it, keeping the cash and the credit cards and the photos of Bohannon's husband and three-year-old son. Spending the money; filing the rest under "Souvenirs."

His drawing of the woman showed her to be round-faced, fair-haired, pleasant-looking even in death. Wood fibers embedded in her hair said Doebbler hadn't discovered the magic of plastic.

June 28, 1991: Back in Philly, another computer conference. A year before, Doebbler had obtained work with an on-line start-up in San Mateo, only to be laid off, no reason given. Selling optioned stock bought him the house in Oakland and some time to try life as a freelance. A sculptor in Lucite.

At one-fifteen A.M., the body of Melvyn Lassiter, a room-service waiter at the Inn at Penn, was found on a street in West Philadelphia. Crushed skull, missing wallet. Lassiter's wife reported that Melvyn routinely brought home food from the hotel kitchen. No trace of such near the corpse.

"Pasta primavera, broiled salmon. Yummy. The Caesar salad was a bit limp, but once I got rid of the soggy croutons, not half-bad."

June 28, 1992: Denver, Colorado. Animation conference. Ethel Ferguson, fifty-six, a breeder of standard poodles, was found bludgeoned in a wooded area near her home.

June 28, 1995: Oceanside, California, Matthias Delano Brown, seaman, USN, brained near the docks. Thad Doebbler has taken a three-day vacation in La Jolla, traveling solo, staying at the La Valencia Hotel. *("Lovely; a well-deserved splurge. I saw dolphins from my window.")*

Then: sister-in-law Marta.

Lover Marta.

Thad accounted the affair in prurient detail, rhapsodizing equally about the release of Marta's "pent-up, Teutonic sexuality" and the pleasure at demeaning Ever Pedestrian Kurt. *("Henceforth referred to as EPT.")*

During the three-month adultery, he traveled to L.A. twelve times, telling his brother that he'd gotten an illustration job at a Beverly Hills ad agency.

"In reality, my job was waiting until EPT had departed for his ever pedestrian employment, then fucking Marta's brains out—ah, the irony— in her marital bed. She'd start off pretending to be reluctant, but always gave in. She ended up being one hell of a screamer. I decided it would be nice to hear different kinds of screams pouring out of her starting-to-

pucker, hausfrau *mouth. She was beginning to grow emotional and tiresome."*

A near-disaster was averted when Kurt returned home shortly after leaving to get a trade journal he'd left near his recliner. *"EPT didn't even bother to come upstairs to say hi to M, just collected his mag and left. He has no social skills, never did. Lucky for M and me, as we were in the throes, connected rather, ahem, deeply. I placed a hand over her mouth and succeeded in not laughing myself."*

After that, Marta insisted they tryst at motels over the hill, in Hollywood and West Hollywood.

The "downtown errands" she'd lied about to her friends.

When Marta announced to Thad that she loved him, was ready to leave Kurt and Katya, he decided to kill her.

He thought it out, waited until her theater night. Phoned her cell from a nearby booth, telling her he was just around the corner, had planned a surprise: meeting her at her car after the show. He'd booked a room at the Hollywood Roosevelt hotel—a suite, actually. But now, he wasn't feeling well. Chest pains, probably nothing more than indigestion, but he was going to drive himself over to the Hollywood Presbyterian emergency room just to make sure. He'd call her when he was through.

She freaked and insisted on taking him. Met him at her car. Before she knew it, he was sitting behind the wheel. Driving away. Looking fine.

She said, *Thought you were sick.*

He laughed, told her they were through.

She began sobbing, wanted to know why. *Begged* to know why.

He parked on a dark side street. Took her in his arms, kissed her. Shoved her away roughly and got out.

She went after him. Tried to hit him.

He got hold of her arm, twisted, shoved her to the ground and smashed the back of her skull with the Lucite club he'd concealed in his coat. The specially stitched internal pocket he'd fashioned. Good with his hands, ol' Thad.

She whimpered. Stopped.

"I'd had this woman at will, knew her as intimately as one can know anyone. Yet her jelly was no different to me than any other. Nevertheless, this jaunt solidified my goals; this was the closest I'd come to ecstasy. And

to honoring the memory of that sage, O.R. Something worth appreciating. Worth celebrating yearly."

Feeling her emotions begin to click off, Petra read the rest of it quickly, turned to the back of the notebook, found the postmortem sketches of Marta Doebbler. And the others.

Something different about his portrait of Marta. Something searching—needy and adoring—in the woman's eyes.

Dead, but he'd drawn her eyes full of life.

That evening, in her room at the Jack London Inn, she took a very long, very hot bath, watched Court TV, and managed to keep a room service cheeseburger down.

Pleasant room: white walls, blue bedding. Rates higher than the department would normally compensate but she'd found a good deal on the Internet.

Outside was activity. The hotel was right in the heart of Jack London Square. Another time and place she'd have explored. Tonight she had no intention of leaving until the airport ride tomorrow morning.

Washing the burger down with a Coke, she went to the mini-bar, studied the cute little bottles of booze and mixers. Contemplated the advisability of a homemade Tanqueray and tonic. Decided against it.

Her cell phone rattled on the nightstand. Still on vibrator; she hadn't altered it since the stakeout at Kurt Doebbler's.

Another potential career disaster. Busting the door in, rushing Kurt and handcuffing him. Waking the poor daughter, too.

Exigent circumstances was her excuse.

Deputy Chief Diaz said that made sense to him.

Kurt Doebbler, lying pinioned on his living room floor, had threatened to sue.

He would've—might've won big—if not for his brother's bad behavior.

Blood on the clothing in the closet. Kurt claimed he had no idea Thad was sleeping with Marta, let alone using his house as a crash pad for his yearly murder jaunts.

Probably telling the truth, the clueless nerd. But the D.A.'s theatrical skepticism and the threat of bad publicity had led Pacific Dynamics to lean on Kurt and he'd backed off.

No harm, no foul. Petra felt bad for Katya but that was someone else's business.

Maybe, at some point, she'd call Delaware about the kid . . .

No, she wouldn't, she was a cop, not a social worker. Thad Doebbler would never bash anyone's brains out again, case closed.

With a little help from a friend.

Isaac, a shooter. His little gift from Flaco Jaramillo. Finally, he'd told her why.

A touch of deviousness in the kid's makeup that she hadn't imagined.

Thank God.

She picked up the phone, studied the numerical read-out, hoped it was Eric. They had a dinner date tomorrow back in L.A. Big splurge at Ivy at the Shore. Intimations—as much as Eric was capable of intimating—of serious talk, career plans.

Whatever.

The phone read out a 213 number. Not Eric, but someone she didn't mind talking to.

"Hi," she said.

"Hi," said Isaac. "Hope I'm not bothering you."

"Not at all. What's up?"

"I just thought I'd tell you I was by the station today and there's a new captain. Someone named Stuart Bishop. He made a point of coming up to me, said he knows you. He seems friendly."

"Stu? You're kidding."

"Is there a problem?"

"No," said Petra. "Not at all. No problem." Her mouth hung open. Unbelievable.

Isaac said, "He seemed like a very decent person."

"He's terrific. Used to be my partner until he left the department."

"Oh. I guess he's back."

Like Eric, Stu had talked about going private. Unlike Eric, he had family money and connections that could've led to the corporate world. So now he was back in the department. He'd said nothing to lead her in that direction.

Then again, they hadn't talked in months.

Back as a captain. How had he pulled that off?

There'll be changes in your division.

"So that's good news for you," said Isaac.

"I'd imagine so," said Petra, talking through her grin. "How're *you* doing, hero? When's the ceremony?"

"Sometime next week. I hope they cancel it."

"Hey," she said, "enjoy the moment. You and Councilman Reyes, adoring citizens, the press. You deserve it."

"I'm no hero, Petra. I was lucky."

"You were smart. Heather Salcido was lucky."

Cute little Heather from Brea, California. Dark-haired, big-eyed, petite, and twenty-three. Cheerleader-pretty despite all those cheek abrasions. A newly graduated R.N., she'd worked Pediatric Pulmonary for less than a year. Still lived at home. Traditional family: dad a retired sheriff, mom a housewife, one older brother a mucho-macho CHP motorcycle officer.

From the way the girl had gazed at Isaac from her hospital bed, from the way he'd looked at her, the kid's relationship to the world of law enforcement might take on a whole new twist.

Petra kept grinning.

"No," he said. "It was luck, that's all."

"Then you're a lucky guy," she said. "And I thank you for that."

"I should thank you. For teaching me so much."

"My pleasure, Dr. Gomez."

"One more thing . . ."

"The gun," she said.

"I—"

"It's been logged into evidence as a legally registered firearm, Isaac. Registered to you last January, you even merited a concealed-weapon permit. Because of your law enforcement activities combined with living in a high-crime area. As things turned out, that was a good call, wasn't it?"

Silence.

"Thanks," he said.

"Sure," she said. "Now go have some fun."

CHAPTER

56

Isaac cut into his hangar steak. Big as a baseball mitt. Soft as a
doughnut.

"Like it?" said Heather. She'd made unbelievable headway with
her T-bone and sirloin tip combo. How could a girl that small pack
away so much prime beef?

"It's great," he told her. Meaning it.

"I love this place," she said. "Partly because of the food, but also
because of all these memories I have. Back when my dad was with the
sheriff's, and he had to be in court late, he'd take us here. Rather than
battle the traffic back to Brea, Mom and Gary and I would meet him
and we'd have a huge meal. It was kind of like Sunday during the
week."

She patted her mouth with a corner of snow-white napkin. Pretty
mouth. Bow-shaped, and some of her lip gloss remained. The scratches
on her smooth, olive cheek were healing nicely. She'd concealed the
dark marks with makeup. Did a lot better than he had with his bruise.

"My family doesn't eat out." *Why had he said that?*

Heather said, "A lot of families don't. Actually, we don't very often. That makes it more special, don't you think?" She rubbed a corner of a linen napkin between tapered fingers. "I love the feel of this."

He smiled. She smiled back and they both ate. Drank wine. Red wine; a six-year-old California cabernet way past his budget. He'd faked out choosing from the five-page wine list, knowing that red went with beef but not much more than that. Pretending to contemplate, he'd finally jabbed randomly and hoped for the best.

Then the whole sniffing, swirling routine, the way he'd seen it done in movies.

Gomez. *James* Gomez.

Agent Double 0 Phony.

"Fine," he'd told the sommelier.

"Very good, sir."

Heather took one sip and said, "Oh, man, this is fantastic. You know your wine."

He'd visited her twice in the hospital, but this was their first date. Spur-of-the-moment thing, after the ceremony on the front steps of City Hall.

She'd occupied his thoughts from the first time he saw her.

The ceremony had turned out to be Councilman Gilbert Reyes, a couple of flunkies, the media, Isaac, and his family.

His parents beaming and his brothers squirming as he accepted the calligraphy-laden official commendation on mock-parchment, then made a cursory speech. All those microphones jammed in his face, cameras clicking and whirring.

He hated every minute of it. Longed for the solitude of the library, his laptop and books and the opera of deduction. Not Klara in his lap, she was too much for him, way too much, but he would work at keeping her friendship.

He got through the ordeal, shaking hands and smiling and waiting for an opportunity to escape.

Then Heather came up to him—where had she been? Before he could ask her, Councilman Gilbert Reyes spotted her and had her pose for stills, sandwiched between himself and Isaac.

Later, Isaac found out she'd wanted to be present for the whole thing but had arrived late because of traffic.

"I heard your entire speech, though," she assured him. "And the ceremony was on KFWB. Daddy always listens to news and talk radio—oh, here he is."

A big square truck of a man stepped out from behind the departing media hounds. White hair and mustache, outdoor skin. Iron grip. Then a small, slender, vivacious woman, young-looking for her age, who Heather resembled strikingly.

Heather would age well.

Nancy and Robert Salcido thanked him, then turned to converse in Spanish with Irma and Isaiah Gomez Sr.

Somehow, Isaac and Heather drifted away from the crowd, over to a shady spot just north of the steps. Somehow, she got him talking about himself.

"A Ph.D. and an M.D.," she said. "That's ambitious—that's unbelievable! Don't tell anyone, but I've been thinking of med school, too. My grades were good and my adviser thought I should apply. But all those years seemed daunting. I thought the R.N. would be enough for me, but now I'm not sure."

"You should go for it," he said.

"Think so?"

"Sure, you can do it." As if he knew what he was talking about.

"Well," she said, "thanks for the vote of confidence. I don't know. Maybe I will . . . well, it was nice seeing you again."

"It doesn't have to end."

She gave a puzzled look that made his heart sink. Then a smile that inflated the damned hunk of cardiac muscle.

"As in lunch," he said. "As in now."

Smooooth . . . stupid!

"Now? Okay. I'll tell my parents. They were figuring to go out as a family, but I like your idea better."

At a loss for a restaurant, phony cool guy that he was, he was grateful when she came up with Leonard's. Despite the fact that it would empty his wallet. Reyes had intimated some kind of reward would be forthcoming. Maybe true, maybe not. What the heck, live dangerously.

Now he watched Heather slice pink meat off the bone, chew, swallow. Everything she did was adorable.

She said, "What?"

"Pardon?"

"You got really quiet, Isaac."

"I'm just enjoying myself," he said. "The peace and quiet."

"Of course," she said, reaching over and placing her hand atop his. He felt his skin go hot.

She said, "Life's so funny, you know? You plan and scheme and then, out of nowhere, something happens."

"I know," he said. "I'm so sorry you had to go through that."

"Oh, no," she said, squeezing his fingers. Smiling. "I wasn't talking about *that.*"